PRAIS

HALSTEAD HOUSE

"The most beautiful, engrossing story of a woman finding her strength and confidence, all wrapped up in sweet romance with an attractive, grumpy hero!"

—Sarah Adams, author of *The Match*

"Hadley captures the essence of breaking out of your shell and falling in love in this delightfully charming romance. Character growth, slow-burn romance, and a setting as charming as Hadley's prose make this book a winner."

—Esther Hatch, author of *A Proper Scoundrel*

OTHER BOOKS BY ASPEN HADLEY

Simply Starstruck

Blind Dates, Bridesmaids & Other Disasters

Suits and Spark Plugs

ASPEN HADLEY

SWEETWATER
BOOKS

An imprint of Cedar Fort, Inc.
Springville, Utah

ISBN 13: 978-1-4621-3907-1

Published by Sweetwater Books, an imprint of Cedar Fort, Inc.
2373 W. 700 S., Springville, UT, 84663
Distributed by Cedar Fort, Inc., www.cedarfort.com

Library of Congress Control Number: 2021902972

Cover design by Shawnda T. Craig
Cover design © 2021 Cedar Fort, Inc.

Printed in the United States of America

10 9 8 7 6 5 4 3 2 1

Printed on acid-free paper

FOR MY PARENTS, RAND AND MARLA RIDGES.

FOR MAKING LAUGHTER THE SOUNDTRACK OF MY CHILDHOOD.

FOR YOUR GRACE AND GRIT IN FACING THE HARD PARTS OF LIFE.

FOR NEVER PUTTING YOUR IDEAS FOR MY LIFE ABOVE MY OWN.

FOR LOVING ME IN EVERY PHASE OF MY EVOLUTION,
AND EVERY MOOD THAT CAME WITH IT.

"FRIENDS MAY COME AND GO, BUT FAMILY IS FOREVER."

CHAPTER 1

IT WAS THE CANDLES THAT DID IT. ALL TWENTY-FIVE OF THEM, glowing ridiculously, wax dripping, marring the perfect white frosting. The light they cast flickered on the faces of the three unfortunate people that Mother had strong-armed into coming to my sham of a birthday celebration. Could it really be considered a party when those three guests—a humiliatingly low number—had stood stiffly in their pressed pant suits, clutching the purses they hadn't bothered to set down when they'd entered my office?

That's right—my office, a tiny twelve-by-twelve square. Mother hadn't even managed to snare enough people to force a move to the staff conference room down the hall. To make matters worse, she had insisted on switching off the florescent overhead light, and I'd watched as the flames of the candles danced across three plastic smiles. They'd sung in stilted voices, and can I just say that if you've never heard the happy birthday song sung under duress, you're not missing out on anything? It's not pretty. Their eyes told the real story. They'd wanted to be gone, and I'd neither blamed them nor taken it personally.

Twenty-five candles. Twenty-five was old enough, finally, wasn't it? After all, there was no such thing as the magical age at which a person was suddenly *allowed* to have a mid-life crisis. Sometimes a person just had to follow their gut, assuming I still had one after so many years of being a puppet. Mary had once told me that if you never got into an argument with someone, you had the personality of a sheep. So, yeah, I'd known I was a sheep for a very long time. At least on the outside.

Standing there with my own plastic smile, wearing my own pressed paint suit while Mother proudly held that horrifying cake with twenty-five glowing candles on it—yes, twenty-five, because Lillian Burke wasn't one to break with tradition regardless of the fire hazard—it had felt like a lightning bolt lanced straight down through my heart. I'd taken a deep breath, trying to restore calm and order even though I'd known that something big had shifted inside of me at that moment. It had sloughed off in disappointment, sure, but even sloughing required a shift.

Grace, those dancing flames had said to me, *you want more than this.*

* * *

I made my way through Boston Logan International Airport, the squeaking wheels of my rolling carry-on luggage, along with the staccato taps of my heels, drawing eyes to me as I made my way to the gate. The attention made me squirm, although years of practice kept my head high and my face calm even as I felt the familiar dreaded flush of embarrassment warm my neck and up into my hairline. It was a cruel trick of nature that I had light, almost china doll coloring along with that tendency to blush. Some girls were tall, some were short, and some, like, me, turned the color of a tomato at the worst possible times. I was grateful when the carpeting near the chairs muffled my movements and the curious eyes sought out other things to watch.

I found an empty seat near a window where the early sunlight was sparkling off the floor, and tucked my cheapo luggage up against my leg. It was plastic, almost an exact match to the chair where I sat. I ran a light hand over it, remembering how I'd actually had to wipe it down with a wet rag the night before to get the dust of storage off. When Mother had given me the luggage as a high school graduation gift almost seven years ago, I had foolishly thought it meant I'd finally see more than the sights of towns within a two-hour drive of

Providence, Rhode Island. Instead it had been living under my bed along with the boogeyman, who made a terrible housekeeper.

I tapped the boarding pass I held in my hand against my knee. My palms were sweaty with determination, and I'd officially wrinkled the poor piece of paper nearly beyond recognition. An image flashed in my mind of the expression on the security guard's face when I'd handed him the slightly damp paper pass rather than holding up my phone to scan. He'd definitely expected something different from someone my age. I'd have to figure out electronic boarding passes for my flight home . . . whenever that would be.

My flight to San Antonio, Texas, was going to take most of the day. With two layovers, I wouldn't be arriving until almost ten o'clock at night. I'd brought two books and had loaded my phone with music, but I still worried about all the thinking time I'd have ahead of me. Thinking made me fidget and caused that uncomfortable thing in the center of my chest to build pressure. Thinking led nowhere I wanted to go.

To say my mother had been angry last night when I'd told her my plans would be like saying the Avengers were mildly annoyed with Thanos. She didn't understand, couldn't. Why would I fly across the country to visit a place that was nothing more than a childhood fairy tale? Why would I take a three-month sabbatical from my job with the Rhode Island State Historical Society in order to chase a dream? How could a dream take three months? A weekend, or possibly a week, she could understand and forgive, but three entire months? Across the country? Away from her? It was unimaginable.

Actually, truth be told, what was unimaginable was that I'd gone through with it. I'd listened to the candles. I, Grace Natalie Burke, sitting alone in an airport at eight o'clock in the morning, holding a boarding pass, with nothing more than a purse, a carry-on suitcase, a quickly fading dose of back bone, and zero plans for a return flight—*that* was the real shocker.

Mother had been wrong about a lot of things in my life, but this one was a biggie. I wasn't chasing a fairy tale. I was chasing something that felt truer to me than my sensible condo, my marvelous retirement plan, or my secure job. I was heeding the call of soft waves, warm breezes, verandas, and a fern-filled conservatory. I was finally, finally, following Mary, my safe haven and only true friend, despite our eighty-year age difference.

Mary, who had always put me first, and reached past my learned reserve to my true heart. She was the first person to fill my mind with magic and to be given a glimpse of the slightly sarcastic nature I kept well hidden. I had allowed myself to truly love her without fear or hesitation, understanding even as a child that blood wasn't the only thing that forged soul deep bonds.

"I'm doing it, Mary," I whispered to myself. "I'm going to Halstead House." The house of fairy tales, her childhood home. It had been calling to me deep down in my bones for as long as I could remember.

*　*　*

I'll tell you what. Ten p.m. in San Antonio, Texas, in the month of March is worlds away from the same time of day in Providence, Rhode Island. The twenty-degree temperature difference was one thing, but the humidity surprised me most. Texas felt humid in a heavy and warm way, while home felt chilly and crisp. I casually wondered how much more humid Lavender Island, my destination among the gulf islands, was going to be.

While I was very much looking forward to getting my first glimpse of Texas, I was too tired, and it was too dark, to do much about the scenery around me as I pulled my little rental car out of the airport and into the city streets. Slightly over fourteen hours after hitting the freedom highway, I was feeling the pull of a bed to stretch out in. The adrenaline that had sustained me was waning, and the barrage of doubting thoughts I'd had to fight off all day had worn me further.

I pulled off at the first exit that had the glowing light of a motel sign. Mother's ever-present, disappointed voice rang in my ear. I should have carefully mapped out more than just a flight plan and music playlist. I had no idea what type of lodging lay ahead. A proper lady was always prepared and in control. I could feel my heart beating in my throat as I signaled into the parking lot of the small motel. I'd been taught well all the horror stories of ill-prepared and naive young women, so I half-expected a drugged-up mugger to jump straight out of the bushes and attack at the first sight of me.

I put the car in park but left the engine running as I looked over the building before me. My lifelong training to seek high standards was butting up against the crumbly red brick and flickering lights that offered rest. As I worked to silence Mother's voice, I was surprised to realize that it wasn't I who actually cared about perfect accommodations. As long as it was clean and available, I would make do.

Decision made, I turned off the engine but didn't immediately open my door. Clean was one thing, safety was another. I wove the keys in between my fingers so that they stuck up like weapons. I'd seen this on TV one time, and knew to jab for the eyes. A squirmy sensation gripped my stomach as I imagined an eyeball exploding, so I did a little breathing to relax and let the silence surround me sink in.

How sad that something as small as checking in to a motel room was monumental and made me feel unsafe. In truth, I had never even pulled into the parking lot of a motel before. I'd certainly never reserved a room for myself. On the extremely rare occasions I did travel, Mother had always accompanied me and insisted on making all the arrangements. We'd always shared a room.

At the thought of how alone I was at the moment, a surge of something resembling nervous glee zipped through my body. I was truly, truly independent. I was miles and miles from my comfy little life. I was miles and miles from the policies and procedures of Mrs. Lillian Burke. And even better, I was miles and miles closer to seeing my dream become a reality. All this sudden freedom felt overwhelming, like stepping into the bright sunlight after sitting in a darkened theater.

Hands shaking slightly, I reached for my purse with my key-free hand and pushed the car door open. I couldn't take my eyes off the neon blinking 'open' sign. The walk into the motel office was accompanied by the clacking of my heels on the asphalt. Even in my escape, I was dressed in a business suit.

The process of getting a room was so simple that I actually felt embarrassed it had taken me twenty-five years to accomplish it. After being handed the key, while pretending to ignore the desk clerk staring at my Wolverine hand, I gathered my things from my car and rolled my suitcase across the bumpy sidewalk into the first-floor room. A room that was all mine.

The door slammed behind me as the cheap florescent lights flickered before coming on full strength, bathing the already depressing room in a blue-green hue. The curtains were pulled shut, making the room appear even shabbier in the shadows.

I loved it.

I loved everything about it, from the old TV, to the yellowed lamp shade, to the chips of missing paint. Even the thought of what kind of shady business had occurred in this rundown room couldn't bring me down.

I set my suitcases on the second bed, worked the keys out of my fingers, and took a few deep breaths as a smile tickled at the corners of my mouth. I carefully took off my skirt suit and hung it in the closet before taking out my toiletry items and a nightgown. Entering the bathroom, I flipped on the light to find it was even more dreary than the sleeping space had been. A small laugh burst out as I looked around.

As I washed my face and brushed my teeth, I took a moment to look at myself in the mirror. With so many new emotions battling within after just this one day, I half expected to see it all reflected in my face, but no. Still the same me: straight, shoulder-length, light blonde hair pulled back into a slick chignon, round face, and gray eyes that always looked serene. My skin was as pale as milk, my cheeks full, and my lips slightly pink. Nothing about the way I looked told the story of what went on inside.

It had always been that way. I had the coloring of a faded china doll combined with the big innocent eyes of a toddler. My smile, on the occasions that I allowed it to fully bloom, was large and seemed to surprise people, as though the doll had mysteriously transformed into a stranger. Mother had always preferred that I keep my smiles demure and close-lipped. In point of truth, it had served me well to look so faded and harmless as I grew up under an iron thumb. Didn't mean I'd never flashed it at her back, though.

Once I heard a story about a wolf in sheep's clothing. It was supposed to be some moralistic tale about avoiding people pretending to be one thing while actually being another. Wolves were supposed to be bad, out there mingling with the innocent sheep who didn't know what was about to hit them. Yet, the image had been stuck in my head for a long time, and it gave me comfort to think that maybe I too was a wolf in sheep's clothing—that there was more to me than what I showed people. That somewhere inside this inno-cent-looking shell, I was swift and strong, ready to stand my ground and take what I wanted.

I had been named after two of Mother's favorite actresses—Grace Kelly and Natalie Wood—but sadly I hadn't been born with any of their apparently flawless traits. Mother had done her best to mold me into the perfect daughter, and I had learned to act like one.

She had even placed a picture of Natalie Wood on one side of my mirror and Grace Kelly on the other when I was a young girl. I had often wondered what went on behind their smiles. As a teenager I had looked into the details of their lives, and it seemed to me that there wasn't much in their real lives worth imitating. I was smart enough to never mention that to Mother, however. Even wolves have a self-preservation instinct.

I changed into my silky nightgown and left the bathroom to crawl under the scratchy covers before leaning against the head-board and opening a file folder I had brought along. When Mary passed, I had inherited a small nest egg—which I'd used as the down payment on my condo—and her personal pictures of her beloved Halstead House. With those two gifts she had given me both my first real taste of freedom, and allowed me to keep a piece of her nearby.

Each time I pulled out the pictures I could still feel the flush of pleasure I'd hidden at the reading of Mary's will when the lawyer had handed me the folder and the prizes that lay within. I had demurely thanked him for the money, but my eyes had glowed brightly over the priceless pictures. Mother had started to make a comment about a silly old woman's pictures, but Mary's son Richard had put a staying hand on her shoulder and smiled at me.

Under the soft glow of the worn lamp I shook off those memories and let my eyes drink in the photographs. Worn snapshots of the sand-colored stone and stucco front, the great staircase with its enormous stained-glass window, the library full of warm cherry wood shelving, the conservatory blooming in ferns. Even though I didn't need to, I read the descriptions on the back, my heart pricking slightly at the familiar handwriting as I gently ran my fingertips over the fraying edges of the well-loved prints.

When I'd had my fill, I deposited the folder on the bedside table and felt duty-bound to turn on my phone and check for missed calls. Tension I hadn't realized I'd been holding drained when the screen remained blank. No messages from Mother. I was selfishly happy to have more time before she called to see how my 'ill-advised rebellion' was going.

I turned off the lamp and settled down into bed. Despite my deep exhaustion, sleep didn't come easily. When it did eventually come, it rode on the warm humid breezes that Mary had woven in to her tales.

* * *

My phone began to ring, Mother's number flashing across the screen, just as I made it to the outskirts of San Antonio the next day. Until that moment, I hadn't realized that it was possible for a phone to ring with an attitude. Mentally crossing my fingers that she'd have had time to accept my choice, I muted the velvety sounds of Fleetwood Mac and hit the hands-free phone button on the steering wheel.

"Hello?" I said as cheerfully as possible.

"Well, at least now I don't have to worry that you're dead somewhere on the side of a highway." Mother's husky voice blared through the speakers of the car. It didn't matter how many times I'd told her she didn't need to yell; she was a loud phone talker, and I hurried to turn down the volume.

Mother's voice had always had the hoarse sounds of someone being pulled from a deep sleep. As a child, I had learned to listen past the scratchiness for the tones underneath, clues as to her mood. This time I didn't have to listen too hard. She had accepted nothing.

"I'm sorry. My flight got in late and I didn't want to wake you," I replied calmly.

"Where are you?"

"I'm just leaving San Antonio, heading toward the Gulf." I tried to inject some lightheartedness into the comment, like I did this sort of thing all the time, but my hands began to shake at the reality of where I was.

"You're still determined to see that place?" Mother's disappointment was so palpable that it actually felt like she was sitting in the passenger seat.

I bit my lips together to keep from placating her. I thought of birthday candles glowing on hollow faces. I pictured Mary, her gnarled hands so soft as they held mine. Finally, I thought of a small girl who had never dared to speak up for herself, and the yellow-eyed wolf who'd been biding her time.

I swallowed hard and cleared my throat. "I am."

Mother made a noise of annoyance and shifted gears. "Where did you stay last night?"

"In a little motel not too far from the airport," I replied.

"A motel?" She paused, but I didn't reply. "I worry about you, Grace. You've never traveled alone. You're young and know so little of the world."

Forget the wolf. I was wrong. Beads of sweat rose up on my forehead, my palms sticky as they clung to the steering wheel. She was right. What was I thinking? I had no preparation for this type of thing. I hadn't even gone away to college. I'd lived at home until just a few years ago. Suddenly my eyes refocused as a little red sports car cut in front of me and I had to slam on my brakes. Traffic! I couldn't afford to zone out, just as I couldn't go back. I clung to the idea like a lifeline.

"Actually, Mother, I really need to go. I'm driving through a city I'm not familiar with and I need to focus. I'm safe and well, and I'll be in touch."

She sighed. "Fine. Promise you'll call the minute you arrive. Otherwise I'll start calling the state troopers. I can't bear the thought of you suffering while the life bleeds out of you at the hands of a carjacker."

"Mother, I'll be fine. I promise to keep in touch."

"You're all I have, Grace. I can't help but worry about you."

This time it was my turn to sigh, but I did it silently. "I know. I'll be careful."

We said our goodbyes and I clicked the 'end call' button. I pushed out a deep breath as Mother's voice disappeared. I had officially planted myself on a path of no return. Still sweating and shaking, although with slightly steadier hands, I restarted the song I'd been listening to. I felt my shoulders begin to relax as I let the music fill the silence. Music had always served this purpose for me.

The miles passed as I did my best to deliver a pep talk to myself. "You are twenty-five years old, Grace. Twenty-five-year-old professional women travel alone every single day. You don't need your mother's permission, or her company." I told myself this multiple times. The words didn't fully penetrate through the worried ache, but they scratched the surface enough to keep me moving forward. This freedom thing was going to take some time.

At last I came to the bridge connecting the islands to the continent. My eyes devoured my first view of the Gulf of Mexico. I couldn't seem to get close enough, so I rolled down the windows and allowed the salty breeze to enter the car. I didn't want to just look at everything, I wanted to touch it. My heart began to beat in a slow, heavy rhythm as I noticed that the blue-gray color of the water matched my eyes. I'd often thought them a boring color, not really blue, just faded, but they were the same color as the Gulf waters that had been calling to me through the years. The realization brought with it an odd sort of excitement. Maybe, just maybe, here, in this salty, gray, humid part of the world I would find what I'd been searching for.

After another hour of GPS navigating small islands, along with a ferry ride that had caused me to question my resolve, I pulled into the parking lot of the Sand Dollar Motel on Lavender Island. The vacancy sign was flipped open, and I smiled to myself as I confidently entered the motel to book a room for a week. I wasn't sure what exactly my plans were, but I knew I'd need to find something a little more permanent if I decided to stay for the entire three months of my sabbatical.

The Sand Dollar wasn't nearly as depressing as the previous night's room had been. Of course, I allowed, that might be because this motel was given a huge boost by being located right across the street from the ocean. Done in whites and blues, the room was small but refreshingly beachy. I opened the curtains and smiled at the sight of the people walking past my window, casting shadows on the sand, set against the backdrop of waves. I was darn near waxing poetic over the entire scene. I needed to get closer.

I propped open the window and breathed it all in.

For a woman who lived life in quiet lulls, what greeted me felt explosive. The constant sound of gulls calling to each to each other, of waves gently reaching land, the happy chatter of tourists, skateboards clattering over pavement, and the shrill whistle of a lifeguard in his shack were mesmerizing. The sounds were in harmony with the sights: kites caught on the breeze and colorful beach umbrellas swaying in place. The humidity was indescribable. It was as though I could feel the heavier air entering my lungs and sticking to my skin. It was heaven.

It wasn't heaven for the temperature of my room, though, so I closed the window and let the AC do its job of keeping things cool. I efficiently unpacked my bags and hung my clothing before flopping down on the bed. In this state of happiness, I decided not to listen to Mother's warnings at all. She'd been convinced that I was walking into the biggest disappointment of my life. However, I told myself that of course, Halstead House would be as beautiful as I'd always imagined. Of course, the island would live up to my expectations. Of course, everything would be fine.

Of course . . .

CHAPTER 2

I stood on the street facing Halstead House mid-morning of the next day, soaking up the sunlight that felt like divine approval of my decision to be here. This, this was how I was meant to see it for the first time, with its proud and timeless face bathed in golden island light. I'd always loved sunlight, but here on Lavender Island it felt thick enough to reach out and touch. I imagined that the old house was preening under the warm beams.

Curls of excitement traveled upward from the soles of my feet as I surveyed the grounds. Palm trees lined the path to a large sweeping staircase, inviting visitors to come inside, the same way they had for a hundred years. The color of the mansion was slightly different in person than it had been in the photographs Mary had given me, along with the pictures I'd seen when doing online research. That was okay. I liked this color better. It had more reds in it, and somehow it looked even better against the backdrop of well-manicured greenery than I'd imagined it would.

A smile lifted my lips. The movement alerted my dazed brain, and I mentally shook myself. Here I was, standing on the public street, ogling a building with a look most people reserved for people they were head over heels in love with. Years of training kicked in, quickly wiping the smile away in favor of a calm expression, and I reminded myself of the plan.

I'd given it a lot of thought on my flight, and overnight, and decided that I didn't want to simply barge in and present myself to the Halsteads. To be totally honest, I still wasn't sure how that conversation should go down. *"Hey, I'm Grace, the non-relative who your Great Aunt Mary took under her wing as an honorary granddaughter. I know she's passed away, but here I am. Surprise!"*

I'd decided that I wanted to take the tour first. I wanted the quiet moments to gaze in wonder at all the mysteries the house had to share. I wanted to scope it out and let the old building tell me its stories in an unbiased way. Okay, truth moment: I'd used most of my bravery in just getting here, and I needed a bit of processing time to pump myself up for introductions. There were only so many ways to pop in and announce one's self . . . and none of them made my stomach happy.

I tightened my grip on my purse and turned away from the inviting glow of the mansion's front entrance in order to follow the ticket office signs, which led me to a side path that was paved in cobblestone. My heels click-clacked on the worn stones while my starved gaze drew it all in. I felt as though I knew every detail of this house thanks to Mary's stories, and it was a little puzzling to know it so well but to be seeing it for the first time.

I passed through more beautiful gardens and allowed myself a small pause to look closer at a fountain to the side of one path. It was a simple two-tier fountain with a small wishing pool at the bottom. Mary's husband, Charles, had proposed to her at that fountain. Her eyes had crinkled as she'd described his fear that she'd knock the ring into the water before he could get it onto her finger.

A few birds sat on the side, dipping their beaks into the water and then chattering at each other. It was so ridiculously idyllic that I couldn't help the small laugh that bubbled up. Places like this were meant for storybooks, not for the real world. I had always known that I wasn't a princess, but that didn't mean I couldn't appreciate a fairy-tale castle when I saw one.

I stopped to look between two buildings as the cobblestone path transitioned into a large red-bricked courtyard. Both buildings were made of that same red brick that was now under my feet. The first building was straight ahead and had three large, rounded doors that looked as though they'd once been open archways. I recognized it at once as the carriage house. The second building, to my right, was much smaller with one regular-sized door flanked by two small windows. It had originally been a dual work and storage shed but now functioned as a ticket office and the beginning of the public tour. It could have been a porta-potty and I'd have thought it was the loveliest thing I'd ever seen.

Stepping out of the morning sunlight into the dark little building came as a bit of a shock, and I blinked a few times while I waited for my eyes to adjust. When my vision was restored, I gazed around to see the former storage shed had been turned into a gift shop. There were some books and calendars, a few jars of food preserves, and some post cards. Signs above two doors in the back wall marked them as restrooms. Finally, in a side corner, I saw a counter top with a computer monitor and a young woman, her head down, reading a magazine and bopping her head to some music only she could hear through her headphones.

The girl's head popped up as I walked toward the counter, her short dark curls continuing to bop for a moment with the sudden movement, and she smiled as she removed her headphones.

"Hi," she said in a rich, deep voice. "Sorry, I didn't realize we already had people coming to see the house. We usually don't get much business in here until the afternoon when it gets hot on the beaches and people are looking for something to do indoors." Her smile reached her dark eyes, making her entire face seem to glow.

"It's not a problem at all," I returned with a small smile. "How much are tickets?"

"How many?"

"Oh, just me," I said easily, used to doing things on my own.

"That's ten dollars," the girl stated before turning slightly to type something into the screen in front of her.

I dug out a crisp ten-dollar bill and handed it to the girl whose name tag said Jayla. As soon as the money was put in a cash box under the counter, Jayla reached into another box and pulled out what looked like a small handheld radio attached to an earbud. She began wiping it with a disinfecting cloth while explaining that it was the guided audio tour of the mansion and that I should simply follow the instructions, push the buttons when prompted, and enjoy myself at my own pace. When I was done, I should bring it back to the ticket office.

I lifted one side of my mouth and nodded before putting the ear bud in and giving Jayla a thumbs-up sign. Jayla gave me one in return and I turned around, thrilled to begin the tour I'd been waiting to take my entire life.

The recording suggested I start the tour in the carriage house, but I didn't have the patience for it. I was itching to get inside. I'd been itching for that for as long as I could remember, and now that I was here, I wasn't going to waste one precious moment with modes of transportation. I'd circle around to the carriage house later, assuming I could get myself out of the mansion.

Walking through the majestic front doors into the large grand foyer felt like a dream. It was the equivalent to me of having had a dream as a child of owning a unicorn, but now as an adult someone telling me they were real and buying one for me. It was thrilling. Pure magic.

I stayed in that dream-like state for the entire tour. At long last I was seeing for myself the rooms, the colorful wallpaper, the enormous gaudily framed mirrors, the large stained-glass window, the floors creaking just where Mary said they would. The only person I encountered was the tour guide, who was available to answer questions, but had only smiled as I'd walked by. When the tour came to an end, I couldn't bear to be done, so I slipped silently back to the carriage house and started it over at the actual, recommended beginning.

If I had been forced to express to someone how I felt, or what I was thinking, I doubt I would have been able to find the words. How does a person describe finding something like home in a strange new place? All I could say for sure was that I was feeling more deeply about this mansion than I ever had about a home I had lived in. Somehow the barrage of joy as I ran my hand along the handrails and let my eyes caress the furniture felt almost like fear.

My stomach began to growl as the second tour drew to a close. I'd been too excited to eat much for breakfast. I made my way back to the grand foyer, intending to return to the ticket office and hand back the hand-held tour recording. My footsteps were slow even though I was starving. I didn't have a reason to stay, and I really needed to eat, but there was nowhere else I wanted to be.

I once again came upon the cheerful tour guide as I dragged my feet through the entrance hall. He was tall and lean, with the look of someone who had been athletic in their youth. His white hair was cut close, his face clean-shaven, his blue eyes warm and bright. This time he did more than offer a friendly smile.

"You seem to be in love with the place," he greeted. "I'm guessing my face looked just like yours the first time I walked through those doors."

I nodded, a self-deprecating grin on my face. "You have no idea."

"Oh, I think I do. After all, I begged them for a job on the spot."

He gestured for me to enter the front formal parlor to the side of the hall. With nowhere else to be, and a strong desire not to leave this place, I happily shoved down the hunger pangs and walked beside him into the beautifully wallpapered room.

"Did they give you a job right then?" I asked as I took a seat on a bench that had been put in the room for guests to sit on. It was lovely, but definitely not one of the original family pieces.

The man sat next to me. "No, they didn't. They're pretty picky around here," he said with an amused expression. "But I kept coming back, learned all I could about this old place, and finally wore them down. They let me start by helping with maintenance. It didn't take them long to notice that the house was crumbling because I was too busy answering all the guests' questions rather than doing my job. They hired a new maintenance man and made me the official tour guide. It's been a great couple of years here. The house is back in shape, and the tourists are happy."

I smiled at him. "It seems like everyone came out a winner then. I think working here would be a dream come true."

"It's become my second home," he replied matter-of-factly. "I'd say it's my first home, but my wife gets all tied up in knots if I don't at least pretend." His laugh was soft and gravelly in the large room. My smile grew more natural in response.

He allowed silence to fall, and we sat companionably for a few moments, looking at the beautiful blue and gold wallpaper and the gauzy gold curtains swaying lazily in the coastal breeze, each lost in our own thoughts. I tried to picture Mary, age seven, moving into this big beautiful home with her parents and her older brother, John Edward. The happiness they'd felt here still floated around me, making the house feel alive.

"You know, they're looking for an assistant event planner." He broke the silence. "I don't suppose you have experience with that sort of thing?"

An odd thundering began in my veins as my heart rate picked up. As an exhibit coordinator and fundraiser volunteer, I had spent countless hours organizing events, putting together everything from displays to food, approving invitation designs, and calling sponsors. Every single cell in my body knew, absolutely knew, that I could assistant-event-plan the heck out of this place.

A job here would be the answer to several of my open-ended questions. I could spend all day soaking up Halstead House and getting involved in a way that a simple tourist never could. I'd find a place to stay and extend my car rental, because the money from this job would cover those expenses. I was practically shaking with the possibilities.

While inside I was flipping out, I sat sedately with my hands clasped in my lap to keep them from shaking and looked thoughtfully back at him. "Actually, I do have some experience in that area."

"Something told me you might."

Of course, they'd have to know up front that I'd be a temporary employee, which might kick all this opportunity right into the proverbial chum bucket. "I might be interested, but things are kind of complicated."

His brows raised. "Complicated, you say?"

I nodded.

"Sounds interesting. I'm Steven, by the way." A glimmer had entered Steven's eye, as though he saw right through my display to the heart beating for joy inside of me.

"Grace," I stated, sticking out my hand and grasping his larger one.

"Well, Grace, let's see if we can't get you a meeting with Ms. Halstead." He squeezed my hand lightly before standing up and turning to leave the room.

I scrambled to my feet, caught off guard, and hurried to follow. "Wait, do you mean see her right now?" I definitely wanted the job, but I'd need to apply, prepare a resume, and set an appointment to interview. I needed time to shop for an appropriate outfit and clean up my manicure. I probably needed a breath mint. Aaah!

"Yes, ma'am." He nodded over his shoulder at me. "Right now."

I'd never had problems with my hearing, but I couldn't quite believe he meant we were going to meet Ms. Halstead immediately. My heart rate spiked again. I was going to meet Mary's great-niece, current matron of the family and caretaker of their legacy. I was excited, but I wasn't prepared.

My heel clicks kept time with my heartbeats as we crossed into the entry hall and up the grand staircase. We passed the open second floor and made our way up the last flight to the private top floor of the mansion.

Steven was annoyingly un-winded when we reached the top of the staircase and entered a large foyer area. He was acting as if this was all routine. "Wait one moment, please."

Telling me to wait there was totally unnecessary. I couldn't have walked another step if my life depended on it. A lump rose in my throat as I looked around the private foyer and hallways leading off of it. Mary's own bedroom had been in this part of the house. Maybe a little of her love still lingered near.

Not five minutes later I found myself sitting in a brown leather chair and facing the mistress of Halstead House. My hungry eyes raked over her, seeing enough resemblance to Mary to make my toes curl. I was truly here, talking to an actual Halstead. Really, it was just too much. My typical reserve was going to crack if things didn't slow down a bit. This little sheep was about to shed her wool.

Ms. Halstead was looking directly at me, her green eyes an exact match to the tailored blazer she wore. Her short gray hair was styled immaculately and tucked behind each ear, showing off earrings that would have made even Mother take a second glance. I felt frumpy in comparison.

"Steven tells me he found a job candidate touring the home," she said matter-of-factly.

"Yes, ma'am. I took the tour twice," I replied.

"What did you think?" She leaned back in her chair and clasped her jeweled fingers together. Her fingernails were perfectly manicured. I wanted to tuck mine under my legs.

"I think it's probably the most beautiful place I've ever seen."

Her lips relaxed into a soft smile at the obvious sincerity. "Well, on that we can agree. You've been told that I'm looking for an assistant event planner?"

I nodded.

"I handle the events, the charitable fundraising, the advertising, the household staff, and really anything else that has to do with Halstead House itself. It's becoming a bigger job, and I need an assistant. Someone with experience."

"I understand. I have experience in all those areas."

"Well, it's easy to say so, but with no resume and no references it would be difficult for me to verify that." One eyebrow raised slightly in timeless challenge.

I had seen worse. I lifted my chin a notch and calmly met her look. "Of course. However, you understand that I did not come here looking for a job, nor do I carry a resume in my purse in case tour guides attempt to drop one in my lap."

Ms. Halstead's face was unreadable for a moment before a large grin broke out. "Very well said. Now, tell me your name and all about you."

I relaxed and returned the smile, although I kept it small and demure as I'd been taught. No one liked all those teeth flashing in their faces, Mother's voice reminded. "My name is Grace Burke. I'm from Rhode Island. I've been working as an exhibit and content coordinator for the State Historical Society. I also do a lot of fundraising volunteer work in the area."

"Grace Burke, you say?" She tapped her manicured finger to her lips. "From Providence?"

"Yes, ma'am."

She shook her head as if clearing it. "No, it would be too great a coincidence," she mumbled to herself while continuing to look me over. Finally, she seemed to come to a conclusion and she leaned forward in her chair. "Is there any chance you knew my great aunt, Mary Reed?"

At the mention of Mary's name, I let my smile grow. "Yes. She was my . . . well . . . adopted grandmother, I suppose."

"You're George and Lillian's daughter?" Ms. Halstead was beaming now, her smile so like Mary's that I was surprised to find happy tears threaten.

"I am."

"How wonderful. If I remember correctly, she always called you her 'sweet Gracie'. Mary told me several times how much she wanted you to see Halstead House and to meet us all."

"Yes. It's all she spoke of while I was growing up," I replied.

"I do believe she left you some pictures when she passed away?" She leaned back again, a nostalgic smile on her face.

"Yes. I still have them."

"How lovely that you've found your way to us at last."

I nodded, yet again.

"And Steven tried to offer you a job. Mary would just love this twist!"

I too could imagine Mary's delighted laughter over this turn of events. She was dancing a heavenly jig, for sure.

"Actually, ma'am, I really would love the job if you feel I'm qualified," I said. The words popped out so suddenly and without thought that my smile died and I pressed my fingertips to my mouth in surprise.

"I'm sure you'd be perfect for the job, dear, but don't you have a job in Providence?"

I cleared my throat and dropped my hand. "Yes, I'd have to be a temporary solution, but I took a three-month sabbatical and can stay through June."

"Three months?"

"Yes. I might be having a mid-life crisis." More unplanned words popped out.

20

Ms. Halstead's eyes crinkled as I clamped my mouth shut once more. I couldn't understand why I was acting so out of character. What was going on with me? Did all Halstead women have the gift of pulling me out of myself like Mary had?

"I'll bet Lillian is just beside herself." She raised an eyebrow and gave me a look, letting me know that she knew all about Lillian Burke.

"Let's just say I'm doing my best to avoid any conversations with her right now," I whispered through tight lips, sharing a secret and feeling a prickle of delight over it.

Ms. Halstead's eyes widened a split second before she threw her head back and laughed out loud. I enjoyed her amusement, and by some miracle her reaction washed away my feelings of embarrassment.

"I do believe I simply must have you as my assistant," she stated. "Also, please call me Eliza."

Eliza. She wanted me to call her Eliza. It was too wonderful for words. "Are you sure? I have to mention again that I can only stay for three months."

"Of course I'm sure. A lot can happen in that amount of time. Perhaps we'll make you fall so in love with our little island that you won't be able to leave."

I refrained from commenting, knowing better than to actually entertain the thought, even if my stomach did a little flip at the idea of becoming a permanent part of life on Lavender Island. The beauty of it was that no matter what happened, I was going to get three months to really dive right in. It was more than I'd ever hoped for.

Eliza rose from behind her desk when we'd finished talking through the details, and I followed suit. We walked together to the door, where Eliza surprised me by reaching out and gathering me into a hug. The soft floral scent of her perfume wrapped me in a second hug. Although Eliza was smaller than me, her arms pulled me in firmly, and she pressed her soft, wrinkled cheek against mine.

"Since Mary can't be here to say it, I'll say it for her. Welcome to Halstead House, Grace."

I allowed myself to relax for one brief moment before gently pulling away.

"Now, let's get your things and get you a bedroom. We've much to do and there's little time for dawdling."

"A bedroom?" I stuttered.

Eliza waved a casual hand above her shoulder in my direction as she proceeded down the hall toward the stairs. "Of course, dear. You'll live on-site."

Well, then. Always obedient, but not always this willing, I turned and followed Eliza out the door. As far as mid-life crises went, this one was working out rather well.

CHAPTER 3

I SHOULD HAVE KNOWN THE MOMENT I BROKE SCRIPT AND HOPPED a plane to a distant island across the country from my home that my comfort zone would be destroyed. "Astonishing" was the only word adequate enough to describe the sudden upheaval in my life.

After my impromptu job interview, I had eaten a light lunch with Eliza. The first floor conservatory where we had eaten was paradise. The women of the Halstead family had dedicated themselves to cultivating ferns for decades, and the results were incomparable. We'd eaten surrounded by air heavy with the smells of earth and salt.

My head was spinning so quickly that I couldn't say for sure what food had been on my plate. I'd vacillated between excitement and horror, amazement and a crippling fear that I'd made a huge mistake. I'd never made a choice about employment without Mother's input. It didn't seem to matter that I was famished; the knots in my stomach had kept me from being able to get much down.

I'd heard other staff members around, and caught the impression of a smaller, dark-haired woman as she'd bustled in with our food, but other than Steven, I had been introduced to no one.

Lunch had been a slow affair, with Eliza treating me as a welcome guest. Conversation had steered clear of heavier topics, for which I was grateful. After we finished eating, I was dismissed back to my little motel room with instructions to do any errands I had and then bring myself and my belongings directly back. Eliza would have a bedroom prepared for me, and I would begin work first thing the next morning.

After making a list of necessary items, I had run a few errands, taken myself out to a celebratory dinner, and just as a chime on my watch dinged the hour of eight o'clock, I had arrived back on the grounds. It was the very first day I'd ever laid eyes on the place, and I was about to become a resident.

I slammed the trunk closed on my little sensible rental car and took a deep breath. Eliza had told me where I could find a ground level side door that the staff used, as the main entrance would be locked for the evening. I carried my luggage to where she'd told me I'd find the door, anticipation zinging up my spine like little flickers of flame. My fingers shook as I pressed a doorbell and waited.

The door opened after only a moment, revealing a small, younger, beautiful woman with her dark hair braided down to her waist. Her eyes quickly and curiously raked over me before she smiled, big and wide and welcoming.

"You must be Grace Burke. Eliza told me you'd be coming tonight." Her voice was cheerful with a slight accent that gave it a musical quality. She swung the door wide and gestured for me to walk past her into the dimly lit basement hallway. "I'm Ana. I'll show you to your room."

I followed with butterflies tickling inside. I couldn't remember the last time I'd felt butterflies. Ana kept a brisk pace, forcing me to hurry along even though I was easily a head taller. She led me through what felt like a maze of twisting hallways before stopping in front of a metallic door and pushing a button. I was surprised to realize there was an elevator in the house, and even more so that I'd be riding it.

"Aren't staff bedrooms here in the basement?" I asked. "I'd assumed my room would be down here."

"Yep. You're a little different because you'll be Eliza's personal assistant and she wants you close to her. Your room is on the top floor. In case you ever need me after hours, mine is down here, right across the hall from the elevator," Ana stated, gesturing to a door nearby.

Eliza could have assigned me the tool shed out back and I wouldn't have cared one bit, but to be told that I'd been given a room on the top floor was a pleasant surprise. That was the family floor. For the next three months I was going to live at Halstead House in the family quarters. A faint prickle of Mother's voice teased at my mind, reminding me to not get overly attached or assume anything.

Ana was still talking, and with some effort I tuned back in. "Chef Lou is next to me. Around the corner is Marshall. He's head of maintenance, and you'll like him. Chef Lou, well, he's nice, but I think he uses a fake accent. You listen and tell me what you think, okay?" Ana wiggled her eyebrows playfully.

I wasn't used to eyebrows being wiggled at me, and my reply came out wooden and unsure. "Okay. Sure." Which is the exact technique I'd always used to attract friends. Sigh.

The elevator dinged and Ana politely stood to the side, allowing me and my luggage to roll in first. We rode up in silence, in that unspoken elevator way, until we reached the top floor and stepped out into the large open foyer where I'd first met Eliza. Her office door was straight ahead and sat slightly ajar. To the left was a side hallway. To the right was another side hallway and the grand staircase that I'd climbed earlier.

Ana turned toward the shorter hallway on the left, and I was quick to follow. At the end were two doors. She swung open the one on the left and gestured for me to enter.

"This is you. The other door in this hall is a bathroom that you can use. Mr. Halstead and Ms. Eliza have bedrooms down the other hallway. I have a couple things to do, but I'll see you at breakfast tomorrow morning. We eat at eight. Chef Lou's accent might be fake, but the man knows how to cook. You'll be chubby soon if you aren't careful." Ana chuckled. "Welcome, Ms. Burke."

I set my luggage down and hesitantly returned her smile. "Please, call me Grace."

Ana nodded once. "Okay." Then she turned, braid flying, and made good time getting down the hall and out of sight.

I wondered for a moment what Ana's role was in the household, but I'd been too distracted to ask. Guess I'd have to ask at breakfast the next morning.

I closed the door behind me and turned to take in the room. It was at least the same size as my bedroom in Providence, if not a little bigger. It was done in rich dark woods, the walls papered in wonderful sea green. The bedspread was white, the bed soft and fluffy. It wasn't modern, but instead retained much of its original 1900s style. I adored it immediately.

A lamp was glowing on the nightstand, a warm sign of welcome and a reminder that I wasn't totally alone in this new place. Sitting propped up under the lamp was an envelope with my name written in delicate, curvy handwriting. I left my luggage near the door and went to the note. When I opened the envelope a key slid out, falling to the carpet. I bent to retrieve it and looked with wonder at the old-fashioned design. It was bronze and heavy, and I felt ridiculously elated that it hadn't been modernized. I lazily played with the key as I opened the note.

It was from Eliza, welcoming me to the house and explaining that the key could be used to enter the same side entrance in the basement that I had just come in. I was free to come and go as needed. I looked back at the key, happiness crawling up inside of me like a living thing, before setting it back down on the side table and refolding the note.

A light breeze drew my attention toward the open window. I kicked off my heels and crossed the room to take in the view. I was greeted first by a soft breeze wafting over my face and arms. Next my eyes were pulled to the view. From here it seemed I could see the entire island. The smells and sounds were new and invigorating.

To my right were the outbuildings, including the gift shop and the carriage house. A bit farther to the right was the ocean. It was too dark now to see it clearly, but I could hear the waves crashing on the sand, and it felt like a friendly greeting. Straight ahead and to the left lay the city. The strip of city lights was tiny compared to home, twinkling here and there, occasionally hidden by shadowy leaves dancing slightly.

I took a few moments to breathe deeply and attempt to shake off the last of the worries I'd harbored about my plan to come here.

So far things were working out just fine, even if the speed with which things had fallen together was a bit unnerving. I'd always been so methodical in my decision making, weighing in Mother's input heavily and rarely trusting my gut. Today I'd used my heart, throwing logic to the proverbial wind, and my head was reeling.

"Mary," I whispered into the breeze. "Do you see me here? Can you believe I made it?" I knew no answer would come, but I smiled to myself, imagining Mary taking my hand in her soft, bony one.

Eventually I pulled myself away from the window and set to work unpacking. It didn't take long, as I only had one suitcase. I hung clothes in the closet, filled a single dresser drawer, and then simply sat on the bed for a moment to soak in the room.

Satisfied with my arrangements, I flopped back on the bed and looked up at the ceiling. I'd been avoiding the thought all day, but I was going to have to call Mother at some point. Especially now that I had a job and was definitely going to be staying for a while.

I sighed as I sat up. I didn't want Mother to ruin my first actual day at Halstead House the next day, so I figured it best to get it over with now. I stood and reached to the ceiling, stretching my arms and back as I took slow, deep breaths. Then I bent and touched my hands to the floor, still breathing deeply and letting my eyes close. Finally, I stood straight and shook out my arms and legs as I finished getting myself into the right mental zone. I needed to be cool and calm because this phone call would not go well if I showed any signs of agitation.

The phone rang only twice before Mother's crisp voice answered. "Grace, thank goodness you're alive. I've been beside myself with worry."

I hoped this wasn't going to be how every conversation started for the next three months. "Hello, Mother. I'm alive and well. The island is beautiful, and Halstead House was as amazing as I'd always thought."

She made a scoffing noise. "I'm not surprised you feel that way. You love anything Mrs. Reed said to love."

As a child I'd been hurt by Mother's coolness toward Mary, but as an adult I'd come to realize that Mother had been jealous of my relationship with the other woman. I found her feelings perplexing, as Mother was the center that my entire world was formed around. I'd tried to comfort and reassure her over the years, but she'd staunchly refused to call Mary by anything other than her last name.

"It really is a beautiful home. So well preserved. The history buff inside of me is loving it," I responded kindly.

"Was it worth deserting your poor, lonely, aging mother?"

I took a silent, slow, fortifying breath. "I didn't desert you."

"It depends upon your perspective," she stated. "When will you be coming home?"

"I'll be here until June."

"June!" Mother shrieked and I shrank back, even though she was nowhere near. I hated her anger. "Grace Natalie, you do realize that June is three months away?"

"I do." I forced my voice to sound confident.

"You just expect me to sit here and wait for you to return, and not care about where you are or what kind of things you're doing?"

"I know you'll worry. I'm sorry about that."

I could practically hear it as Mother shifted from anger to her ice mode. "Very well. I'll put you out of my mind."

"You know that's not what I want," I habitually soothed.

"Clearly it is. Your actions have made that obvious. I will see you in June. Hopefully you will still remember me by then."

I heard the line click as she disconnected the call. I rubbed a hand over my face and let my phone fall to the bed. Well, at least it had been predictable. Manipulation, anger, freeze out. The order remained forever the same. Guilt, the fourth step, was setting in, and I needed to fight it or this argument would go the way of all the rest—with me caving and begging for forgiveness. Although it had been a long time since we'd made it to freeze out. Usually I caved at anger.

Glancing at the clock, I saw that it was almost nine. My body was tired enough to sleep, but my mind needed to settle. A walk around the property would do the trick. The gardens had been so beautiful, the fountain especially.

I slipped out of my dress, happy to change into the more worn and soft fabrics that I wore in the privacy of my own home.

After putting on comfortable pants, a silky shirt, and sandals, I grabbed the key to the house from the side table and quietly slipped into the hallway. I opted to take the elevator, as I didn't want to draw attention to myself by taking the stairs through the house. The ride down was silent other than the creaking of the pulley system. After getting off in the basement, I made only one false turn before finding the door I was looking for and exiting into the darkened night.

I was surprised to feel a chill in the air when I left the house behind. The daytime temperature on this island had been deceptive. With the sun down, I rubbed my arms for warmth. From somewhere close I could hear the waves lapping up onto the sand and feel the constant breeze that swept across the island. I inhaled deeply, pulling the new smells in and pushing the old hurts out.

I truly loved my mother, but I when I'd made my birthday wish and blown out the candles a week ago I'd made a promise to myself that now was the time. I was going to discover who Grace Burke really was, and it was hard to know how to go about that with her pressing on my mind.

I strolled slowly, letting my hands run over the flowers, or caress the rough prickly bark of the palm trees that I found so fascinating. A light caught my attention from off to the side, and I turned toward the outbuildings to see that the carriage house was lit up. Tour hours had long passed, so it seemed like something I should check out.

The door was unlocked and I let myself in. I did not, however, close the door behind me. If one of Mother's psychopath killers was in here I needed to have an escape route at the ready. The only sound was that of my sandals working their way across the cement floor into the main gallery area where the two carriages and three cars were on display. They were beautiful, shiny, and well cared for. There was no sign of anyone else, and my historian's eye verified that they were too valuable to be left with lights blazing and doors open overnight.

"Hello?" I called into the stillness. If no one was out here I'd let Ana know so someone could lock up.

"Over here," a muffled male voice replied.

The voice startled me, a fact that I found amusing since I'd been the one to call out first. I spun quickly to the side, putting a hand up to my chest as I saw his shape start to form out of the corner of my eye.

He was fairly tall, with black hair and olive skin. His hair was cut close, as was his tidy beard. His t-shirt showed broad shoulders and arms, as would be expected of a mechanic who worked with cars and other machinery every day. I didn't remember mention of a mechanic, but then again, I was new and my head was still spinning a bit. His eyes seemed tense as he watched me, and I had the feeling that he saw me as a threat to be analyzed. That was a first. Me, the little lamb, a threat?

"Can I help you with something?" he asked, breaking what had become an awkward silence.

I had intended to weave my way past the carriages to where he was standing near the cars, but something about his tone stopped me from getting closer. "Oh, well . . . I was just curious. I saw the light on. I wanted to make sure everything was okay out here."

He nodded, one flick of his head that I would have missed if my eyes hadn't been glued to his face as realization dawned. I'd seen this man before, but only in pictures.

With a rag in his hand, he gestured to the black car that I hadn't noticed before. "Everything is just fine. I'm waxing the cars." I nodded, unable to speak over the thoughts coursing through my mind. "After hours is the only time I can do that," he added quietly.

"Yes, of course." I felt a nervous tingle in my toes as he stoically met my gaze. His eyes were cautious and unwelcoming, and I struggled to know how to proceed.

This was John Lucas Halstead, Eliza's nephew, and last in the Halstead line. He oversaw the business side of the Halstead empire. He had visited Mary a couple of times with his parents, but I'd never had the chance to meet him. I knew he was several years older than me, and strictly dedicated to the family businesses. Thanks to some shameless internet stalking, I also knew he was a well-dressed, well-traveled professional, who apparently made the ladies swoon. Mary had loved her great-great nephew with the same fierce devotion she'd given to me, and she'd often spoken of her desire for John Lucas and me to meet. For my part, I'd never been that eager to meet him. I'd seriously doubted we'd have much in common.

It was a total out-of-body moment to see him standing there across from me. I knew I was staring, but I couldn't help but catalog the differences from the pictures I'd seen. He looked a little less perfect in person, his nose a little larger, his eyes more hooded, his gaze shuttered. I couldn't decide if I should tell him who I was or not, and the one-sided recognition made me stumble when words finally came.

"I just got hired on today," I said. Smooth.

He nodded again, his stance relaxing slightly. "Well, in that case I hope you won't mind if I get back to work." He waved the cloth again and crouched down to resume his polishing.

"Sure, no problem." I decided to be brave and introduce myself properly, so I zigged around the two cars and came around to look down at him. "I'm . . ." I stuttered to a stop, my desire to make the connection squelched by the look on his face. He wanted me gone. I took an involuntary step backwards. "I'm so sorry. I can see that I interrupted you. I was going to introduce myself, but . . ." My eyes glanced behind me toward the door I'd come in.

Our eyes caught again when I looked back. He remained crouched but pressed his lips into a practiced smile that did nothing to make him look happier. "What's your name?"

"It's, um, my name is Grace." I tried to maintain my cheerful greeting by offering a half smile. It fell after a brief second. He didn't recognize me. And why would he, really? I deflated a hair.

"Hey, Grace." His dark eyes held no interest before they dropped back to the cloth he had in his hand.

He didn't offer his name in return, even though he had no possible way of knowing that I knew who he was. He asked no further questions, and I didn't offer more information as he dipped the cloth into the polish and began wiping where he had left off.

I recognized a brush off when I saw one. He clearly wasn't interested in company. Still, I was a little surprised at how stand-offish he was to a new employee. Maybe Mother had been right, after all, that not everyone was going to welcome me with open arms. It was clear that he had a mile-high wall and that pushing at that wall would be unwelcome. As far as walls went, I understood, perhaps better than most.

CHAPTER 4

I AWOKE THE NEXT MORNING DISORIENTED WHILE STARING AT the cream-colored ceiling above me, as though the past few days had been nothing more than a dream. But no, I was, in fact, watching the sun light up the third-story room before my eyes. This was real. This was the answer to so many unvoiced prayers. Ripples of disbelief coursed through me and settled in my stomach as the reality of this moment sank in. With that came a raging moment of doubt and worry.

With those two emotions creeping along my skin like the devil on my shoulder, a wave of need to call my mother crashed over me. I'd never, ever found myself so far from home without her. My father passed away in a boating accident when I was three years old. My memories of him were not my own, but made up of pictures I'd been shown and stories I'd been told. I couldn't imagine a life where I had not become the object of obsession for my mother. No one could blame her for clinging so tightly to me.

Yet . . . those same people who clicked their tongues, and patted my arm, and told me what a good daughter I was for staying close to my poor mother had never actually lived with Lillian Burke.

I threw the covers back and strode with determination to the closet door. I would not cave. I would remember the candles, and the loneliness, and the pain of having my spirit cry out for more. I would call Mother later, not from a place of worry, but from a

33

place of strength. Today had to be about me. Today had to be about moving forward. I couldn't afford to look over my shoulder.

It was all fine and dandy to give oneself a pep talk, but it was quite another to keep the fires burning when I discovered that my favorite dove gray skirt suit was wrinkled beyond repair. I'm talking next level wrinkles. I had packed it carefully, but clearly underestimated the toll that humidity would take. Even hanging it in the closet overnight had done nothing to help the situation. Without actually sniffing it I could tell that the slightly damp material would be repellent. Nothing but a full dry clean was going to make it wearable. My fairy godmother had fulfilled all my dreams by getting me here; she definitely wasn't going to come back and clean my suit with her magic wand.

I stood in the middle of my cozy room and tapped my bare foot against the hardwood floor in agitation. I needed that suit. I couldn't be expected to face this new day wearing anything less than perfection. My hands were shaking badly enough as it was. Even the mellow sound of the waves lapping on the beach nearby wasn't calming me the way it should.

I'd been too excited last night to think about preparing my clothing, and I berated myself for the oversight, especially when I had such meager offerings to begin with. I certainly hadn't planned to be professionally employed while on the island and had only hastily thrown in a couple of passable garments. My trusty gray suit had been one of those because, well, according to Mother a lady was always prepared. And I had been raised to be a lady right down to the tips of my china doll toes.

I paced to the window to clear my head and think. The view this morning was lovely, with dense gray humidity teasing around the edges. I could finally see those waves I'd only heard the night before. The smile that came to my face at the sight of the much-envisioned dips and swells didn't last long. I was finally here, and instead of making a good first impression, I was fighting with a pile of wrinkled, possibly rank, clothing.

I could do nothing but hope Eliza was still upstairs and ask her about an iron and some de-funking spray. She was a woman who would appreciate an effort toward being presentable.

I cracked the door open to peek down the hallway. No one was in sight, thankfully. I tiptoed across the large foyer to the hallway containing Eliza's room. I knocked lightly on the first door I came to, fingers crossed and prayers to heaven that it wasn't John Lucas's. After our awkward encounter in the carriage house I didn't need him thinking I was a stalker. No one answered that door.

I knocked on the second door, my stomach in knots. Same result. My last efforts were given to Eliza's office door back in the foyer. Third strike, I was out. I slumped in both relief and disappointment. No embarrassing interaction with John Lucas, but no solution to my clothing problem. I chewed on my bottom lip while I thought, a habit my mother greatly disapproved of.

"Can I help you with something?" A deep voice behind me caused me to whirl around.

The first thing I noticed about him was his size. He looked ridiculously large standing in front of the elevator door, his frame hiding it from sight. His skin was such a dark, smooth brown that he seemed to merge into the shadow he cast. He saw my surprise at his sudden appearance, and a slow, bright smile bloomed on his face.

"People always tell me a guy this size shouldn't be so quiet," he chuckled.

"I think they have a point," I stuttered out with a wobbly smile, amused by his comment and embarrassed to be caught standing in my night clothes in the hallway.

He tilted his head and studied me in a friendly way that caused me to relax. "I assume you're our new friend, Grace?"

I nodded.

"I'm Marshall. If you're looking for Eliza, she's up and about before the sun. Anything I can help you with?"

I hurried to him and stuck out a hand. "Nice to meet you, Marshall." He took my smaller hand in his and squeezed it firmly before releasing it.

"Happy to meet you."

"I'm trying to find an iron so I can attempt to resurrect my suit. It got horribly wrinkled while I was traveling here."

Marshall shrugged his shadow-casting shoulders and shook his head. "Wish I could help, but I never iron anything. Ana could tell you where to find one if you can wait until after breakfast."

I recognized a lost battle and made a face. "I suppose I'll have to admit defeat and choose something else to wear. Thanks for your help, though."

Marshall nodded and turned down the hallway toward Eliza's and John Lucas's rooms. I went the opposite direction and stood in front of the mostly empty closet again. After some more careful consideration, I chose a blush pink silk button-up top and black slacks, with shiny black heels to finish off the outfit. It wasn't my first choice, but beggars can't be choosers. While I had a small handful of nicer clothing I could mix and match to get by, the truth was I hadn't wanted to bring all my best clothing. I had purposely left it behind, wanting to be someone else for a while. I hadn't realized that leaving all that behind would feel like I'd left my protection behind too. Every wolf needs her lamb-skin around her.

I quickly applied my makeup and pulled my hair into a loose chignon, careful to squash any fly-aways. I stood in the bedroom doorway and crossed my fingers on both hands in front of me for a moment, willing nothing but happiness to come from this. I was as ready as I'd ever be.

I made my way down the back staircase, what would have been considered the service stairs when the mansion was built, and wondered what I'd find in the kitchen. While I had never been anything less than upper middle class, household staff was far out of my experience, and I felt unsure of what I would find. Would they accept me into their group? Would they know I was sort of family and keep a distance between us? Were they a group at all, or more like some of the museum staff I worked with who went independently about their duties, uninterested in friendships? Would the Halsteads be eating there too, or did they dine separately?

I had never been good at inserting myself into a group. I was too afraid of making a misstep or pushing myself on someone who didn't want my company. I'd been so isolated as a child, with home tutors and only adults for company, that my first public schooling experience was college. I marveled at the ease others had in talking to each other, forming study groups, and comfortably chatting about whatever crossed their minds. Even more eye-opening had been the light-hearted debating between peers. I couldn't understand how disagreeing with each other didn't destroy relationships. I'd obsessively watched how the others behaved, wanting desperately to fit in, but my desperation had exacerbated my shyness, leaving me forever on the sidelines, until I'd given up and accepted my place. Lately, however, I'd felt a sneaking loneliness, like the starving child pressing her nose up to the bakery window, wanting to be fed, wanting what those rosy-cheeked people inside had.

I paused outside the large swinging kitchen door and took a deep breath as I pushed a lifetime of experiences down, allowing myself a moment of quiet. Getting out of bed this morning and choosing to not call Mother had been my first big speed bump of today. Now, a second decision had to be made in this moment, before I entered that room and first impressions were made. I had come to this island mansion because I was tired of being lonely and predictable. Now it was time to face the social scene, and I could go forward as I had for the past twenty-five years, or I could try something new. I could open my mouth, speak some words, and try to let inner Grace have a little breathing room.

I had to believe that given a true chance I could learn to have friends and open up. It was either that or accept that the future would never be brighter than the past. One thing I knew for sure: I wasn't dead yet. As long as my lungs were pulling air, I had a chance to change.

With head high and heart attempting to beat straight out of my chest, I opened the door and entered a world I'd never expected to inhabit. It was a world of swirling steam, banging pots, conversation, and delicious smells. It was in absolute contrast to my sterile life. My eyes hardly knew where to look first.

An older man, who was as pale as his white coat, stood next to a stove top, his face red from the heat, barely legible words flowing out of his mouth quicker than I could pick them up while steam rose around him. Ana and Marshall were sitting around a large wooden table in the center of the room, eating and chatting comfortably with smiles on their faces, oblivious to the chef's constant chatter. To me it looked like a scene from a sitcom. My lips curved at the corners as my stomach responded to the heavenly smells.

Ana was the first person to notice me. "Hey, Grace. Good morning. How did you sleep?" She gestured for me to come all the way in. "Marshall tells me you needed an iron? Your clothes look fine to me."

"Girl, don't you listen?" Marshall pointed at me with his fork. "I said she wanted to wear her suit. Does that look like a suit to you?"

Ana pulled a face at Marshall before looking back at me. "Don't let us keep you from getting some breakfast." She tipped her head slightly toward the cooking area. "That's Chef Lou."

I aimed toward the stove top, where several dishes were being kept warm—cinnamon rolls, a veggie frittata, and what appeared to be the makings of eggs Benedict. Chef Lou was finishing the hollandaise sauce as I took a plate and stepped up to make my selection.

"The fruit is there," he said in what sounded like a French accent, barely pulling his eyes away from the pan he was studying.

"Thank you. This all looks delicious."

"It is," Lou returned confidently enough that I felt a bubble of amusement rise. "I'm Lou. I cook, you eat, you like. Simple."

I immediately nodded my understanding. "I'm Grace. You cook, I eat. Got it." I happily added the delicious-looking food to my plate, stopping to get fruit at another cook station, and joined the group at the table.

"Well?" Ana asked. Marshall lifted his eyes to see my reply.

"Definitely a fake accent." I nodded and Ana grinned.

Marshall's eyes crinkled as he took a bite of a roll. "I don't know why he bothers when we all know he's from somewhere like Kentucky."

"Maybe he thinks it's the reason Eliza hired him," Ana supplied.

"His cooking is what got him hired. She don't care where he says he's from." Marshall shook his head and took another bite.

"Do the Halsteads not eat with you?" I asked as I cut my frittata into precise pieces.

"Nah, they eat in the dining room, or Ana will take them a plate up to their rooms if they want," Marshall replied. I nodded my understanding. His friendly way of speaking took any possible sting out of his words.

I took another glance around the sunshine-filled kitchen. "I think it's nice that you all dine together. I usually eat alone. This is much better."

"With Marshall smacking his food and that crazy chef talking all the time to himself in his fake accent?" Ana laughed. "I think I'd rather eat alone in my room too."

"You'd miss all this," Marshall said.

"I'm willing to give it a try," Ana teased.

"Where you from, Grace?" Marshall asked.

"Oh, sure, play getting to know you with her on the first day. You didn't talk to me for my first entire week here." Ana rolled her eyes.

"I took one look at you and knew I'd need to step light," Marshall replied. Turning to me he said, "Don't you mind Ana. She's always trying to put on like she's the most picked on person around."

"I have the power to make your life miserable, Marshall. One snap of my fingers and the day staff leaves your sheets unwashed and your bathroom uncleaned. You'd better show me some respect." Ana pursed her lips and raised her chin.

Marshall grinned and playfully raised an eyebrow. "You aren't the only one who can make things hard. How do you feel about no power, or a door that hangs off its hinges?"

I was in awe watching them talk and tease each other like it was the most natural thing in the world. They hardly chewed their food before they spoke, their silverware clinked on the plates, and their elbows were on the table. Both sets of brown eyes, laughing, glanced my way. For a moment I'd almost forgotten that I'd been asked a question. I snapped back to attention.

"Oh, um, I'm from Providence, Rhode Island," I said.

"You have family there?" Ana asked.

"Yes, my mother."

"Just her?" She seemed perplexed by that answer.

"Yes. My father passed when I was very little."

"No brothers or sisters?" Marshall asked around a big bite of fruit.

"No. I'm an only child."

Ana nodded. "Wow. Now we know why she dresses so nice, Marshall. No hand-me-downs. Sounds nice."

Marshall smiled. "It's probably why she eats so nice too. She never had to protect her plate from other hungry mouths."

"All that food and clothes just for you," Ana sighed dreamily. "I bet you even had your own bedroom, didn't you?"

Marshall chuckled. "Of course she did. Not like she was sharing with her mama."

I simply nodded at Ana's inquisitive look.

"What size bed did you have in that room?" Ana asked.

"Queen," I replied.

"Well, that does it. You're the luckiest girl I know. Sleeping in your fresh pajamas, in your queen bed, in your own room." Ana grinned and stood. "Well, the ladies will be here soon, so I'm off to work. I'll have Josie put an iron in your room, Grace, so you'll have it when you need one."

Marshall waved lightly as Ana took her dishes to the sink and slipped through the swinging door. "Don't mind her, Grace. I'm sure it wasn't all easy being an only child."

"I may have had all the space I wanted, but it could be pretty lonely," I admitted. My nerves tingled as I told a truth that made my life look imperfect.

"Well, you're sure never gonna have a chance to feel lonely here." Marshall smiled as he too stood. "I'll see you around."

* * *

"Life as my assistant will be busy over the next three months," Eliza shot over her shoulder as she rifled through a filing cabinet. "We have a charity luncheon, a wedding, a fortieth birthday party, a fiftieth wedding anniversary . . ." Her voice trailed off as she found the paper she was looking for and began to scan it. "Ah, here." She turned and sat gracefully at her desk.

I quickly shifted my expression to a professional, interested look rather than the "how in the world am I sitting across the desk from

Eliza Halstead right now?" jaw-dropped expression I'd been wearing. I was sitting across the desk from her, legs demurely crossed at the ankles, with a note pad and pen at the ready, hoping I was the picture of patience and decorum.

Eliza glanced at me for perhaps the first time that morning and smiled warmly. "Well, aren't you looking professional? You're dressed quite elegantly for our little island."

"I only wish I could have worn my dove gray suit," I bemoaned, the words slipping out almost without thought. Something about Eliza kept making that happen. It was most likely the fact that she looked so much like my beloved Mary.

"This dove gray suit is important somehow?"

"It's my best suit," I replied. My cheeks warmed at the admission.

"Ah, I see. So you can't do your best work in what you're currently wearing?"

I blinked a bit. "Well, not exactly. An outfit won't affect my work."

"Wonderful. Then the gray suit is forgotten."

A dimple poked out on Eliza's cheek, and I couldn't take my eyes off another trait she and Mary shared. She slid the paper she'd been scanning across the spotless, highly polished desk. It stopped in front of me.

I reached out to pick up the offered page, feeling slightly bemused. I wasn't sure how to take Eliza's comment. Of course, I knew the suit didn't give me superpowers, but the importance of a flawless façade was a tune I'd long been marching to. Eliza was beautifully put together herself. I would have expected her to be an ally in the wardrobe department, but . . .

She interrupted my musings. "Now, to quickly go over how the household divvies up tasks for events. Ana really does oversee it all, but to drill down for you, Chef Lou handles the catering. Marshall handles room set up of the tables, chairs, etc. Ana and the rest of her staff make sure the room is clean, and they prepare all linens. She also leads the clean-up after the event. You will assist in planning, gathering decor, running errands, and written correspondence, along with helping me to set up and take down the decor. In reality, we all pitch in where we're needed, but it helps to have a basic understanding of what our main responsibilities are. During an event I will need you to be discreetly ready in the background to handle any issues that arise. I meet with the clients, personally attend and oversee the event, tie up loose ends, handle verbal communication with the clientele, and all hostess duties. Any questions?"

My first thought was that I was terribly overqualified for this job. Back home I was the one overseeing and assigning out duties. Yet, I found the idea of stepping down a notch and doing the background work to be quite appealing. It would be like a three-month-long game of playing hooky. Besides, in my experience, being the one in charge seemed to be another blockade to forming true friendships. Lumping in as a regular old staff member could be a great opportunity.

"That sounds great to me," I replied with a succinct nod and smile.

"On that paper is the information for the charity luncheon we'll be hosting next week. One week from today, actually."

I glanced down and quickly scanned the list, along with a handful of beautiful drawings. The decor and layout ideas took up space on both front and back.

"Who drew this?" I asked.

"I did." Eliza's attention had moved on to more rifling, this time in her desk drawer.

I felt immediately silly for asking the question. Of course, it was her. "It's lovely," I said.

Eliza's head popped up. "Thank you, dear. I should hope it is. I have my degree in interior design."

"I know some people in Providence who would kill to have you working with them."

"There are enough killers on Lavender Island, I assure you," Eliza replied in a lightly amused tone.

I looked back up and blushed slightly. "I'm sorry. Of course you have work enough here. I just . . ."

Eliza cut me off with a wave. "It's nothing, dear. I consider it a compliment, so thank you. Moving along. After the charity luncheon comes the wedding. I'm currently fifty–fifty on if the bride will end up being terrible or not. Her mother seems sane, which is always a good start. You never know, though. As a wedding draws closer, the sanity tends to come in shorter supply." She pushed a second paper my way. "I had a meeting with the bride a couple of months ago and this is her idea for decor. What do you think?"

I looked over the second sheet and was taken aback to find that the wedding colors were a bright fuchsia pink and a rust orange. I glanced back up to Eliza, who had a poker face on.

"I'm surprised by the colors. They seem a little . . ." I searched for an appropriate word.

"Gaudy and ill-matching are the words you're looking for," Eliza stated. "This is why I'm waiting for the bride to lose her mind. These are not sensible colors, yet she insists they'll go beautifully together." Eliza snatched the paper back and jotted something down before handing it to me once more. "Regardless, it'll be your job to gather the necessary decor."

"When is the wedding?"

"Two weeks."

I swallowed a big lump. That was soon. "That's not much time."

"That's true. But never fear, we're down to the details at this point. I've been doing it all on my own, but I'm so happy to have you to help wrap up the little things. Food and catering staff are ready to go. Marshall has hired outside staff and knows the required layout. Ana is fantastic at her job. We'll be just fine." Eliza smiled warmly, which helped me relax.

"Great."

Eliza leaned back into a more relaxed position and asked, "How's your room?"

"My room?"

"Yes, dear. The place you slept last night. Was it to your liking?"

My lips curved up. Eliza's thoughts seemed to flit like a hummingbird. "It's a charming room."

"I hoped you'd like it. It was my room when I was a girl."

Without thinking, I allowed a full smile to bloom across my face. "Really?"

Eliza's face softened. "Yes. I loved the view from that window. It seemed like the whole world was at my feet. As a visitor I thought you would enjoy seeing the island from up there."

"I do. I looked out for quite a while last night. It was so kind of you to give me a room upstairs. I would have been more than happy in the basement with the other staff."

"Except you're not merely staff, are you?" Eliza let out a breath and hopped to her feet. "As if I'm going to take a chance on having Aunt Mary haunt me from her grave. I'm happy you like the room. Now, let's give you the private tour of this place. First stop, the linen closet near your bathroom. I think you'll be pleased with the assortment of chocolates I keep in the bin labeled 'Clothespins'. My darling nephew still hasn't caught on."

Eliza swooped around her desk and out the door while I hurried to follow, a smile on my lips.

CHAPTER 5

THE FIRST MONDAY AFTER MY ARRIVAL WAS A BREEZY, SUN-KISSED morning and, as happened every Monday, Halstead House was closed and paychecks were given out. Not direct-deposited paychecks every two weeks, but weekly checks, handwritten by Eliza. Everyone had an entire day off to do whatever they wanted or needed to do. Number one on my list was finding some new clothes.

Even though I'd scrimped up enough to be presentable, I was obsessing over the need to bring my wardrobe up to par. I could send for all the stylish pieces in my condo, but the more I thought about it, the more I realized I'd worked too hard over the past five days in trying to relax a bit, join in the chitchat, and present a new side of myself. Old clothes that my mother had shopped for and approved weren't welcome to the new party. I needed to figure out what my actual style was. Also, all the travel shows I've ever watched say to immerse yourself in the local scenes, which I'd assume would include clothes shopping, in order to get a better feel for wherever you find yourself. Lavender Island was a place I wanted to fully experience.

Okay, in the interest of total honesty, number two on my list was to find a dry cleaner. Despite Eliza's easy attitude, and my own metamorphosis, I could not let the dove gray superpower suit go. I fully planned to wear it on the day of the charity luncheon, which was to be my first working event. It had only been five days, after all. I couldn't be expected to give up all my old ways that fast.

Maybe number three needed to be to find a therapist and ask if this roller coaster of thought, this wanting the old while aching for the new, was normal.

With the kitchen closed for the day, I decided I'd hunt down breakfast on the touristy main strip. I sat at the desk in my room and made a to-do list for the day before slipping into khaki slacks and a loose button-down blouse. My one nod to a beachy day off was a pair of strappy sandals. With my hair pulled back perfectly, makeup artfully applied, and power suit slung over my arm, I was ready to head out.

Opting for the main stairway, I paused two floors down to let the colored light coming through the stained-glass window tickle my eyes. I took advantage of any chance I got to linger here. The grand staircase was two full stories high, and the window made the most of it, standing a regal twenty feet. The colored glass scene was that of a family in a garden, surrounded by roses, sitting on the grass. Father and Mother leaned close while their three children lounged at their feet. After so many years of seeing it in pictures, the reality of it had left me speechless. I had fallen in love with the vibrant greens, reds, and blues, but especially with the softer colors woven throughout that had been lost in the photographs. It was a powerful work of art that made a simple statement about the value of family.

"Where you off to today, Grace?" Ana called from the grand foyer below, causing me to turn and look down the last flight of stairs toward her happily upturned face.

After only a few days it was unusual to see her without a couple of people following her and taking her orders. I'd learned that Ana was over the smooth running of the entire household. Lou and Marshall technically reported to her, along with a staff of a half dozen day workers who worked on anything from cleaning, to gardening, to grocery shopping, and helping Lou with food preparation. It all fell under Ana. She was young, probably only a couple of years older than me, but she bore the responsibility well and the household felt cheerful and alive under her hand. So different from the cold way I was raised.

This morning she was dressed casually in shorts and a tank, with what looked to be swim suit straps peeking out. She had flip flops on her feet and sunglasses propped up on her head. A big beach bag was hanging from one slender shoulder. She looked like a beach day postcard.

I smiled and descended the stairs. "Dry cleaners first. Then I have a list of errands."

Her brow puckered. "A list?"

"Yes, a list. I have several things to do today." I nodded as I came to stand near her.

"This is your first full day off."

"Which is why I have a list of errands," I confirmed.

"Who makes lists for their day off?" Now her lips pursed.

That familiar feeling of being somehow different from everyone else clogged my throat, and I resisted the urge to clear it or cough. "I'm sure Eliza makes lists," I defended, unwilling to admit that I'd been practicing the fine art of making lists since learning to write.

"Well, of course. She's a Halstead. They practically invented list making. The rest of us islanders wouldn't dream of it."

"Yes, but I'm not an islander." That bright realization made the tension woosh out. It was okay. I was different because I was from a different place. "If only you could meet my mother."

Ana sighed. "Fair enough. Let me see it."

"What?"

She held out her hand and wiggled her fingers. "This important list of yours." I opened my purse and carefully retrieved the rose-colored stationary. Ana was shaking her head before even taking a look at it. "This is very disappointing," she said while looking over what I'd written.

"Did I forget something?"

"Yes. You did." Ana looked up at me as the side of her mouth lifted. "You forgot to have some fun." She tore the list into pieces and tucked them into the pocket of her shorts before I could react. My mouth opened and my eyes grew round, but no words came out. "Don't worry, I tucked the scraps in my pocket so they wouldn't litter the foyer." Ana grinned broadly. "This will never do for your first full, uninterrupted day here."

"But, Ana, I . . ."

"You can shop after work another day. Today is too perfect to pass up. We're going to the beach."

I felt like my feet had been knocked out from beneath me. "I'm not dressed for that, and this dry cleaning must be taken in."

"No problem. I'll have Derek take it with Eliza's things tomorrow."

"I can't possibly let you charge it to the household accounts." My face heated at the very idea.

"Did I say I was going to charge it to the house? No. I said I'd have it dropped off tomorrow. You can pick it up on your own time and pay with your own money." Ana put her hands on her hips and gave me a look.

"I . . . " I blinked a few times.

"You what?"

"I . . ." My lips pursed in an effort to keep my amusement from showing. "You sure put the 'bull' in bulldozer."

Her eyes swung toward the ceiling like she was thinking hard about it. Then she shrugged, having apparently decided I was correct and she accepted the assessment.

"Have you never taken a day off before?" she asked.

"Of course I have."

"Without a list?" Her head tilted and raised her eyebrows.

"Maybe." I allowed a small smile.

It worked. Ana laughed and I felt like the man who walked on the moon. "Well, buckle up, newbie. Today I introduce you to list-free living here on Lavender. We're having a full-fledged beach day. Go change into a swimsuit. Fair warning, if I see anything with buttons or creases I'm sending you back upstairs. Meet me here in five minutes."

My heart rate sped up at the realization that I was being invited along to a beach day. Well, pushed into going, but still . . . "I haven't had breakfast yet."

"It's not a big deal. I'll grab something from the kitchen while you change into your suit."

I chewed my lower lip. An unplanned, totally spontaneous day on the beach with Ana sounded like exactly the kind of thing I'd always dreamed of doing. It was so tempting that I was practically paralyzed by worry.

"Grace, get moving. I'm not wasting my day off trying to convince you to take that rod out of your spine. It's now or never. Your list is gone. Your dry cleaning will be handled. Move it!"

I jumped, finding some precious familiarity in her commanding tones. With my body obeying and my mind whirling, I headed back up the grand staircase quickly. The sound of Ana's amusement filled the air. My heart rate sped up from the combination of speed stair climbing and nervous excitement. I was going to the beach. Someone had invited me to a day out. I couldn't remember the last time that had happened.

I scrambled into my room, lungs pumping, and found my sensible, navy blue, one-piece bathing suit neatly folded in a drawer. I quickly stripped off my clothing. Tugging the suit on with shaking hands wasn't working well. I forced myself to stop what I was doing and take a deep breath.

"Grace Natalie, get it together. If Mother could see you now she'd be horrified by your behavior," I said aloud in a stern voice.

Then I began to laugh. Really laugh. My laughing fit calmed the shaking hands and allowed the suit to slide on. I laughed as I put my swim cover-up on and tied the strings into a neat bow at my side. I laughed because if Mother *could* see me in that moment she *would* be horrified, but she couldn't see me. I was free to take Ana up on her offer, mistake or not.

I didn't own flip flops, but I did have some slip-on canvas loafers, which I slid my feet into and wiggled my toes. I looked in the mirror when I was all dressed and did a little happy dance in a tight circle.

I left my room and walked briskly down the gleaming wooden staircase to where Ana was waiting with a large striped towel in her arms and a grocery bag full of something that smelled great.

"You own something with no buttons!" Ana said when she saw me. "I guess I owe myself five dollars, because I bet myself you didn't."

"Even people with rods in their spines know that visiting an island requires swimwear." I gestured at my outfit. "Perhaps you owe *me* that five dollars." I teased in a way I didn't know I could.

Ana's eyes crinkled. "You've made your point. I'll pay you back with this breakfast I brought you. Where's your flip flops?"

"I don't have a pair. You'll have to forgive this island novice," I replied.

"Your feet, your problem."

Ana handed me my towel and the plastic bag of food before she turned and marched out of the front hall, through the kitchen, and to the service stairs in the back. I followed, loving the slapping sounds that Ana's flip flops made on the gleaming floors. I thought maybe I'd like to own a pair of shoes that slapped around in total disregard for subtlety.

After descending the last flight to the basement, we exited the side entrance and headed toward the waves that lapped lazily at the private beach three hundred feet away. We left the manicured back gardens through a gate, and came to stand on top of a large cement retaining wall that ran as far as I could see in either direction. It abruptly dropped several feet down, requiring use of a stone staircase that started at the top of the wall, where we were standing, and ended in marshy grass that quickly thinned out into beach sand.

"Back in 1900 there was a huge hurricane that came through here and tried to destroy everything. So a lot of the city has seawalls like this to protect in case of another big storm," Ana related as we climbed carefully down the steps.

"Are these steps original from 1900?" I asked, noticing how worn they were.

She shrugged. "Probably."

The marsh grass tickled at my ankles as we walked. The air felt somehow thicker here as we neared the water, and the smell was pleasantly salty. We left the marsh grass for the open sand, and I was surprised to find it was rock free and had tracks in it.

"What are these tracks?" I asked.

"They're from a tractor. A bunch of the homes along here get the sand groomed." Ana kicked off her flip flops and used her toes to pick them up and put them into her hand. "It's not like it's really bad on the ungroomed beaches, but who wouldn't choose a groomed beach if they could? Perk of the job that I take full advantage of."

I slid out of my loafers and paused to enjoy the first feel of Lavender Island sand under my feet. It wasn't all that different from other sand I'd felt, but it made my heart smile. *Mary, if you're listening, I'm wiggling my toes in your sand right now.* I tilted my face up to the sky and closed my eyes, my lips relaxing into a toothless smile.

"When you're done smiling at the sun, I'll be over at that beach umbrella," Ana teased.

I abruptly opened my eyes and blushed. "Sorry."

"For what? Sun worship is an important part of island life," she replied easily.

We made our way to a large umbrella and two chairs. The cheery yellow and blue striped umbrella danced in the ocean breeze. The chairs were larger than normal beach chairs, which promised comfort.

"Are we okay to use these?" I asked when Ana set down her things.

"Yep. The same people who groom the beach set these up." Ana wiggled her hips as she worked her shorts down her legs. "It's kind of nice to be rich. Or, at least to live with the rich." She grinned.

"It would seem so." I smiled back.

Ana set her shorts and tank on one of the chairs and looked out at the water. "You ready?"

"To swim?"

"Yes."

"It's only nine o'clock," I stated.

"What would be an appropriate time to swim?" Ana tilted her head in a way that I was beginning to be familiar with.

"I don't mean that there's an appropriate time, but won't the water still be cold?"

She shook her head. "Nah. Gulf water is pretty warm, even this time of year."

I was intrigued and ridiculously happy over the news that I wasn't about to do a polar bear plunge. My stomach growled lightly, reminding both of us that I hadn't eaten yet. I blushed when Ana laughed, having heard the sound.

"Go ahead and eat something. I'll meet you out there when you're ready. Oh, and with skin as pale as yours, you'd better spray on some of my sunscreen."

"Sorry."

"For what?" Ana asked.

"Making you wait. Letting you hear my stomach growl," I replied quietly.

"Are you going to do that all the time?"

"What?"

"Apologize? By my count you've apologized to me three times already this morning."

"Oh. Well . . ."

"Well, what? Stop saying you're sorry all the time. You haven't done anything to hurt me. You step on my toe, or use all the hot water, or eat the last piece of cake, then you say sorry. Otherwise, you don't owe me any apologies." Ana walked the last couple of feet to where the water licked the sand and poked her toe in.

I was speechless. Ana was unlike anyone I knew in my real life. I always apologized when I felt I'd done something to inconvenience someone. It was polite. Wasn't it? I mentally ran through the times I'd apologized to Ana that morning and could see nothing wrong with what I'd done. Yet, Ana's statement gave me something to think about as I ate the still-warm breakfast sandwich and piece of fruit she had brought for me.

I ate quickly, tore off my cover-up, coated myself in sunblock, and walked toward the water, trying not to care about the time I'd spent on my hair and makeup that morning that was now wasted. Spontaneous women didn't worry about that sort of thing, I assumed. The moment my foot touched the waves I couldn't help but gasp. It was warm. Ana had been telling the truth. It was like entering a lukewarm bath. I released a breath I'd been holding and walked to where Ana was floating on her back in the waist-deep water, eyes closed, bobbing along on the soft waves.

One eye popped open. "Hey."

"You were right." I ran a hand through the water.

"My three favorite words." She chuckled. "You should join me."

I lay back in the water and let my arms reach out to the side. I couldn't believe how buoyant I felt. I'd never been able to float so effortlessly on my back. The waves were relaxing, the sun warm on my face and the fronts of my legs. The last time I'd been in the ocean had been off the coast of Massachusetts on a week away with my mother. The waves had been chilly, knocking roughly against my knees and sending me back to my towel on the sand. Mother had sighed and given me her 'I tried to warn you' look. Here the waves were shallow, calm, drawing me in to their embrace.

I opened my eyes and watched the brown pelicans fly around us, occasionally diving into the water for their own breakfast. A little farther out, fish were jumping.

"Nice, huh?" I heard Ana say.

"Quite."

"Tell me about this list-making mother of yours."

"I'd rather not."

"Why?"

"Because talking about all of that will ruin this beautiful morning," I replied.

"Oh, it's like that?"

"It's like that."

"Would it make you feel better if I told you that my mama always burns the eggs?"

"Burnt eggs?"

"I swear it's true. Sometimes she even burns the enchilada recipe that my abuelas have handed down for generations."

"I'm sorry to hear that."

"It's a great tragedy," Ana stated.

A laugh burst out of me, strange and a little rough. Ana joined in. The wide open air stole the sound away as we floated in the sun. The waves seemed to push me forward, while at the same time carrying the tightness of Mother's embrace away to places I couldn't see.

After floating aimlessly for a while we made our way back to the beach where we sat in comfy chairs, listening to the ebb and flow of the water. I leaned back in the chair and closed my eyes. My breath slowed, and time held still in the humid air. I couldn't remember an occasion where I'd felt more peaceful.

A familiar booming voice woke me from a light doze. "Hey, Ana and Grace, how you ladies doing?"

I opened my eyes and glanced to the side to see two figures heading toward us. I recognized Marshall right away, but the other man had his head down and was focused on the fishing pole and tackle box he was carrying. Both men were wearing t-shirts, shorts, and hats that shaded their faces. Their feet were bare, leaving prints in the wet sand as they neared.

"We were having a lovely time until you woke us from our beauty sleep," Ana called back.

Marshall laughed. "I see I didn't do any harm. You both still look as pretty to me as you ever did."

I sat up straighter in my chair and offered Marshall a smile before my eyes shifted again to his companion. Up close I was surprised to realize it was John Lucas. He was as rugged-looking and handsome as I remembered. At the sight of him a little tingle started in my toes. It was a feeling I'd experienced for the first time in the carriage house the other night.

I felt agonizingly awake and absolutely petrified as he drew near with Marshall. His eyes were shadowed by his hat, but I felt it when he glanced my way. They sparked in recognition, but he said nothing. I flexed my toes, willing the feeling away, wishing he didn't make me so nervous.

Ana's voice interrupted my thoughts. "Flirting won't get you anywhere with us, Marshall. We're two strong and independent women."

"What if I told you I caught some fish and was offering to cook it up for lunch?"

Ana raised her brows as she gazed back at him. "I'm listening."

"On the beach. Over a fire." Marshall grinned.

"See, big guy, it's food that does all the talking. I'm in. Grace?" Ana turned to me, and I realized I was still staring at John Lucas. How embarrassing.

His face was unreadable. Serious. His already dark coloring shaded by the hat made his unusually light green eyes seem to glow. He had the same expression as the night I'd first seen him. It pushed me out of the trance I'd been in. I tore my eyes away and looked to Marshall.

"Um, thanks, but . . ." I began.

Predictably, Ana interrupted me. "Jeez, Grace, don't undo all the work I've done here today." She lightly swatted my arm. "This girl was really in need of some island therapy."

"That so?" Marshall smiled. I shook my head and sighed. "Well, Ana is the girl to help you out with that."

"She can be very persuasive," I replied.

"Does that mean you'll join us?" Marshall asked. I took a deep breath and then nodded. "That's just fine then." Marshall turned to John Lucas. "Would you like to come too?"

"I'm sorry. I have a commitment this afternoon," he replied. It sounded like a canned, habitual response, and I didn't get the feeling he was actually sorry.

"Well, shoot. Maybe some other time?" Marshall offered.

"Sure." His gaze skittered away toward the house.

"Okay. I'm heading back to the house to clean up these fish and get some supplies. I won't be too long," Marshall said to me and Ana.

Both Marshall and John Lucas touched the brims of their hats in a gentlemanly salute as they turned to walk away. The gesture was a nice surprise. I allowed my eyes to follow the men as they climbed the stairs and disappeared through the gate.

Ana's voice pulled me back. "Talk about luck. A fish fry on your first day off. The stars are smiling at you today," she said as she sank back down to her napping position.

I also relaxed back into my chair with the smallest of smiles on my face. I'd never jinx it by saying anything out loud, but it wasn't just the stars smiling down on me . . . it was the entire universe.

CHAPTER 6

I floated on the feelings of that beach experience for two full days. Sitting around an open fire with Ana and Marshall was the happiest I had felt in a long time. Marshall had teased and flirted harmlessly while the popping and sizzling sounds of fish cooking filled me before I'd even taken a bite. Stories had been told—most of which I was certain were made up—and there had been so much laughter that my face still felt a little sore. My poor face muscles weren't used to that much work.

I replayed the fire-lit scenes in my mind a million times over, wanting to make sure no detail would fade from memory when I had to rerurn to Providence.

The crash of a chair hitting the floor snapped me out of my reverie.

"Sorry, ma'am," Marshall said with an apologetic look toward Eliza.

"Did it scuff the floor?" she asked, walking briskly toward him.

The rest of their conversation was lost as I chastised myself for my daydreaming. The charity luncheon was today, and I had no time to be in another world. I hustled from the room to gather more tablecloths from the housekeeping room, where the crisp blue linens were being ironed.

Eliza guided the entire thing like a conductor with her orchestra. Marshall had set up the tables the night before and was now bringing in chairs. There would be ten tables with eight seats around each. Eighty guests was a pretty respectable showing, I thought, for an island this size. When I'd voiced that opinion, I'd been reminded that people were always amiable to traveling from bigger cities to spend an afternoon on the island.

Ana and the day staff had made the room sparkle the day before, and if the sounds and smells from the kitchen were any indication, the guests would be dining well. Chef Lou had insisted that the live-in staff stay out while he and his hired catering team prepared. We'd been dining on a back patio, and it hadn't felt like punishment to me at all.

"What was that crash?" Ana asked as I entered the housekeeping room off the kitchen. It was part laundry facility, part cleaning closet, and Ana's personal office.

"Marshall dropped a chair." I reached out for the ironed tablecloths on a table nearby.

"I swear if that man messes up that room . . ." she grumbled as she turned back to the basket of linens and grabbed another.

"I think it's okay." I offered her a small smile.

"If you see Josie out there, will you tell her these tablecloths aren't going to iron themselves? Or, rather, I'm not going to keep doing her job. I have other things to check on." She sounded more annoyed than I'd heard before, so I quickly agreed and hustled back out to the ballroom.

The house seemed larger than ever as I made the return trip. Funny how when I was wandering around leisurely it felt cozy, but when I was dashing to and fro it felt cavernous. Context was everything.

I was briefly sidelined when I saw Josie dusting the parlor. I quickly sent her on her way before hustling back to the front of the house. Thankfully things seemed to be back in hand as I put more tablecloths in place. Eliza grabbed one from the stack and pitched in. No one was talking, but soft jazz music played over cleverly concealed speakers in the ceiling. There was a sense of calm urgency as we worked together, everyone knowing their part.

When all the tablecloths were arranged Eliza got us started on centerpieces. I loved the elegant simplicity of her design. Short, round, clear glass vases were to be filled with some water and then blue and green hydrangeas and cream roses. Around the vases would be small tealights. The china was done in matching cream with simple silver adornments around the edges.

I quickly worked to transport empty vases to each table, followed by the tealights. Next I filled pitchers of water from a sink in the conservatory and began to fill them one-third full as instructed. When they were filled, Eliza brought in the fresh flowers and arranged them while Marshall wheeled in the stacks of clean china from the kitchen.

"Thank you, Marshall," Eliza said as the last load was brought in and set carefully along one side of the room. "We should be ready for take down by four p.m."

"Yes, ma'am." Marshall nodded, shot a smile to me, and left the room.

Eliza and I worked in silence other than her occasional humming along to the music. She artfully arranged flowers as I set up the china and silverware. It was a familiar routine, working with others to set up an event. The difference today was that the silence was companionable, rather than heavy. I wasn't grasping for things to talk about or stumbling over my words. Instead my mind wandered peacefully.

Ana and Josie joined us before we were finished and lent a hand to the process by placing pressed napkins at each place. Ana kept making funny faces at me whenever Eliza would turn away until I finally gave in and giggled.

Eliza smiled up at me as I walked past. "It's good to hear you laugh, my dear."

"Grace has been laughing more and more these days," Ana said.

"It's mostly because Ana's only goal in life is to get a reaction out of me," I replied with a chuckle.

"You need me," Ana stated so matter-of-factly that I shook my head.

I turned to Eliza. "Ana believes herself to be the Great Island Therapist."

"Well, whatever she's doing, it seems to be working." Eliza smiled warmly back. "There's a reason I have her running my home."

"Next step will be getting Grace to let her hair down. I mean that literally. Do you ever do anything other than that bun?" Ana teased as she moved to the next table.

"This is not a bun, Ana. I'll have you know it's a chignon. And it's very fashionable and professional," I replied in a mock stern voice.

"Says your ninety-two-year-old grandma," Ana snorted. "You're not old, so why do your hair like you are?"

"I do not do my hair like an old lady," I burst out, the light-hearted feeling popping.

"How many bobby pins do you own?" Ana darted me a look.

"I refuse to answer that," I replied, fighting to stay away from the humiliation that wanted in. I knew Ana well enough now to feel easier around her, but I hated any reminder of my differences. For some people differences were a strength, but for me it had never felt that way. It wouldn't be easy to let those old hurts go.

"I'm just saying, your hair is such a pretty color. You should be like a peacock, fanning it out everywhere. Not tucking it behind you like you're trying to hide it," Ana pressed.

"Good grief, Ana, I am not trying to be a peacock!" I stopped what I was doing and looked at her with big eyes. "Besides, peacocks are colorful. I am colorless. Big difference."

"Colorless? Please. Women spend a lot of money trying to get their hair that color."

"She's right, dear." Eliza surprised me by entering the conversation. "It's quite lovely."

"Do *you* think I do my hair like an old lady?" I asked Eliza as I walked past her carrying more place settings.

"I think you do your hair in a way that makes you feel comfortable," Eliza replied simply.

I had nothing to say in reply to that shocking burst of insight. I'd done my hair in some type of chignon for years. But why? Did I really like the style? I wasn't even sure what I liked. On a scale of one to ten, my self-knowledge was squeaking in at a zero point five. How did a person get to their twenty-fifth birthday without knowing how they liked their hair styled? The wolf inside me moaned and flopped to the ground.

"Well, it doesn't matter today," I said after a short pause. "Peacocks take time, which is something we don't have."

Ana grinned. "You might be right, for now, but don't think you'll get away from me that easily."

The moment we finished setting up, I checked in on Chef Lou and then raced to my room to clean up and prepare for my first event. While Eliza would handle the official hostess duties, I was expected to stand by to take care of anything that needed to happen outside of the ballroom. Escorting guests to the restroom, alerting Chef Lou when the next course should be served, telling Ana of any spills—those were all tasks I would be in charge of, among other things. I felt confident as I slipped into my freshly dry-cleaned dove gray power suit and put the finishing touches on my makeup.

Yes, my hair had been pulled into my signature style. And yes, I was questioning it as I gazed at my reflection in the mirror. Darn Ana for putting doubts in my mind. Did this severe style make me look old and unapproachable? Would softening up my look help in some way I was unaware of? I'd always blamed my lack of friends on my reserve, but perhaps my style was compounding the problem. Aargh! I did not have time for this right now.

I slipped into black pumps, spritzed on a lightly scented spray, and left my room. It was quarter to one, and guests would be starting to arrive, as it was common knowledge that Eliza served promptly on the hour.

The service stairs were quiet as I hustled down. The heartbeat in my throat seemed louder to me than my footsteps. *"There's only once chance for a first impression,"* Mother's voice reminded as I passed by the kitchen. The loud clanking of dishes let me know the staff was hard at work. Ana's office and housekeeping room were empty, which meant Ana had changed into her uniform. Everyone was ready to go.

I silenced Mother's voice and squared my shoulders as I rounded the corner into the dining room and passed quietly through into the conservatory, which was attached to the ballroom by a set of large French doors. Ana was hovering behind the partially parted doors, exactly where I expected her to be. Her lovely brown hair was plaited in one thick braid down to her waist. She'd changed into a tailored gray button-down shirt and black slacks, which designated her as staff to anyone who bothered to look at her. I knew from experience that most of them wouldn't. People tended to let staff stay part of the background.

"Nice bun," Ana said out of the side of her mouth as I came to stand next to her.

"Careful, someone might think you're being improper," I replied quietly with a straight face as she peeked through the open door.

Ana's eyes lit up, a look of delighted surprise on her face as she turned to face me fully. How sad that my cracking a joke would be worth a double take.

"My apologies. Nice chi-non, or whatever you called it."

"Thank you. I think it's one of my best yet." I ran a hand lightly over my flyaway-free hair.

"Oh my gosh, I have so much work to do with you." She sighed theatrically.

Eliza appeared directly in front of us before I could reply, slipping gracefully through one side of the French doors.

"Ladies, good, you're ready." Eliza gave us both a once over. "Your super suit, I presume?" She tipped her head toward me with a smile.

"The very one." I lifted a corner of my mouth.

"Then I expect your very best work today," she stated.

"Ma'am." I nodded once.

"She wore her extra special power bun too," Ana supplied cheerfully, which made Eliza chuckle and me roll my eyes.

It also made me pause for a moment to watch the two women together. It was clear that Ana respected Eliza and understood her position in the household, but it was also clear that their relationship was warm and friendly. I wondered if I could build that camaraderie with my staff when I went home. I was certainly willing to try.

Eliza transitioned briskly back to business mode. "The guests are arriving, and my nephew is at the door greeting them. I'll be here in the room when they arrive. You two know what's expected of you?"

"Yes, ma'am," Ana said.

I nodded vaguely, startled at the news that the elusive John Lucas was greeting guests. There had been no mention of him regarding this luncheon. In fact, I'd been living in the house for a solid week and Eliza had yet to introduce us or really speak of him to me at all.

The first cluster of women entered the room just then, and Eliza turned, flashing her bright smile on them as she exited the conservatory and walked to where they were. I stepped into the doorway but didn't fully enter the room, at attention and ready if I was needed. I was surprised by what I saw. The three women began to flush a bit and appeared to lose their cool, polished exteriors as Eliza took their hands one-by-one in her own.

"They sure seem in awe of Eliza," I whispered in amazement to Ana who was still hidden behind the door.

"Of course, they do. Everyone is in awe of Eliza," Ana said plainly.

"No one around the house seems to be," I replied.

"You can't spend every day cleaning a person's toilet, cooking all their meals, fixing their broken items, and washing their sheets, and still be in awe of them."

I nodded at the truth of Ana's statement. "Well, it'll be interesting to actually see John Lucas doing the hosting thing," I mumbled distractedly as I glanced around the room. "I've only seen him twice, and he wasn't very friendly, but I've heard about him for years."

"What do you mean, you've heard about him for years?"

"What?" I was only half listening.

"Are you stalking him or something? Is that why you really came here?" Ana's tone became oddly cool.

I turned to face her. "What? Stalking?" As the words sank in, I let a full natural smile fill my face. Ana blinked. People always blinked at my megawatt smile. "No. Not at all. His Aunt Mary used to tell me about him and what he was up to, that's all."

"Aunt Mary?"

"Oh, you don't know? I guess I thought Eliza would have told you. Her great Aunt Mary Halstead Reed is my adopted grandmother. Her and my actual grandmother were best friends, and she acted as an aunt to my father. My grandmother passed away before I was born, so Mary stepped in."

"Really?" Ana pinched her face up as she focused closer on mine.

"Really." I let my smile linger as I nodded.

"Huh. That is a detail that I should have known. Any self-respecting house manager knows all the dirty laundry." She looked back to the ballroom and pointed through the entryway we were standing to the side of. "Here he comes now."

I had understood the concept of having your breath leave your body due to a surprise, but this was the first time I'd actually experienced it. It came with a rush of lightheadedness and a feeling that my knees were about to give way. I had met John Lucas already, but he'd been a dressed down version of himself. This version was wearing a tailored suit with his hair cropped close, his beard short and expertly trimmed, and shoes that were as shiny as his bright, white smile. It was the first time I'd seen him smile, and even though it looked a little fake to me, it was no less attractive. Ooh, boy. The tingles were back and they weren't welcome. This was bad. So bad. Why him and why now? I'd met many wealthy, self-assured men in my life and not found a single one even remotely interesting. If I'd thought the Garage Guy version was unapproachable, this side of John Lucas Halstead looked to me like manicured ice. Here was a man full of drive and control with no discernible softness.

"Careful, Grace, or I'll think you're ogling him." Ana elbowed me lightly in the side.

"I am not ogling the man." I startled myself by getting snippy. I put a fluttering hand to my chest. "I didn't realize . . ." I wasn't sure how to finish the sentence. Leave it to Ana to want me to anyhow.

"Realize what?"

I wasn't about to let her know I was experiencing the first zing of my life over this total stranger who was in no way inviting any of those feelings. In truth, he appeared to be the polar—and I do mean polar—opposite of everything I'd ever hoped to find in a man. Mother would love him. Mother loved power and purpose and cool interactions. Well, I'd had enough of controlled anything. All the zinging had left me nauseated, and the impressions he gave off made me somehow melancholy. I probably needed more than a Snickers bar to get me through this one.

I waved a casual hand in the direction of Eliza and John Lucas, hoping to redirect Ana. "Look how everyone is fawning over them. If you'll remember, I grew up in Providence. I was over two thousand miles away," I whispered. It wasn't the whole truth, but my face felt warm and I was hoping I looked uncomfortable enough to convince Ana that this was nothing more than a case of being starstruck.

"This Aunt Mary never showed you any pictures?"

"What?"

"Of the man you're staring at."

I blinked, stunned that she could see through me so clearly. "What?"

"Tailored suit, black hair, olive skin, dreamy dimples."

"He does not have dreamy dimples," I muttered. "He has a beard." I actually would not be surprised to find out he did have dimples under that facial hair.

"Yeah, well, you'll have to take my word for it," she joked.

"Oh, Ana." I put a hand over my face. "I was not . . . forget it. Any pictures I saw of him were when he was a lot younger, wearing glasses, with a face dirty from eating berries in Mary's yard." I wasn't about to mention that I'd also seen grown-up pictures of him on the internet, dressed just like this, but they hadn't done him justice. In person he gave off a vibe that didn't translate through a computer screen.

"You saw him at the beach the other day."

"Yes, but he was dressed down and didn't look so . . ."

"Impressive?"

"Unapproachable, standoffish, aloof."

"Huh. Well, you'd better pull yourself together. Eliza is going to officially introduce you to him. If that gray suit of yours really does have superpowers, you'll want to call on them now."

"Now?" My hand fell to my side.

"Eliza is standing next to him and gesturing to you. Better scoot." Ana tapped me on the back.

The tap rebooted my brain and settled the tingling feeling I'd had. I took a deep breath and willed myself to relax one muscle at a time as I walked the length of the room. I weaved as gracefully as I could between tables and guests, to where Eliza and John Lucas stood.

"Grace, dear, you haven't had a chance to meet my nephew, Lucas." Eliza smiled warmly as she reached a hand out and grasped my slightly cold one. "I've been meaning to introduce you, but he's been so hard to catch. Here he is now."

My face slid into its familiar plastic society smile as I forced my eyes up to his. So . . . he went by Lucas, not John Lucas. Okay. All the Halstead men had the first name of John and had for generations. Most of them had gone by the dual name, but somehow just Lucas suited him better. He offered an abrupt nod in greeting.

"Grace and I have bumped into each other once or twice already," he said.

"Wonderful. Did she tell you who she is?" Eliza beamed at her nephew.

His light eyes clouded for a just a moment. "I don't believe so." The look said he'd been surprised in the past and didn't like it.

"Oh, she must have been feeling shy." Eliza squeezed my numb fingers. "This is Miss Grace Burke. Aunt Mary's 'little Gracie'."

Lucas's eyes zoned in on me, truly looking for possibly the first time. His gaze seemed to hit every point of my face, and I held perfectly still under his scrutiny. There were things in his eyes I didn't understand. After what felt like hours, but couldn't have been longer than three seconds, his shoulders relaxed.

I tried to relax a bit as well, but my smile couldn't quite slip into its natural state. "Yes, well, I'm not in the habit of telling my full genealogy to everyone I meet." I was gratified when Eliza chuckled softly. Lucas didn't, which wasn't great, but also wasn't unexpected.

We were interrupted by the head of the charitable organization, whose luncheon this was, before we could make any more conversation. I didn't mind. I needed to gather my thoughts.

"Please, excuse me," I said tactfully, my professional façade back in place. "There are a few things I need to attend to."

With one last small nod to Eliza and Lucas, I returned to my place in the conservatory. Ana greeted me with a knowing smile that I didn't bother to respond to. Instead I ran wobbly fingers over my hair and suit jacket, my nerves seeking the soothing motions.

My mind was racing. For years and years Mary had teased me, saying I should look up Lucas someday. I had seen through her match-making attempts and allowed the older woman her fun. I'd never imagined that when I did finally meet him, he'd be someone who made my toes tingle. Nor did I imagine he'd be such a cold statue. It had been ten years since Mary had passed. Enough years for the happy and loving young man she'd always described to turn into the cool, reserved man I'd just officially met.

Watching Eliza and Lucas Halstead work the adoring crowd over the next two hours was eye opening. I'd had no idea. Eliza had welcomed me so warmly and effortlessly that I'd not realized the true social status of the beautiful gray-haired lady. She had simply felt like family. However, Ana was right; the Halsteads were Lavender Island royalty.

Having seen Eliza in her relaxed, familial state, I could easily recognize the mask she wore for the guests. Lucas's was the same aloofness he'd used with me in our short interactions. While I knew that Eliza took her public persona off at the end of the day, I didn't know if Lucas did or not. And I wasn't sure if I was brave enough— or interested enough—to find out.

CHAPTER 7

Ana was speeding along Lavender Island's little coastal highway a few days later with me as a helpless and terrified passenger. We were heading toward the bridge that would take us to the mainland. At the rate she was driving, I had to wonder if her plan to get there involved launching us into the air and skipping the bridge all together.

"I would have been happy to drive," I said through gritted teeth. I hadn't planned to come to the island to die, after all.

"I've seen your rental car. No thanks. My abuela drives a more exciting car."

I was momentarily distracted from my horror by a chunk of Ana's long hair whipping across my face when she turned her head quickly. I had only ever seen it braided, but today Ana had left it down and it seemed like it had a life of its own, filling the tiny car with its dark waves while the breeze from the window tossed it recklessly around.

A honking horn brought me back to reality. Ana's own horn honked, and she laughed as she swung the car to the right and then whiplashed back into our lane. I did not want to know what I'd missed.

"There's nothing wrong with my rental," I argued.

"That's true, if you're out to impress the women at the senior center." She turned to look at me with pursed lips and raised eyebrows. I pointed out the front windshield in an effort to get her eyes back on the road, even though it seemed to do little good.

"Seriously, Grace, you have got to be less of a cheapskate and do something fun just because you want to."

"I got the blue car instead of a more sensible champagne color," I defended.

"Stop my racing heart." Her eyes rolled.

"Hurtling down the highway in this death trap certainly isn't sensible, now, is it?" I replied in a haughty tone that sounded so much like Mother I actually cringed with regret. "I'm sorry . . ." I started to say.

"Nope, don't say it. You're probably right." She shrugged. "Now's as good a time as any to tell you that we aren't going to the movie you thought we were seeing." She cranked her head to look over her shoulder before zipping into the next lane. It was the first safety conscious thing I'd had seen her do. "You're about to start phase two of your therapy."

"Phase two? What was phase one?" I asked curiously.

"The day I made you go to the beach instead of dropping off your dry cleaning."

"Oh." I paused. "Quick question. Do you suppose the therapy counts if the patient doesn't realize they're in the middle of a session?" I quirked a smile.

"Are you kidding me? Sneak attack therapy is the best kind." She changed lanes again, making my elbow slam against the door. I made a noise of complaint, and she sent an apologetic smile my way.

"Do I want to know what movie you're actually taking me to see? Assuming we arrive there in one piece," I said.

"Hey, I've been driving for years and haven't died yet," she chirped. "We're going to the biggest action, alien adventure, super-hero show I could find."

I processed that for a moment. I liked to think of myself as a reasonably intelligent person, but it would be best to make sure I'd heard correctly before deciding how I felt about this tidbit of news.

"If I'm understanding correctly, you're taking me to a blow-em-up show?" I finally asked.

"Yep."

My fright-filled brain needed another few seconds to process before asking, "Why?"

"Because I'm guessing that you've never seen one."

Annoyingly, she was right. I only went to festival award winners, or independent films, or classics like *Casablanca*. Still, I lied. "How do you know I don't love those kinds of movies?"

"I don't think you get out much," Ana supplied.

"I get out just as much as anyone else," I defended.

Her only reply was to huff out a loud sigh and shake her head.

"You could have warned me," I murmured.

"Would you have come?"

"I'm not sure," I replied honestly. "I think those kinds of movies are good for some people, just not me."

"You can stop pretending you have any idea of what's good for you." She snorted. I was amused, but before I could respond, she glanced over at me. "I think it'll probably be kind of fun. The show, I mean." She steered the car off an exit that lead us onto the bridge. "And if it's not, at least you can say you tried something new."

I thought about that. She was right. I had been making an effort to say 'yes' a lot more lately. "Okay. I'll try to have an open mind."

"Good." She smiled and reached out her hand. "Now, can you hand me the bag of chips that's in the glove box? I'm snacky."

"What are the chances of you being able to focus on driving and eat those chips at the same time?" I hedged.

"Our chances of *you* arriving alive are higher if you hand me those chips."

I handed her the chips and tried to relax. Pretending to be on an amusement park ride helped. A little. I'd always gotten sick on those rides.

By the time we arrived I had made some firm decisions about asking more questions next time I was invited to go somewhere. Also, I'd be doing the driving, grandma car or not.

Ana pulled her little red sports car into the parking lot of a beach-side movie theater called The Lux—and I almost grinned at the irony. It wasn't luxurious at all. We both got out, stretching our legs and taking in the view. It didn't seem to matter that I had now been on the Gulf Coast for almost two weeks; the scenery still felt new. I loved the tang of the air and the way the humidity made my skin feel soft. The constant warm breeze was a miracle to me after living my entire life in a cooler eastern seaboard climate.

I turned away from the view to see Ana watching me from the other side of the car. I pulled a face and said, "I see you've delivered me alive, as promised."

"All part of the therapy, my friend." She cheerfully grinned.

"Something about staring down death?"

"Yep."

We fell into step, Ana's flip flops slapping as we followed a handful of other people in through the front doors of the theater. The lobby was large and light, decorated in a surprisingly bold color pallet of reds, oranges, and creams.

It didn't take me long to spot the enormous poster board picture of a muscled guy with dirt smears on his face wearing a tank top and snarling as he looked down the barrel of a gun. I took a deep breath and let it out slowly.

"That the show?" I asked.

"Yep." Ana made a popping noise with her lips and headed to the ticket counter.

"I think I'll probably hate it, even with the open mind." I followed slowly.

"Yep."

True to my words, I hated the show. Luckily Ana hated it too. Which meant we found ourselves spending the entire second half of the movie fighting the giggles and making fun of it. Which obviously ended up being really fun. So, in the end, Ana thought she'd won this round.

On the drive home Ana insisted on trying out some of the sweet moves—her words, not mine—that the stunt drivers had pulled. To get me to stop screaming she made me say five nice things about the movie. But the only thing I could come up with was that the guy's biceps were drool worthy. I had to give credit where credit was due.

"They'd have been even better if he'd ever washed them. The dirt ruined the view," Ana said with a serious face as she zipped between traffic.

And I laughed the whole way home.

The day would have gone down as a surprise favorite in my book had it not been for the phone call from Mother just as I'd reached my bedroom at Halstead House that evening.

"Hello, Mother," I answered as I crossed the threshold and closed the door softly.

"Thank goodness you answered. I needed to hear your voice. It's been nearly two weeks that we've been apart, and I'm so lonely that I can't eat, I can't sleep, I'm worrying all day about where you are and how you're doing." Mother's crisp way of speaking was a shock after the time spent among the slower, softer, Southern way I'd become familiar with.

An image of her sitting alone at her dinner table flashed through my mind, and guilt prickled behind my eyes. "I'm doing just fine," I replied in deceptive calm.

"How can you be doing just fine when you know you've left me?" she asked.

The familiar stone fell into my stomach. "I'm not trying to hurt you."

"Then what are you trying to do? What am I to think? You ran away to some island as though you had nothing here to worry about leaving."

I swallowed hard. I didn't want to see it from her point of view, but Mother did have a point. She was as unfamiliar with me rebelling as I was with making my own choices. We were both charting new waters here.

"I'm . . ."

"You need to come home right now," Mother snapped before I had a chance to offer up the apology I'd been starting. "You've been there long enough. I tolerated this little *episode* of yours, but two weeks is plenty of time to see the sights."

My mouth froze, the apology dying on my lips. While I was sorry that I'd worried my mother and that she felt all alone and abandoned, I wasn't at all sorry I had come to Lavender Island. I most definitely was not sorry for the things I'd experienced in the past two weeks. In my mind I rephrased what I'd been about to say.

"I'm sorry you're lonely," I offered softly.

Mother was silent for a split second. "That's all you're sorry for?"

"I'm also sorry that you feel hurt by my choice to come here." I was suddenly desperately grateful for the protection of a long-distance phone call. Even with that, I'd started biting my lip. No one made me feel as unsure as my mother did.

"I don't know what to you say to you, Grace. I don't recognize this side of you. You've never been troublesome and dramatic."

"I'm not trying to . . ." I stopped myself. I did not want to grovel. Groveling Grace was in the process of being put to rest.

Mother didn't seem to notice I'd stopped myself from finishing my phrase. "Well, you are. I raised you better than this. I have no idea what's gotten into you. Did you join a cult? Have you been brainwashed?"

I somehow managed to make a sound of amusement I didn't feel. "Of course I didn't. All I've done is made a decision without consulting you first." The statement echoed in the stillness of what I could only assume was surprise on her part—because I was certainly surprised that I'd dared to say it.

After a few beats of heavy silence she was back on the attack. "You say this as though I'm a monster who has you under her thumb. You're my only child, my only family. You're asking me to shut that off and not care where you are or what you're doing?" Mother's voice had gained a shrill edge that caused me to close my eyes tightly against the emotion boiling up. "Am I supposed to just allow you to run around the country freely?"

I bristled at the word *allow*. At my age my mother shouldn't be *allowing* me to do anything. Still, I didn't have the guts to say that, so instead I said, "I'm asking you to trust me."

We were at a stalemate. It was the first stalemate of our relationship. It wasn't lost on me that this conversation was long overdue. I was having a conversation that most people had at age sixteen.

But even with that knowledge, oh how I wanted to cave. Twenty-five long, long years of indoctrination had taught me that my mother's love required obedience and conformity. I opened my mouth several times, almost letting the words slip out that would heal this breech. The temptation was so great that

I finally put a hand over my mouth, using all my willpower to fight this battle.

"Fine," Mother sighed at last. "If family means so little to you, then you can forget you even have a mother."

The line went dead.

Well. That was new. She'd never disowned me before. I clicked off my phone and let it fall to the bed. I didn't have the energy to move, for fear I'd break into pieces. I'd finally discovered how it felt to defy my mother, and it didn't feel good. It felt like I'd been gutted. Hot tears filled my eyes and threatened to fall.

A soft knock at the door caused me to jump a bit, and I went to answer it on autopilot, wiping under my eyes as I walked across the room. I didn't have enough brain power left to wonder if I should be answering, or to consider how I might look to the person on the other side. I was a robot.

I opened the door and it turned out I could still feel something, because I was horrified to see Lucas standing on the other side. He was dressed in a business suit, although his tie was hanging loose and the top button of his shirt was undone. I couldn't help but notice how the olive skin of his throat contrasted with the white shirt before I glanced up to his face. He looked as stoic as ever, which gave me a little comfort. In my current state stoic was welcome. Kindness would have broken me.

I shifted my gaze to the side and wiped at my eyes while I cleared my throat and blinked away the stray tears. He remained a silent wall of man. For some reason his muteness almost made me smile. Almost. Instead I took a deep breath and let it out slowly. Still he said nothing and the silence grew strained until I met his eyes once more. They were wary. He'd obviously seen the emotion on my face.

All I knew was that I couldn't stand there all night, so I breathed in and said, "I hope you don't take this the wrong way, but is there something I can help you with?" I tried to soften my expression to let him know I wasn't trying to be unkind. He didn't reciprocate. I noticed a file folder in his hand and gestured toward it. "Is that for me?"

He looked down, as though he'd forgotten it was there. "Aunt Eliza left town tonight and won't be back until late tomorrow. She remembered this at the last minute. I was on my way to bed and thought to save her the trip back upstairs. It's for the wedding next week. She'll check in with you when she returns day after tomorrow to go over whatever's in here." He handed over the folder.

While I knew Lucas slept on the same floor as me, this was the first time I'd seen him there. The reminder was followed by a deep embarrassment, like I was somewhere I really shouldn't be.

"Thanks." I nodded and stepped back into my room. "Have a good night, then."

Lucas nodded. I started to close the door, but one large hand reached to stop it. The movement wasn't aggressive, but it startled me and my eyes flew up to his.

He pursed his lips as though his words were being forced out against his will. "Are you okay?"

I wasn't sure how to answer. It was obvious he was just asking to be polite, but still, he had asked. And while the look in his eyes wasn't warm and welcoming, it wasn't hostile either.

"I just got off the phone with my mother," I replied after a brief pause.

He nodded again. Apparently the man thought of nodding as communication. "Lillian?"

Another surprise. "Yes. You know her?"

"I've heard of her."

"I see. Well, the good news is that I'll be just fine." I managed a small lifting of my lips.

He nodded again. "Good night, then."

I closed the door as he turned away, not wanting to be tempted to watch him walk down the hall. I didn't know how I felt after this roller coaster day. A near-death car ride, a blockbuster action film, a phone call with my mother, and Lucas acting slightly human. The only thing I did know was that it was straight to bed for me. Things always looked better in the morning.

CHAPTER 8

I knocked lightly on Eliza's mostly closed office door, the folder Lucas had given me clutched to my chest, and smoothed down my navy pencil skirt while I waited to be invited in. She was back from her quick trip, and I had taken the time to go over each detail I'd been given.

Selfishly it had been nice to have a quiet workday after the strange events of the movie night and Mother's phone call. I had been left feeling off-center and vulnerable. Opening up to new experiences, and new friendships, while simultaneously closing myself off to my mother's demands, was hard work for a woman who had launched herself out of her comfort zone. I had sequestered myself in my room for the majority of the day, working at my little desk and enjoying the view from my dormer window. Being tucked away in the eaves had felt peaceful and safe.

"Come in," Eliza's warm voice called.

I entered to find her head bent over her desk, studying her phone screen. Her lovely silver hair was flawlessly styled. She was dressed elegantly in a rose-colored suit that flattered her coloring tremendously.

"Good morning," I greeted quietly as I sat across from her. I didn't want to interrupt whatever she was working on.

"Good morning, dear. I received an email from the people who are having a fortieth birthday party here in a couple of weeks.

Something about a clown. I'm praying I read that wrong." After another moment of scrolling through her email, Eliza's head popped up. "How disappointing to find that I did read that right. They want a clown. We don't do clowns at Halstead House, I'm afraid. I'll have to get back with them." She looked at me thoughtfully for a moment. "How old are you, Grace?"

I was caught off guard by the question. "I turned twenty-five a couple of weeks ago."

"Do you think that in fifteen years you're going to want a clown at your birthday party?" Her lips pursed as she considered it.

I smiled, amused at her train of thought. "I doubt it."

"Lucas is thirty-two. Do you think in a few years he'll want a clown?"

I couldn't imagine that Lucas had wanted a clown even as a child, so it was a definite no from me. I shook my head.

Eliza's head bobbed. "Yes, that's what I thought too. Although I was worried for a moment that at sixty-six years old I was officially out of touch and perhaps I should retire." She sat thoughtfully for another second before huffing out a laugh. "No, I think retirement is great for John David and Elena. Not for me. I'll say no to the clowns and that'll be that."

"John David is your brother? And Elena is his wife?" I asked, unable to pass up a chance to learn more about them. I knew the family tree well but not much about the people themselves.

"Yes. John David is my twin brother. He's wonderful even though he handed his half of the business to his son and took off to California." Eliza smiled warmly at the thought of her brother. "His wife, Elena, is the most beautiful and elegant woman. Her Mexican heritage is what gives Lucas his dark coloring. She has the most beautiful way of speaking." She paused again with another soft smile. I experienced a prick of envy over the familial warmth I could see on Eliza's face, something I'd longed for but had never known. Oh, Mother cared for me, but our relationship wasn't what anyone would consider affectionate. "Anyhow, enough about that. We have a wedding to throw in precisely five days. Did you go over the contents of the folder?"

"Yes, ma'am." I opened the folder and put it on the desk. "Would you like to start at the top of the list and work our way down?"

"I find that's always best." Eliza smiled and settled back into her chair. "Do they still want fuchsia and rust for their colors?"

"I'm afraid so." I nodded. "I spoke with the bride yesterday."

"Well, I suppose it's for the best, as we've already ordered everything in those colors. However, this was one time I would have been willing to scrap it and work like a mad person to redo it."

I grinned. "It works well for me to remember the guests will blame the bride."

Eliza's eyes lit up as her lips curved. "A happy thought indeed."

We worked companionably through the rest of the morning, hammering out details and making new lists of what needed to be done each day leading up to the wedding. It would be busy, and quite different from other functions I'd put together. It honestly felt a little overwhelming, but I loved learning from Eliza. Spending time with her was bittersweet at times—a comfort enjoying the warm relationship with an older woman that I'd missed so much after Mary's passing, but making me miss her all over again.

When we broke for lunch, each with our own to-do lists ready to go, Eliza walked me to the door and put a hand on my arm.

"Dear, I don't mean to pry, but Lucas mentioned that you seemed upset when he took you the files the other night. Are you okay?"

I was thoroughly shocked that he'd said anything at all. "Oh, really?"

Eliza squeezed my arm lightly. "I hope you're doing well here. Is there anything I can help with?"

I paused, not used to being open with others. I'd only recently begun showing more of myself in casual conversation or making little jokes here and there. But this was Eliza. She knew my mother—or at least of her—and could understand what I was facing. I had to be brave.

"Did he mention that he caught me right after a phone call with my mother?"

Eliza raised her brows. "Ah, I see."

"I've hurt her with my choice to come here. I didn't discuss it with her first, or get her permission, so to her it feels as though I took off with no warning and don't care about her needs or feelings. I'd told her I wouldn't be returning until June." I chewed my lip. "I've never done anything like this. She's concerned."

"I doubt concern is her only emotion," Eliza stated. I nodded. All was quiet for a moment as her gaze delved into mine. At last her features softened and she said, "Take courage, sweet Grace. You're wise to trust your heart. We want you here, and we'll do our best to make your stay a happy one."

I was unable to answer. A lump had formed in my throat that was impossible to swallow. Eliza seemed to understand and reached out to give my hand a soft squeeze. Then she was gone, leaving me to lean against the door frame while I pulled myself back together—because in one short moment, Eliza had seen more of me than Mother had ever bothered to look for.

* * *

Ana informed me over breakfast two days later that therapy session number three would be happening that afternoon.

I looked up from my waffle. "Do I dare ask?"

"New clothes. You can't live on this island wearing slacks and button-downs all the time. Don't even get me started on that pencil skirt I saw you in a couple of days ago. Is it fun to have your legs stuck together all day long?"

I pushed down a giggle. Then, my eyes grew round as I realized that my initial reaction had been to laugh rather than worry. It was good to no longer feel threatened by Ana's pronouncements. "There is nothing wrong with looking professional. I care about my appearance," I responded with a smile.

"Trust me when I say you need some wardrobe adjustments. Right, Marshall?" Ana elbowed him in the side.

"I think Grace should dress however she wants to dress," Marshall mumbled through a mouthful of fruit. "She looks nice."

I rewarded him with one of my full smiles. "Thank you, kind sir."

Ana rolled her eyes. "Don't you be giving him one of your smiles. And you, Marshall, do not encourage her or I'll assign you rain gutter duty for a month. She's on the island now. She needs to have some casual clothes. She needs to let down that hair and relax into life here."

Marshall looked at me a little more closely. "My granny used to do her hair just like that. It's classy."

I knew he was trying to compliment me, but my heart sank as I maintained a pleasant expression. Being lumped in with someone's grandmother wasn't as flattering as he'd meant it to be.

"Oh, boy. Grace, he called your chi-non a 'granny style'." Ana sighed playfully.

"My granny was a beautiful woman with classy hair." Marshall scowled. "If I tell you that you're anything like my granny, you take that as a straight-up compliment."

I reached across the table and laid my hand over his larger one, startling myself in the process. When had I started being comfortable initiating affection? "Thank you, Marshall, for saying something so kind about me." I squeezed. "It's not our fault that Ana is so uneducated in these things."

Marshall's face relaxed, and he patted my hand with his free one. "You're right, Grace." Ana slapped his arm. "I guess Ana is a little bit right too. It might be nice for you to get some more casual clothes. You might feel more comfortable on your time off."

"So this is the next step on your grand therapy plan?" I turned to Ana. "New clothing?" Maybe Ana had a point, at least about my off-work time. A tiny, miniscule, pin-prick of a point, but still a point.

"I'm beginning to think of myself as an archeologist and you're the long-buried treasure. I'm embarking on the excavation of Grace," she replied cheerily.

I raised my eyebrows. "So long as you don't accidentally cut off an important part of me as you dig around."

"I'll do my best, but I've got to warn you, some days nothing but a jack hammer will do." She stood to take her plate to the sink. "Meet me near the carriage house at one o'clock sharp. We'll do some shopping down in the historic distract. You can be touristy at the same time." She left the room without waiting for an answer.

"Should I be worried about what kind of clothing she'll insist I buy?" I asked Marshall.

He nodded. "Stay strong, Grace." His loud sounds of amusement followed him as he too cleared his place and left the kitchen.

"She means well," Chef Lou suddenly said from the stove in his thick fake accent.

I startled when he spoke, having forgotten he was there. When I turned to face him, I was surprised to see him looking at me. Really looking. We'd never made eye contact before this. He meant what he was saying, and it warmed my heart to see evidence of the ties among the staff.

"She's a good friend." I nodded as I stood with my plate.

"Yes, but even good friends should not be allowed to choose *all* your clothes." He turned back to whatever he'd been working on.

"That's good advice, Chef," I agreed as I put my plate in the sink and left the kitchen.

I wasn't totally surprised when at one o'clock sharp I found myself standing alone in the courtyard area outside of the carriage house, no sign of Ana. Knowing I may be waiting for a bit, I made my way over to a small bench situated in the shade underneath a tree at the edge of the courtyard. It looked so appealing, and got my fair skin out of the warming afternoon sun. I sat down, content to enjoy the quiet, and fully prepared to tease Ana about her tardiness.

My solitude was interrupted by the arrival of a motorcycle. The rider came to a fast stop near the large carriage house doors and cut the engine as he placed his booted feet down on the red brick pavers. He was wearing jeans with a black leather jacket and a helmet.

Before taking the time to think about it, I jumped up from where I'd been sitting and marched over to where the man was now swinging a leg over his bike. While I wasn't blind or immune to how . . . well, masculine . . . he looked in his gear, I couldn't believe the audacity of his behavior. This was private property and definitely not a parking area. The tires from the bike could scuff the beautiful old red brick that the courtyard had been painstakingly paved with decades earlier. Events were hosted there, and I knew the Halsteads wouldn't stand for it. While I was reticent in my real life, I'd had to chasten my fair share of people for being disrespectful of historical artifacts. I put on my historian hat and didn't hesitate.

"Sir," I called. He didn't hear me. "Sir!" I called louder. "You can't park there."

He rose from his bike as I was about to reach his side, but the moment his helmet came off I stumbled to a halt. Then again, maybe I'd been mistaken about him parking there. It was Lucas, and his Garage Guy persona had returned in full force. I desperately hoped he hadn't heard me and did my best to back pedal my way into looking like I was headed into the ticket office.

No luck. His light green eyes speared me from beneath his dark eyebrows with the same shuttered look they always wore. He didn't smile, his posture inflexible beneath the black leather jacket as he hung his helmet from the handlebars.

"You always go around telling people what they can't do?" he asked as he shrugged out of his jacket and folded it over the seat.

I had been taking small steps backward in hopes of giving him space, but his words halted me. "I didn't realize it was you."

He broke eye contact as he pulled keys out of the bike's ignition and hit a button on the key chain that caused the huge doors of the carriage house to open. They didn't bend and roll up into the ceiling like my garage doors at home did. Instead they went straight out into the air, coming to rest at a ninety-degree angle to the building and leaving a great shadow underneath them.

Still he remained quiet. My mind raced, wanting to fill the awkward silence. "I am aware that my duties don't involve being a guard dog," I stuttered. He tossed me a quick look over his shoulder. "It's just that I didn't think the family would want tire tracks on this beautiful brick courtyard."

He nodded. "I'm sure you're right." Then he turned and rolled his bike into the carriage house and disappeared from view.

Of all the rude . . . I couldn't even begin to understand how he, Mary, and Eliza shared blood. What had I ever done to him?

"Hey, Grace," Ana called just then from behind.

I jumped and spun to face her. "Let's go." I walked quickly across the bricks toward a parking area on the other side of the gift shop building where Ana's car had its own stall.

"Hold up, lady. My legs aren't keeping up with yours. Why the hurry?" Ana called. "Why is that carriage house door open? I'll bet Carl left it open when he was sweeping before the ticket office opened. How irritating. I'd better let Marshall know before we leave." Ana stopped walking and pulled out her phone.

Ugh. Just, for once . . . "It's not a big deal. Lu-, uh, Mr. Halstead was just out here on his motorcycle and he opened the doors." I anxiously retreated to where Ana was standing and grabbed her arm. "So, let's get moving." Please, please, please.

"Okay. Okay. Easy." Ana tugged her arm away and put her phone back in her pocket, but she still didn't move. She put her hands on her hips and gave me a once-over. "What's going on with you?"

If there was ever a time to forget my etiquette training, slap a palm to my face, and wail at the sky, this was that moment. I didn't have an answer that I was willing to give her, because my emotions made no sense. I just wanted to get away before I had yet another agonizingly awkward and slightly disappointing encounter with Lucas.

I'd never felt the conflicting emotions of attraction and anger like this, and I was scared. He was not the person I thought he would be. I had expected him to be welcoming and warm like Eliza, not aloof and wary. None of the smiling internet pictures had told me to expect his cool attitude. Nor had those pictures prepared me for the things he was making me feel. It was messy and confusing and sort of hurt my feelings somehow. Explaining all of that to Ana seemed like a terrible idea. The only good idea here was a tactical retreat—even if it would require brute force.

The whirring sound of the carriage doors closing kept me from manhandling her out of the courtyard. I groaned as her attention—okay, and mine—shifted to him, who was now carrying his jacket in his hand and striding toward us. He brought with him those annoying tingles in the soles of my feet. It was simply the worst.

"Afternoon." Ana smiled at him. "Did you have a good ride?"

"I did," he replied.

At that exact moment Eliza came out of the ticket office. Her normally serene expression looked troubled as she took in Lucas's attire.

"I thought I heard that motorcycle out here. Did you ride it on my bricks again?" she asked. Lucas gave her a succinct nod in return. "I swear, dear, I'm going to be forced to send you to military school if you don't stop. These bricks are irreplaceable and part of our history."

"I'm a little old to be shipped off to military school," Lucas replied with a hint of a smile, his face softening in a way that made my stomach swoop as he looked at his aunt.

Eliza pursed her lips. "Perhaps. However, you're still young enough to clean all the toilets." I'd have felt a little bad for him, being scolded in front of Ana and me, if I thought for a moment he cared. Eliza turned to Ana and me with a smile. "Where are you two off to?" she asked.

Ana replied cheerily, "We're off to the Historic District to try to breathe some life into Grace's wardrobe." I managed to not melt into a puddle of mortification, but then it got worse. "You can see for yourself that her outfits need some help relaxing into island life." She gestured to me.

I blushed hard as the two Halsteads took quick stock of my outfit, my light coloring making it impossible for them not to notice my face reddening. How embarrassing. I'd been so proud of myself for the more casual attire today. I was wearing a floral print blouse and cream slacks with flat sandals. I thought I looked relaxed and touristy.

"What's wrong with it?" I found my voice.

"It still looks a little . . ."

I held up a hand and closed my eyes. "Don't finish that thought. If you compare me to your abuela, or Marshall's granny, I will have to kick your shins."

Eliza chuckled as Ana said, "Kick my shins?"

I opened my eyes and looked firmly at Ana. "Yes. Your shins are in danger. No comments about my outfit. This is why you wanted to shop, right?'

"Sounds like you've got an interesting afternoon ahead of you," Eliza said. I wasn't sure if I was insulted or not. "You two up for some company?"

I smiled warmly at her. "Of course." I meant it. It would be fun to have one of those shopping trips I'd always heard girls talk about taking with their mother. Eliza would fit into that role very neatly.

"Wonderful. Lucas here has been working too hard. I think an afternoon off with two lovely ladies would be just the thing."

Lucas, Ana, and I looked at each other with raised eyebrows, wearing the same expression of complete shock on our faces, then back to Eliza, and then back at each other.

Her request surprised us so much that even Ana stayed silent as I counted my own heartbeats pounding in my ears. Lucas shopping with us? For clothing for me? I was knocking on death's door at the moment, grasping for a reply as my entire face flooded with twice the heat it had before. There was no way he was invited to my therapy session. No way. Ever.

"I have a few things that I need to work on . . ." Lucas began stiffly.

"Nonsense. How could you possibly turn down the company of two such beautiful young women?" Eliza returned before he could finish. "Besides, I don't believe that you actually have any friends, which is quite tragic." She sniffed a little and looked away, and I swore she was stifling a laugh, knowing she was poking at him and meaning none of it.

His mouth fell open, his expression reminding me of a highly insulted six-year-old. "I have friends."

Eliza shrugged. "Well, I never see any."

"Fine." His smile was patently false as he turned to face Ana and me. "I'll drive." He turned back in the direction he'd just come from, obviously confident that we'd follow, and began heading around the large building, toward the back side of the carriage house. "My car is in the garage."

He was right about one thing, because after a nod and a chipper little wave from Eliza, we did follow him. What else were we supposed to do? The battle had been won and the general had spoken. The two of us stumbled along, bemused.

As soon as we rounded the corner Ana turned to me with big eyes. "What is happening?" she mouthed.

"You. You did this," I mouthed back, pointing my finger at her.

"Me?" She shook her head violently.

"You. You . . . are . . . dead . . . meat," I whispered, enunciating each word precisely.

"Just through this side door here." Lucas looked back at us. We both pasted on smiles and nodded.

He opened a man-door and held it, letting us through before he came behind and closed it. I was in an area of the property I hadn't known about until now. It was a large garage that housed two sleek black sedans and a luxury sports car of some kind.

Lucas led us to one of the two sedans and opened both of the passenger side doors. Ana and I stood in front of the doors and looked at each other.

"After you, Ana." I smiled stiffly and motioned for her to get in the front seat.

Ana waved her arm toward the car. "No, no, please, you take the front seat," she said as she dove for the back.

Lucas made a noise that could have been amusement, or it could have been him swallowing down something cynical and annoying. This was bad. I had no choice but to sit down in the front passenger seat. Lucas bent down slightly to look in at his passengers.

"I need to change out of these motorcycle boots before we go. I have a change of shoes in my trunk. It'll just take a minute to switch." He closed the doors and walked around to the trunk of the car. I made good use of the time.

My head whipped around as I whispered to Ana, "How do we get out of this?"

"You tell me. Have you ever managed to tell Eliza no?" she hissed.

"Well, no, but, aaah." I chewed my lip. "You have to tell him we changed our minds."

"Me? Stir up trouble? Yeah, right." She made a face and sat back in her seat.

I wanted to tell her that she'd done nothing *but* stir up trouble in my life, but I settled for saying, "I will not survive trying clothing on in front of John Lucas Halstead," I squeaked.

She waved a careless hand and looked out the window. "He'll wait outside at the tables along the sidewalk," she said.

"You'd better pray you're right, Ana."

"Again, how is this my fault?"

"If you'd been on time to meet me, then we would have been gone when he showed up riding his motorcycle," I muttered at the last second before he reappeared.

The driver's door clicked open, cutting off our conversation as Lucas entered the car. He was wearing some sneakers now, and it looked as though he'd run his hands through his hair to tidy it up a bit.

"So . . . " He looked over at me as he took his own seat.

Be brave, Grace, I thought, *just let him off the hook*. "Look, you don't have to do this," I managed. "It won't bother us."

"Fair enough. Which one of you is going to tell my aunt that I'm not coming?" he raised an eyebrow.

"Ready or not, then, huh?" Ana said cheerfully from the back.

I looked straight ahead and Lucas started the car. The hum of the motor was the only sound as we cruised along, and I appreciated the silence. I needed it to get my emotions pushed back into their comfortable hidey hole. I had no idea what had happened in that courtyard today, but somehow we were being forced to have what was the equivalent of an adult play date.

I had mostly calmed down by the time we arrived at the the historic district. It helped a lot that everything around me was eye candy. I was enthralled with the century-old buildings, their worn railings, and siding speaking of the harshness of life next to the gulf. Every building was vibrant with colors. Houses in reds, blues, yellows, and greens captivated my attention. Many of the homes were on stilts, with cars parked underneath them, evidence of a community prepared for life alongside the water.

Before long we entered an area of town with cobblestone streets. Lucas guided the car into a parallel parking space and turned off the motor. It was silent for a beat.

"Where to?" I turned over my shoulder to look at Ana, studiously avoiding eye contact with Lucas.

"Um, well, I thought we could combine a little tourism with the shopping, seeing as you're new to our island. Let's start at one end and work our way down." Ana opened her door.

Lucas and I followed suit, stepping out into sights and sounds that were completely foreign to me. I took a moment to look around before moving to join Ana where she was standing on the sidewalk. I was so busy looking around that when I stepped up from street level I was caught off guard by both how high I'd had to step and how tilted the cement was. I wobbled for a moment before a warm hand pressed against my upper back, steadying me.

"Careful," Lucas said from behind as he released me.

"They're so tall, and tilted," I breathed out, looking down at my feet.

"For flooding. During storm season the water runs away from the stores and back down into the streets, which act as canals to take the water out of town. Turns out the old-timers knew their stuff," Ana said. I nodded my understanding. "Let's do this. By the end of the day phase three will be complete."

Ana—a woman quite comfortable giving orders—didn't wait for us but headed off up the street. Neither Lucas nor I had moved to follow her, and I looked over at him.

"Phase three?" he asked.

I sighed. "It would have been nice if she'd kept that little bit of information to herself." I began walking.

"I don't believe Ana keeps much to herself," he quipped.

"I'm beginning to understand that."

"So. . . phase three?" He wasn't letting it drop.

I pulled a face. On the bright side, I wasn't trying to impress him, so I might as well answer the question. "Ana sees me as some kind of archeological dig site. She's working in phases to uncover the real me."

"That sounds painful."

"It is." I glanced over to see if I could read his tone from his facial expression, but he was looking back at me and I was too nervous to maintain the contact. I looked away quickly. "I'm sorry I yelled at you about driving your motorcycle on the bricks." I'd been thinking it the entire drive, and it felt good to get it off my chest.

He made a sound. "No, you're not." I didn't dare to respond, but I did allow a small smile to form. Okay, I wasn't *that* sorry. "What were phases one and two?" he asked.

"One was the day we saw you and Marshall on the beach. She tells me the lesson there was spontaneity."

"Phase two?"

I nearly grinned at the memory. "She took me to some block-buster action film in Corpus Christi."

Lucas's face remained mostly passive, but one eyebrow furrowed. "An action show?"

"Yes. Guns blazing and muscles flexing. I don't think anyone spoke below a yell. The lesson in that was to try new things."

"Huh."

"It turned out to be really interesting and entertaining." Warmth spread in my chest at the memory of mocking the movie and trying to suppress our laughter.

Ana had disappeared into a shop three more doors down, and I amazed myself by finding a way to talk lightly and casually with Lucas until we caught up. It wasn't painless and he didn't give a lot back, but he wasn't rude and I was relieved to feel an easing of the tension between us—at least on my part. I couldn't speak for him.

As the unease flowed out, I was able to think more logically. In fact, I told myself, it was natural to feel tingly around Lucas. He was handsome and confident, yes. Even more than that, though, he was in some ways the Prince Charming of my childhood fairy tales. Mary had wanted so desperately for us to meet and had inadvertently built Lucas up on a pedestal. Now that I was finally meeting him, it would make sense that I'd be excited and a little emotional about the entire thing. I was a late bloomer when it came to interactions with the opposite gender. The feelings would settle.

We spent the afternoon walking on tilted sidewalks, entering stores with colorful clothing, touristy items, strange smells, and so much variety in music that my ears were downright exhausted by the time dinner rolled around. Ana's prediction about Lucas waiting at sidewalk tables and benches had proven true. He'd only entered one or two stores himself, but mostly waited as we shopped. He'd been the epitome of patience, never showing any frustration at idling away the hours. Then again, I doubted it had been a trial for him as I'd noticed several people stopping to visit with him along the way. He was clearly a well-known figure on the island.

By the time we headed back to Halstead House I had managed to get a few items of new clothing that I was excited about, a few souvenir items that would look lovely in my condo, and best of all I had spent yet another day doing friend things with Ana. Even having Lucas along hadn't ruined the afternoon. Only one month earlier I'd never have dared hope for those simple things. Gratitude filled my heart as I put my purchases away, serenaded by calls of pelicans outside my window.

CHAPTER 9

With all the new experiences that had been thrown my way lately, it hardly seemed possibly that there would be room for another, but today I was directing Marshall's hired trio of workers in arranging the dining room, ballroom, and formal front parlor for the wedding that would happen in two days. While Ana and her day staff could usually handle event setup, a wedding brought on enough extra work that Marshall got a staff of his own to direct. One of those men, Jonathan, was someone—or something—I had never seen coming.

As I said before, my experience with men was limited. They either took one look at my stiff posture and no-nonsense demeanor, or gave up after one stilted attempt at conversation, deciding rather quickly that I wouldn't be worth the effort. I couldn't blame them. Even I grew frustrated with myself.

However, thanks to Ana's encouragement—or, to be precise, verbal threats—I had shed yet another layer of my old self and was currently wearing jeans and a top that had no buttons. When I'd reported to the main floor of the house that morning, I'd actually felt a little embarrassed about it. While I understood that this casual clothing made sense for the activities of lifting, moving, and decorating that I'd be doing all day . . . well . . . I hadn't worn jeans since graduating from high school nearly eight years before. Not even around my condo on the weekends. Ana had whistled and clapped when I'd entered the kitchen for breakfast.

"The transformation is stunning," she'd cheered. "Tomorrow I expect to see your hair down."

I'd blushed and pulled a face. "Baby steps, Ana."

Ana had picked up on my discomfort and said nothing in reply. I was surprised but grateful. Bubbly, cheerful, confident Ana could have no real idea of what it was costing me to transform myself. A part of me wanted to crawl back into the cocoon—no matter how dark it had been in there.

After breakfast I'd followed Marshall to the front of the house to meet his crew, feeling self-conscious about how the jeans hugged my legs. Yes, I did occasionally wear a pencil skirt that fit snuggly, and I understood that skirts didn't always cover my legs from the knee down, yet the pants felt different somehow.

I'd walked with Marshall, my mind focused on trying to remember all the arguments Ana had made while insisting that skinny jeans were in. The sales people had, predictably, agreed with Ana. Big surprise there. Lucas's opinion had not been asked.

Eventually Marshall and I had reached the front porch, where his temporary crew was waiting. Jonathan had given me a slow, interested perusal when Marshall had introduced me to the three men who would be assisting us. My eyes had widened, but I'd managed to remain passive.

After that introduction, Jonathan had been everywhere I turned. He would smile or nod at me each time we made eye contact. Nothing inappropriate or creepy, just making sure I knew that he was aware of me. Eventually the blushes had broken through, and they hadn't stopped in over an hour.

Now I was leading the way as Jonathan and Marshall each carried one end of a table that would be moved to the side of the dining room as a serving area.

"Where are you from, Grace?" Jonathan asked, speaking directly to me for the first time as we entered the large room.

"Where Grace is from isn't something you need to be worried about," Marshall warned grumpily.

"I'm curious, that's all." Jonathan shrugged and sent me that easy smile of his when Marshall wasn't looking.

His chin-length mahogany hair was slightly wavy and tucked behind each ear, his build lean, his skin sun-bronzed and his eyes as blue as the sky. He wasn't traditionally handsome, but he was appealing and charmingly confident, and just about everything I would have steered clear of in the past.

"Be less curious," Marshall replied sternly.

Jonathan met my eyes and raised a side of his mouth in apparent amusement. I felt a return smile raise the corner of my mouth, more as a result of Marshall's reaction than Jonathan's behavior, before I realized it was happening. Jonathan saw it, misinterpreted it, and grinned. Rats.

I turned away as the other two men Marshall had hired entered the room rolling round tables, grateful for the distraction.

"That large table should go up against that wall, please." I gestured to Marshall and Jonathan. "I'm going to the parlor to start decorating. I'll leave you men to begin setting up the tables and chairs in here. Marshall knows the layout we need."

"Anything for you," Jonathan replied, straightening up after releasing his end of the table.

I didn't respond but turned and began walking out of the dining room toward the front parlor, where the wedding ceremony itself would take place.

"Really, man?" I heard Marshall state flatly. "You leave Grace alone. She's too good for you."

The front formal parlor was one of my favorite rooms, perfect to host a wedding ceremony. It was open and light, with a high ceiling and gauzy draperies in the large bay windows that took up two of the walls. The glitzy sea green and gold silk wallpaper made the room feel elegant and timeless. Its swirling patterns brought images of afternoon tea and ladies come to call in their finest. Each time I entered the room I felt the brush of history like a shot through my veins. I absolutely loved it.

The bride and groom had only been able to invite immediate family because the parlor was one of the smaller rooms in the mansion. Afterward there would be closer to one hundred guests for a luncheon and reception to be held in the large dining and ballrooms.

I was grateful that Eliza had talked the bride into dropping her personal color choice for the ceremony itself. The rust and fuchsia would have been a color-clashing eyesore in such a graceful room. Instead, the bride had wisely chosen to highlight the colors of the wallpaper by bringing in gold chair covers, sea green highlights, and some well-placed greenery.

"It looks marvelous in here, dear." Eliza's voice interrupted my thoughts, causing me to jump. "I'm so glad our bride saw the wisdom in making use of the decor of this room."

Eliza entered wearing slacks and canvas slip-on shoes with a boat-necked striped shirt. She looked relaxed and breezy, her smile warm and big.

I stood from where I'd been tying a sea green bow around one of the chair covers. "I totally agree. This is one of my favorite rooms in the house."

"My parents and grandparents were married in this room." Eliza's eyes were dreamy as her gaze roamed the room.

"Really?" My smile bloomed. "How romantic." I was practically swooning over the very thought.

"Lucas's parents were married here as well. It's something of a family tradition." Eliza sighed. "If I'd ever been married, I'd have loved to do it here too."

Having met her, I could honestly say I was stumped as to why she had never married. However, I kept my mouth closed and my thoughts to myself. Eliza must have sensed them anyhow.

"I had opportunity, Grace. Don't doubt that. With my name, my money, my family . . . well, there were certainly men willing enough to offer. I was chased for many years. The problem was that I could see through all of them. They weren't chasing Eliza. They were chasing Halstead. I'm afraid there is a big difference between the two." She smiled softly.

I came to stand next to her. "Their loss."

Eliza reached out and squeezed my hand. "You're a doll to say that. At this point I'm too set in my ways and wouldn't be interested even if Prince Charming showed up on my doorstep." She grinned a little devilishly. "And far too demanding for one poor man to handle." She was quiet for one more short moment before she shook her head and released my hand, ending that topic of conversation. "I've been to check on the food. Everything is coming along nicely. How is setup going?"

I verbally ran through the list I kept in my head and updated Eliza on the status of preparations. She seemed pleased with the progress and left to check in with Marshall in the dining room.

I opted to take my sandwich out to the garden when lunch eventually rolled around. I found a bench under a palm tree and let out a deep sigh of contentment. I couldn't get over the feeling of the island. The warm, soft, steady breeze and salty floral scents were so different from the region I'd grown up in. I did miss some things about home, but I reveled in the sound of waves nearby, lulling in their steadiness. Perhaps best of all, no sounds of traffic interrupted the lazy afternoon.

A shadow fell over my shoulder, quickly followed by the appearance of Jonathan. "Mind if I join you?" He beamed down at me. His shadow blocked out the sun and left him highlighted from behind.

Cue the dreaded and mortifying blushes. I wasn't sure if I wanted him to join me or not, but I nodded.

"Thanks." Jonathan sat on the grass near the bench.

I relaxed at the distance he'd put between us. Slightly.

"How long have you worked at Halstead House?" he asked around a bite of his own sandwich. He kept his gaze forward, as though taking in the same view I was so interested in, yet it still felt like his eyes were on me.

"A few weeks," I replied.

"I thought so. I've worked some events here for Marshall and never seen you before." I simply nodded, having nothing to add. He pressed on. "I'm kind of afraid to ask, since Marshall wasn't happy about me bothering you, but where are you from? I haven't seen you around the island before. I'd remember."

"I'm guessing it's my accent that gave me away."

Jonathan's eyes crinkled up. "That might be part of it."

"I'm from Rhode Island."

"What brought you here?"

I took a bite of sandwich, deliberately making it impossible to answer while I considered what to say. While I wasn't in the business of rudeness, I certainly wouldn't be sharing my entire life story. At last I swallowed and dared to meet his eyes again. "Vacation, actually. Which ended up in a job offer I just couldn't pass up."

Jonathan nodded slowly. "So now you're on permanent vacation?"

"It feels that way most days. Not today."

He grinned. "The events here are always a big deal. I appreciate the extra work they give me. They're good people."

He took a large bite of his own sandwich and allowed silence to fall. I couldn't hear the waves over my heartbeat. I was both terrified and excited to be having a normal conversation, with a man I didn't know, that wasn't work-related. Okay, it kind of was work related, but still.

"Have you lived on the island your whole life, then?" I pushed out through numb lips.

"Pretty much. Don't remember anywhere else, at least. It's a good place to put down roots," Jonathan replied.

"What kind of work do you do here?" I swallowed.

My hands were feeling a little fidgety as I continued to work outside my comfort zone and practice some of the things I'd been learning from life with Ana and Marshall. Like how to talk to people.

"I'm a contractor. I do a steady business. It's a benefit of living on an island with so many historic buildings. Between the salt, sun, and sea they're always needing repair."

"So you just help out Marshall here and there?"

Jonathan nodded. "It works for both of us. The extra money doesn't hurt, and the Halsteads don't have to keep on a full staff."

I nodded and pushed a stray hair behind my ear. My food was almost gone. Lunch was almost over. I'd been chatting with a man for more than five minutes. Sure, it wasn't earth-shattering conversation. It was small talk. Still, I thought Ana would be proud. Heck, I was proud of myself.

"You always this nervous talking to new people?" Jonathan broke in to my thoughts.

Oh, well, maybe I wasn't pulling it off. I looked toward him to find him looking steadily at me, his blue eyes kind and interested, maybe a little teasing.

My face heated while a soft smile tugged at my mouth. "Yes."

"I don't see why, you're doing just fine. It's almost like you've talked to people before and have some experience," he joked.

My smile grew. "That might be the most glowing report I've ever received."

His smile did the same, and dang it, he was actually really attractive when it filled his face. I gulped and raced right back to terrified, tucking my sheep's skin around me protectively. The silence fell again.

"Why, Grace." Ana's laughing voice preceded her by a split second. "First you wear jeans, then you start cavorting with strange men. Praise heaven, I knew this day would come. Makes me darn proud to have been part of the transformation."

I pulled a face at her teasing. "Hi, Ana."

"She peels back another layer every day." Ana plopped down on the bench next to me. "How you doing, Jonathan?"

Jonathan smiled up at her, although it felt slightly less genuine than the smiles he'd been giving me all day. "I'm good, you?"

"Oh, you know, busy as always. I was pretty surprised to see Grace sitting out here having what looked to be an actual conversation." Ana nudged my side playfully. "And with the catch of Lavender Island. I'm impressed."

"I have normal conversations every day," I replied with a shake of my head.

"I'm no great prize, Ana," Jonathan replied lightly.

"Grace, your heart isn't safe with Jonathan, here. Please tell me you haven't given it to him already?" Ana said.

"It's still where it belongs," I confirmed.

Jonathan sighed and shook his head. "Ana, you're killing me here. I'm just trying to get to know our new friend."

"Well, get to know her *slowly*." Ana's voice held a note of warning, but her face remained open and cheerful as she jumped up and grabbed my hand. "Break's over and Eliza is looking for you."

I stood at once and smiled down at Jonathan. "Thanks for the conversation."

Jonathan hurried to stand and gave me a warm look. "I hope we have the chance again."

Neither Ana nor I said anything as we made our way back toward the house. My mind was racing, and my chest fluttered. I could see why Ana called Jonathan a catch. I just wasn't sure if it was deserved or not. Then again, Ana would be the one to know.

Work in the house continued full steam for the rest of the day. I felt that same flutter in my chest whenever I was in the same room as Jonathan. I analyzed, over-analyzed, and obsessed over what he meant by all the looks and grins. When six o'clock rolled around and Eliza called quitting time for the day, I was so tied in knots I could hardly tell up from down.

Jonathan came to where I was standing in the dining room. I could tell by his stance that I was finally going to get some answers to my questions. "Grace, can I chat with you for just a second?" he asked. I nodded. "Outside, privately?" I nodded again.

I put down the vase I was holding and followed him through the entrance hall to the large front porch. He rubbed his hands on his pants and then shoved them in his pockets. He looked away from me, toward the street, the very picture of nonchalance. I waited.

"I'm wondering if I could take you out sometime?" he finally asked.

"Oh," I whispered.

"You can't tell me you didn't see that coming," he teased, turning to me.

"Uh, actually, no, I don't, um . . ." I paused. It didn't seem like the best idea to tell Jonathan that I never got asked out.

"Nothing big. Dinner some night after the wedding festivities are over."

"I'm not sure," I replied honestly.

"Is it because of what Ana said?" He shook his head and made a face. "Don't listen to her. We've known each other forever. When you've lived on the same island long enough, you know how to get under someone's skin."

I didn't respond immediately. I needed to think. From my professional career I'd always been told not to date co-workers. Yet Jonathan wasn't really a co-worker. However, he was someone so free and open and flirtatious that I knew it would be a night of blushing and awkwardness for me. Then again, should I actually turn down the first date invitation I'd received in years?

"Well," I finally began, taking a deep breath.

"Well?" He took a step closer, gazing at me with those sky blue eyes that looked oddly intent at the moment.

It wasn't that it was bad, or there were warning bells suggesting danger. It was more like he had something in mind and I couldn't begin to guess what it was. I didn't understand the game, or the rules, at all.

His intensity sparked my own vulnerability, and I realized that I wasn't ready to throw dating into the mix just yet. I was trying to stand on my own two feet, to figure out who I was, to see the truth about myself. Adding romance into that equation seemed like a recipe for disaster.

"Actually, I hope you don't take this personally, but I'm not ready to date anyone just yet." I spoke as honestly as I could.

"Bad relationship?" he asked sympathetically.

"Um, I suppose you could say that," I replied. Technically, my relationship with my mother wasn't a good one.

"I guess I'll just have to hope I see you later then."

I merely smiled and nodded as he hopped down the front stairs and turned toward the parking lot behind the mansion. Nerves tickled restlessly at my stomach, wondering if I'd made the right decision. On the one hand, I didn't know anything about this man, other than he was attractive and apparently interested in me. On the other, well, should I be turning down date offers when I was only getting them . . . never?

I sat on the front steps and propped my elbows on my knees rather than returning inside immediately. I put my chin in my hands and thought about what a strange day it had been. Maybe Ana was right and clothing did have power. Either jeans were magical, or buttons were poison. The idea had merit. I'd have to keep testing it out.

I heard the front door open behind me, and I turned to see Lucas coming out. I hadn't known he was around today. He was dressed immaculately in a pressed and tailored navy suit, pin straight tie, and shiny dress shoes. He looked as handsome as ever. I couldn't help but notice the difference between how I reacted to him and how I'd felt around Jonathon. One was simply scary, the other was completely and overwhelmingly terrifying.

I turned to face the street again, expecting him to keep walking down the front steps. Instead he came to stand near me. I waited, but he remained silent.

"You on your way out?" I finally asked.

"Yes." He walked a few steps down and turned to face me at eye level. "Did I see you out here with Jonathan?"

"Yes."

"Marshall's worried that Jonathan is bothering you."

I was more than a little caught off guard that Marshall would have taken it to Lucas. It was both sweet and a little overbearing for him to have complained to the boss rather than talking with me. In my real life, my mother was constantly overbearing, and Marshall's tattling—as I saw it in that moment—sparked annoyance in the pit of my stomach.

I'd been working so hard to choose my own way these past weeks. Add to that the fact that Marshall took it to the one person on the property who I wouldn't have wanted him to talk to, well, to be totally honest here, it rubbed. I was not happy. Fortunately, I had a lot of experience in looking serene when I was angry inside.

I took a slow, quiet, deep breath, not wanting Lucas to see any of the thoughts that were racing through my mind. It took a moment to quell the frustration, even though I knew Marshall had good intentions. Ana had warned me to be cautious too, after all.

"It's kind of Marshall to worry," I said at last. "But I'm fine."

"I assume Jonathan asked you out?" His voice was flat and I nodded. "Not surprising." My jaw tensed. There was history behind that remark, and I wasn't privy to any of it. "Did you agree to go?"

I debated how to respond. Cowardice and bravery warred within. "Since it would be during my private time, I'm not sure that's any of your business," I replied at last. One point for bravery. Ignoring the shaking knees and the fact that I'd had to look away from him as I said it.

"So that's a yes."

A blush warmed the tips of my cheekbones as I fought to keep my face passive. I was really not liking this moment. "Actually, it's a no."

"Really?"

I couldn't read his tone, and I certainly wasn't going to look at him, as I'd inadvertently just humiliated myself. I shook my head and closed my eyes. "Can we be done talking about this now?"

"I'm just surprised." His voice shifted into a less abrasive tone.

"Why?" I scoffed.

He didn't answer right away, although I could feel his eyes on me. Finally he said, "You seemed to enjoy talking to him."

How would he know that? I glanced up at him. "Were you spying on us just now?"

"I wouldn't call it spying so much as looking out the front window to see if my ride was here and accidentally watching you and Jonathan talk."

Oh. I cleared my throat. I stood and gestured down to my pants. "I think I have these ridiculously tight jeans to thank for any interest. Ana will be thrilled."

Lucas actually chuckled. It was the first time I'd heard that sound out of him, and it caused a swell of tingles to rise from my stomach into that fluttery spot in my chest. I chided myself immediately. Enough of that. If I allowed myself to think of Lucas romantically, well, it would make my whole experience on the island a miserable one, and I hadn't come here for misery.

Two staccato beeps from a sports car pulling up in front of the house was a welcome distraction. His ride was here. I watched as a woman stepped out of the driver's door and waved to Lucas. She was dressed as formally as Lucas, and her evening gown sparkled in the last rays of the sun. He waved back and she didn't make an effort to come any closer, waiting next to the car instead.

"Good luck with wherever you're off to tonight." I turned to go inside.

"Grace?" he called. I looked back over my shoulder to see he hadn't moved. "If it changes, with Jonathan, from fun and flirting to being bothered, let me know. Okay?"

I shrugged, which was becoming one of my new favorite gestures. It may have something to do with the fact that Mother abhorred shrugging. "It's no big deal. I'm not sure that I'll ever see him again anyhow."

"Okay, but, I'd like to know if there's ever a problem," he reiterated.

My features relaxed and I offered him a small smile. With a final nod in my direction he walked down the steps toward the glittering woman waiting for him. I made my way inside with a truckload of thoughts bouncing around.

I understood that as my employer and host he was trying to look out for me, but something about the way he'd said it didn't totally sound like it was only because I was an employee of the family. This feeling of being looked after was different somehow. Instead of bristling and making decrees, like Mother always did, he'd simply asked if I was okay and made it clear that should I need him, he'd be there.

The night was so beautiful that I decided to go to the garden fountain and sit for a moment. I wasn't quite ready for bed, and there was more over-analyzing to be done about Jonathan and Lucas. I sat down and listened to the fountain water against the back drop of the ocean waves nearby. It was soothing. I methodically relaxed every major muscle group in my body as I reviewed the day and its conversations. From what I could tell Jonathan seemed nice enough. It warmed me to think that he wanted to see me again. It warmed me even more that Lucas wanted to make sure I was okay. Which was silly, because I couldn't decide if Lucas thought of me as a pest or a person.

The sudden vibration of my phone jarred me out of my head space. I'd turned off the ringer while we were all working, and now I fumbled around in my pocket trying to locate it. I answered without checking, afraid to miss the call. What if Jonathan had gotten my number from someone else and was going to ask again? I was willing to be chased a little, I thought, maybe.

"Grace." Mother's husky voice came at me like a wave crashing against the side of my head.

My spine snapped straight out of habit. "Mother?"

"Who else were you expecting?"

Anyone but her. Last time we'd talked she'd disowned me. I hadn't been made aware that we were back on again. "Oh, well, I just had a man ask me out and thought maybe it was . . ." I bit my lip but it was too late. My guard had been down and I'd said more than I'd meant to.

"A date? Oh, Grace, there are plenty of single, eligible men here in Providence. You didn't need to run away to find someone. In fact, I've had a few in mind . . ."

"No, Mother, no." I hurried to get that thought out of her head.

"Are you sure?"

"Yes, I'm sure." Truly, I did not want her list of eligible bachelors. I wasn't in the market for a bow-tied yes-man who'd flow right along with her plans.

"How is it that you've been down there for such a short amount of time and you're dating, but you never date here at home?" she asked.

"Maybe the men in Providence are idiots?" I tried to joke.

"Or maybe you're trying to be someone else and lying to the men there," Mother replied. Ouch. I felt a stab in my stomach, but said nothing. "How am I to know what you're up to? You never call and I haven't seen any pictures at all. For all I know you've dyed your hair black and started dressing like a floozy."

"I'm still me," I said.

"Hmm . . . I should hope so." Mother made another noise but didn't say any more about that particular topic. "I've decided that I'm not all that surprised that you've decided to stay until June. You've been enamored of that house ever since Mrs. Reed told you her fairy tales. She filled your head with fluff and nonsense. What a complete waste of time. I can't imagine that the house is half as wonderful as she led you to believe. If by some chance it is, they're going to see you as a gold-digging upstart trying to claim a connection to a family that isn't even

yours. I hope you haven't totally embarrassed yourself yet."
She was really getting a head of steam. "Never mind, of course
you have. Dating around the island like you are, you're probably making a name for yourself. How humiliating. Now the
Halsteads really won't want anything to do with you. I raised
you better than this."

The blows came one upon the other in a way that I couldn't
seem to handle. I'd been gradually letting my wall down, releasing
chunks of the protection I'd so meticulously built. Her arrows were
finding the cracks. They stung more than they had since I'd been
too young to know that mothers could hurt you.

Tears of humiliation and defeat filled my eyes. Her voice echoed
in the secret places of my heart. I understood that she was spouting
lies and manipulations, but I was unable to pull up the slick glass
shield I'd often used to let them slide off.

Alone, in the darkness, sitting on a bench in the garden of my
dream house, I let the tears fall. She couldn't see me. As long as I
was able to keep myself from making any noise she would have no
idea that I was upset. I was an expert at the silent cry.

"What are you planning to do until June?" she said as her tirade
ended.

I filled my lungs with a slow breath and released it silently, gain-
ing control of my voice before I spoke. While tears still made tracks
down my face, my voice was steady.

"I'm staying in the house with the family and helping them with
event planning," I said.

"You haven't changed your mind, then? You're slaving yourself
out for them? In hopes of what? Sucking up any crumbs they throw
you?"

My throat felt dry and raw as the accusation hit. "No, Mother.
I was hired on as a staff member before they knew who I was." The
slight fib felt necessary.

"Let me get this straight. You took a sabbatical from your perfectly respectful job in Providence to chase your dream, and ended
up taking a grunt job on an island somewhere?" A response was not
going to be necessary or helpful. "Your silence tells me everything

I need to know. Well, I sincerely hope you'll get this out of your system and return my real daughter to me at that time."

The line went dead. She'd now hung up on me twice in my life. It was jarring. I dropped my phone onto the bench next to me before I let my head fall back and looked at the sky. The irony of her timing, and her words, wasn't lost on me. I'd just come from a personal high—getting asked on a date—and it was as though her instincts had screamed at her across the distance to cut me down. A new round of tears threatened as I thought of all the things I wanted to say to her but never would, and of all the times that she'd managed to bring me to my knees.

CHAPTER 10

My world didn't stop spinning for a few days after my phone call with Mother. She'd knocked me clear off my axis. I sought refuge as I had after the last confrontation: by diving in to my responsibilities as Eliza's assistant. When I was technically off the clock I stayed on the property. I had a feeling that this adventure would end sooner than I wanted it to, and I needed to not waste a single moment.

I was in Eliza's office on Friday morning, just before the doors were set to open to the public for tours, looking over the paperwork for the next week's fortieth birthday party. I was happy to see that there would be no clown, and was about to ask Eliza what she'd had to say to the birthday boy, when the tour guide Steven called. A stomach bug had caught him, and while he was discreet in his description, it didn't sound like something that would allow him freedom of movement that day.

Eliza offered her sympathies and understanding before hanging up the phone. Her thoughtful gaze met mine and I sat up straighter, as was my habit under any kind of scrutiny.

"I'm guessing you know as much about Halstead House as Steven does," she said.

I nodded in what I hoped was a modest way, even as my inner wolf rustled in her sheepskin. "Possibly."

"How would you feel about taking over for him today? Tours go from ten to six. They're self-guided, but occasionally someone wants more details or gets lost—heaven only knows how."

My stomach flipped happily at the idea. "What about our plans for today? That fortieth birthday party is next week." I tried not to sound too anxious.

Eliza waved away my concern. "We can talk when Steven is back tomorrow. We're down to details, and I can manage without you for one day."

I smiled. "Well, if you're sure . . ."

She chuckled. "I have to give you credit for trying to pretend you didn't want to run straight out of this room the moment you heard." My smile grew. "Go have your fun day."

I stood quickly and put the paperwork that I'd been sorting through on her desk. "Thank you."

"Just don't cross the line by trying to steal Steven's job after this," she called as I left the room.

"No promises," I teased and was rewarded by the sound of Eliza's full laughter.

I hustled to my room to put on something I thought was more "tour-guidey." What that would be, hey, who knew. It wasn't like I hadn't already dressed for the day in business clothing. Steven was usually dressed in a polo shirt and khaki pants. I threw open the wardrobe and honestly considered the dove gray suit for my first foray into being the official face of Halstead House. I ran my hand over the suit and imagined people listening to me in rapture, their eyes glistening with unshed tears as their hearts were tugged by stories of generations of familial happiness. I started to lift the suit off the hanging rod when I caught myself. This was "old Grace" business, and I'd slipped dangerous down the slope into la la land.

I had to get a grip and remember that no one actually judged me as harshly as I judged myself. In all actuality, most of the tourists came through in shorts and flip flops, and they'd give no consideration to what I had on. I hung the suit back in the closet and left my room without changing.

I had a new mission in mind—to share my good fortune with someone, and I knew just who that would be. Ana was in her office when I finally tracked her down. She was sitting behind her desk, bent over what looked like account books and a pile of receipts. I didn't want to scare her, so I waited until her head was out of the pile and she turned. She squealed and pressed a hand to her chest. Guess I scared her anyhow. Oops.

"What are you doing standing there being creepy and silent?" she asked.

"I didn't want to call out and scare you while you were wrestling with the paper mountain," I replied.

"They say it's the thought that counts." She pulled a face. "What's up?"

"Steven called in sick today."

"Oh, man. Does this mean I need to get Michelle started sterilizing all the public rooms so he doesn't spread some disease to our guests? I was going to have her handle the fresh floral arrangements this morning."

"I honestly have no idea." I drew my eyebrows down. "You could ask Eliza, but it sounds like a good idea to me."

"No need to bother her when it's up to me." She sighed and made a thoughtful face. "I'll make adjustments."

I smiled big and pointed at myself when she focused in on me again. "Ana, I get to take his place today. I'm the substitute tour guide!"

She sat up straighter in her chair, eyes dancing. "Well, congrats, Grace. That's very exciting news."

"Thank you." I stood smiling like an idiot but said nothing more. This was the type of things friends shared with each other, right? The smiling thing, maybe not so much. I worked to clamp my mouth shut and paste on some serenity.

"Anything else?"

"No, I don't think so." I shook my head. "Well, what if . . ." I took a deep breath and shoved myself into the abyss of uncertainty. "Uh, maybe we could have a celebratory dinner somewhere afterwards?" In for a penny, in for a pound. It had been longer than I could remember since I'd extended anyone a social invitation.

Relief flooded through me when she chuckled and replied, "Sure. I mean, who doesn't celebrate when a co-worker gets sick and they have to do their job for them?"

"Seems normal," I cracked.

"I'm in. If you don't already have somewhere in mind, I have just the place," she replied. I clapped my hands. "On one condition." My hands dropped like lead.

"Oh, no, Ana. This is not going to be therapy session number four or something. This is my night out."

Ana laughed. "My only request is that we go casual. As in you wear some of those new clothes we bought."

"Okay."

She wasn't done. "Plus, you wear your hair down."

I pulled a face at her.

"I'm serious. I'm not taking you to this place while you're still uptight."

"What kind of questionable place are you taking me?"

"You're going to have to trust the island master."

Our gazes locked for a moment, until I caved. "I'm not sure how to style it if I leave it down," I admitted.

Her hands froze in the act of leaning back over her paperwork. "Seriously?"

"Truly."

Her questioning look said a lot, but she kindly replied, "Okay, I'll come up to your room at six thirty and teach you how to do your hair." I gave her an unsure look and she grinned. "It'll be worth it. Now, go impress some people with your knowledge of this house and I'll impress some people with my knowledge of accounting. I'll see you tonight."

I nodded and left her office to go into the front entrance. It would be my job this morning to unlock the big front doors and officially open the house. My heels made quick staccato sounds as I unabashedly trotted across the floor to the huge double doors. I turned the three locks and tugged. And it was open. That simple. Like a thousand other doors I'd opened in my life. Still, today Halstead House sort of belonged to me . . . and it was going to be awesome.

* * *

"If you pull any harder, I'll be bald, and then all your plans about me leaving my hair down will be ruined," I said through gritted teeth as Ana ran a brush through my hair later that evening.

It came as no surprise that Ana wouldn't be a gentle teacher of hair arts. Nothing she'd done around me had ever been gentle. She was a tiny bulldozer, and now I'd handed her a brush and given her free reign of my hair. This was my own fault.

"Stop whining," she grumbled.

"My neighbor's German grandmother didn't pull hair as hard as you do."

"Are German grandmothers heavy-handed hair brushers? Because that sounds a lot like stereotyping to me."

"Everyone knows they are," I replied, trying not to laugh.

"Please, even if that were true, it's not like you've actually had a German grandma brush your hair," Ana scoffed.

"Well, I watched her brush my friend's hair."

"What was your friend's name?"

"Gretel," I responded.

"Uh-huh. She sounds super real." She rolled her eyes. "Do you have a flat iron?"

"I don't."

"I have a question, and I need you to answer me honestly."

"Okay."

"Do you actually know what a flat iron is?"

"Yes."

"Hmm."

I tried to turn my head to give her a look over my shoulder, but she yanked it back into place. "This is the second time in the last five minutes that you've accused me of lying," I growled.

"Well, you've been talking about German grandmothers. I have reason to wonder."

"Hey, Gretel's grandmother was a tough cookie. And I do know what a flat iron is. I just have no idea how to use one."

"Fine. I'll be back. Change your clothes while I'm gone."

Ana dropped the brush on my bed and was out the door before I had a chance to fully process her instructions. I stared into my closet, unsure what look Ana wanted me to go for that night. I rifled through some options before settling on jeans and a sleeveless, flowy tunic type shirt. Ana entered the room holding her flat iron just as I finished getting dressed and was starting to re-hang my business outfit. She paused long enough to take in my outfit, give me a brief nod, and find an outlet near my mirror for her to plug in the device.

"My hair is kind of thin, Ana. Don't burn it," I said.

"I know what I'm doing," she replied.

I sat down in the chair she'd pulled over and tried not to be too tense. Before I knew it she had brushed and ironed and curled my hair into soft waves that fell around my face and brushed my shoulders. I hardly recognized myself.

"Wow," I said.

"I know. You have great hair," Ana replied as she unplugged her flat iron. "You're lucky. A lot of people spend a lot of money to get platinum hair."

My face warmed at her compliment. I'd often felt washed out and plain, a fact my own dark-haired mother had also lamented. My father had been fair, but somehow I had been considered a disappointing anomaly. Forget the fact that Grace Kelly had been blonde. My blondeness had gone too far.

"Let's go," Ana said before I had a chance to reply.

"I'm driving," I called after her as I hurried to grab my purse and follow.

"Fat chance." Ana grinned when I caught up to her at the elevator door.

"This is supposed to be my special night," I reminded her as we stepped inside. "Cheating death doesn't make me feel special."

"Oh, it's going to be perfect. Trust me."

Ana's words caused a few nerves to race across my heart. I knew it. Ana was turning this into a therapy session. She was going to force me to face something I wasn't prepared for. I almost bailed. Almost. Yet memories of a beach day and an action film kept me going. Both of those had turned out pretty well. Maybe this would be the same.

She didn't let me drive, but at least this time I was prepared for her crazed auto-gymnastics. I also figured we'd be staying on the island, which meant the drive wasn't going to be terribly long. I hoped. Assumptions didn't always play out, but I was too apprehensive to ask many questions.

Thankfully I was right about the drive time. We passed through the historic district and made our way out to the wharves on the north side of the island. I hadn't been here but had noticed the taller warehouses peaking up from my bedroom window. The buildings were gray and brown, victims of being so close to the ocean. To me they had a menacing feel, unwelcoming and strange when compared to the colorful historic homes nearby.

"Where are we?" I asked as Ana parked in front of the largest building in the group.

"It's called the Warehouse," she replied. "Us locals pride ourselves on keeping the place a secret from tourists." She pushed her car door open and got out.

"How cleverly named," I mumbled.

"They have the best true Southern food on Lavender. Plus, it's Friday night so there will be dancing. A lot of people come around. You're going to have a great time."

I remained quiet as I followed Ana through a dark alley that felt like a murderer's paradise before we came around to the dockside front doors where the cheerful sunlight returned. The sound of ocean water slapping up against the cement walkway was nearly drowned out by the music coming from inside the weather-worn building.

Ana paused for a moment, her hand on the door. "You ready?"

"Probably not," I replied.

She chuckled. "Come on, you chicken. Remember who you are. You're the power suit wearing, substitute tour guide at Halstead House." She grabbed my arm and tugged me in behind her.

The Warehouse was just as off beat as its outer shell had promised. Tools of the fishing industry hung haphazardly above our heads. Tables were strewn here and there with no immediate sense of order. In the back was an already crowded dance floor. Loud music blared from a DJ stand in one corner, its heavy beat echoing the pounding of my heart.

It didn't appear that any walls had ever been painted. Everything was gray or brown, with occasional rust, and a lot of steel. No tablecloths, china, or glassware softened its rough-hewn appearance. Everything was serviceable and not one inch more. Not exactly cozy, and definitely not my usual style. I felt immediately out of place but did my best to keep from folding in on myself.

"Come on," Ana tugged. "Let's get a table."

I followed along, my eyes barely able to take everything in. Ana's hand pulling on my wrist was the only thing keeping me tethered to reality. If I hung around with her much more I was going to crack.

She found a small table pressed against the wall near the dance floor. I was grateful for the sense of security the wall afforded me. Something solid to lean against, and possibly hide next to if I needed it.

"Here's your menu." A piece of laminated paper was pushed toward me. "Literally everything is good."

I perused the menu and was pleased to see that she had been right about the food options. Everything had a distinctly Southern flair. I wasn't sure where to start. My experience with that type of food was lacking.

"What do you recommend?" I lifted my eyes to find Ana looking at me. "What?"

"Just making sure your head doesn't explode," she replied.

I raised my eyebrows. "I think your therapy sessions might kill me."

"Nah. I'm seeing improvements every day."

"May I offer some feedback for the future?"

"Why not?"

"Clients don't appreciate you promising a celebration activity and then surprising them with another therapy session cloaked as fun."

She made a thoughtful face and playfully rubbed at her chin. "I'll take that under advisement."

I returned to the menu. "So, really, what should I try?"

"Well, if you trust me, I'll order for both of us," she offered, and I nodded. "You allergic to anything?" I shook my head. "Great. Prepare to be amazed."

Ana ordered, and while we were waiting on our food we watched the dancers on the floor. Songs alternated between fast songs, line dancing, and slow songs where couples moved together to the music. Some couples were fun to watch, their complicated dance steps showing a lot of skill. Other couples seemed to think the dance floor was their own private love space, making me distinctly uncomfortable.

When our food came Ana explained the various dishes. Blackened catfish, steaming jambalaya, fried green tomatoes, creamed corn, and hush puppies filled the small table top. Last were the beignets, fried dough covered in clouds of powered sugar that I'd always wanted to sample. My eyes grew large at the display.

"We'll never be able to eat all of this," I said as I looked up at Ana's happy face.

"That's not the point, Grace. The point is to try all the things. If you have to unbutton your jeans and roll out of this place, then it was a successful night."

I looked back at all the food and felt a smile begin to lift my lips. "Okay. I'm game. What should I try first?"

"Doesn't matter. Try it all."

I loaded my plate with spoonfuls of everything. I followed Ana's lead, using my fork for some dishes and picking up the hush puppies and fried green tomatoes with my fingers. If Mother could see me now, hair down, wearing jeans, eating with my fingers while people danced all around me, well, I wasn't sure she *was* going to get her 'real' Grace home after all of this.

Our conversation was relaxed and comfortable as we stuffed ourselves full. Turns out I'd worked up quite the appetite playing show and tell. The crowd continued to grow, and before we had finished eating, all the tables were filled. The dance floor surged with people, and that end of the workweek feeling grew.

"So, Grace, what do you think of this place?" Ana asked as she leaned back in her chair and patted her stomach.

"It's definitely eye-opening," I answered, taking a sip of water and leaning back myself.

"Worthy of a celebration dinner?" she said with a grin.

"Yes. Even if you did try to sneak attack therapy me."

Ana started to reply, but her grin faltered as she looked over my shoulder. She opened her mouth to say something, but a low male voice beat her to the punch.

"Hello, ladies. What a surprise finding the two of you here tonight." Jonathan's smiling face came into view as he stepped from behind me to stand next to our table.

"Hi, Jonathan." Ana's greeting was pleasant if not exactly happy.

He turned his gaze to me, and my stomach felt full of wiggly worms. The gummy type, not the gross slimy ones. "What brings you two out tonight?" he asked.

"I'm celebrating," I replied. I felt shy, remembering that the last time I'd seen him he'd wanted to take me out.

"What's the special occasion?" He snagged a chair that wasn't being used at a nearby table, tugged it over, and sat on it backwards, his arms resting against the back and his legs splayed, confidence and charisma oozing from his pores.

I suddenly felt ridiculous and didn't want to tell him. "Um, well, just a good day at work," I replied.

"It's worth celebrating when those come around." He nodded. "Looks like you've got a great spread here." He gestured to the food with a slight flick of the wrist.

"I liked it a lot. Ana ordered and had me try some of everything," I replied.

"You hungry?" Ana asked. "We hardly made a dent." Her words were polite, but her tone less so. My gaze shot to her, but she was looking at Jonathan in a way I couldn't decipher. This was the first I'd seen of Ana without her more-the-merrier attitude.

"That's real nice of you, Ana. Thank you, but I've eaten already. I was making my way to the dance floor when I saw you two over here. Thought I'd see if Grace wants to take a twirl with me." He looked to me, and I read the hint of challenge in his expression.

My stomach clenched. "I'm afraid I've never done this type of dancing," I hedged.

"What type of dancing do you mean?" he asked.

"I mean, I've never line danced or done any of the couple dances with their intricate steps." I felt my face warm and cursed it for the millionth time.

"Don't worry about that. Everybody has to learn sometime. I'm a great teacher."

He stood up from his chair, kicking it back toward the table he'd taken it from and held out a hand to me. I looked to Ana, who just shrugged. I was on my own to decide. It should have been a simple decision: to dance or not to dance. But it wasn't. There was true potential for me to embarrass myself or cause some kind of disturbance, and I couldn't be relaxed about that. A Burke was always proper in public. No scandal should ever be attached to my name.

While I realized that I lived a strict set of rules, I did agree fundamentally with some of them. The way Ana was acting toward Jonathan made me think that dancing with him would cause some unwelcome consequences—whatever that meant. I didn't want anything to be said about the Halstead family because of me. Then again, this was the man I'd recently shared a nice conversation with over a sandwich, and we had worked side-by-side. He seemed harmless enough for one little dance.

"Come on, baby girl, nothing to worry about," Jonathan said in a soothing tone as he took my hand.

Turns out I didn't like being called baby girl. I was learning new things about myself every day. Still . . . I had worn my hair down, and it seemed like an awful waste of hair-tugging if I turned down this opportunity.

I took his hand and a deep breath at the same time. "Okay. One dance."

"We'll start with one and see how it goes." He smiled his handsome smile. My eyes practically crossed at the sight of all that male beauty, and all arguments flew out of my head. He was dangerous.

As luck would have it, a line dance was starting when we found some space on the dance floor. My eyes were wide as I turned to Jonathan, but he grinned and nodded.

"Just follow along and you'll pick it up." He let go of my hand after giving it a reassuring squeeze.

I looked to where Ana was still sitting at our table. I understood the words Jonathan had said, but I wasn't exactly comforted by them. Thankfully Ana understood my panicked look and hurried out to join us. She shoved her way in to stand next to me.

"Okay, Grace, nothing to worry about. Line dances repeat the same movements over and over. We're in the middle of the crowd, so no one will notice you. I promise you aren't the only one learning this dance tonight," she said quietly.

I bit my lip and nodded. "Okay. That makes sense."

I was comforted by Ana's presence next to me as the music started and all around me people began moving as one. Arms and legs kicked and flew in unison. People whistled and called out words as they got into the groove. I noticed two girls in the row behind me laughing as they stumbled through the moves, trying to learn. The only difference between them and me was that I was doing it stiffly while they were relaxed, not self-conscious, and laughing. I tried to make my muscles unclench.

I made a mistake as we rotated and allowed myself a small laugh. Jonathan heard me and smiled. "See, this is fun."

I looked to Ana, who was on the other side of me, eyes glowing as she did the moves perfectly. "You could have taught me these dances before we came," I said off to her side.

"And miss watching Miss Perfect Pants struggle? I don't think so."

"I'm not perfect," I argued as we turned again.

"Obviously." Ana tapped me on the shoulder to get me moving in the right direction.

After another full rotation I got the hang of the steps and began to feel freer and more confident. By the time we turned again I was smiling. Another turn and I was laughing. When the song ended I had my full megawatt smile shining.

I felt sweat trickle down my back as I thanked Ana for coming out to dance with me. She gave me a spontaneous hug, which lodged something new and sweet in my throat, before heading back to our table. A feeling of affection washed over me as I watched her walk away. She'd seen my need and come to my side for no reason other than to help me. I had a friend. The feeling was remarkable.

I turned to Jonathan, smile still shining, as the music slowed to another couple's dance. "Thank you, that was fun," I said.

"You can't leave now," he responded, grabbing at my hand. "This is the good part."

"I really should . . ."

"Come on. You wouldn't let me take you to dinner. At least share one slow dance with me."

My argument died and he saw his chance to pull me in close to him and put both hands on my waist. I instinctively reached for his shoulders as he guided me into some simple footsteps. As soon as I gave in to his directions we were moving gracefully across the floor, weaving through the other couples.

As my apprehension melted into the soothing movements of the dance, he pressed me gently closer, moving his hands from my waist to my lower back and making it so that our heads were side-by-side. I went hesitantly into his less formal embrace but held my distance when he tried to squeeze me tighter.

I felt his hot breath on my ear as he chuckled. "Feeling shy?"

"I hardly know you," I replied.

"Relax, Grace. You're on island life now. No one here will think anything of two beautiful people dancing together." He guided me into a twirl and brought me back up against him, stealing back the space I'd asked for. My mind stuttered over the fact that he'd called me beautiful. Of course, he'd called himself beautiful in the same sentence. "If you're just uncomfortable because it's me, well, I can back off." He released me abruptly, taking a step back and holding only my hands as we swayed a foot or so apart.

His plan worked, and I laughed at the absurd picture we made, dancing like two sixth graders at their elementary school Valentine's Day dance. I tugged on his hands and he quickly put his arms around me again.

"See, not so bad," he said. I pulled a face but said nothing.

As we continued to dance so closely, I felt a new tension radiating from him that I'd never felt from a man before. His arm muscles seemed to alternate between flexing and relaxing as we moved, both holding me close and guiding me along. He was quiet, but it wasn't a bored type of quiet; it was focused. It felt like it was focused on me, as though he was aware of every move I was making and trying to anticipate the next. Was this what it felt like when a man was attracted to you?

My mind was spinning as the song ended. Rather than walking me back to my table, Jonathan took my hand and asked me if

I wanted to step out for some fresh air. I agreed as a bead of sweat ran down my forehead and into my eye. The room was crowded and warm, and my heart was pounding in an unfamiliar rhythm.

I signaled Ana from across the room, letting her know I was stepping outside with Jonathan. She waved. Jonathan tugged on my hand and wove his fingers through mine. I liked the feeling in the same way I had liked Ana's hug. This connection to other people was something I'd wanted for a long time.

We walked out a side door and onto a raised veranda. It was a bit overcrowded as other people joined us in seeking some reprieve from the stale air inside. Jonathan held my hand and wove us through the crowd before leading me down the steps from the veranda. I wasn't sure why we were leaving the open area until he turned sharply at the bottom of the stairs and walked into the welcome shade below. The veranda was high enough that we could both stand up straight. The blessed island breeze, combined with the shade, began its work of cooling us down.

Jonathan looked to me and his dazzling smile flashed. "You're a better dancer than you give yourself credit for," he said.

"Thank you. You did a great job leading me. It was fun to learn some new steps."

"Oh yeah?" His voice had become a bit rough sounding.

"Yeah," I replied, my eyebrows dropping in confusion.

He was close enough to my height for us to be nearly eye level. His sky blue eyes looked darker this close. I felt nerves zip up my back when he shuffled forward a step, but I held my ground.

"I'd really like to kiss you, Grace." He reached out a hand to touch my cheek.

"Oh," I breathed, startled.

"Is that okay?" His hand came to rest on my shoulder.

"I don't know," I whispered.

In hindsight, I should have seen it coming. I'd read enough romance novels and watched enough Hallmark channel to know that after dancing came kissing. Plus, honestly, the guy had taken me into a dark place away from other people. We were obviously not here for the shade. Logically, my astonishment didn't make much sense. I suppose the surprise was because *this stuff did not happen to me.*

I didn't even want to think about the last time I'd been kissed. Okay, I'd only been kissed one time in my entire life. The night of senior prom. And that had mostly happened because everyone got kissed on prom night and even though my date had been arranged by our mothers, he wanted a piece of the action that all the other kids were getting that night. It hadn't been great, but it had technically been a kiss. Or two. Two awkward kisses. In fact, even thinking the name of that poor boy still made me shudder. I had the feeling kissing Jonathan would be very different. Did I want to kiss him?

His low voice brought my thoughts back to him. "Are you afraid?"

Yes. Definitely. Still, I was a bit affronted about him saying it. "No," I stated.

"You sure?"

I thought maybe being kissed would be a nice thing. I was twenty-five years old, and while I was in no way falling for Jonathan, he was the only guy offering. Plus, I was trying so hard to say yes more often. Then again, if he'd asked me to jump off a cliff . . . Mother's voice in my head verbally berated me over even considering kissing a man I had no feelings for. So, obviously, that meant I was going for it. I mean, I'd kissed that poor kid in high school and nothing bad had come of it.

I couldn't make the words actually come out, so I just nodded. Jonathan's eyes gleamed and his other hand came to rest on my face before moving slowly around to the back of my neck. He tugged gently and I closed my eyes in preparation. My body remained stiff, but I tried to relax my lips as he pressed his softly to mine.

It took me several breaths to decide if I was okay with him kissing me. When I decided I was, it took a couple more breaths to kiss him back. I haltingly opened up my senses, taking in the feel of his arms around me, the prickle of his beard growth coming in, the way his lips were softer than I'd have expected, and his obvious skill at kissing. This was nothing like Stuart, boy of prom fame. And I waited.

This was my moment. The worries of my first real kiss were behind me. I was choosing to engage in this kiss. It was butterfly and tingly feet time. And I waited.

Then the worry hit. Where were those darn butterflies? Why were the only tingles I was feeling the ones coming from my rib cage as I started to realize I couldn't breathe? I was supposed to be transported, but I knew exactly where I was. In fact, I'd bet money that a girl on the veranda directly above me was wearing stiletto heels because of the sound it was making as she walked back and forth.

I knew it couldn't be normal to think about someone else's stiletto heels while I was given what I could only assume was a great kiss. But, sadly, there it was.

I pulled away as gently as I could and pasted a smile of contrition on my face, my lifelong habits instructing me to make sure I hadn't caused any offense. I opened my mouth to apologize when it hit me that I had nothing to feel sorry for. It didn't matter if he was going to be offended or not. I was done kissing him.

The feeling of liberation that came from that thought stole my breath in a way his kiss had not. I was free to act for myself and not apologize for it. A wave of dizziness hit, causing me to blink a few times and reach above me to brace myself on the floor beams.

His face went quickly from surprise at me pulling away back to his typical confidence when he saw what appeared to be my reaction to his kiss. "Sorry," he said with a knowing look. "You're just so beautiful that I forgot myself."

As I came back to the present, I felt my head cock to the side like Ana's so often did, and I met his gaze. Huh. So that's what it felt like to have a line delivered. He was the first guy to ever try that kind of thing on me, and I found it kind of funny. Did girls go for that?

"I need to get back to Ana," I stated as I turned and walked out from under the veranda.

"Can I see you again sometime?" he asked when we entered the crowded building.

I stopped walking and turned to face him. He really was incredibly handsome and quite charming, and he'd been kind to me. Which made turning him down even harder. "I don't think that's a good idea."

Thankfully he took it stoically and offered me a small nod and smile before going back to wherever he'd come from. Ana looked me once over as I approached the table and sat down.

"So?" she asked.

"So, he took me under the veranda," I replied.

"Ah, the make-out zone. Did he kiss you?" I nodded. "Are you okay?" Her face was full of concern, and I hurried to put her at ease.

"I'm totally fine. Well, sort of. I'm new to all of this, but there were no butterflies and I kept thinking about the stiletto heels on the veranda floor above me, so I broke off the kiss and came back inside."

"So, not a love match." Ana's face lightened.

"No."

"Was he angry?"

"I don't think so. But, the strangest thing happened. I was getting ready to apologize for ending it, when I suddenly realized I had nothing to say sorry for. He can be angry if he wants to be angry." I said the last part in a whisper as my mind reeled once more.

Ana laughed out loud and patted my arm. "Therapy session complete, thanks to an unexpected assist from Jonathan."

I snapped out of my musings and grinned. "Having me kiss a near stranger and then turn him down with no regard for his feelings was the goal for this session?"

"Of course not. We aren't terrible humans, mostly. This lesson is a biggie, and it happened a little differently than I would have planned, is all. The thing is, it's okay to care about what you want, or don't want, and to stop apologizing for that."

I nodded and gazed at the dance floor. "Besides," I said, casually taking a sip of my drink, "it's obvious he only loves me for my hair, which would bring nothing but problems."

For the second time that night Ana laughed out loud, but this time I joined her.

CHAPTER 11

THE FORTIETH BIRTHDAY PARTY WAS IN FULL SWING, SPILLING OUT from the ballroom, through the conservatory, and down into the garden. People were everywhere, and the sound of their laughter and the tinkling sounds of endless toasts permeated the air. There was a sense of celebratory abandon that I'd seen often from the outside but had never fully understood.

Women were dressed in deceptively casual-looking sundresses and hats that I knew cost a small fortune. Their teeth were glaringly white and their spray tans perfect. The men looked equally polished in button-up shirts of varying prints and pressed shorts. It was clear that the birthday boy was doing quite well for himself, which made me wonder why on earth he'd wanted a clown. There weren't even children in attendance. Odd.

Then again, maybe he was like me and he'd finally broken free of a strict upbringing and wanted to celebrate with the clown he'd always been denied as a child. Or, his buddies tried to order the clown without him knowing. I'd heard guys did things like that.

Eliza had asked me to station myself in the garden, while Ana would be in the conservatory and she, herself, would be in the ballroom. I had happily agreed, always enjoying the atmosphere of the garden. A gigantic white canopy had been set up near the fountain with groupings of chairs here and there. All were filled with women and their carefree chatter.

I moved about the periphery, watching for anyone who may need my help. So far that had entailed one broken sandal strap, two cases of drippy mascara (this humidity), and a yappy purse pooch trying to steal the food off another woman's plate.

As I strolled around, I caught snippets of conversations. Most of them revolved around relationships. Husbands, boyfriends, children, in-laws, parents, siblings—the people who made up their world. It seemed to be a universal topic, from what I'd observed. And I'd observed a lot.

It had been a while since the old envious feelings had cropped up behind my passive expression. I'd become adept at not thinking about how hollow my life was. However, today felt different. Here these women were, some professional, some homemakers, sharing the things that made them the same. They laughed and doled out tips, suggestions, and support, the whole while having no idea how lucky they were.

After an hour or so I decided maybe it would be nice to trade places with Ana. The conservatory was more of a pass-through room as people moved between the ballroom and the garden. I was feeling melancholy after comparing my lonely existence to the rich and full lives of the garden ladies.

Ana agreed, and I spent the remaining hours of the party tucked away among the ferns. It didn't have the effect I was going for, however. I watched the guests through windows, making up stories about their lives that had no basis in fact. No one's life was perfect, and I knew that. It didn't matter. In short, I was feeling ugly and resentful inside by the time the guests left. Those were emotions I'd made little room for in my life, and now they were baring their teeth and begging to be embraced.

My stoic demeanor during cleanup didn't invite conversation, and I was grateful to Eliza and the others for not pressing. The work was a good distraction, and I used it to my advantage. When the cleanup was done I grabbed a plate of leftovers as my dinner and went straight to my room.

Unfortunately, being alone in my room didn't do the trick. By the time the sun began to set I was going stir crazy on top of my feelings of injustice and disappointment. I had slipped into full-on wallow mode and needed to break free.

The waves called to me from my open window. I answered by slipping into shorts and a tank top. I was grateful that I met no one on my way out of the house, nor did I see anyone on my way to the beach. The sand stretched farther than I could see, and it was empty. I was blissfully alone.

I kicked off my shoes and left them next to the stairs before I waded through the sea grass and onto the open sand. The soft breeze greeted me and cooled off my overheated skin. I stood still, facing the ocean, and closed my eyes as I took a slow, deep breath, filling my lungs until they felt like they would burst. I released the breath slowly and repeated the process a few times. I loved the feeling of the humid air flowing over my closed eyelids and making stray hairs tickle my ears. My chignon suddenly felt restrictive, so I reached back and took out the pins, shaking it free.

It didn't take long to feel the hurt start to flow out of me. I'd read once that taking deep breaths turned off the primitive part of the brain and got the logical brain thinking again. While I liked to think I was more evolved than that, today had proven otherwise.

I opened my eyes and walked in the opposite direction of the city. Ana had said there were more private residences farther down this same stretch of beach, along with a few jetties sticking out into the ocean, but all I cared about was that it was the quiet side of the island. I got close enough to the water's edge to have the waves cross over my feet as they glided back and forth across the sand.

The sky gradually grew darker until I noticed lights starting to blink on in the houses. It wasn't full dark, but twilight. The sky was losing its blue color and fading to match the gray of the murky horizon. I kept walking. I wasn't making good time, and that was fine. I occasionally paused to spread my toes and let water run between them. I dug my toes into the sand and wiggled them, all the while keeping my mind empty. There was something about water that was so serene and healing. I'd never realized it before, and I knew that I would miss this when I returned to my city life.

I had leisurely walked perhaps a mile and was getting ready to turn around when I heard the sounds of a boat pulling up next to a rocky jetty slightly ahead of me. The jetties were few and far between, so this was the first time I'd actually seen someone using one of them. Curious, I paused to watch. It was too dark to see details, but to my untrained eye the boat looked slick and neat, unlike other boats I'd seen on occasion in the area. Whoever they were, they had money. The driver expertly slid the boat into position next to the rock formation as the bright light on the front of the boat lit up the beach nearby. A man's shape jumped agilely from boat to rock and then caught what looked to be fishing gear that was tossed his way.

I continued to watch as the man waved to the boat and made his way up the jetty to the beach. Something about the way he moved was so unashamedly masculine that it made my mouth curve into a small, toothless smile. As an observer I'd seen many men walking about, proclaiming who they were by the way they moved. I'd often wondered how much of it was show. With this man, who had no idea he was being watched, I knew it wasn't show.

I startled as he turned my direction, his long strides eating up the ground between us. I doubted he'd noticed me yet, but I didn't want to be caught staring. Nor did I want to have an awkward encounter on the beach with a stranger in the dark. I glanced around, seeking cover. There weren't many options on the wide open sand, but I thought if I headed toward the houses that maybe he'd think I was one of the residents heading home and not give me a second look. Unless I happened to choose his house. Oh, good grief. There was nothing for it but to make a choice and hope for the best.

I spun on my heel and began walking toward the closest home behind me. I kept my head down and let my hair cover the sides of my face. The plan was solid, until I felt a sharp slicing pain across the bottom of my bare foot. I let out an involuntary exclamation and reached down to check the damage. I couldn't see well, but my hand met something warm and oozing. Blood.

I sat directly down on the sand and pulled my foot toward me to try and examine the wound, but it was too dark. I shifted around until my foot was lit slightly by the moonlight shining, and squinted my eyes, hoping that would help.

"Ma'am, are you okay?" a male voice behind me asked.

Shoot, shoot, double shoot. The man. I kept my head down. "I must have stepped on something, but it's fine. I'm almost home," I lied.

A flashlight suddenly shone on my foot, revealing a neat slice that was about two inches long. It didn't look terribly deep, but it stung like the dickens and was bleeding more than I'd have liked to see. A broken bottle shimmered in the same light near where I was sitting. Ah, so that was the culprit. Stinking litterers.

The flashlight moved to my head. "Grace?"

My eyes shot up to meet the rarely readable eyes of Lucas Halstead. I wondered how many women—heck, people—had spent their time trying to decipher what went on in his steel-trap mind. I didn't envy those who met him in a boardroom.

I didn't respond verbally, just nodded and blushed. Fantastic.

"You're *not* almost home," he stated.

I swallowed hard and scrambled to think of something while looking innocent. *Think sheep, think sheep*, I chanted before saying, "Oh, I meant almost to *a* home. I was going to visit a friend in this house here." I pointed to the house I'd been heading for. Let him think I was a social butterfly making friends all over the island.

He raised his eyebrows. "That dark house that's closed down while the owners spend the warmer months up north?"

Nervous, totally humiliated laughter tickled in my chest. Still, I played it cool. "I think they leave next week." I nodded as though what he'd said didn't throw me a bit.

He blinked, slowly and suspiciously, before shaking his head. That motion called me out on my lie without actually saying anything, and we both knew it.

I sighed and owned up. "The truth is I didn't know it was you and I was just trying to avoid running into a strange man on the beach at night."

His flashlight beam moved back to my foot. "It doesn't look too bad. Hard to tell for sure, though, in the dark."

"I think it's fine. I'll just finish what I was doing here and head back soon." I tried to smile up at him, but my lips seemed to have frozen in place, and a drop of blood landed on my thigh where my foot was resting on it. His eyes followed the trail of blood before looking back to me.

"On second thought, there's a chance you'll need stitches. You'll have to break into that empty neighbor's home another night." His eyes sparked, but in the falling darkness I couldn't read if he was teasing me or being an A-class jerk.

I felt completely mortified, and him calling my bluff was the worst. I'd never, ever found myself in this type of situation. I was known in my world as intelligent and level-headed. I had no idea how to respond, so I said nothing, just sat there holding my foot and looking anywhere but at him.

He puffed out a breath that seemed full of words he wasn't saying. "I have some first aid supplies in my tackle box."

He set down the box he'd been carrying and clicked the lid open. His flashlight moved from my foot to the inside of the ridiculously tidy box. I wished it would've been a mess—you know, even the playing field somehow, but no dice. It was as flawless as could be.

He pulled out a length of unopened gauze wrap and tore the packaging before handing it to me. I wrapped it a few times around my foot and tied the end as best as I could, while he watched wordlessly.

"That'll do, Donkey," I said, quoting a movie I hadn't even seen in an uncomfortable attempt at humor. I knew it would fail the minute the words left my mouth. I had never been a joker, and he certainly wouldn't be the person for me to try it out on.

His eyes flicked briefly to mine and then back to the box as he clicked it closed. "Can you walk on it?" He stood and picked up his box.

I rolled my ankle a bit to make sure the gauze was going to hold before squirming around to use my good foot to stand. I was pleased with how easily I stood up, but when I put some weight on my injured foot to start walking it cried out in protest, causing me to stumble. Lucas's hand caught my elbow, righting me as I got my balance back. He released my arm almost as quickly as he'd taken it.

"Thanks," I mumbled. He said nothing.

I played around with a few different ways of holding my foot to keep weight off the cut and finally settled on walking on the side of my foot. It worked if I moved slowly and cautiously. It wasn't going to be the best mile of my life, that was for sure.

I took a few steps to get into the groove, and when I felt confident, I looked to where Lucas was walking silently next to me. He'd turned off his flashlight, and we were guided along by the moon. I took a few breaths, trying to regain that sense of peace I'd had earlier. This didn't have to be awkward. We'd gone shopping together that one time, and it seemed like we should be able to act sort of normal-ish around each other at this point. Another breath—engaging the logical brain. This was totally fine. All I had to do was shake off my own issues and just talk to him. I'd need another breath . . .

He looked over. "You're breathing pretty hard. Does it hurt too much to walk on?"

I shook my head but then realized he probably couldn't see the motion. "No. I'll be okay. Just need to walk slow." It was going to be the longest mile of my life if he kept walking with me and my cave man brain. "You know, it's okay if you want to go on ahead."

He made a low sound "Eliza would kill me."

"She doesn't have to know," I replied.

"I would know."

Okay, so the flair of integrity was interesting. A gentleman existed inside there. I wasn't about to come right out and tell him that his presence made me squirm, so I continued hobbling along at a snail's pace. The longer we walked, the more I stopped caring about the silence. I didn't have the energy or interest to decipher his thoughts. *In fact, maybe he should be the one worrying about what I'm thinking,* I told myself. The thought cheered me up.

I stumbled over a camouflaged piece of drift wood and stubbed the toe of my injured foot. Once again, before I could eat sand, Lucas caught me. This time his hand wrapped around my upper arm. His hold was strong but not painful as he waited for me to balance. I couldn't help but notice the contrast between his warm hand and my chilled skin. My foot was really aching, and I took a few moments to wiggle it around before stepping on it again. Pain, annoying pain. I locked my jaw and forced myself to move again. I was descended from strong people, I had a backbone of iron, I would not be defeated. Blah, blah, blah, this hurt.

Lucas must have noticed my adjusted gait because he slid his hand down to my elbow and helped keep me steady as we moved forward again. Goose flesh broke out on my arm, chilling me further. I didn't especially want to be in constant contact with him, even though I kind of wanted to be wrapped up in the warmth coming off of him. I casually pulled my arm out of his hold, and he was quick to oblige.

The quiet between us continued until I stumbled a third time. This time Lucas wasn't fast enough, and I landed on my hands and knees. Stupid sand with its hills and valleys. I remained in that position, head down, hair touching the sand as I took a few deep breaths. I had no idea what had tripped me, but I was ticked about it. Ticked. I wanted to get back to my bedroom and crawl into the soft covers and pretend this entire day away.

His hand lightly touched my shoulder, asking a question without words. I nodded and pushed up into a kneeling position. Mother's voice came out of nowhere, berating me for my foolish nighttime walk, telling me it was no wonder I was alone in this life. No one would want someone who made such a fool of herself. I shivered in reaction.

"Can you stand?" Lucas interrupted Mother's lecture.

I looked up at him and nodded again, although I didn't really believe it. He must have had night vision and seen the look on my face, because he reached a hand down to me this time. I really didn't want to take it, but I really needed to. So, I did.

My hand slid into his grip and he hauled me to my feet. I reached out my free hand to steady myself and came into contact with his shoulder. The shock of it made me forget the ache in my foot for a split second. I could smell the ocean on his skin from this close, and it caused a shiver to run up my spine.

"Come on," he said somewhat gruffly.

I dropped my hand from his shoulder and let go of his other hand before I turned to walk again. Relief flooded me at the sight of the mansion around a small bend. I was sweating with the effort of walking somewhat normally on a foot that was throbbing. I wondered if I would need stitches after all.

When we got to the stairs, I retrieved my shoes and Lucas gestured for me to go up first. I did so, leaning heavily on the railing as I climbed. When I reached the top, I turned to see why I hadn't heard Lucas behind me. He was shining his flashlight on the wooden stairs. Everywhere my injured foot had stepped was a dark patch. I lifted my foot to look at it, and sure enough, I was bleeding through the gauze. I looked back to Lucas as he climbed the stairs.

"Why didn't you tell me it was still bleeding that much?" he asked as he took them two at a time.

"I didn't know," I said, because saying I was too emotionally shuttered to tell someone I was hurt didn't seem like the right reply.

Something about that answer bothered him greatly, although I had no idea what, and he scowled. His scowl was the last straw. I had gone to the beach to be alone, not to follow him around, cut my foot, and ruin his evening. How had my injury become his annoyance? Not cool.

I glared at him, wishing I could give him what for. I'd perfected the art of telling people off in my mind, angry words I knew I'd never say but that felt good nonetheless. Then it hit me. Just like I'd stuck up for myself with Jonathan, I could stick up for myself with Lucas. An exhilarating sense of freedom, even greater than the one I'd experienced under the veranda with Jonathan, washed over me as our gazes locked. How many times had I gone over something in my mind and wished I'd said this or that, picturing the event happening a different way?

I took a deep breath. "Of course, it's bleeding. I just walked a mile on it. You didn't offer to come back and get, I don't know, a golf cart or something to give me a ride. You weren't offering up your personal services as a pack mule. What did you want me to do?" I threw him one last look and turned for the mansion.

I was shaking so hard I could hardly walk, even if my foot hadn't been injured. I'd just done it. Take that, world. I'd said what I was thinking, and while it was liberating, I was definitely about to vomit. Maybe that pack mule comment had been a bit much. I felt dizzy, elated, and so upset with myself for my rudeness, while also patting myself on the back. It was just so much sensation.

"You've got to be kidding me," I heard him mumble an instant before his tackle box clattered to the ground and he swooped me up into his arms.

The unexpected momentum caused my arms to flail around looking for purchase. They found it around his neck. My surprised eyes met his angry ones before skirting away in discomfort.

"What are you doing?" I asked in a high-pitched voice.

"I'm offering my services as a pack mule," he stated, in my opinion, sarcastically. I could feel the vibration of his low voice where my side pressed to his chest. It tingled.

The fact that it tingled brought me up short. I didn't want tingles with this man. I wanted nothing to do with tingles. Yet here I was, noticing the smell of his laundry detergent, the way his dark hair and beard were swallowed up in the moonlight, the fluid way he walked that kept me from bouncing around in his arms.

Clumsy warmth began to gather in my limbs and work its way up to my face. While romantic comedy movies everywhere told me I should be rejoicing over this moment, it was the single most awkward thing ever, and I had caused it by speaking my mind. It had been a gamble and I had lost. I was never doing it again. At least with Lucas.

"I'm sorry. You can put me down," I whispered, humbled. Yeah, the pack mule comment had crossed the line.

Lucas's rigid posture relaxed as he shook his head. "You've probably done some damage by walking as far as you did. Let's just get you back to the house and Ana can take a look at it."

"I shouldn't have yelled at you."

His mouth twitched a bit, but he kept looking straight forward. "Maybe."

In all fairness, when he relaxed there was a tiny second where being held close to a man wasn't quite as terrible as I'd initially thought.

It didn't take Lucas long to stride across the yard to the small basement door that the staff used for coming and going. It made sense that he'd go to that door. There were no stairs to climb here, and Ana's room was on this floor.

When we reached the door, Lucas set me on my feet but instructed me to not put weight on my injured foot. I balanced myself on the door frame while Lucas unlocked the door and let us in. This time he didn't pick me up, but he put an arm around my waist and supported me while I hopped down the hall with my own arm around him.

"Do you know what time is it?" I asked when we reached Ana's door. "I hope she's not asleep."

"It's late," was his reply. Helpful.

We released our holds on each other, and he decisively knocked on Ana's door. I used the door jamb for support as I balanced on one foot. We waited in silence for her to answer. It took a moment, and when the door did finally open she blinked and raised her hand up to block the light.

"What's going on?" she asked after it became obvious the Silent Twins weren't going to say anything.

"Grace hurt her foot," Lucas finally replied formally. Gone were the flashing eyes and annoyed tone he'd used with me. He sounded almost disinterested.

Ana opened her door wider and reached for the light switch. After spending so much time in the moonlight, the light felt jarring. I glanced to Lucas as he turned to leave. His face had slid back into that self-contained mask he typically wore.

"Thanks," I said through numb lips, even though his expression didn't invite my gratitude. He nodded and turned to go back out the way we'd come. He'd left his perfect tackle box near the stairs and probably went to retrieve it.

"Tell me everything," Ana said as she ushered me into her room. "Don't leave out one single detail."

I took her outstretched hand and hobbled toward her bed. "Not much to tell."

"Oh, please. John Lucas Halstead delivers you to my room late at night with an injured foot and you want me to believe there isn't a story there?" Ana pursed her lips and cocked her head. "Uh-uh, no way. Spill it."

I couldn't help the laugh that sprang out. Oh, it was good to be back with Ana. "I'm afraid you'll be terribly disappointed at the truth."

"I doubt it."

So, while Ana doctored my foot, I told her about my rough day, my walk on the beach, my running away from the strange man, and our uneasy journey back to the mansion. She was silent for the entire story. When I was done, she patted my newly bandaged foot and grinned.

"You like to act all stiff and proper, but I knew under the mask was someone ready to shake things up." She stood and opened her door. "Let's get you on up to bed. You should probably go to the clinic when it opens in the morning to see if you need stitches. I can drive you once the staff has their assignments."

"Your driving might make it worse," I teased, rising to stand on my good foot.

She wrapped an arm around my waist as we made our way to the elevator. "I can't wait to see what will happen next."

"What do you mean?"

"I mean around here. With you. With Lucas."

My jaw dropped as a wave of worry washed over me. "Nothing, Ana. Nothing will happen next. I lied to him, I said rude things to him, and he dropped his perfect tackle box because of me. If he didn't hate me before, he does now."

"It's called teasing," Ana soothed.

"I don't think I'm the type who does good with teasing," I said as we entered the elevator.

"Sure you do. I've done nothing but tease and push you since the moment we met. You're stronger than you think."

The comment warmed me as the elevator doors opened to the large foyer on the top floor. Ana put her arm around my waist again, and I around her shoulders, as I hopped down the hallway to my room. Ana said nothing until she'd helped me change into pajamas and pull up the covers. It was such a comforting gesture.

Instead of leaving, she sat on the edge of my bed. Her face was serious and kind. "Look, I know you're upset about what happened tonight, so I apologize for messing with you about it. You going to be okay?"

I pushed up to a sitting position against my headboard. A cheerless smile tugged at my lips as I met her gaze. Ana, my first true friend. I was caught off guard by the emotion that welled up at the thought.

"I acted so out of character tonight, and I feel sick about it. I don't find myself in these types of scrapes and it makes me feel . . . like I'm spinning out of control."

Ana nodded. "Well, I wasn't there, but I'd say you were due for a spin. Thanks to my efforts you had one."

I laughed, which was her intention. "Your efforts?"

"Obviously. Would you have ever dared to stand up to Lucas Halstead if you hadn't had practice standing up to me? You're turning into a real nice lady."

"How does speaking my mind make me a real nice lady?" I asked.

"I'm not sure, but that's not the point."

I laughed while she pulled a face. "Honestly, Ana, I don't have the faintest idea what goes on in his head."

"Who does? Still, when it really mattered, he was a gentleman."

"Does it still count as gentlemanly behavior when it was done grumpily?"

"All the best heroes are broody." She nodded.

I rolled my eyes. "I'm not sure I totally agree, but I will agree that he didn't leave me stranded."

"Lucas just protects himself the same way you do." Ana stood and yawned. "Now it really is the middle of the night. I'll see you tomorrow. Sleep well."

"Thanks, Ana, for everything," I called as she crossed my room.

"All in a day's work for the Great Island Therapist." The door closed on the sound of my laughter.

CHAPTER 12

Sitting in the conservatory several days later, my injured foot resting comfortably on an ottoman and my laptop on my lap, I allowed myself a moment to ponder over that fact that even after five weeks, give or take a bit, of living at Halstead House, it all still felt magical. I felt safe here in a way I'd only dreamed of.

"You're looking rather pleased with yourself," Eliza remarked cheerfully as she came into the room carrying what looked like an overnight bag.

"Being here is a dream come true," I replied.

"For us as well, dear. How is your foot?"

"It's feeling much better. Ana did a wonderful job bandaging it, and her healing ointment has to be worth millions. The doctor was pretty impressed."

It was true. My foot was healing much faster than I'd imagined possible. I hadn't ended up needing stitches, but skin glue and surgical tape had been used to pull the skin back together. I'd been instructed to stay off of it for the first few days and was looking forward to being able to start walking a little tomorrow. Another day or two after that and I should be getting back into my groove.

"I'm so happy to hear that. Ana is definitely an asset to us." Eliza nodded. "What are you working on this morning?"

"I'm finalizing the plan for Lucas's business luncheon next week. I hope it's okay with you if I work in here. I love this room."

The conservatory was one of my favorite rooms in the mansion. Being surrounded by the lush plants and glass walls made me feel as though I'd entered another world. The smells were earthy and warm, and I'd cracked two windows to allow a through-breeze. It was heaven.

"Of course, that's just fine. I'm off to . . ." Eliza began, but was interrupted by Lucas as he marched into the room.

"I just ran into Derek in the foyer," he stated, referring to a member of the day staff.

"I'd imagine that happens on occasion," Eliza replied with a serene face.

A muscle in Lucas's cheek twitched and he took a deep breath. "Yes, but it's not often he's hauling your luggage along behind him. Where are you going?"

I had been fascinated at the sight of Lucas losing his cool exterior, but that immediately shifted as the words he'd said penetrated.

"Wait. You're going somewhere?" I squeaked out to Eliza.

Derek entered the room just then with luggage under each skinny arm. He couldn't have been more than eighteen and looked funny juggling the large bags. "I'm ready whenever you are," he said to Eliza, unaware of the tension in the air.

"Excellent. Let's go." She spun around and exited the conservatory doors without saying another word.

Lucas was hot on her heals, with Derek following directly behind him. There was nothing for it but for me to join in the procession while doing my best to figure out what was happening. Based on Lucas's face, and the rigidity of his movements, this was not a happy, celebratory parade but a parade of horrors. I grabbed my crutches and tried to keep up.

"What's going on?" Lucas asked Eliza as I navigated the stairs down to the gardens.

"I always spend a few weeks in Maine each summer and . . ." Eliza began.

Lucas jumped in. "It's not summer yet. It's the first week of May."

"True. *However* . . ." She drew out the word when she saw his mouth begin to open again. He slapped it shut. "Some things have come up and I'm going now. I'll be back before you know it."

Lucas tried to shift in front of her, but she skillfully dodged him while continuing to walk purposefully ahead. "What about our upcoming events?"

Eek, the events! I had been more concerned with her leaving—and what that meant for me emotionally—than about the events. I would now be solely in charge of those in her absence. She just said *weeks*, right? As in plural? Lucas was right. What was she thinking?

We had reached the garage, although I was a few paces behind and my armpits were getting the workout of their life trying to keep the crutches from falling. Lucas paused to hold the door for Derek and Eliza before turning to wait for me as well. I hustled to enter, not wanting to redirect his frustration toward myself.

"I have total confidence in Grace," Eliza said as Lucas and I entered the garage. "She knows everything you need for the luncheon next week. The next big event we have isn't until the end of the month. I'll be back by then."

"But . . ." Lucas tried again.

"Not to mention this glorious technology we have that will make it possible to keep in touch. I'm not needed here right now."

I begged to differ. Truly, I did.

"Which car did you want to take today, ma'am?" Derek squeaked politely.

"My sedan will be fine, thank you." Eliza gestured to a sleek, shiny black car parked next to Lucas's.

"Oh, no, no, no." Lucas strode up and planted himself in front of the trunk before poor Derek could heave a bag in.

Eliza's face opened into a delighted smile, and she leaned up to kiss Lucas on the cheek. "How wonderful, darling. I'd love for you to drive me."

While Lucas blinked at her sugary sweet manipulation, Eliza turned to Derek and told him to put the bags in Lucas's car. He did so, and then with a polite nod to all of us he returned to the mansion and his other duties. I wished I could do the same, but my duties were being directly affected by what was happening here.

What exactly *was* happening here? All I knew was that no more than five minutes ago I'd been happily basking in ferns and sunlight. Now, things were crumbling and I couldn't seem to gather my thoughts. Eliza had said she'd be back by the end of the month. That was a long time. A really long time. Weeks. The word made me shudder.

"Do you need anything from me before I leave?" Eliza turned to me, pulling me out of my inner thoughts.

I almost laughed at the absurdity of her question. "I'm still trying to process you leaving. I don't even know what questions to ask."

She walked to me and put a hand on my arm. "You'll do wonderfully. If I didn't trust you, I wouldn't be leaving."

"Eliza, I don't have much time left here," I said before I realized I'd been thinking it. The truth of the sentiment hit me as her face softened. "Do you have to go now? Can't you postpone leaving?"

"I'll miss you too, dear."

"This is madness," Lucas inserted as he came to stand next to us. He looked at me and gestured toward his aunt. "Can you try to talk some sense into her?"

I glanced at Lucas and then back to Eliza. They both wanted what they wanted, and I was powerless to change either of their minds, nor did I want to. The entire reason I was standing there was that I'd dared to make a choice for myself regardless of what anyone else wanted me to do.

"It's her choice," I mumbled.

Lucas glared and Eliza leveled a look at him. "Don't you be unkind to Grace."

He took a breath and closed his eyes briefly. "I'm sorry," he said to me. It was enough. I understood why he felt snappish.

Her attention turned back to me. "Be brave, dear. You've done many events, and you'll make us proud."

"I'll try," I replied.

I leaned in for a quick hug and then spun around on my good foot and left the garage. I couldn't bear to watch her drive away. It didn't make sense, but I felt like she was abandoning me. I'd meant what I'd said: I only had so much time on Lavender Island. Why would she choose to miss some of that time together?

I leisurely hobbled back to the house. It wasn't that I truly felt like I'd fail at running Lucas's luncheon or handling some of the smaller details that came up day to day. I was well trained and experienced in such matters. It was that I had grown to truly enjoy the camaraderie of working as part of a team for the first time in my life, and I felt a little lost knowing half of our partnership would be gone.

I eventually made my way up the outside stairs from the garden and into the conservatory. My laptop was still on, sitting on the couch where I'd dropped it in my haste to figure out what was happening. It hadn't even had time to go into power saving mode. My head was reeling as I sat back down and propped my foot up. I wasn't wearing shoes. I'd been so incredibly surprised that I'd chucked my laptop and gone barefoot out to the garage. I almost smiled over it.

I picked my laptop back up and opened the folder with notes on Lucas's luncheon. One week was plenty of time to manage the last details, but I didn't want to take any chances on not knowing every last detail.

* * *

My insides wanted to jump out of my throat as I entered the large dining room one week later to prepare for Lucas's luncheon. The head count wasn't high enough to require the use of the larger ballroom next door, so the more intimate feel of the smaller room was ideal. I arrived just in time to step aside while Marshall rolled one of the five round tables in from the back of the house.

"Morning, Grace," he greeted with a smile. "Didn't see you at breakfast today. You doing okay?"

I returned his smile. "Busy morning," I lied. My body wasn't accepting food at this time. "Did you hire a crew? Or can I help?"

"Nah, I didn't need a crew for a small job like this. Your help would be nice."

I helped him unfold the legs of the table he'd been rolling and lift it to standing. We slid it around into position, and I followed Marshall back past the kitchen into a large storage area.

We worked quietly, Marshall occasionally saying something about the weather, or projects he'd been working on around the house. I appreciated his light chatter and the fact that he didn't need me to join in.

When we finished adding in the other tables and the thirty chairs, I went to find Ana and see if the tablecloths were ready. She wasn't in the housekeeping room, but the small stack of cream tablecloths was sitting on the laundry counter near an ironing board. I turned on the iron, needing something else to keep me busy. I was certainly capable of ironing five tablecloths.

I'd finished two by the time Ana found me. I didn't hear her come in, but I did hear the overly loud "Ahem!" when she said it. I turned to find her, lips pinched and her hands on her hips.

"Just what do you think you're doing?" she asked.

"Eliza left town." I frowned.

"I heard. It's been a week and news travels. Is ironing tablecloths how you deal with life's disappointments?"

I chuckled despite my melancholy. "No. I already helped Marshall set up tables and chairs for today, so I thought I'd get going on the rest."

"Well, then I'll just pull up a chair, tell the others to take a break, and get me a cold glass of lemonade. There's sheets to wash too." Ana's lips twitched. "Honestly, scoot over and let me finish up." Her hands fell from her hips as she walked toward me, waving one hand to shoo me away from the ironing board. "There's an art to this."

"Okay, okay." I snatched up the two I'd already ironed and took them to the dining room to drape over the tables.

Lucas was standing in the middle of the room surveying tables when I entered. His head rose when he heard me, but the eye contact was very brief before he walked to one of the tables, slid it over a few inches, and made a non-committal noise that I wasn't sure how to interpret.

I walked to the table farthest from him and spread out the first tablecloth. I repeated the procedure on the next table. By the time I'd smoothed it out, he had moved the other three tables back and forth a few times. Chairs were scattered around him as he glanced around the room.

"Is there something wrong with the room setup?" I asked.

He walked to a table he'd already moved twice and shifted it again, rather than answer. Then he walked between all the tables, zig-zagging back and forth. "Did Eliza come up with this seating arrangement before she left?"

My heart rate picked up at his expression. "No, this arrangement was my idea."

"Well, that explains it." He pushed another table over an inch with his toe. "The flow is totally different than I'm used to. The tables are laid out all wrong," he mumbled.

Different didn't have to be wrong, but my throat felt tight at the thought of bombing my first solo event. "Eliza never said there was a particular layout."

"She knows my preferences," he responded, toeing a chair out of his way as he once again moved around the room.

"Unfortunately, she didn't share those preferences with me," I said, keeping my tone apologetic.

"Perhaps you should have thought to ask." He glanced my way.

The look he gave me wasn't unkind, but it made me feel about two inches tall, which was something I hadn't felt for a while now. I didn't like it. Not one bit. It no longer fit, as though it was a pair of shoes I'd outgrown. I'd made myself two promises recently. One was to stand up for myself more, and the other was to not push back at Lucas again. I was in a no-win situation here.

After some thought I said, "I have a lot of experience with this type of thing, and Eliza left it in my care, with her trust."

Lucas's expression didn't change. "Then surely you understand that part of the process is finding out what the customer would prefer."

Our eyes locked and I felt that familiar feeling in my brain that choked off arguments and demanded obedience. I opened my mouth, ready to ask him what his chosen setup would be, but after a strong inner struggle I instead turned and walked back to the house-keeping room. That's right, in the choice between fight and flight, I flew. Inner wolf, schminner wolf.

Ana was no longer there—she really was having a busy day—but the last three tablecloths were ironed and waiting for me. I paused next to the stack and hung my head, sucking in deep gulps of air and trying to loosen my tongue again. I had to face him, and I had to do so professionally. I couldn't for the life of me figure out why, after so many years of dealing with difficult and demanding people, he should be the one to get under my skin and make me want to argue back. He was not the right person to try out New Grace on.

When I reentered the dining room, Lucas was standing exactly where I'd left him, and he watched me with a remarkably stiff countenance as I walked toward the tables.

"Do you always walk away during a discussion?" he asked.

I shook my head. "No, I don't." I headed for the nearest empty table to begin spreading out cloths once more, this time with shaky hands. "Would you have questioned it if it had been Eliza who had opted for a new setup?" I asked.

"If I'm the customer and I want it a different way, then yes."

"I see. So you have a complaint with the work I'm doing."

A lump was forming, rock hard and large, in my throat. Moisture rose behind my eyes as we stood staring at each other. I tried not to blink or show any sign that I was truly upset, yet something shifted in his gaze, softened. His shoulders relaxed and he took a breath while running a hand over his beard.

"We'll try it this once, but if I'm not satisfied with the new arrangement, I hope you'll be willing to accept that in the future," he stated in a quiet voice, then turned and walked from the room without a backwards glance.

I looked around at the haphazard placement of tables and scattered chairs. He'd shifted and pushed things around until there was no reason to where they were sitting. It was a perfect outward expression of how I felt inside. I wondered if the same was true for him. Perhaps we were both on edge over handling this event without Eliza.

The rest of the morning sped by with preparations, and before it seemed possible, Lucas's guests had begun arriving. I was stiffly attired in my dove gray super suit, hair in the tightest chignon I'd ever managed, makeup done with precision, and still feeling shaken over the conversation with Lucas earlier.

I pushed emotion away and smiled warmly as I welcomed guests and showed them to their seats, all the while wondering what made this luncheon so different from the hundreds of others I'd attended and arranged. I knew how to greet, seat, and feed people. But, still . . .

Lucas caught my eye as he worked his way around the room. He looked superb in his tailored suit. His grooming was, as always, impeccable. His expression was one of casual welcome. He had been smiling at his last guest when he glanced up in my direction. My breath hitched in my throat as his gaze met mine, his eyes still slightly crinkled at the edges.

We hadn't ended on a good note earlier in the day and hadn't spoken a word to each other since, even though he had come down to double check the details before returning to his room to get dressed. Still, I had a job to do. I offered a small nod and moved on.

The luncheon itself began with Lucas calling the meeting to order. He was an engaging and knowledgeable speaker as he addressed the crowd. It was obvious from my place standing in the back corner that he had the group riveted and absorbed by what he had to say about their various business interests. The Halsteads had always known how to build an empire, and Lucas was no exception to the rule. It was amazing to me to think that a family who had started off manufacturing tools for oil companies now had their hands in fishing and hotel chains. It was a diverse portfolio, and Lucas had been raised to manage it all.

He didn't once look my way while he spoke, and I was grateful. I was also thankful for the chance it gave me, for perhaps the first time, to truly study him without it being strange. It was totally acceptable for me to watch the speaker at a business lunch.

The more I watched him, the more I began to feel things I was afraid of. He was not the most handsome man I'd ever seen, but he was definitely on the list. Worse, he was attractive to me in a way others hadn't been. He was tall, athletic, well-spoken, and carried himself with confidence. I couldn't for the life of me understand why he so often treated me with such remoteness. I was certain Mary had told him about me. He'd known about my mother, after all. I would have been perfectly happy to strike up a friendship with him, but the feeling was not mutual.

Perhaps it was because that when I was around him I was someone different. When he pushed, I wanted to push back. When he was unkind, I didn't handle it in a docile way, but instead felt red hot anger bubbling under the surface. I didn't seem to be able to blow Lucas Halstead off like I had so many of life's other little hurts. I didn't understand it. He terrified me. It was strange and new, and it was bringing out a side of me that I had never explored.

A small smile tugged at my lips as I thought about telling Ana that Lucas was giving me free therapy without realizing it.

When I focused back in on Lucas, he had just wrapped up his speech and was returning to the front table where he would be seated. Our eyes caught again, and my smile dimmed as I saw a curious look on his face. At first I didn't understand it, but then I realized that the end of his speech was my signal to get the food service started. I had missed my cue in all the woolgathering I'd been doing. Shoot!

I walked as gracefully as I could to the side door and signaled to Chef Lou and his catering staff to begin. I had asked him to hire one server for each table in order to keep things flowing smoothly. The five uniformed people entered with the first course and began serving with a military precision. Lou only worked with the best.

As I observed each table one by one, my eyes were repeatedly drawn to Lucas. I was ridiculously fascinated by watching him in his element. The unfortunate thing was how many times he caught me looking. I hoped it seemed natural to him, a way for the host and planner to be in communication, but I knew the truth was that I couldn't stop watching . . . and I had no idea why.

This same dance went on for another hour and a half. Lucas's gaze tangling with mine, his nods letting me know what needed to happen, me watching him and feeling more and more confused by the prickles of some unidentifiable and uncomfortable emotion.

A lightning bolt of insight hit me between the eyes as dessert was being served. I found him interesting, and not in a textbook way. I was jealous of the people who had his undivided and charming attention. Dear heaven, I wanted that for myself. I'd chosen the worst possible candidate with which to experience my first infatuation. Why couldn't it have been Jonathan? He was willing and available, and I'd pushed him away. I closed my eyes for a moment against a wave of misery.

At last dessert was cleared, and Lucas began to cleverly and graciously usher his guests out the door. I had followed the stream of people into the great hall as I assisted with hosting duties, amusement making me smile as the last guests left. They had no idea they'd basically been kicked out. When the door closed with a click, I turned to share a relieved smile with Lucas, only to find that he and a woman attendee had moved into the formal parlor and were sharing a quiet conversation.

I stood for longer than I should have, watching the way she rested her hand on his arm and leaned in to talk to him. He wasn't pulling away, and I couldn't read his expression—heck, I couldn't have even if I'd been looking directly at him. When he responded to her with a smile I nudged myself away. I was better than this. Spying was beneath me.

My shoulders relaxed as I entered the now empty room, and I let my stinging, aching, clenched hands release and fall to my side as I returned to oversee take down in the dining room. It had been a smashing success, and confusing feelings aside, I had something to celebrate. Eliza would have been proud.

The catering staff were nearly done clearing dishware from tables. I shrugged out of my suit jacket and hung it over a side table before starting to fold up the tablecloths on empty tables. I worked alone for just a moment before I heard footsteps behind me.

"Grace?" It was Lucas. I turned to face him with a questioning look, hoping my polite mask was firmly in place. "I owe you an apology. Everything went well today. The setup worked just fine. Thank you."

Surprise kept me from answering immediately, but it didn't keep my face from warming with pleasure. "One more satisfied customer," I replied in a lightly teasing tone I hadn't known I was capable of using around him.

One side of his mouth tugged up as he shrugged out of his own suit jacket and placed it next to mine. He took off his tie, undid the top button, rolled up his sleeves, and began taking chairs down alongside me.

"What are you doing?" I asked.

"I think that's pretty obvious," he replied in a casual voice.

"I, um, please don't." I hugged the tablecloth I'd just finished folding close to my chest.

He straightened up, a relaxed expression on his face that I'd never seen, and passed his folded tablecloth to me. "Last time I checked, you weren't supposed to tell the boss what to do."

"Oh, looks like everyone's helping today," Ana called cheerfully, offering Lucas a nod as she entered the room and went for another empty table.

"Uh, no, he's . . ." I stammered.

"Yes, I am," Lucas replied, moving to the next table.

"Has he ever done this before?" I hustled to Ana's side and whispered.

"Nope," she whispered back, eyes dancing. I had no idea why her eyes were all sparkly, but I didn't like it one bit.

"Let's get the after party started," Marshall's voice boomed as he appeared from the kitchen. He pulled out a small portable speaker and placed it on one of the shelves before pulling out his phone and asking Ana, "What's your music mood this afternoon?"

"Ask Grace," Ana replied. "This is her show."

"I don't . . ." was all I managed.

Ana paused in folding a chair and came to stand near me. She reached out to take the tablecloths I was still crushing to my chest, then pushed me toward where Marshall was holding his phone.

"Tell him what kind of music you want to listen to," she instructed. "We call this an after . . . party . . ."

I looked to Marshall, who was grinning, and back to Ana, who was also smiling, then finally to Lucas, who still stood still, simply watching.

I cleared my throat. "Well, okay. Do you have any Aerosmith?"

"Aerosmith?" Ana's voice sounded a bit surprised.

I nodded, feeling terribly vulnerable and totally ridiculous as I kept my eyes fixed directly on Marshall. "Yes. The early years?"

Marshall grinned. "I sure do. I have to say, Grace, I never pegged you as an 'early years Aerosmith' kind of gal."

I relaxed into a smile. "I've always been told not to judge a book by its cover."

Marshall's shoulders shook with amusement, and he pushed some buttons on his phone. The sounds of Aerosmith filled the room while we cleaned and restored everything to its proper place. Marshall sang along to the songs while Ana teased him for his singing voice. Lucas, although more reserved than the others, was the most relaxed I'd ever seen him. I tried not to think too much about it, or how attractive it made him appear.

I excused myself abruptly when everything was done, and retrieved my jacket from under Lucas's things. I hustled out of the room and up the back staircase, not willing to wait on the elevator, until I was safe in my room. Only then did I allow myself to take a deep breath. Unsettling things were happening in my head regarding Lucas, and I didn't appreciate it. I wished there was someone to give me advice on how to control it, or at least words of comfort. I certainly wasn't going to mention it to Eliza or Ana, and Lucas himself could never find out. Never.

CHAPTER 13

I SUCCESSFULLY AVOIDED SEEING LUCAS FOR A FEW DAYS, DURING which I was able to re-shore my defenses and convince myself I had imagined any and all emotions radiating toward him. This was made easier by knowing that he in no way radiated anything toward me . . . and a little bit easier because I was a pro at talking myself out of emotion. Which is a sad state of affairs when I really think about it.

I spoke with Eliza a few times over the phone and fielded a few event-related phone calls. I spent most of my time working in my room, and I spent the evenings going on walks with Ana or reading in the garden. The pace had slowed down with Eliza gone, but I was okay with that. My life in Providence had been full speed ahead all the time. I'd choose slower and filled with new friends over fast and empty any day.

Lucas shattered my illusions of peace by appearing in the kitchen during breakfast on Friday morning with our tour guide, Steven, following closely behind. I nearly choked on the soft-boiled egg I'd been chewing.

"Good morning, everyone," he said.

The way everyone's eyes grew large as they swung his way proved that I wasn't the only one caught off guard by his appearance. In the nearly seven weeks I'd been in residence, this was the first time I'd seen him in this particular room.

"Good morning," Ana finally replied.

Her speaking seemed to jog everyone else's brains, and we all joined her in greeting him.

"I wanted to thank everyone for the excellent work you've all been doing, especially picking up the slack while Eliza has been away. I've organized a dolphin watching harbor tour for this evening at seven. There will be food and drinks provided. I hope you'll join me, and we'll have some fun." The room was quiet. I gathered that this had never happened before. To his credit, he held the smile in place through the silence before he pressed on. "I'm aware it's a Friday night, and this is sudden. If you had plans already, you're welcome to invite a guest if you'd like." His gaze moved around the room.

"Sounds fun. The wife and I love harbor cruises," Steven—bless him—said.

Chef Lou piped up, his accent thicker than ever. "I do not need plus one. Just me."

"Thank you," Ana said happily. "I'll be there."

"Yeah, sounds like fun," Marshall agreed, nodding. "I'll change my plans and bring my date along."

Lucas's eyes swung to me, and I had to blink a few times. I hated boats and being out on the open water. I loved walking the beach, and even swimming in the shallows. Swimming pools were fine as well. However, I broke into hives over the thought of anything deeper than five feet. It had everything to do with the fact that my father had drowned in a boating accident. While I didn't remember him, I did remember the trepidation that my mother had instilled into me for deep water. Plus, wool shrinks, and I was a water-fearing little lamb.

I met his steady gaze, then looked to the others who were smiling and nodding. Old Grace reared her ugly head and instructed me to make everyone happy at my own expense, so I nodded as well.

His shoulders seemed to relax a smidgen. "Great. It's through Lavender Island Cruises at Pier 17. Boat leaves at seven o'clock sharp. Be on board by 6:45." He turned to Ana. "Ana, will you please let the day staff know they're invited as well? They can bring a plus one too if they'd like." Ana nodded and then he was gone, leaving a wake behind him that seemed to keep us all off balance.

My inner wolf whimpered.

"Well, that's a first," Marshall said, breaking the silence.

I was too panicky to ask what he meant, and was grateful when they all returned to eating breakfast with no further comment.

I was miserable the entire day. I couldn't focus on my work. My palms and the soles of my feet were sweaty, and my neck felt tight. I wanted so desperately to find Lucas and tell him that I couldn't go on the harbor tour, but he was trying to do something kind, which made it impossible for me to speak up.

Perhaps I could make myself sick. It wouldn't be too hard to fake that. All I'd need to do was induce vomiting and let Ana catch me in the act. I could moan about my stomach aching and with how much I was already sweating, it would be believable. It was worth a try.

In the end I did nothing.

I had made a lot of progress in standing up for myself, but not quite enough when it came to the idea of disappointing these people I cared about. Ana, Marshall, Lou, and Steven had become my friends, and I'd had so few friendships that I didn't dare do anything to taint, or even worse, end, these new ones. The concept of unconditional affection was still so new to me that I didn't dare test it. Logical or not, I worked it up in my head that the success of this entire adventure lay on my shoulders.

Besides, honesty moment, I hadn't actually been out on a boat before. I'd avoided them my entire life. Maybe I'd be just fine. I'd lived through the ferry ride when I'd made my way here from Providence, after all. Perhaps this was a mind-over-matter situation.

I mean, for many years I never tried sushi because Mother said it would poison my insides, give me a worm, and leave me suffering in agony. Then one day I decided to try it on a whim, and I'd loved it. I was still living worm-free. Maybe boating would be the same way.

But probably not.

Ana offered to drive out to Pier 17 in her fatality-mobile. This time Chef Lou joined us. I had insisted he sit in the front, not only to be polite and to prevent me from such an up close view of all the near accidents we would experience, but also to make it unnecessary for me to keep up conversation. They cheerfully chattered about the adventure while I was mostly silent. My lips were numb with worry. I could hardly squeak words out of my dry throat. I kept chewing on my lips and squeezing my hands together.

My legs wobbled when we got out of Ana's car and walked toward the docks. It took massive self-control to keep up with the others. Marshall and Steven were already standing near the small shack with two women, waving at us as we approached. I couldn't return their smiles. Some of the day staff were there too, and I studiously avoided their greetings.

Ana placed a hand on my shoulder. "Are you okay? You look a little sick, and you had nothing to say on the drive over."

I licked my parched, white lips. "Uh . . ."

"Do you get sea sick?" she asked, a frown tugging her lips down.

Oh, how I wanted to grab onto that excuse with both hands, but honesty won out. "I don't think so." How was I to know?

"Well, do you need to go back to the house?"

"I can't."

She tilted her head and furrowed her brow. "Explain."

"I . . ." I shook my head and tucked my hands into the pockets of the shorts I'd put on. "It's nothing. I'm being silly. I'm fine." I attempted a smile. My lips were too frozen to know if I'd succeeded or not.

Ana didn't seem convinced. "This doesn't have to be another therapy session."

"Oh, no." I laughed nervously. "It's just that I've never been on a boat before." Hey, a way to be honest without giving it all away. Hooray.

Her face relaxed a bit. "I can see why you'd be nervous. Don't worry, you'll like it. Your hair looks great, by the way. Very islandy."

I fingered a few pieces of the hair that were hanging free around my shoulders. "Thanks. I tried to do it how you showed me."

The truth was that I'd left my hair down in hopes it would hide the horrified expressions I was sure to make as we got underway.

It was my plan to let the ever present island breeze whip my hair around and keep my face hidden.

Lucas came striding up the boardwalk at the same time that Ana and I joined the rest of the group. He looked wonderful in a t-shirt, shorts, and a baseball cap—warm and approachable. My stomach swooped at the sight before sinking even further at the reminder that I needed to keep my inconvenient feelings for him tamped down. That was a dead end road.

For his part, Lucas looked confident and actually happy, a smile on his face and his eyes welcoming. This was the Lucas I'd seen pictures of on the internet. I had a sudden vision of how he must be when he traveled around conducting business and attending social events. How would it be to have that charisma focused at you? I'd never know. My stomach heaved harder. I was now entering Barfsville.

"I'm so glad you're all here," Lucas said. "The boat is this way." He turned and motioned for us to follow him down to the water.

The boardwalk quickly gave way to a floating dock. It rocked back and forth as we stepped on, forcing a giggle out of Ana as she gripped the railing. I gripped it too, but without the giggle.

Lucas stood next to the boat entrance, legs spread wide to keep his balance, one hand on the boat railing itself and the other reaching out to assist anyone who needed it. A few people took his hand, but most didn't. I almost broke out of my terror sweats when small Ana tried to make the leap onto the boat, but it suddenly shifted and Lucas caught her arm, saving her from a very wet experience. Next it was my turn. He reached his hand out to me. Although I was taller than Ana by several inches, I was too shaky and scared to try casually jumping on board. I took his hand, warm in contrast to my icy fingers, and somehow convinced myself to climb onto the floating morgue.

"Where are the life jackets?" I said to Lucas as soon as he landed on board next to me.

His eyebrows pulled together. "Life jackets?"

"Yes," I replied, my voice airy with worry, "those things that keep you afloat if the boat goes down."

"I'm sure the captain will tell us when he gives us the safety talk." He passed me and walked to the middle of the boat, where he turned a slow circle. "Welcome, everyone. Let's have some fun. The food and drinks are all paid for, so help yourself. The tour lasts about an hour and a half."

Everyone but me clapped. I found a space on the side where I could sit and wrap my arms around a railing. I tried to do it in a way that said I was casually resting there, but I didn't know a lot of people who relaxed by hugging a railing hard enough to form a permanent indentation in their forearm.

The loud rumbling of a motorcycle engine broke through the chatter as a flashy bike careened around the corner and parked near the ticket shed. A scruffy-looking man, who appeared to be in his mid-sixties, hopped off and took his time sauntering down to the boat. He climbed aboard and came to stand next to Lucas, toothpick swirling around in his mouth as he eyed our small group.

He proceeded to give the least helpful safety speech I'd ever heard. It basically consisted of, "If the boat goes down, hope you can swim," after which he chuckled and disappeared into the pilot house.

"Did he say where the life jackets are located?" I asked Josie. She shook her head. I chewed on my lip and tried to play it cool.

"Are you nervous on boats?" she asked kindly.

"Oh, no, I'm fine." I tried to laugh lightly.

Josie exchanged a glance with Derek, who was sitting next to her, but they were kind enough to not push. Still, their dubious expressions hadn't escaped me. After a few moments they stood to go find a drink, and I didn't blame them for leaving my side. It was that or sit by the ghostly pale, sickly looking china doll, who was hugging the railing as though she expected the boat to go 'boom' at any second.

It took me a solid twenty minutes of smooth harbor cruising to relax. I started to notice how many other boats were around. If ours went down, certainly help could arrive quickly. This was an active, busy harbor. I knew from swimming that the water was warm, not the rough and freezing waters of the north Atlantic that had claimed

Father. In fact, the waves were gentle, almost non-existent. Everyone else was relaxed, pointing out marine life and sipping their drinks. I was the only one missing out.

I slowly released one hand and put it in my lap. Releasing the other arm took another ten minutes. In the meantime, I tried to focus on the dolphins, seagulls, pelicans, and nameless fish jumping out of the water. The sun had fallen from its peak, and the feeling was tranquil as it began to descend.

My second arm finally released the railing, and I focused on breathing deep, soothing breaths. This was good. I was okay. Everyone was having fun. I wasn't having fun, but the terror had seeped out and I was no longer in danger of screaming. For now.

As we hit the hour mark, I finally became brave enough to stand and walk to where the others had discovered a pod of dolphins following a shrimping boat that was coming in. They laughed in amusement at the hoard of seagulls that were also following the boat, diving and trying to steal the precious cargo. The shirtless men aboard seemed immune to their attackers and just kept busily tugging in the nets.

"Is that a couch on top of the pilot house?" Ana asked, squinting toward the boat.

"I'm not sure I'd call it a couch, but it might have started life as one." Steven laughed.

"I've seen a lot of strange things on boats in my day," Marshall replied, "but a boat with a couch up top is new."

"This is much better than a movie," his date—I think her name was Olivia—said.

Everyone cheerfully agreed and went back to their food. I hadn't made it to the point where I thought eating would be a good idea. There was still the danger of fear purging, and I didn't want to tempt the fates.

"What do you think of our little harbor?" Lucas came up beside me. At least, I think that's what he asked. I was only functioning at 30 percent brain capacity.

"I've never been anywhere like Lavender Island." I smiled up at him, grateful my lips had unfrozen. "You're very lucky to call it home."

Lucas's eyes moved from mine to gaze out. "I am." After a small pause he said, "I think everyone's enjoying the evening."

"Mmm," I managed.

"I've been boating in these waters since I was born," he went on. "I love to be on the water." He turned back to me. "Do you enjoy boats, Grace?"

I gulped. "Oh," I faked a chuckle, "sure." Because lying to Lucas always went so well for me.

He nodded. "Good. So, you're having fun?"

I didn't want to outright lie . . . for the second time. It seemed like I should spread the lies out a little more than once per sentence. Fun was a little strong for how I was feeling, but what harm could it do to let him think it? So, I offered a smile in reply.

Ana walked up just then and patted me on the shoulder. "As if you even needed to ask. Who wouldn't be having fun?"

I tried to remember to smile, but just then a huge cargo freighter came past, pushing a mammoth wave toward us. I wasn't at all surprised, because that's what happens to fibbers. I'd brought it on myself.

Everyone who knew what to expect calmly spread their legs for balance and found a hand hold until the wave passed. I, Grace Natalie Burke, panicked. I was standing in the middle of the boat watching what felt like a tsunami coming to consume us, and I had nothing to grab onto. Oh, wait, I did. Lucas.

Without conscious thought I let out a squeal, closed my eyes tightly, and turned to him. I forcefully wrapped my arms around his waist and buried my face in his chest with my eyes tightly closed. His arms were both above his head, holding on to some stabilizing handles that hung from the ceiling. I, very unfortunately, hadn't noticed them before I reacted, and was now unable to release my survive-at-all-costs grip and reach for them. I pressed my face closer to him and fought to take normal breaths.

When the wave hit, the boat tipped sideways, and my hands dug deeper into the muscles around his spine. I was terrified. This was it. The boat was going to tip over and I'd be trapped underneath it and it would be the end of Grace Burke, the lying liar. One of his hands dropped down to press against my upper back and steady me through the rocking. He said nothing as I smothered my squeals in his shirt.

Before long—really, it was probably no more than ten seconds total—the boat righted itself. I still held on. Seconds passed as I counted my breaths and held my eyes shut. Thankfully Lucas didn't push me away. Instead, he dropped his other hand and placed it on my back as well. It wasn't exactly an embrace meant for comfort, but I felt the stability of his hold. I gradually noticed the silence, followed by an awareness of how tense his body was under my grip. His hands felt large and warm on my back, and I could hear his heartbeat under my ear. What I couldn't hear was any conversation.

"Well," someone whispered, "that was . . ."

"Grace?" Ana's voice nearby pulled me fully back to reality. "The wave has passed. It's no big deal."

I wanted to hide away, but I forced my arms to let go as ripple after ripple of humiliation poured over me. Lucas's hands fell to his sides. I kept my eyes glued to the floor, unable to bear looking at anyone. I still hadn't taken a step away from him, and even though my arms weren't holding onto him anymore, we were so close I could feel the heat and unease coming off of him.

"Do you want to sit down, Grace?" Marshall's voice was near.

I nodded my head and risked a glance up at Lucas. His light eyes were distant and cold. Gone were the sparks of friendliness I'd seen earlier that evening. I stepped clumsily away.

"I . . . " I looked around at everyone. Lucas took several steps back while I stuttered out, "I'm not afraid of water. I'm afraid of boats." There was a difference.

There were a few intelligible mumbles from the group as I let Marshall lead me to a seat, followed by Ana. She sat next to me, one of her small arms draped around my back in a comforting way. We fell silent as the boat began to turn around and head back to the pier. Was Lucas cutting the cruise short?

"I'm so sorry, everyone," I said in a louder voice. "I didn't mean to ruin the fun. We can keep going."

"You didn't ruin anything, Grace," Marshall said from where he still stood nearby. "We were getting ready to head back anyway."

It was kind of him, but I knew the truth. I had done this by not speaking up. I didn't know how I could have avoided it, though. I'd have either ruined it in the kitchen this morning, or on the boat tonight. It had been a no-win situation for me. The worst part of it all was seeing Lucas's face. I'd ruined it for my boss. If he fired me, Eliza wasn't here to stop it and I'd have no reason to stay on the island anymore. I hadn't been able to act the part tonight, and it may have ruined more than just a harbor cruise. Heavy, mournful tears threatened. I refused them. I'd caused enough of a scene for one lifetime.

The cruise back to the pier had lost its festive spirit. My friends tried to bring it back by chatting with each other and joking around, but I could read a room. I'd been reading rooms since I was four years old. In all honesty, I did believe them that they weren't upset with me. I knew I wouldn't have been upset with any of them. No, the problem was that we all knew Lucas was upset, and nothing could be done to change that.

As the pier came into sight, I began to feel angry with the hopeless situation. I hadn't meant to ruin anything. In fact, the worst I could be accused of was trying to be a team player. I was afraid of boats, but I'd come along in order to make everyone happy.

I had intended to apologize to Lucas privately later, but now I had doubts about that. What did I need to be sorry for? Making people uncomfortable? Possibly. But why did it always have to be me who apologized? Hadn't I been made to feel uncomfortable by the fact that I'd felt pressured to come along?

The boat gently bumped against the dock, and I sprang to my feet. No one argued about me being the first off. While I'd come on timidly, I leaped off onto the dock with no support and raced up to the parking lot. Ana's shorter legs couldn't keep up, and she was breathing hard by the time we arrived at her car. Chef Lou was nowhere to be seen, and I figured he was smart enough to get a ride back with someone else.

"You okay?" Ana asked breathlessly.

"Not all of this was my fault and I won't apologize for it," I stated.

She blinked. "I'm not sure where you're going with this, but it might be one of those things that you sleep on."

I nodded stiffly, unwilling to argue with her over nothing.

The drive home was silent, and it gave me time to fume. I couldn't pin down what I was feeling. Ashamed, embarrassed, sad over letting my friends down. Anger, irritation, and frustration over feeling like I'd had no choice in yet another situation I hadn't wanted to be in. Disappointed in myself for having a meltdown in front of everyone. That image was now the only one those people—some of them total strangers—would have of me. All those emotions boiled inside of me until I thought I'd burst with the nastiness of it all.

Underneath all of this sensation was confusion. I couldn't recall ever feeling so jumbled up. I'd learned to live life in a way where I experienced emotion, but I never released it. I'd learned long ago that expressing those feeling got me nowhere. I was the master of pushing it all back down until I was calm and untouchable once more. I was ice.

In this island sun the ice had cracked. I knew better than to spread blame, but in that moment I blamed all of them. Eliza for hiring me and showering me with affection, Ana for her therapy sessions and being my first friend, Marshall for comparing me to his beloved granny. The list went on and on. They were undoing a lifetime of hiding.

I had to put myself back together. I would have to return to Providence soon, and I wouldn't survive it without my invincible shell.

Ana parked behind the carriage house, and I thanked her for the ride before heading straight past the house to the beach. It seemed ironic to be going back to the water, but I needed to breathe, deeply. I needed the cool air on my heated skin. I needed to cry a little too. Then I needed to figure out how to move forward. Maybe I'd pushed myself too far, too soon, and needed a tactical retreat. Maybe, although it tore me up to even think it, just maybe, I was better off in my shell.

I reached the steps to the sand quickly and hurried down, once again tossing my shoes next to the stairs as I made my way to the water. This time my intention wasn't to walk, but to be still. I stood facing the gulf and let the warm water lap at my feet as the sky finished its transition into dark. I sat on the damp sand and finally let the tears free. So many years of them. I imagined the ocean sucking them away as they fell.

I sat alone on the beach long enough to have no idea what time it was. The sky had been fully dark for a while when I heard someone approaching. I knew it was him before he spoke. I didn't bother to turn, and he came to stand next to me.

I heard him take a deep breath, as though he already hated this conversation, before he said, "I'm still trying to understand why you lied to me today." At least he sounded more disappointed than angry.

I already hated this conversation too. "I had no choice."

"There's always a choice."

Now it was my turn to release a sigh. "No, not really. My only choice was to ruin the trip before we went, or ruin the trip while we were there. No matter that I did, I was going to ruin it somehow."

Lucas didn't reply, and long moments passed while I counted waves and breathed with them, in and out. He continued to stand next to me.

When he finally spoke, it was said quietly, like a secret not to be shared out loud. "I've had enough of people telling me what they think I want to hear. Enough to last two lifetimes."

To my surprise, I felt words slipping out in the same soft tones. "I've had enough of people telling me I have a choice, when what they really expect is that I'll do what they want me to do."

"I wasn't strong-arming you into doing something, Grace," he replied. "I was trying to offer a fun activity, not force you to face your deepest fear. I honestly had no idea it would be a problem."

"I understand that, but from my point of view, my boss had arranged something fun and all my friends were excited. It was a work group activity, and I sincerely doubt you would have been happy about it if I'd refused to come along," I dared to say. Then I dared a little more. "Bosses don't get to pout, by the way, when things don't go their way."

He took a slight step back, his eyes flying down to look at me, as though my words had actually touched him. "You think I was pouting?"

"It felt that way. You'd been friendly up to that point, and then suddenly you were standing by the pilot house talking to no one. The trip didn't have to be ruined. If you'd have just laughed it off, the others would have followed your guidance."

"I was not in a mood. Honestly, Grace." He pursed his lips as he looked away for a moment. "I had no idea how to act or how to feel, so I did nothing. Would it have been better if I'd laughed off your very public panic attack?" I couldn't tell if he was genuinely asking, or if sarcasm had entered the conversation.

"You could have taken a moment to let me catch my breath and then reassured everyone that things were fine to carry on."

"You didn't see yourself. You were whimpering and clinging to me with a surprisingly strong grip. You did not look fine to carry on."

"I was not whimpering," I grumbled out.

He pulled a face, letting me know that he strongly disagreed with my statement and was choosing not to press the point. "Not to mention that you had just lied to me. To my face. You looked at me and said you were having fun."

"No. I smiled at you. I never said one word."

"So silence was honesty?"

I pulled a face. He had a point. "I'll admit that lying to you wasn't a good idea."

"It was a terrible one."

"I only did it because it was what you wanted to hear."

He stared at me like I'd sprouted another head. "I just told you that I'm tired of people telling me what I want to hear."

"How was I supposed to know that about you? You don't encourage much conversation, which only makes me feel like I should keep my thoughts to myself."

"Your thoughts to yourself? Several times you've told me exactly what you thought. This time, you didn't, and I was supposed to know that this *one* time was the lie?"

"I only tell you the truth when I'm mad at you," I huffed.

He grinned at that. "You must be mad at me every time we see each other then." I felt an answering grin but kept my lips shut. "So, let me get this straight. You only lie to me when I'm being nice?"

"It appears that way."

"Why?"

"Because in my experience kindness isn't all that kind. Ultimatums are often delivered with a sweet word, packaged as gifts."

I turned back to face the open ocean, unable to meet his eyes after that confession. Admitting that to him had been too much, an accident that I couldn't take back or bear to acknowledge. Why him? Why could I finally say what I felt to the one person I didn't want to be having sharing time with?

"Grace," he whispered, finally sitting on the sand next to me. His voice was low and filled with sympathy, and I suddenly remembered how rock solid he had felt when I'd been holding onto him on the boat.

My throat went dry with fear and something even scarier. Maybe I did want to have sharing time with him. Gulp. It was awful.

I held up a trembling hand as though trying to ward off any more words. "I shouldn't have said that." Another moment of silence descended, each of us lost in our own thoughts as we looked out into the dark gulf.

He was the one to finally speak again. "So, if I have this straight, I'm tired of people feeding me lines, and you're tired of people telling you what to do and then punishing you if you don't." It wasn't a question, but a statement of fact. I nodded. "I think we're more alike than I realized."

I looked back to him. "How do you figure?"

"We're both being fed lines all the time, neither of us knowing who or what to trust. It sounds lonely when I say it out loud."

"You can't possibly be lonely," I replied. "Everywhere you go people know you and chat you up."

"I understand how my life looks from the outside. I also understand how lucky I am to have this life. I have all the comfort, stability, and money I could ever need." He took a deep breath before pushing on. "Money doesn't buy honesty, genuine friendship, or any of the things I really want in life. Yes, I know a lot of people, but it doesn't always mean much."

This had been an interestingly vulnerable conversation. I remembered Eliza saying the same thing to me. That people had been interested in the Halstead name, but not Eliza herself. It was startling, and perhaps a little humbling, to realize that Lucas felt the same way. The images I'd found online had been slices of a life I knew nothing about. The truth about Lucas Halstead was something very different. A strange warmth bloomed in the general vicinity of my heart.

"These weeks at Halstead House have been the first time in my life I've had actual friends," I admitted haltingly.

"I haven't been very welcoming to you."

"I noticed."

I expected him to tease me back, but his voice remained serious and thoughtful. "It was childish, but I saw the way everyone immediately cared for you. I've known them for years, but they keep me at arm's length. I'm treated with nothing more than cordial respect."

"I joined them as a fellow staff member. You're the boss, and they want to be respectful of that. Plus, you're kind of standoffish most of the time," I ventured, testing this new openness.

He scoffed. "I am not standoffish."

"Fine, then. Arrogant, superior, snooty?" I hardly recognized my own teasing voice as the words came flying out.

He laughed, the first true laugh I'd heard from him. I felt it shoot down my spine and make my toes curl. I wanted to hear him laugh a million more times.

"I am not snooty," he said.

"Then prove it." I shrugged.

"How?"

"Stop being standoffish." It seemed pretty simple when I said it like that, but I understood how hard it could be to change lifelong behaviors. I'd been struggling with it for weeks now.

"Aunt Mary wanted us to be friends, you know."

I nodded, surprised he'd mention it. "Yes, she told me the same thing."

"Do you want to try it out?" he asked. "Being friends, I mean."

My heart rate sped up as I was asked something I'd never actually been asked by another human being. I considered Ana my friend, but that had sort of just evolved without any conversation.

I wiggled my toes in the sand as I tried to feel courageous and believe he meant it.

I chewed my lip and nodded. "I think so."

"No more telling me what you think I want to hear, even if I'm being nice?"

"I'll try." He snorted in amusement. "Well, turning over a new leaf isn't all that easy," I defended. "For your part, you can't be over-bearing, or cold, and make me feel like you'll end our friendship if I don't live up to your standards."

"We're both taking a risk here, you know," he said. I nodded. It was as exhilarating as it was sobering.

He extended a hand to me, and we shook on it, there in the sand under the stars. Our hands released quickly, but our eyes locked for a moment longer, as though we were both trying to see if we could trust in each other.

"In the spirit of our newfound honesty, why are you afraid of boats?" he asked.

"My father drowned in a boating accident. He was deep sea fishing and something went wrong. The boat sank. I was too young to know him, but trust me when I tell you that Mother exaggerated the story so greatly that I've never dared set foot on a boat until today."

"Today was your first time on a boat?" He seemed shocked, and I didn't blame him.

"Yeah."

"I wish I'd known. It would have been nice if that had gone better." He reached out a hand and gave my arm a light squeeze before releasing me again. I felt that squeeze all the way to the tips of my fingers.

"I was starting to relax tonight until that tsunami came out of nowhere."

"The term *tsunami* is debatable," he said, his mouth shifting in amusement. I pulled a face and he held up his hands. "Okay, okay. It was a matter of perspective."

"My thoughts exactly." I cleared my throat. "I'm sorry about the boat trip." I didn't say it because I felt pressured to. I said it because I felt it, and he deserved to hear it.

"I'm sorry too," he replied.

More silence, but this time I was peaceful as I sorted thoughts through my mind, finally settling on one. "It's going to be hard to say goodbye to this place."

"You say that like you'll never see it again."

"Well, I . . ."

"It doesn't have to be to that way. You're always welcome here," he replied matter-of-factly.

A bubble of pure happiness rose in me at his words. Somewhere in my mind I'd thought of this as an all-or-nothing experience. I'd been desperately trying to soak it all in because I thought I'd never see it again. Lucas had freed something with his statement, and it was all I could do not to laugh out loud like a crazy person.

"You're right." I turned to him with a mega smile growing.

"I think you'll find I usually am." His eyes crinkled, and I rolled my own playfully as I shifted to stand.

He got to his feet before I could and reached a hand down to assist me. I took it without any qualms, releasing it as we turned to walk back, both of us lost in our own thoughts, this time in companionable silence. He wanted to be my friend, and said I could come back any time I wanted. My head said I wanted to be his friend too, but when I'd gazed into his eyes and shook his hand, my heart had whispered something decidedly different.

CHAPTER 14

I HAD COME TO TRULY LOVE MY MONDAYS OFF SINCE ARRIVING ON Lavender Island. To be fair, it wasn't like I was being worked to death the other days. I certainly had plenty of free time in the evenings to spend around the mansion immersing myself in everything it had to offer. Still, Mondays were for adventures, and it felt like playing hooky after so many years of having Saturdays off instead.

Rather than dreading Ana's plans like a kid staring down a needle, I had begun looking forward to them. Perhaps the biggest change of all, though, was that I no longer made plans for myself. No dry cleaner, no banking, no tidy little lists to follow. Instead I cheerfully made my way to breakfast to see what she had up her sleeve for the day. This week I was not disappointed.

She told me her plans before I'd even opened my mouth to ask. "I've rented us E-bikes to take a self-guided island tour. We start along the seawall, make our way to the Historic District where we'll have lunch, then along to the harbor side. We can also do a ferry crossing, but I think Friday night's little . . . situation . . . has motivated me to pass on that."

I pursed my lips, but otherwise ignored the crack about my harbor tour melt down. "E-bikes are what, exactly?"

"Electric bikes."

Huh. "Are you talking motor scooters? Like a Vespa? Because I've seen the way you drive a car, and I'm not sure you should be on something with that type of speed and only two wheels." Actually, between us, I was totally picturing Ana flying along with her legs stuck out to the side trying to keep her balance while pedestrians ran for their lives . . . and it sounded hysterical.

Ana pulled a face. "You're a scaredy cat."

"No, I'm a woman who values human life," I responded with a laugh.

"E-bikes look like a normal bike. They pedal and handle the same. You still have to use your legs to make it go, but it has a motor that helps with things like hills and headwind. Pedaling is easier, and you can bike farther without getting as tired."

"That sounds doable."

"Yeah, well, I'm in pretty good shape since I'm on my feet all day, but you . . ." She shrugged as her words faded out.

"Gee, thanks for keeping my weak desk-job legs in mind. Have you done one of these bike tours before?" I asked.

"No. Locals aren't really into the touristy stuff."

"Ah, so this is just for my benefit?"

"Your hair is still stubbornly in buns at least seventy-five percent of the time, so I'm still pushing you into new things."

"I appreciate you being so willing to suffer for my hair's progress."

Ana stood and gave a theatrical sigh. "The things I do for your golden locks."

She left the kitchen after telling me to meet her at her car in thirty minutes. It didn't give me much time to eat and get dressed properly, but I wasn't going to cycle around the island on an overly full stomach anyhow. It wasn't supposed to be a tour of island restroom locations.

I was surprised to see Lucas coming down the hallway from his bedroom when I reached the top floor landing. The only other time I'd seen him upstairs was when he'd dropped some paperwork off to me one night. I wasn't sure where he spent all his time, but he was very rarely around at the same times as me.

He was dressed in what I thought of as his fishing clothes. Shorts, a t-shirt, baseball cap, and sandals, carrying his tackle box.

He looked a million miles away from the business luncheon host of the week before. I liked him this way.

We hadn't really spoken since agreeing to be friends, and I wasn't sure if that was the kind of thing you jumped right into, or if it would take some time to grow. I'd never officially agreed to be friends with anyone. Thankfully he spoke first.

"What are you up to today?" he asked.

Well, that seemed like a chummy thing friends would ask each other. The easy question helped me relax. "Ana is taking me on another of her therapy adventures. Her mission to stop me from being me, and start being someone a little more normal, is still full steam ahead."

"I see." He paused and his expression changed to something a little puzzled. "No, I don't, actually. What exactly was wrong with you being you?"

"I know it's easy to think I'm perfect, and I hate to burst your bubble, but I have some baggage that makes me act uptight and unapproachable. Ana has gone so far as to call me inflexible and unspontaneous." I managed to keep a straight face even though his smile was growing with each sentence.

"You hide your imperfections well."

"Why, thank you. If you'd be so kind as to tell Ana?" I lifted my eyebrows hopefully.

He shook his head. "Oh, no, I make a habit of never upsetting the person in charge of my life. She has the power to make me suffer."

"Probably best, unless you want her to start therapy on you." I grinned. I felt as though my feet were no longer touching the ground. I sounded so normal, and nothing was shaking or sweating. This conversation made me feel free somehow, and I adored it.

"I'm not sure I'd survive. What's in store for you today?"

"Our adventure involves electric bikes and an island tour."

"That sounds much better than what I'd imagined. You had me thinking she was going to dangle your body over a shark tank."

"Don't give her any ideas." We shared a smile for a long enough moment that a blush began to rise. I cleared my throat and blurted the first thing that came to mind. "Do you want to come too?"

Lucas's first reaction, before he could hide it, appeared to be one of surprise. He quickly slid a casual look back into place, but I had seen it. He rarely got invited to these types of things, and he knew that I knew it.

"I would really like to, but . . ." He swallowed and I suddenly felt embarrassed and foolish for the invitation. The man was holding his tackle box, dressed to go fishing.

"Don't worry about it. I know how busy you are." I waved a hand in the air and turned toward my room to make a hasty retreat.

"Grace, wait."

I froze a few steps away and turned to face him. He stayed where he was on the other side of the foyer. "I'm meeting a business associate today to do some fishing and discuss plans for some production upgrades. My life is so busy, but I . . ." His vibrating phone interrupted him before he could finish the thought. He pulled it out of his back pocket to see who was calling.

"It's okay. We can still be friends even if you're too busy to go on a bike ride with Ana and me today." He must have read the sincerity in my expression, because he relaxed a bit.

"I'd rather go on a bike ride. I'm sorry that I can't." He waved the still ringing phone in the air.

"I'll have to get with your secretary to schedule something next time," I joked.

"If Ana heard how unspontaneous and overly scheduled I am, she wouldn't like it," he replied. I showed my appreciation of his crack by beaming at him and was fascinated to watch his smile grow to match mine. "Thank you for inviting me today. It's nice to have someone want me around for no reason at all."

"To be totally honest, I probably would have hit you up for ice cream," I replied, trying to tamp down on a heart rhythm that was seriously affected by his smile.

"I probably would have bought it."

I wasn't sure if my mind was playing tricks on me or not, but it felt like the room had shrunk down to just the two of us and the temperature had risen by a thousand degrees. I could do nothing but nod.

He touched the brim of his hat and turned to go down the stairs as he answered his phone in a clipped tone. I watched him and wondered when I'd stop being afraid of him in one way or another. This new, relaxed, and approachable Lucas was possibly scarier than the aloof and cold one had ever been.

*   *   *

"Do you think you can get hairline fractures in your buttocks?" Ana asked later that afternoon as we walked from her car back to the mansion.

"Definitely," I replied in a slightly strained voice. "Were bike seats more comfortable when we were kids?"

"Obviously, because I deny the idea that it has anything to do with the size of my bum." Ana came to a stop in a shady garden spot and bent over to touch her hands to her feet. "What stretches do I need to do in order to loose the caboose?"

I giggled at the phrase. "I don't think you can stretch out fractures."

"I knew by the time we were two blocks away from the bike shop that I'd made a terrible mistake. Why didn't you stop me?"

I groaned as I too stretched, tugging my heels up toward my back. "You made it two blocks? I sat on the seat *at the shop* and had the same realization before I'd even started pedaling. I was trying to tough it out for the Great Island Therapist. I was afraid to show weakness."

"Honesty is a virtue." Ana grimaced as she stood straight again.

"I *honestly* think that I won't be able to sit down for a week."

Ana nodded. "Maybe longer. I have no idea how long it takes for broken rear ends to heal."

"It was pretty fun, though, right?" I asked her as she once again leaned into a stretch. "I mean, the temperature couldn't have been above eighty, and the breeze was so nice."

"Yep, blowing on your bare neck."

"Chignons save the day once again." I wiggled my head at her. "Plus, I got to see a lot of fun things I'd never seen before."

169

"Like your friend crying on a sidewalk and rubbing her derriere in the Historic District, and then again by the harbor, and then again on the seawall?"

I beamed. "Exactly. Treasured memories I will keep forever."

Ana stood straight and pulled a face. "If they're going to put electricity in a bike it should be for a massaging seat."

"With a heater."

"No. I refuse to add bum sweat to soreness." She pulled a face that made me laugh. "I'm glad you had a good time. Maybe this was karma for all the terrible things I've been making you do lately."

"You won't get an argument from me," I replied straight-faced.

"If you'd just let your hair down, I could stop all this nonsense," she grumped.

"Are you saying your therapy sessions will end when my hair hangs down?"

"I've gotten you to stop with your lists, you're willing to go with the flow on adventures, you aren't apologizing for every little thing you do, so yes. Your darn hair is all that's left."

"Why didn't you say so?"

"I did say so. This very morning."

I reached up and pulled all the pins from my hair, ran my fingers through it, and let it fall loose. "There you go. Mission accomplished. No more bum fractures for us. You win"

Ana let out a big sigh and gazed upwards. "Finally. Thank heavens it's finally happened. I need a stinking nap."

"May I remind you that you picked today's activity?"

"By all means, remind me. As long as you remember that I may leave you an unpleasant surprise in your bed."

I wrinkled my nose. "I'm afraid to ask, but I have to know. Do you keep unpleasant things in the housekeeping room in case someone defies you?"

"No yet, but I like where you're going with that idea. Sadly, right now all my brain power is focused on healing the deep bruising I'm experiencing in lower areas of my body."

"Those pedals were too hard for your tender feet?"

Ana rolled her eyes. "When did you get so sassy?"

"When you started teaching me to be."

"I've created a monster." Ana began walking again toward the house.

"Yes, but a monster with flowing hair who's never even heard the word *chignon*," I teased.

Ana laughed and reached for me, wrapping her arms around my waist in a spontaneous hug. I hugged her back without thinking, enjoying the quick exchange and understanding the value of it. All joking aside, Ana really had nudged me onto the path of loosening up and becoming courageous. She'd even taught me how to have engaging conversations with others. I loved her for it.

"I take it back," she said when she released me. "I've created the perfect version of you. Watch out, world, Grace Burke is coming for you."

"People in Providence won't know what to make of me," I cheered.

Ana's face immediately fell. "I keep forgetting that you're not here forever. It seems wrong somehow."

Her words sobered me as well. "Yes, well, I'd stay here forever if I could. These past few weeks have been the best of my life. I truly mean that. This is the happiest I've ever been."

"I know." She patted my arm.

"Ana, I can't thank you enough for all you've done for me . . ." I began.

She quickly interrupted. "No thanks necessary, Grace. We're friends. It's that simple."

My throat thickened and tears rose at her words. She was right. I wished I had a way to pay her back, but I couldn't see a thing that Ana needed that I could offer her. For now, I'd have to settle for being the best friend to her that I could be.

We had reached the side stairs leading into the conservatory when my phone began to ring. It pulled me from my thoughts and I fumbled with it before answering.

"Hello?"

"Grace, it's Mother."

My stomach immediately and involuntarily clenched at the sound of her voice. The husky, clipped tones had a way of putting me on edge before I'd even heard what she had to say. I hadn't actually spoken to her in weeks. She'd occasionally sent me a text, but I'd only responded when absolutely necessary. Hearing her voice again broke some of the spell I'd allowed my life on Lavender to weave around me.

"Hello, Mother," I said in a calm voice.

Ana heard and looked to me with concerned expression. She knew enough about Mother to know the relationship was complicated, and enough about me to hear the tension in my voice. She asked me a question with her eyes, and I answered by offering her a smile as I gestured to my favorite bench near the garden fountain, letting her know I'd take the call there. I mouthed a 'thank you' to her. She nodded and continued up the stairs into the house. I was sad to see her disappear into the conservatory and close the door behind her. I was alone.

"It's been seven weeks, Grace. Surely that's long enough to get this, this *house* out of your system."

"My sabbatical was for three months. I plan to use all of it."

"I've had a lot of time to think, and frankly I'm offended and hurt that you didn't discuss this with me. Surely the two of us could have come to an understanding." Her tone changed to one of coaxing and wheedling. This was the tone that was supposed to shift blame to me. To make me look like the unreasonable daughter. It was the same argument she'd used the night I'd told her. She was always hurt and offended when I didn't discuss my life with her— which is why my life had eventually become hers to run.

Time to practice what I'd been learning. Honesty, standing up for myself, and no apologizing when I'd done nothing wrong. "I don't think we would have found common ground, Mother. I think you would have continued to tell me not to visit Halstead House, just as you have my entire life."

Mother huffed. "I don't see how that's my fault. Mrs. Reed was unable to travel that far, and what was the point in visiting her childhood home without her?" I didn't bother with an answer to the timeless argument. "I suppose if you insist on staying there for another month, then I'll have to insist on coming to see you."

A stone the size of Texas itself fell into my stomach at her words. No, no, no, no. She could not come here. I had found a place of refuge and escape. I had found a place of peace. I was learning about myself and growing braver day by day. She would somehow find a way to make it about her and push me back into the box where I'd been wasting away.

My mouth worked to form words into some kind of response, but nothing would come out. She had robbed me of speech with her pronouncement. I swallowed three times, hard, and cleared my throat.

"I didn't think you had any interest in Halstead House," I said at last.

"I don't. What I have an interest in is seeing my daughter, and since she refuses to leave the place, I have no choice."

"I don't think you should come," I replied. It had felt like forcing words through a dense fog, but I was proud of myself for getting them out.

"Why not? I'm all alone here. I miss you. You're what my world revolves around."

That's what I was so afraid of. I didn't want to be the focus of her world again, and I really didn't want her to become the center of mine once more. "Mother, I really feel that you visiting would be a mistake. You'd like very little about Lavender Island, and I'm working, and you wouldn't be able to stay with me." I paused while desperately thinking of other reasons she should stay in Providence.

"Mrs. Reed always spoke about how large the mansion is."

"It is. But it's almost totally open to the public except for a few private bedrooms, and with the upcoming events it'll be even tighter." I rambled as I listed off any reason I could think of to keep her away.

"Grace Natalie, the fact that you're trying so hard to keep me away tells me that I absolutely must come see what you're up to. I've already purchased a non-refundable plane ticket. I arrive Thursday. You don't need to pick me up. I've arranged a car for the week. I won't push to stay with you, since you say I'd be uncomfortable. I'll find a hotel nearby to stay in. You can expect to see me at Halstead House late afternoon." I remained silent, taking agonizingly shallow breaths. "Grace, are you still there?"

"Yes," I squeaked.

"Good. Think of all the wonderful times we've had together. We always have such fun, you and I. This will be our latest adventure."

The truly worst part of the whole thing was knowing that we had indeed shared some good times. Mother wasn't a total monster. She was lonely, deeply controlling, and selfish, but she had given me enough occasional moments of happiness to keep me off balance. The tug-of-war between loving her and wanting to escape her was beyond exhausting.

The line went dead. She may have said goodbye, but I'd been too preoccupied to hear it. I put my phone back in my pocket and remained seated on the bench for a few more minutes. The sound of the fountain gave me something to focus on as I did my best to talk myself out of a total panic attack.

Eventually I found my feet and walked all the way around the house to the basement side entrance, hoping to avoid the main parts of the house. I slipped through to the elevator unnoticed and pushed the button. Luckily it had been on the basement floor already, so it opened quickly. I climbed in and counted my breathing on the way up. Five in, three out.

I once again found myself face to face with Lucas when the doors opened at the top. I couldn't figure out how that was possible. Two times in one day seemed highly unlikely. My mind was too muddled from my worries to process if he was real or not. This time he was dressed in a suit. I had thought I liked him best in casual fishing clothes, but maybe I'd been wrong. He looked like perfection, all groomed and pressed. Untouchable. I couldn't take my eyes off him.

"How was your therapy adventure?" he asked.

I blinked a few times and met his eyes. "Ana thinks she fractured her butt cheeks," I replied in a detached, monotone voice. "I think bike seats should be classified as torture devices."

"Grace?" his voice sounded closer and I blinked again. His eyes held mine as his eyebrows dropped lower. "What's happened?"

"My mother is coming. She just called. She's bought a plane ticket and she'll be here Thursday." My mind suddenly cleared, allowing ice-cold dread to settle in as I said the words out loud. "Oh, my gosh, Lucas . . . my mother is coming." I could hear the fright in my own voice as I said it.

"It's okay. We can handle her." I was grateful that Lucas already knew something about my mother so that I didn't have to explain my horror. Yet, because of that he should be as scared as I was. Why was he not appalled right now?

I shook my head frantically. "That is definitely not true. What am I going to do?" I paced away from where I'd been standing by the elevator door and back again. "I have to think of something. She absolutely cannot come here. It'll ruin everything."

As I came back to where Lucas was standing, he reached out for my hand and tugged me to a gentle stop. I looked down at his hand and back up to his eyes. Something in them was fierce, but not in the cold way he'd looked before. The contact made warmth wash from my hand up to my face, which was luckily already flushed so he wouldn't know it was caused by his touch.

"It's going to be okay."

"I have to leave," I breathed, staring with agonized eyes into his light ones. "It's the only way. She's only coming to see *me*. If I go back to Providence tomorrow, she won't come here."

"You do not have to leave here if you don't want to." His hand enveloping mine seemed to add weight to his words, and I wanted to believe him.

"I don't want to go, but she can't come here." My voice shook and I felt tears well up. I pushed them back, years of practice helping me keep them at bay. I knew he noticed, and appreciated that he didn't say anything.

"Let Lillian come. You won't have to face it alone. We're friends now, remember?" He gave my hand a last squeeze to emphasize before finally releasing me. "You have Ana and Marshall, Chef Lou and Steven, and Eliza will be home in a week."

I took a deep breath and let it out slowly as I repeated his words to myself, barely above a whisper. "I'm not alone." And then, "She'll cause a storm that will rival a hurricane," I said louder.

"Then we'll be your anchor." His voice had taken on a low, earnest quality that was hypnotizing. I nodded shakily. "You're not alone," he murmured once more.

"I'm not alone," I repeated.

I lost track of time as I stood near Lucas, drawing off his calm and letting my eyes glaze over. Soon my breathing slowed to match his. I felt stronger, more capable, and supported in a way I had never known. It was bliss. Dangerous bliss, because I was beginning to feel something a little more than simply comforted.

I stiffened as a new line of thinking emerged. "Oh, Lucas, you're in a suit." I pulled my unfocused vision back and focused on him again.

"I am."

"I've made you late, again, for something important. Do you have a business meeting?" My face reddened at the thought of throwing his schedule off track. Then it reddened further at the thought that he'd made time for me when he had other places to be.

"I do have somewhere to be, but no one will be upset if I'm a few minutes late. I'll blame it on traffic."

I gave him a look. "Lavender Island has no traffic."

"True. But plenty of bad drivers who get in the way." His eyes smiled down at me. "You okay?" I nodded. "Good."

"Thanks. For, you know, everything."

"Oh, you mean for being an actual friend?" His expression was amused and relaxed.

"Yep."

"No problem."

"Have a good night, then." I gave a strange little wave and watched as he pushed the elevator door open.

"You too," he said as he stepped in. Then, just as the doors began to close a bewildered look crossed his face. "Wait, did you say Ana thinks she fractured her bu- . . ."

I laughed out loud at the expression on his face as the doors cut off any further conversation. Having been Lucas's enemy for a while, I could definitely say that being his friend was much, much more enjoyable.

CHAPTER 15

I stood in the grand foyer of Halstead House, sheep skin shaking, watching the front door for any sign of my mother's arrival. The past three days had been both the longest and shortest of my life. I was in my dove gray super suit, hair so tightly pulled into a chignon that my eyes felt like slits, makeup back up to standard, and fingers gripped so tightly I wasn't sure I'd be able to break them apart. My armor had returned, and I was pacing as rigidly as a soldier.

Ana slid into step with me and harrumphed in annoyance. "Weeks of work down the drain. I don't know your mother, but I'm having a hard time not disliking her on principle," she said, referring to my return to Old Grace.

"I can't spring flowing hair and a laissez-faire attitude on her right when she steps of the plane. I need to ease her in. If she saw me in those skinny jeans she'd pop something in her brain."

She harrumphed again as we about-faced. We'd been having this conversation all morning. "I still think you'd be better off waiting in Eliza's office," she said. "Go with the power move. She could ring the front door, and one of the staff could show her to you up there."

"Using a power move with Mother would be a huge mistake."

"Fine. Well, at least wait up there and I'll call you down when she gets here," Ana huffed. "It's not a power move, but it would show her you aren't her puppet." This was yet another argument we'd been having since breakfast, and yes, the word *puppet* wasn't helping me calm myself. It was rude and made me want to lash out, but most brutal honesty feels that way.

I shook my head and pivoted for the hundredth time. "I know when she'll arrive. She knows that I know when she'll arrive. She'll be expecting me to be here to greet her directly. Besides, it would be unkind not to."

"How can you possibly know when she'll arrive? Didn't she just say to expect her Thursday afternoon?"

"No. She said late afternoon Thursday."

"Which is any time between four and six o'clock. You going to pace here for two hours waiting?" She scurried when I turned before she'd expected. "And could you stop for just one second!"

I stopped and she bumped into me as I faced her. "Late afternoon to Mother is five o'clock precisely. Which gives me five more minutes to prepare myself."

Ana looked me over and pulled a disapproving face. "You know what paces like that? Caged wolves," she grumbled, and the irony wasn't lost on me. "You're as stiff as the day you arrived."

"You'll appreciate my need for armor after you've met Lillian Burke."

"I never thought of you as dramatic. I did think of you as an ice queen, to be fair, which is the total opposite of dramatic. Although I suppose freezing people out is a form of drama . . ." She paused and tapped her finger on her lower lip.

"I am not being dramatic." I looked over at her. "You're about to meet the woman who created the ice queen you used to know."

Ana pretended to shiver and then laughed a bit. "This is all so soap opera-ish right now, that I actually find myself excited to meet her. Is it five yet?"

I shook my head and closed my eyes. While I was amused at Ana's antics, I knew for a fact that she didn't quite believe me. Lillian would have her for dinner.

"Listen, Ana, you should be a little less excited and a whole lot more anxious. You may even want to hide in a corner and watch for a while instead of being right in her line of fire when she gets here."

"You think she'll come in guns blazing?" Ana looked a little less amused.

"No. She'll be as polite as she can be. She'll insult you left and right, make you feel two inches tall with the IQ of a sloth, and do it all in a way that makes you wonder if you heard her correctly. She'll have you doubting yourself, your life choices, and our friendship within the first five minutes. In the next five she'll have you agreeing to let her run your life because you obviously cannot be trusted to do it with your pea-sized brain." I was a little out of breath as the last of the words rushed out on the heat of emotion.

"Is that all?" Ana's mouth pinched as her gaze moved to the big doors.

"We're friends, right?" I managed to unclench my hands and touch her shoulder.

"Obviously it's not normal for the therapist and the client to become friends, but I like to think of us as an exception." She shook herself a bit and smiled. This time I returned her amused look. I loved that Ana was strong enough to find humor in tough situations.

"As my friend, I'm asking you to trust me. Go away. I'll introduce her to you when we do the tour of the house. It's really best if Mother doesn't realize we're friends. She's angry with me, which means you'll become a target, a way for her to manipulate me."

She finally—at long last—accepted what I'd been trying to say. She gave one succinct nod, patted my hand that was resting on her shoulder, and turned to head back toward her office. I felt a rush of relief to realize I was alone. Not alone in the old bad way. Rather, alone in a way that would protect these people.

At 5:02—two minutes late, which I took delight in noting—I heard the dong of the front bell. I had already instructed Steven that I would handle this special tour. He had asked no questions but willingly headed for the kitchen, having smelled Chef Lou's pastries baking earlier.

My heels clicking across the foyer felt overly loud without the normal buzz of household activity. It was as though Halstead House itself were holding its breath. I inhaled deeply once more as I reached the door and put my hand on the nob. It was go time.

The door swung open to reveal my mother looking as she always did. Stick thin, stylishly dressed, with her dark graying hair swept into gravity-defying heights. She somehow managed to make her hair large without making it strange. She was holding sunglasses and her purse in her hand. Behind her stood a man in a black suit whom I assumed was her driver.

She turned to him. "That will be all, Stanley. I'll let you know if I need your services again tonight, or if my daughter is willing to handle my transportation needs."

Stanley simply tipped his head and walked back down the front steps to a black sedan that was idling at the curb. I said nothing in response to Mother's cloaked barb but took the moment to look her over. I hadn't been away from her long enough for there to be any real changes in her, yet my eyes did their best to evaluate how she was doing. As I had long been the overseer of her happiness, it was a habit I fell immediately back into. Measuring her, taking stock, trying to determine what she needed from me.

"Please, come in, Mother," I said when she turned back to me. She offered a polite nod and smile in return, and an odd mixture of happiness in seeing her and fear over what it meant warred inside of me. This duality of feeling was something I only felt around her.

She stepped through the door, and I watched with interest as her gaze swung high and low, left and right as she took in what was before her. I knew her well enough to know that she was surprised by the grandeur of the place. It had certainly impressed me with its classic style, well-kept decor, and soaring heights—and I'd been seeing pictures of it for years. Mother had never wanted to see pictures or hear stories. For all intents and purposes, this was her first glimpse of the place.

I also knew her well enough to know she'd never admit to being awed. If it had been any other mansion, anywhere else in the world, she would have taken a delighted breath and told me what a beautiful place it was. Not here.

"Well," Mother sniffed, "it's pretty much what I'd expected." Her eyes finally turned to me, and she perused my outfit from tip to toe. "You don't look any different."

I blinked, unsure of how to respond. "Did you honestly think I would?"

"I don't know what to think about you."

She turned away from me again, gliding further into the home and toward the formal parlor. It was an elegant room, and I wasn't sure I wanted her tainting it with her reviews.

"Would you like a tour?" I asked.

Her eyebrows raised. "The public tour, or the family tour?"

I put a practiced smile on. "The family tour, of course."

"Very well. Show me what's got you so enamored of the place, because at this point, I simply don't see the appeal."

"We'll see some of the staff as we go around, and I'd like to introduce you to them." I chewed on my bottom lip as I worked up the courage to say what I felt needed to be said. She pursed her lips impatiently. "Please be kind to them, Mother. I know you're upset with me, but they are good people and deserve to be respected."

A manicured hand flew straight to her chest as her eyes widened. "I don't know what type of person you think I am, Grace, but I assure you I need no such warning. I don't go around belittling honest, hard-working members of society."

Normally that was true. Mother was polite and respectful even if she was never kind. However, these weren't normal circumstances, and I had a feeling part of her goal in coming was to make me pay for leaving her. She'd take her shots where she could find them.

Having made my request, I moved on. "Are you ready?"

On a typical public tour I would have strolled casually, sharing tidbits about the home's history or funny anecdotes about the family. Mother received the speed-walking tour. We covered the first floor in record time, yet I found myself pausing outside of the kitchen where I knew Chef Lou would be busy working on dinner preparations. Ana's office and the housekeeping area were nearby as well. We'd been lucky so far to not see anyone else. It was go time yet again.

"Well, Grace?" Mother was breathing down my neck as my hand hung in mid-air, reaching toward the swinging door but not quite pushing it open.

"Sorry, Mother. Uh, this is the kitchen. Our chef will most likely be working on dinner at this point in the day." I pushed the door and stepped in, heart in my throat.

Sure enough, Chef Lou was chopping vegetables at one counter while steam rose from a pot on the stove. He was humming lightly to himself. Steven was sitting at the kitchen table flipping through a magazine, the remnants of a crumbly tart crust on his plate.

"Good afternoon, everyone, if I may have a moment?" I called in a clipped, detached, professional tone. I wanted nothing of our warm camaraderie to show in front of Mother. It worked. The two men looked up but extended no greeting. "This is my mother, Mrs. Lillian Burke. She's here to visit for a couple of days, so I'm giving her a tour of the house. Mother, this is Steven. He's the official tour guide."

Steven smiled at her in his easy tour-guide way. "Welcome, Mrs. Burke. I hope you'll enjoy your stay."

"Why is he not giving me the tour?" Mother asked.

Steven jumped in seamlessly. "Grace thought you'd enjoy a more personal touch this afternoon, ma'am. But if she leaves anything out, you let me know and I'll make sure to step in."

Mother gave him a tight smile and turned her gaze to Chef Lou. "And this is?" she asked.

"Mother, this is our chef, Lou. He cooks us three meals a day and handles the catering for any events. His food is always delicious."

"How nice that must be to have someone handle all your meals." Mother offered him a nod.

"How do you do, Mademoiselle?" Chef Lou turned to her and smiled, his accent thick.

I groaned inwardly as Mother's smile warmed a bit and she threw out a string of words in French. Dang French. Mother was fluent, having studied abroad in her youth, and I should have told him to lose the accent today. His eyes grew wide, but he said nothing in return.

Mother's lips pursed as the silence extended painfully. "I see," was all she said, but Chef Lou's face reddened and he turned abruptly away.

"Mother, please," I murmured. "You said you'd be kind."

"I didn't say a word, although I could have. His food might be world class, but that man is lying to everyone who passes through this kitchen. I should have known when he called me Mademoiselle that he was a fraud. Do the Halsteads not worry about having employees with integrity?" she said loud enough to carry.

I shriveled up inside at the look on poor Lou's face. I couldn't imagine the accent would make a reappearance after this. "Let's move along, shall we?"

I attempted to do nothing more than gesture into Ana's office area, but Mother noticed her typing something on her computer and wanted an introduction. I followed along as she pushed her way inside.

"Mother, this is Ana. She's the facility manager. She's over running the household and staff, and keeping everything up to par." Ana gave Mother a warm smile. "Ana, this is my mother, Mrs. Lillian Burke."

"How old are you?" Mother asked abruptly.

Ana's eyes clouded in confusion, but she kept her smile in place. "I'm twenty-eight, ma'am."

"So a little older than Grace? Have the two of you struck up a friendship?" Mother's smile was kind, and I blinked a few times.

"Ana has been very kind to me and taken me on a few sightseeing adventures," I replied before Ana had a chance.

"Yes, I did think you looked a little more relaxed than the last time I'd seen you." Mother reached over to give my cheek a tender pat, her eyes crinkling. As always happened with any displays of affection, my face warmed and I felt pleased. She turned back to Ana. "Thank you for taking care of her." She smiled. Then, the gears shifted. "Just think, only twenty-eight and running a household of this size, on your own."

"Yes, ma'am," Ana said. I could read the questions she shot at me with her eyes. She thought I'd lied to her about my mother. It was only because Mother was currently stringing her sugary web.

"How long have you been doing housekeeping work?"

I felt my face tighten. "Ana isn't a housekeeper, Mother. She runs the entire household, including all the accounting and staffing . . ."

Mother cut me off with a wave of her hand. "Still, you must have had to work your way up?"

Ana looked back to Mother and answered the question. "I started as a day staff member doing all sorts of jobs when I was eighteen."

"Did you attend college?" Mother asked casually, almost as though she didn't really care. I winced inside. Here came the kill.

"No, ma'am."

"What a shame. You seem an intelligent girl. I'm surprised you would choose to give up your life for this house when you have more potential than that. Well, to each their own, I suppose. Sometimes we don't have the strength to crawl from where we were dropped." Mother turned and walked back out the door.

Ana blinked a few times before her eyes met mine. I tried to apologize with a look. She mouthed the word *wow* before shrugging and getting back to her work. She didn't seem devastated, but I promised myself I'd return to check on her later.

"Mother, what on earth was that all about?" I caught up to her as we circled back through the dining room and into the entrance hall.

"What?"

"Telling Ana she's wasting her life here."

"She is," she stated.

"She's not. This is a good career for her. You have no idea what goes into running a business of this size."

Mother scoffed. "A business? It's a family home that they've opened up for entertaining."

"The Halstead Corporation includes this mansion and several businesses. Ana runs this arm of the company." My jaw clenched. "She has a good, steady job working for decent people. There's nothing wrong with that."

"Mmm. Perhaps. It's sad, really." Mother didn't bother to look at me as she said this, but headed for the main staircase.

"What is that supposed to mean?" My warmth at her affection was quickly taking a back seat to the familiar chill.

"Grace, I would suggest you watch your tone." Her eyes snapped to mine with a glare that would have frozen the earth's magma.

I should have stopped talking, but I couldn't quite let it go. I had, after all, learned a little bit about taking a stand recently. "Honestly, that was very offensive to Ana, who is probably the best friend I've ever had. I don't know what to say right now, or how to apologize to her for this."

"Then don't say anything. Are we going up to the next floor or not?"

She turned and gracefully began walking up. She didn't even pause to study the gorgeous stained-glass window that had so often captured my attention. I shook my head and followed her. My stomach was churning with anger and resentment. My heart ached for the things she'd said to my friends. I wanted her gone. So much for the anchor that Lucas had promised. I was drowning here, and she'd only arrived fifteen minutes ago.

The next floor went as quickly as the first had gone. Mother showed no interest in the displays of clothing and personal Halstead family items that had been laid out in each of the bedrooms. She was untouchable and apathetic.

When we climbed to the top floor, where my private quarters were housed along with Eliza and Lucas's, her eyes took on the first hint of interest.

"This is the family's private floor?" she asked.

"Yes."

"Which room is yours?"

I took her down the hall to my room at a snail's pace—a woman off to the gallows. I really didn't want her to see it, as it was, in fact, large enough for her to have stayed with me. My jaw was tight and my stomach in knots as I opened the door. We stepped inside my personal haven.

"Ah," she said as she fully entered and turned a circle. "I can see how there wouldn't have been any room for me, at all. Such a postage stamp of a room." Her eyebrows raised, and she once again faced me. I remained guiltily silent. She walked to the window and took in the view that I so loved. "The view is nice, I suppose." She walked back toward me, lightly trailing a finger over the bed as she passed. "I can see why you love it here, Grace. This room suits you."

"Thank you. I really do like it."

"Still, I have to say, this isn't all that Mrs. Reed built it up to be. I'm a little disappointed."

It had taken her longer to go for the jugular than I'd thought it would. My back stiffened even though I'd known it was coming. Reacting to her statement wouldn't get me anywhere, so I silently waited for her to finish what she was going to say.

"I know you loved her, and I can even understand wanting a vacation here, but to spend three months on this island? Someone of your drive and intelligence . . . well, you need more." My eyes flickered, but I held my tongue. She saw and pressed on. "Oh, I'm sure you feel like you've made some friends here and found a nice new group, but don't be silly." She laughed lightly. "That fake French chef, that lazy tour guide, and that young housekeeper? You could never be truly happy with their company for long."

"They're lovely people, Mother." My jaw was going to snap, but I kept my tone civil.

"Of course, you feel that way. Maybe you always will because this is a situation outside of reality, but I doubt they return that same level of affection. You are, after all, nothing more than a long-term guest. Perhaps a co-worker at best." Mother walked toward the small desk and rifled casually through some papers. "Before you get your feathers ruffled, I think you're a lovely person Grace. Kind, talented, and always so very empathetic with people." She walked closer to me and gave me a soft look that I knew she thought was one of tenderness. "I've had a lot of time to think, and I realize that I've been hard on you over the years. After your father died, I was so terrified of losing you too that I held on tightly. No one could blame me for that, but I can see how you may have felt stifled on occasion. Because of this, I'm willing to take some of the responsibility for your little rebellion here. However, you must admit that the track you're on in life is a good one. I have not led you astray in the past, and I can't watch you throw everything away now. It's truly time you came home, dear." She glued her eyes on mine, which was easy as we were exactly the same height.

My hands began to shake. I'd only been away for two months, yet I'd already forgotten her special mix of loving kindness and cold maneuvering. I could hear the strain in my own voice as I responded. "I'm going to stay, Mother. I have a few more weeks until my sabbatical is over."

She chuckled lightly. "Oh, sweet girl." Her voice dropped back to the gentle, kind tone I knew well. "It's been fun for you, I know. I'm happy that you've had a good time, but I have no intention of leaving here without you."

I shook my head and her eyes changed from warm to cool, but she maintained her friendly expression. We needed to leave my room before she started packing my things.

"I need a few moments to think." I stalled. Mother's expression shifted to one of triumph. She didn't realize I was stalling. Most likely because I'd never stalled with her, or if I'd tried, I'd always ended up capitulating.

"I understand. There were some lovely gardens outside. Why don't you show me those and then we can go to a nice restaurant and discuss your future?" Mother looped her arm through mine, all warmth and kindness, as we walked back down the hallway to the staircase.

I followed in shuttered silence as we made our way through the home. Mother, however, having delivered her ultimatum and feeling secure in my obedience, had blossomed into generosity itself. Suddenly the house was lovely, charming, and winsome in its decor—a true historic treasure. Lavender Island was beautiful. She was grateful I'd had a nice vacation.

While she gave her victory speech, I grew more and more withdrawn. All I knew was that I was not leaving Lavender Island with her. I needed to stay. More than that, I needed it to be my own decision. I was learning to stand on my own two feet, and I couldn't allow her to push me back down.

We strolled through the gardens for a bit, her arm in mine, before heading toward the courtyard that housed the ticket office. Lucas came from behind the carriage house as we passed from the gated fountain area into the bricked yard. I couldn't believe my eyes. It was not quite six o'clock, far too early for his day to be wrapping up. At least, I thought it was. He was still in one of his impeccably tailored suits. This one was black, which only enhanced his dark coloring, and drew attention to his lean, athletic build.

He was still too far away for talking, but relief surged through me, leaving my knees weak as our eyes met across the distance. I soaked him in, wishing he could give me some of his strength and wondering if I could talk him into spiriting me away on the back of that motorcycle of his.

"Oh," Mother breathed. "Who is that?" Even she was impressed with his looks and the way he carried himself.

"That's Mr. Halstead," I replied.

"Really?" Her tone grew thoughtful as she watched him move easily toward us. "The heir?" I nodded, and her raised lips told me she saw something there worth exploring.

"Mr. Halstead," I greeted in a cordial and distant tone before he could say anything, "may I introduce my mother, Mrs. Lillian Burke?"

He immediately understood me and showed no signs of our budding friendship. His smile was reserved. "Good evening," he said.

Mother's hand shot out to shake his, something she hadn't bothered to do with the rest of the staff. "What a divine property you have here," she said, the very definition of warmth and congeniality. I had the strange urge to cry.

"Thank you. I understand you've come to visit for a few days," Lucas replied.

"Yes, my dear Grace simply disappeared on me and came running down here. I had to come check up on her myself and make sure she hadn't gotten into any trouble." She laughed airily. "I truly hope she hasn't been a burden on you and your aunt."

Lucas's eyes met mine. That fierce look was back. He made no indication of what he was thinking, yet somehow I knew that he was debating on how best to respond to Mother, while not hurting me in the process. Gratitude and something sweet flooded from my head to my toes as his body shifted slightly toward mine. The eye contact lasted only a second, but my heart was pounding as he looked back to Mother.

"Grace has been an asset to Halstead House ever since her arrival. You've raised a remarkably kind, intelligent, and hard-working daughter." His voice was firm and low, defensive without giving offense. I wanted to throw myself into his arms and never let go.

"Well." Mother cleared her throat. "I'm grateful that she's carried herself well. I did my very best to instill those traits in her."

"I understand our families have been acquainted for years," Lucas remarked.

"Oh, yes, of course. Your Aunt Mary was the dearest friend of my mother-in-law. She was so gracious to step in as a substitute grandmother for Grace. We've all missed her since her passing." Mother's smile would have been convincing to someone who didn't know her well. Lucas nodded, while I struggled to keep my jaw from hitting the floor over the fact that Mother had actually referred to her as Mary rather than Mrs. Reed. She was up to something. "Grace and I are headed out to dinner. Would you care to join us?" Mother asked.

My startled eyes flew to his face, but his polite mask was on and he showed no sign of being as surprised as I was.

"That's a tempting invitation. However I don't want to get in the way of your reunion. It's up to you, Grace." He turned to me with a masterfully casual expression. He couldn't have possibly had any idea how deferring to me would be taken by my mother. Then again, perhaps he did.

I followed his lead and with great effort kept my eyes on him rather than looking for her reaction. I offered him a polite—if a little wobbly—smile of my own. "We'd be happy to have you join us, of course, but I know how busy your schedule is. Was there somewhere else you were expected tonight?"

"Not at all." He gestured back toward the garage. "After you, ladies."

I seriously considered asking Lucas to drive, as his car would serve to impress Mother further. However, he'd nudged me to take charge, and I wanted so desperately to do just that. So, I led the way to my rental sedan and unlocked the doors. Lucas politely opened the passenger door for Mother before settling himself in the back seat.

"What restaurant do you recommend, Mr. Halstead?" Mother asked when we were all seated.

I caught his look in the rear view mirror. "I'm sure Grace has already considered where to take you, and I'm happy to eat anywhere she chooses."

Mother flashed me an irritated look when I turned my head to start backing out of my stall. "Of course, I'm sure you're right," she said. "It's just that Grace has been quite busy settling in, working a new job, and . . . well, you must know that she's also been going on dates. I'm sure she hasn't had the time to completely plan out my visit," she replied.

Lucas said nothing, but our eyes met once again in the rear view mirror. I could tell he was caught off guard by the announcement I was dating, but I couldn't quite decipher how he felt about it. Either way, Lillian Burke was making an impression.

"Actually, Mother, I thought you might enjoy seeing some of the Historic District. There are some nicer restaurants there to choose from. It's a beautiful place." I pulled out and drove that direction.

Eventually we arrived and I parked. Her pinched face told me she wouldn't be happy with anything that was going to happen that night, and I prepared myself for the worst while wishing I could do the same for Lucas. As it was, he was in the frying pan now.

The food was too 'foreign'. The waitstaff was slow, and she couldn't understand their Southern accents. Rather than eating her food, she picked apart my life, Lavender Island, and even took a few digs at Lucas for still living at home.

The walk back to my car was tense. Mother was several feet ahead, marching along like a general, having given up on her campaign for the evening. Lucas walked next to me. His presence had been an incredible gift that evening. I felt horribly guilty for being grateful that he was there.

"I hesitate to ask if she was on her best behavior tonight or not," he said into the stillness.

A laugh burst out before I caught it back. "You're saying you think it's possible she could be worse?"

"All I can say for sure is that she's not to be underestimated."

The statement brought a smile to my face. "Believe it or not, when I'm doing the things she wants me to do she can be quite pleasant. Tonight was about delivering one shot after another to wear me down."

"I noticed. She brought some pretty heavy artillery to dinner." I made a sound of agreement. "Look, Grace, I'm sorry for not taking you more seriously when you were upset about her coming to town. I thought I knew the type of woman she was, and I've dealt with them before, but now I'm . . ." He seemed unable to finish the thought.

"Sometimes there are no words." I shrugged as he looked down at me for a moment.

Our eyes caught and something in his gaze looked different. It was as though he were actually looking at me. He wasn't just seeing blonde hair and a dove gray power suit, gray eyes, and stuffy heels. He was seeing inside of me. I felt vulnerable as he peeled back the layers.

"I'm an idiot," he finally said.

"Why?"

"For a lot of reasons, none of which we need to discuss right now." He quirked a smile at me, taking any possible sting out of his words, and looked straight ahead once more.

After another few steps he reached out and took my hand in his. I fought to keep from looking at him to see what he was thinking as he wrapped his fingers around my smaller ones. Heat flashed up my arm, and I swallowed hard as warm, gooey, confused happiness ran through my veins. Oh my gosh, this felt good.

"I feel awful that you had to come tonight, and . . ." I stuttered.

His hand squeezed, stopping my tongue-tied apology. "Don't. I could have easily gotten out of dinner if I had wanted to. I'm only sorry I wasn't around earlier. I tried to get home as fast as I could."

My eyes shot to him. "You did?"

A corner of his mouth lifted as he nodded. Well, that was kind of the nicest thing. I let it wrap me up and bring some heat into my chilled body as we strolled along, in no hurry to catch up with my temperamental parent. It was a mistake, but maybe for the smallest of seconds I pretended we were just another couple out for an evening.

Mother was still facing away from us when we neared the car, heavily committed to pouting. Lucas let go of my hand and moved ahead to help Mother in when I unlocked the doors. The drive to her hotel was frosty. I could tell she had a lot she wanted to say to me but was holding back because we weren't alone. Because that had stopped her from being an ogre the rest of the evening. Still, I appreciated the reprieve.

We pulled up to her hotel, and she opened the door, offering no goodbye, not even polite parting words to Lucas. I was getting out to walk her in, but she stopped me with a hand in the air.

"I am a perfectly capable adult. I will be in touch."

Lucas had opened his door to get out, and we sat with our doors wide open watching her disappear. When she was out of sight we turned to each other with identical smirks before we started laughing.

"You might as well move up front." I chuckled.

"You know that my life is crazy sometimes, right?" he asked when he'd entered the front passenger seat and closed his door. I nodded. "Nothing like this. This was a real treat."

"I'm expecting a strongly worded phone call in the morning."

The drive home was much less chilly. Lucas told me a little about his latest business efforts. I shared with him what I'd been up to around the house. It was so normal riding with him in the car—except for the part where he picked a piece of my hair up off my cheek and tucked it behind my ear. That part made my heart thump sweetly.

We rode up the elevator in silence for no other reason than that's what happens in elevators. He took off his tie and undid the top button of his shirt, rotating his neck and running his hands through his hair. I understood the feeling. When we stepped off we turned to face each other to say goodnight. His hair looked a little mussed. His eyes were relaxed and still held hints of amusement as he looked down the few inches between us.

My heart decided to occupy my throat as I thought about how many weeks we'd wasted not liking each other. I'd been so wrong about him. My palms felt sweaty in the hushed hallway. I was in serious trouble of forgetting my resolve and falling for John Lucas Halstead.

"Lucas?" I gulped. He tilted his head, his eyes questioning. "She was an absolute terror to everyone, but you were . . . I'll never . . . she always . . . but . . ." I shook my head, not liking the way the right words wouldn't come. "I'm messing it up."

He took a tiny step closer, and something instinctual inside of me reached for him without asking my brain permission. I closed the distance, raised up on my toes, and put my arms around his neck. The hug started out awkward, but he took over, putting both of his arms around me and turning the hug into something natural as he pulled me a little closer and turned his face toward mine, his beard lightly grazing my cheek.

He felt perfect. He smelled amazing. He'd come home early for me. Who was I kidding—I was already half in love with him. There were butterflies. Millions and millions of them, spreading like warm honey, making my heart beat slow and heavy. I felt overwhelmingly shy—and a little like I was about to pass out—so I started to pull away. His arms tightened around me when I shifted, and he turned his face a little more until I could feel his breath on my ear. We were both quiet for several heartbeats, until he released his hold and took a step back.

"I just wanted to thank you for everything." My voice shook, so I pressed my teeth into my lower lip to stop the flow of nervous words.

"I'm glad I could be there." A side of his mouth raised up, and he tucked his hands into his trouser pockets. "Goodnight, Grace," he said.

"'Night."

CHAPTER 16

M OTHER HAD BEEN IN TOWN FOR FIFTY-TWO AND A HALF GRUELING hours before I snapped. I sat on the bench next to the garden fountain after dropping her off at her hotel, devoid of the energy to make it back to my room. The air had turned full on muggy as the month of May took hold. It dampened my spirits as much as it did my light silk shirt. I could feel it sticking to my skin, but I didn't care enough to pull it back away. The discomfort barely registered at the moment.

What was I going to do? I wasn't sure I'd be able to fend off her strategic, offensive attack for the rest of her week-long visit. My friends had put up a good show, giving me words of encouragement and support, and Chef Lou had even baked me chocolate chip cookies two days in a row. I had thanked them by keeping Mother away from Halstead House. However, even with their support I felt lonelier and lonelier.

I hadn't truly realized it before—or perhaps I hadn't wanted to see it—but Mother was a pro at isolating me. She ate up my time, controlled my decisions, and generally kept me to herself. I was both horrified by the discovery and relieved. Relieved because it meant that perhaps *I* wasn't the only reason my life had been without friendships. Maybe, just maybe, there wasn't anything truly wrong with me other than an overbearing mother. I still wasn't sure what I was going to do with this new understanding, but it gave me courage to keep pressing on in the face of her displeasure.

I pulled my hair out of its chignon and ran my fingers over my scalp, loosening the strands before tilting my head back and letting them hang free. I was hoping to catch at least a little breeze to cool my head where it was aching. I hadn't done my hair so tightly in a while and . . .

Oh. My. Gosh. It hit me like a thundering train as I looked down at my pressed suit and the bobby pins I was still holding in my hands. I was back in uniform. I was wearing exactly what Mother had picked out for me. My hair and makeup were both done to her specifications. I had been loosening up and choosing my own style, and the moment she'd waltzed back in I'd stepped back into her mold. I'd meant to do it that first day, but I hadn't meant to slide fully back into my past self.

Anger, hot and dark, flooded me. My hands and feet felt numb as the blood pumped to my racing heart. How had I not seen it? Ana had seen it the moment I'd walked into Halstead House that first day, and she'd done her best to crack the Lillian shell and find the Grace beneath it. Yet, I'd picked the shell back up and closed myself in the moment Mother showed up. How ridiculous that I'd ever thought there was a wolf inside of me. No, there were just layers and layers of sheep.

If I hadn't known how ridiculous it would be to strip naked in the garden and cut up the suit with garden shears, I'd have done it. As it was, I kicked off my heels and chucked them over the garden wall into the street beyond. I hoped a car ran them over. No, I hoped that ten cars ran them over. The shoes were old and stodgy, and I was neither of those things anymore.

I ran my hands through my hair again. It had gotten a few inches longer in the two months I'd been away. I normally went to the salon every month on the same day and had my hair trimmed exactly one inch. Now I felt a scandalous joy over the fact it was two inches longer. No one would notice. Not one soul on earth would look at me and see anything different, and suddenly I just knew I had to do something that would show the world that I wasn't the same person I had been.

I was going to cut my hair short. Maybe a pixie cut. Or better yet, a pompadour, with the sides shaved and the top a different color. Now *that* would be something no one would overlook.

My eyes flew to the ticket office with one goal in mind: scissors. I jumped up and jogged toward the building. The bricks were warm on my feet as I reached the edge of the lawn and darted into the open courtyard area. The ticket office was dark and I knew it was probably locked, but I tried anyhow. The door didn't budge. I chewed my lip and looked around. I needed another option, and it couldn't be inside the big house where someone would try to talk me out of it.

The carriage house. I knew there was a section I hadn't been in, because I'd never seen Lucas's motorcycle when I'd been inside either the display portion or the garage portion. It was worth checking into. I tried the main door, but it was locked. Next I tramped around back to the garage portion. To my knowledge it was left unlocked, and I was giddy when the knob turned. The inside of the garage was dark, so I turned on my phone flashlight and weaved my way around the cars until I spotted the motorcycle in a back corner that I'd not noticed before. Disappointment over having found nothing helpful began to make my heart slow, but then I spotted a small door behind the motorcycle. I reached for the knob with shaking fingers and was thrilled to find it was unlocked too. How could I be so lucky?

I let myself in and blinked a few times to adjust to the darkness. Even with my phone it was hard to see. The room wasn't big, and there was only one small window up high. It looked to be an office of some sort, with a desk in the center of it. Perfect. Desks have scissors.

I risked flipping on the light and moved to the desk. The top was dusty and worn, and a cloud puffed up when I sat down on the chair, causing me to cough lightly as I waved a hand in the air in front of my face to clear it.

The drawers squeaked as I opened them one by one, searching for scissors. At this point I was pretty sure whatever scissors I found would be rusty, but it wasn't like I was going to cut food, or medical supplies, or my own skin. I was going to cut my hair. I could wash the rust and grime out of it afterwards.

Somewhere in the back of my mind I understood that I did not, in fact, want purple pompadour hair. Nor did I want to cut it myself in the dusty forgotten office of the Halstead House carriage house. I did, actually, care that my hair would be rusty and disgusting, and knew that I'd probably cry as I watched it fall to the floor.

Still, I pressed on, because I also understood that I couldn't go back. I couldn't be the power-suit-wearing, chignon master anymore. I needed to be Grace. It was essential to discover who she was and then let her breathe a little. It had been easy to play New Grace when Mother was far away in Providence, but now was the true test and I needed to prove that I could be myself anywhere and around anyone.

At last, I struck gold, or rust, as the case may be. Scissors, browned and dull, appeared in the next drawer I opened. I pulled them up and held them at eye level, as though I really had unearthed something precious. I turned them this way and that, like Gollum with his ring, staring intently and letting the flickering office light strike off them as I thought about where to make the first cut.

"You look like you're expecting those scissors to answer life's great questions," a familiar voice interrupted from the darkness outside of the office doorway.

The scissors clattered to the desk as I let out a shriek. "Do not sneak up on a person who is holding scissors," I said more sternly than I'd meant to.

Lucas entered the room. "As your friend, it's okay to tell me if you have a scissor fetish. Do you collect them? That pair looks pretty antique." His lips smiled, but his eyes were watching me carefully.

"I'm going to cut my hair," I stated as I picked the scissors back up off the desk.

"With those?"

"Why not?"

"They've got to be completely dull." He came closer to the desk, and his cologne came with him. I nearly closed my eyes in pleasure as the smell reached me.

"Still . . ."

"Still what?"

"I'm going to cut my hair."

He nodded and leaned casually against the desk, as though this was a sane conversation. "What look are you going for?"

"A pompadour." I looked back down at the scissors and put my fingers through the holes. I tried to open and close them a few times, but it took effort. They were old.

"Sorry, but I'm not sure what that style is."

I didn't look up but kept working the scissors. Open, shut, open, shut. "It's where the sides of your hair are cut really close, almost shaved, but the top is still there. Kind of like a mohawk, but not spiked." I finally glanced up at him, and he shook his head like he didn't quite understand. "You'll see soon enough."

"You're doing this yourself?" Rather than answer I lifted the scissors in the air and wiggled them around. He nodded. "Do you need a mirror?"

I chewed my lip. "That would probably be a good idea. Is there one out here somewhere?"

"I'm afraid not. Unless you think a rear view mirror would do the trick."

I went back to looking at the scissors. The anger was wearing off a bit but not quite enough to make me put them away. "It might."

"Well, then, follow me." He stood and gestured for me to join him in the garage. I stood and followed. My feet were still bare, and they slapped lightly on the garage floor as I caught up to him. "No shoes?" he asked when I'd come to stand next to him.

"I threw them into traffic." I shrugged.

He nodded again and exited the office. A light flipped on with a switch I hadn't noticed, and we stood shoulder to shoulder for a moment while he looked around.

"I'm trying to decide which car will be the easiest to get hair out of," he said after a moment. "I guess it's only fair that we use mine, since I did make the offer. It wouldn't be very fair to use Eliza's when she isn't here to defend herself."

I said nothing as he guided us to his car and opened the passenger door for me. I climbed in and popped down the visor as he walked around. The mirror was lighted, as I had suspected it would be, and I angled it to see myself better.

Lucas entered the driver's side of the car and closed the door. "Can you see all right?"

I could see. I could see the desperation, fear, and anger in my eyes. I could see the flushed cheeks, the lips red from my chewing, and the tears begging to fall. I could see everything happening inside of me. I didn't want to see any of it.

I held up a piece of my hair and looked at it for a long moment. Lucas was silent, letting me fight the battle myself even though I was sure he had opinions about what he'd stumbled into. I was grateful. He knew that I was tired of people running my life. Lucas was a man of action, a man used to controlling things, and yet he sat in silence and let me be.

It was probably the kindest thing he could have done, talking to me like this situation was normal, walking me to the car and helping me get all settled to chop my hair off. The tears escaped as a sob forced its way out on the sound of brittle laughter.

"This has to be the stupidest thing you've ever seen," I said in a strangled voice as I turned to him.

He shook his head. "Nah. I've seen worse."

I laughed, releasing more tears, and sniffled. "I would look terrible in a purple pompadour."

"Purple?" His eyes grew wide for the first time since he'd walked in on me. "This is the first I've heard of purple."

"It would have made a statement." I tried to form my wobbling lips into a smile, but all I did was grimace.

"No doubt."

I handed him the scissors and closed the visor mirror. I thought I heard him sigh softly, the sound of someone who'd been practically holding their breath, as he took the scissors and set them out of the way.

"I hate who I am around my mother," I said. And then I was crying. Really crying.

A lot of people say they can't remember the last time they truly cried, but I could because it happened so rarely. It had been the day I'd gotten the call that Mary had been laid to rest. Her body had been sent back to her beloved Lavender Island, and I hadn't been able—okay, allowed—to attend. I had kept a stiff upper lip about it, pretending to understand my mother's dictates, but when I'd been alone I had sobbed out my broken heart.

Lucas reached across the console and took my hand in his. His larger hand enveloped mine as his thumb caressed my knuckles. I ducked my head, embarrassed for him to see my tears, and clung harder to his hand.

"I'm so sorry," he said. It was enough. What else was there to say, anyhow?

I allowed myself to release the emotions for a few more minutes, all the while loving the feeling of my hand in Lucas's and the comfort it brought.

I wasn't sure how much time passed, but when the tears wound up I was left feeling gutted, raw and exposed, and absolutely exhausted. I dried my eyes on my sleeve—like a child—and finally dared to look up at Lucas. I felt my cheeks warm as we made eye contact.

"So, having me as a friend might be more than you bargained for," I said in a still unsteady voice.

He smiled and reached over to push a stray hair way from my face, and every single nerve in my body stood on alert. "It might be fun to have a friend with purple hair. It would lend me some street cred."

I blinked a few more times and then started laughing, hard, my head leaned back against the seat, shoulders shaking. After a few moments I looked over to him. He was grinning, happy to see me smiling. He lifted our still entwined hands to his lips and kissed the back of my hand. My laughter stopped abruptly, replaced by the most glorious sensation.

"Do you want to talk about it?" he asked, dropping our hands back to my lap.

Did I? I wasn't sure. I wasn't used to being open, and it felt like a really heavy thing to start out with. Figuring out that my mother had been more abusive than I'd understood was something I needed more time to process.

"I don't think I can yet," I responded.

He nodded his acceptance. "Fair enough. Can I trust you around scissors?" I rolled my eyes, but my head bobbed. "Good."

He let go of my hand and we exited the car. The sound of my bare feet against the garage floor made him look down as I walked around the back of the car to where he was standing.

"You really threw your shoes into the road?" he asked, his eyes amused.

"I hate them," I stated with a shrug.

"Is that considered littering?"

"Probably."

He held the door for me and waited until I'd walked through before following and closing it behind us. Before I could take more than a few steps, he snagged my hand again and turned me to face him. I didn't have long enough to ask what was happening before I was pulled up against him and wrapped in a hug.

My arms worked their way around his waist, and I pressed my cheek against his chest. I was surrounded, cocooned in his embrace, safe and sound.

"Hugs have magical powers," he said against my hair. I grinned, even though he couldn't see me. I'd never have guessed he had a silly side, and I loved it. "It seemed like you might need a little magic tonight."

I wasn't about to argue with that logic. Nope, not one little bit.

* * *

I made it through Sunday and Monday with my mother, thanks to Lucas's support. Simply knowing someone cared about what I was going through made a big difference in my ability to handle it.

Thanks to my shedding off of old thoughts, I saw her actions with new eyes. It was a long two days. It was a heart-wrenching two days. Those days confirmed my feelings that it was time to find a way to move permanently out of Mother's control and search out my own path. Still, we were each other's only family, and while I no longer wanted to be a puppet, I wanted some sort of healthier relationship. But figuring out what that was would take time.

Tuesday morning was bright, warm, and hazy as most mornings were on the island. I was supposed to pick Mother up at ten for brunch before she would return to Halstead House with me. I had successfully kept her away since her first tour on Thursday, but she wasn't taking any more of that. I needed to begin setup for the fiftieth wedding anniversary party that would be happening the following evening and figured Mother could be of use in that area. It also meant I wouldn't have to find ways to entertain her. Mother may be severe in some ways, but she had impeccable taste and an eye for detail.

But, before I picked her up, there was something I had to do. And I needed Ana's help. I'd been thinking a lot about my hair and my style, and I wanted to make a change. Now that my sanity had reappeared, I wasn't going for a purple pompadour, but I did want to get my hair done. I found Ana eating her breakfast, and I hustled to sit next to her.

"I need a haircut."

She swallowed and looked over to me. "Okaaay . . ."

"Now. This morning. Before I pick up my mother for brunch. You know everyone there is to know on the island."

"I am a handy person to have around." Ana's eyes crinkled in amusement.

"Will you help me or not? It's time to take that last plunge. I hate my chignons and everything they represent. I want to do something that fits who I really am."

Ana kept chewing, but her gaze wandered over my face for a few seconds before she swallowed and replied, "Are you serious about this?"

"Yes. I am."

"I never thought I'd see the day."

"You're seeing it right now. It's staring you in the face and begging you for one of your super island local contact things."

"What did you have in mind? Just cut, or cut and color?"

I chewed on my lip. While it was tempting to do something drastic, I also knew that there was nothing wrong with taking small steps to my new self.

"Just cut."

"Okay. Meet me at my car in fifteen minutes. My friend Gwen owes me."

I smiled, letting it fill my face. "Perfect. Thanks, Ana." I squealed as I leaned over to give her a hug. "I can't wait." Before she could answer I raced out of the room.

I beat Ana to her car, and she was smiling as she strolled up to me. We got in the car and zipped out of the parking lot. This time I laughed at her horrible driving. It was so Ana, and so Lavender Island, and so freeing to let go of the door handle.

"Are you okay?" Ana asked.

"Never better."

"You seem to be having a breakdown," she replied.

"What you are seeing is the crumbling of an old life."

Her brows furrowed as she glanced back ahead to the traffic. "Is that a good thing?"

"Yes. I think so. Now I rise from my cocoon." I'd purposely said the last part in an overly cheery tone while lifting my hands skyward, and it paid off as Ana snorted.

"The beautiful butterfly?"

"Obviously."

She parked her car in front of a tiny salon and shut off the engine. "Well, come on out, Miss Monarch. Let's see what Gwen can do with that mop on your head."

Gwen chopped my shoulder-length hair to a chin-length bob with fringe bangs that swept across my forehead. Then she added a few waves to it and turned me to face the mirror. I was amazed. The cut really flattered my features. Instead of my eyes and mouth looking so disproportionately large, they fit. Until that moment I hadn't really comprehended that by pulling my hair back every day I was making my features look bigger than they actually were. I still looked professional, but in a stylish and relaxed way.

"You look amazing," Ana said as she stood next to me and fingered a piece of hair. "I'm glad you had your breakdown, because this is so much more you than the old you was."

I cleared my throat and nodded in agreement. "Thank you so much, Gwen." I turned to the friend of Ana's who had welcomed us in and cut my hair on the spot.

She patted my shoulder and gave me a smile. "It's a pleasure to help out a girl who needs a big change."

I insisted on paying even though Ana said there was an *understanding* between the two women. The only understanding I had was that I paid for services received. They could keep their deal between the two of them.

The entire drive back to Halstead I was in a reflective zone. I kept reaching up and playing with the choppy pieces of hair that tickled my chin. This haircut made me feel more different than I'd felt over Ana making me change up my wardrobe. I wouldn't be able to pull this short hair back, even if I wanted to. It was almost silly that this small tweak felt so enormous.

I thanked Ana again before we went our separate ways, her to her office and me upstairs to change and get ready to pick up Mother. It was going to be close, but I'd make it.

I decided to wear shorts and a sleeveless, flowy shirt to brunch with Mother. Not only would it send a subtle statement to her, but it was a beautiful island day, and afterwards we'd be working hard in the house.

As I was hustling through the garden to get to my parking space I ran into Lucas coming from the garage. He was in his motorcycle gear, and the attraction I felt for him caused me to miss a step. I stumbled to a stop. I hadn't seen him since Saturday night, and I wasn't sure how things would be between us, but I'd give anything to have his arms around me again.

"Hey." A side of his mouth quirked up as he came to a stop near me.

"You're home and you're not in a suit," I blurted.

"Can't sneak anything past you." He chuckled.

I immediately blushed and wished the ground would swallow me up. Of course, I knew that his job didn't stick to the normal nine-to-five routine and dress code. He'd most likely been at some breakfast or something and was returning home to change for his next round.

"Stating the obvious is one of the services I provide as a good employee." I smiled and was grateful when he returned the look.

He reached out and took a piece of my hair between his fingers. "I thought I could trust you around scissors."

"It wasn't me. Ana's friend cut and styled it."

"It's not purple."

"Baby steps."

"So, should I consider myself warned that it may be purple at some point?"

I tried to casually shrug, but the way his eyes were roaming over my face and hair was making me feel out of breath. "Who knows. I'm a butterfly coming out of her cocoon." I attempted to joke like I'd done with Ana.

"I won't argue with that." He took a step closer and to the side, as though he was going to pass me and carry on into the house, but he surprised me by pausing for a second and reaching out to take my hand. "I can't wait to see what happens next in the evolution of Grace Burke." He grinned as he squeezed my hand. Then he gently tugged me toward him and placed a light-as-air kiss on my temple before whispering, "The new style suits you."

I managed a smile, my hand tingling and my feet trying to float to the sky. A few more of those moments and the new Grace Burke's heart was going to find itself in even more trouble than it already was.

CHAPTER 17

You know how when you're watching one of those documentaries about mountain goats and you think to yourself, "How does that big furry goat not topple right off the mountain?" Well, I was that goat, and Mother was an earthquake about to send the mountain plunging into the sea.

It was the day of the fiftieth wedding anniversary dinner. Guests would begin arriving in two hours. Marshall, who had finished his portion of the setup the night before, had skedaddled. Ana was making herself scarce in the housekeeping room with her office door closed. Closed! Ana's door was never, ever, ever closed. Chef Lou, who was now speaking in his American accent at all times, had sent catering staff to ask me any questions rather than ask me himself. Worst of all, ten minutes ago Lucas had come down the main staircase and into the dining room where we were working, taken in the scene, raised his eyebrows at me, and gone back to wherever he'd come from, which had left me feeling irrationally irritated.

My plan to keep Mother busy helping me decorate had flopped spectacularly. She'd succeeded only at scaring everyone else away, and now I was wound tight as a spring, ready to snap at any moment.

Tomorrow, I told myself for the millionth time, *tomorrow she goes back to Providence.* I was going to have my work cut out for me apologizing to every person who lived and worked in Halstead House. I was only hoping that list would still include me.

The tables were dressed, and we were working on final decor around the ballroom where there would be dancing after dinner. Eliza and the couple celebrating had met several months before and decided on colors, floral arrangements, and music. All I needed to do was execute the detailed plan I'd been left.

Oh, how I missed Eliza. I was expecting her home any time, but I would have given anything for her to be here now. Then again, I couldn't picture her and Mother working together in any way, so perhaps it was for the best. I didn't need a blizzard on top of everything else.

"Imagine choosing magnolias for your main flower," Mother scoffed as she passed by a large arrangement on the side table.

"I think they're lovely," I replied, head down, looking over my notes.

"Of course you do. You also thought this new haircut of yours would be lovely . . ." she trailed off, letting me remember her heated words from the day before, when she'd come out of her hotel room to discover this "strange hippie island girl" standing there in place of her daughter.

I had watched in silence as her lips had pursed and she'd run her gaze over me. She'd wanted to know what on earth had possessed me to do something so unflattering to my face shape. Then she'd wanted to know how I expected myself to be taken seriously as a professional woman when I looked so interchangeable with all the other young women in the world.

I hadn't raised to the bait then, and I didn't now. She disappeared into the dining room to retrieve another arrangement that would be added in the ballroom. I could hear her grumbling under her breath, but I didn't care to know what she was saying.

"How are the lovely Burke women today?" Lucas reappeared just as Mother entered the room, her arm full of flowers.

He'd changed out of his suit and was wearing shorts and a t-shirt, his feet in sandals. He looked like a life preserver, and I took back everything I'd thought about him just minutes ago.

"We're just fine, I'm sure," Mother replied with a stiff smile. She'd long ago given up on schmoozing him.

"What can I do to help?" he asked me.

Surprise stole my thoughts, and Mother replied before I had a chance to. "Well, I suppose since you're here you could carry those two large floor arrangements into the ballroom and place them on either side of the doorway," she said. "They're too heavy for me, and Grace is more intent on checking her lists than on actually doing the work."

Lucas shot a look at me and opened his mouth to reply, but I shook my head, letting him know it was pointless. His polite public mask slid into place as he nodded to my mother and walked toward the far side of the dining room, where the florist had left them.

I understood something in that moment. That mask was his armor. A short two weeks ago when we'd decided to be friends he'd said we had more in common that we'd realized. At the time I hadn't totally understood, but now a little part of me did. We both dealt with difficulties in life, and we both had our coping strategies. I was just so grateful to know Lucas without the mask.

"Who chose these arrangements?" Mother asked after a moment.

"Eliza did," I replied.

"I question her taste," she harrumphed.

"I don't believe it's good manners to badmouth the lady of the house," Lucas said as he passed through the room, his arms wrapped around a huge pot full of flowers and greenery. His tone said he was teasing, but his eyes told a different story.

"I'm sure you're right. Still, these are definitely not something I would have chosen," Mother said.

I put the list down on a table and moved to face her. "It's not your party, though, Mother. The couple celebrating worked with Eliza to make the choices. Our job is to facilitate what the customers want, not the other way around." Yeah. Take that. Verbal jujitsu for the win. From my victory stand I couldn't resist adding with a saucy chuckle, "Be glad you weren't here for the fuchsia and rust wedding."

Mother's entire face was pinched with displeasure. "You're right. I wasn't here, because I was back in Providence worrying over my wayward daughter and where she'd gotten off to."

Oops. Fatal miscalculation.

Lucas left the room again to get the second large floor piece. Our eyes caught, and he offered me a nod of encouragement. I took a deep breath and nodded back. I wasn't in this alone. Lucas had come back down and was braving the firestorm. I only hoped he wasn't a casualty of the war.

"I'm returning to Providence tomorrow, you remember?" Mother's voice pulled me back into the ring.

"Yes, I remember."

"When we finish here, the two of us need to get a start on packing your things."

Even though I knew her plan all along had been for me to return with her, this was the first time she'd said the words out loud since the day she'd arrived. Ice crawled from the top of my head down to my feet, freezing me in place.

"What?" I asked through numb lips.

"We need to get you packed. I've purchased us seats together on the return flight first thing in the morning."

My silence alerted her, and her head lifted from where she'd been fidgeting with the flowers. Lucas had entered the room to catch the last part, and I met his eyes over Mother's head. He set down the large pot and gave me a puzzled look.

I took a deep breath and clasped my hands together in front of me. "I'm not going back to Providence with you tomorrow, Mother," I said, although I'd have liked it if my voice had sounded more sure.

"Pish, of course you are. That was the understanding all along." Mother laughed, a brittle and hollow sound that I didn't hear often.

"I don't plan to leave for another few weeks."

"You've been here two months already. What difference will another make?"

"It might make all the difference in the world, to me." I whispered the words, terrified to say them out loud, but knowing I had to.

"Yes, well, thank you for reminding me that this is all about you. Forget poor widowed Lillian back in Providence. Forget all the sleepless nights, worry, prayer, time, and money I've spent trying to do my best for you," Mother whined. "You're my only friend, my treasured daughter."

"I'm sure Grace is grateful for all you've done for her . . ." Lucas stepped past her to come stand by my side, and our shoulders brushed.

"Are you a father, Mr. Halstead, and I'm unaware of it?" Mother interrupted. "Obviously not."

His jaw clenched.

"Then you have nothing of value to add to this discussion. This is between a parent and her rebellious child," she stated.

Lucas and I both spoke at the same time.

"I'm not rebellious for wanting to make a choice for myself," I said.

"Grace is old enough to decide what she wants to do," he stated.

Mother turned a hateful glare on Lucas, obviously seeing him as the bigger threat, and I felt him stiffen at my side. "So now you're an expert on my daughter? I don't think so. You need to stay out of this conversation and away from Grace."

"Do I need to remind you that you are in my home where Grace is both my friend and employee?" Lucas seemed to grow three inches in that moment. "You have no say in who I speak to or spend my time with."

Mother met him with silence, her eyes appraising. I could see the wheels turning in her mind, trying to figure out what angle to work, where to poke and prod, what would make him see her side of things.

I didn't give her the chance. "I'm staying, Mother."

She seemed hesitant to look away from Lucas, but she finally turned to me. "Against my wishes?" I chewed on my lip and nodded. "I'd like to know why."

"She doesn't owe you any explanation," Lucas, still in giant mode, stated firmly.

"It's okay, Lucas, really, I . . ." My throat was unexpectedly dry and I had to swallow.

His hand found its way to mine, the backs of our fingers tangling lightly, but not quite gripping. Courage like liquid fire chased up my spine, almost as though he'd given me a portion of strength to stay the course. I looked up to him, my mouth relaxing into a soft smile as our eyes met.

"Oh." Mother's face transformed from cold disdain to mocking humor. "You've set your cap for the Halstead heir. You think that he'll take you and make all your fantasies come true. You'll get to live in the fairy tale castle that Mary told you all about." She laughed, but it was without amusement. "Darling girl, you're a fool to think that a worldly man like him will be interested in ever settling down. I've protected you your entire life, and I can't stand by and watch you be hurt this way."

Mother had blown a hole right to the tender spot in the center of me. Of course I hadn't come down to Lavender Island to seek out Lucas and try to live out my wildest dreams. He hadn't even been on the list of reasons for me to run away. But he didn't know that. He had no idea why I'd come. Her words made sense in the most bizarre way, and I was terrified that he'd believe them.

Mother pressed on. "Look around you, Grace, there's no place for you here. They gave you a small job as an assistant so that you could feel useful and so that they could honor Mary somehow. That's all. As soon as you leave, things will return to normal and they won't miss you one little bit."

Lucas tensed next to me and I knew he was preparing to say something, but I didn't want that. I wanted to say it for myself, from my own place of self-worth.

"That's not true." I shoved the words through the lump forming in my throat. "They've become my friends."

"They aren't your friends." She laughed again, a scratchy sound that made my ears hurt.

Lucas had had enough. His hand moved from near mine to rest on the small of my back, and I so wanted to lean into his side and let him hold me up. "I'm having a hard time understanding how a mother can speak to her daughter this way. Grace is welcome here for as long as she'd like to stay." His voice sounded different, and I looked up at his face. Gone was the polite mask, and in its place was something fierce and almost primal. "You've insulted this entire household at this point. I should ask you to leave."

His hand reached further to my waist, pulling me against his side, his grip strong as he seemed to hear my thoughts. He couldn't have realized that he was literally holding me upright. My legs were rubber. I hated confrontation. I hated the words spilling around us and the anxiety they brought.

"Please, Mother," I pled, "let's drop this and finish our work here. You and I can talk later when we've settled down."

"There's nothing to discuss. If you won't come home, and Mr. Halstead has asked me to leave his home, what else is there to say?" She raised her chin a notch. "It hasn't been easy spending my life protecting you from your stubborn and difficult ways, but now you'll have to live with the consequences."

"I've always done my best to please you," I replied.

I was surprised to feel stung again. I should have been horrified past feeling. Yet instead of feeling the heat of anger, I felt so wooden in that moment that I may as well have grown roots out of my feet. I opened my mouth to say more, defend myself, but words were trapped. My hair tickled my chin and I almost laughed. I had a small glimpse into what Mother must be seeing. My short hair, my shorts and button-free shirt, my sandals, my nearly makeup free face. She thought that all she'd molded was coming undone. If I'd been in a more forgiving state I may have felt sorry for her. As things stood, though, I couldn't.

"I'm sorry, Mother," I managed at last.

"Then come with me! None of this is real life, Grace. None of it!" Mother's voice raised a notch. "This is all an illusion. Our life in Providence, that's real. My love for you, that's real."

Her words caused a conflicting swirl of emotion. I knew that she loved me, but her love was hard to bear and difficult to understand. It wasn't the kind of love that bred trust and closeness. It was a suffocating, devastating love, and I couldn't go back to that frigid place quite yet.

When I did nothing but blink a few times, Lucas gave my side a squeeze and stepped in. "Mrs. Burke, no one is saying you don't love your daughter, or that you're wrong to want to keep her safe. However, this conversation is going nowhere, and she is working right now. Perhaps you really should leave." Lucas's voice, no matter how firm and controlled, no matter how reasonable and polite his words, left nothing to the imagination as far as what he felt for Mother.

I turned agonized eyes to him as humiliation washed over me. How embarrassing to have this family meltdown in front of him. He had promised I wouldn't have to face my mother alone, and I was torn between gratitude for him keeping his word and horror over the airing of our private business in front of someone I was coming to care about. Things had spiraled so far out of control that I didn't know what I wanted to do.

"I just need a second to think," I pleaded with them both.

Lucas's nostrils flared as he sucked in a big breath, but he kept his mouth closed and gave a succinct nod. I pulled my lower lip under my teeth and looked back at Mother. I was completely unprepared for this situation. I had no idea what to say or how to deal with it.

"Well?" Mother said through a clenched jaw.

"I think you should leave the ballroom, but . . ." Before I could tell her I meant for her to return to my room and I'd meet her there to discuss things, she cut me off. Again.

"Are you truly going to send your own mother away?"

"No, but I might." A new voice joined us from the doorway and we all swung around.

It was Eliza, and she looked like an avenging angel. Her eyes were alight with something I'd never seen as she walked over to our battling trio.

"Hello, Eliza." Mother's entire body language changed into polite warmth. It was an astonishing transformation.

"Lillian," Eliza returned.

My heart rate slogged back to life. "You've met?" I blurted out. The two women nodded.

"Years ago," Mother replied.

"Yes, it's been quite a while," Eliza agreed. She turned to Lucas and me, her eyes not missing the fact that his arm was wrapped around me. "I expected to come home to the happy house I left, but I see that's not the case. Nonetheless, I'm so glad to see you both."

She came to Lucas and gave him a kiss on the cheek. He released me as he hugged his aunt, and I felt the loss. Next she came to me with a brief kiss and hug as well. She said nothing, but the comfort flowed into me anyhow.

She stepped away from Lucas and me and turned to take all three of us in. "I'd ask what's going on, but I think I heard enough from the doorway to guess. Lillian, it sounds to me like your daughter would like to stay on here for the rest of her sabbatical. Let me ease your mind by telling you we'd love to have her. Grace plays an important role here and has fit in seamlessly. You can take comfort in knowing you've raised a very capable, friendly, and kind daughter. She's been my right hand these past months, and when *she* decides to return home she'll be missed."

"This trip was never discussed with me," Mother couldn't help but interject.

"As Grace is twenty-five, I never thought to ask if she'd received her mother's permission," Eliza responded. Lucas coughed, and for the first time in a few days I felt like smiling myself.

Mother's eyes narrowed. "I believe this is something Grace and I should discuss in private."

Lucas's demeanor went back to cold and commanding. "You expect us to just let you take her off somewhere to . . . "

Before he could say any more, I tugged on his arm. "Lucas, you have to let me handle this," I said softly.

He grabbed my hand and pulled me a few steps away. "She's . . . well . . . she's the worst and I don't want you to have to be alone with her," he replied with an intensity I'd never experienced from him before.

He was bossy, flustered, and stubborn, and he made my head feel like it was disconnecting from my body. I was seriously twitterpated with Lucas Halstead. The thought caused a corner of my mouth to tug up.

He must have seen something in my gaze, because his became more alert and he leaned toward me, his voice dropping to a near whisper. "I know you don't want someone managing your life, and I know you can decide what's best for you, but if she makes you cry, I'm going to push her down the front stairs."

"Without a safety mat at the bottom?" I asked as my heart rate increased at the look in his eyes.

"You'd better believe it," he replied.

Then he did the most amazing, unimaginable thing. He put a large, warm hand on the side of my neck, and pulled my face to his, pressing his lips to my forehead. He didn't linger, but the contact between us was electric. As brief as the kiss was, I could feel the emotion behind it, and a wave of some magic feeling flowed through me as he pulled away and walked out of the room.

I straightened back up, my cheeks blazing, as I turned to Mother and Eliza. Mother's glare was icy. If looks could kill, I'd be toast. Eliza's, however, was delighted. Ooh, boy, that was another conversation I'd be having soon.

"Mother, let's go up to my room and sort this all out," I said.

She nodded and we moved together to the doorway leaving the ballroom.

"Oh, and Lillian, a quick word?" Eliza called, causing us to pause and turn to face her. "I'm home now and I'd appreciate it if you'd be sure to treat my household with courtesy. That includes your daughter."

Mother's jaw clenched, but she simply nodded and we continued on our way. Eliza was home and Lucas had my back. That kiss, though not the first one he'd given me, had gifted me something to hold on to as I made my way upstairs to face the dragon lady head to head.

* * *

Sheer grit and determination had helped me get through the rest of that afternoon and evening. Happily, the anniversary party had gone off without a hitch and been efficiently cleaned up. It was late now, after ten. Mother had been gone for hours, and in spite of knowing I wouldn't see her again for a little while, I still felt the pull of our mother-daughter bond in my hollowed-out heartbeats. I'd spent the past thirty minutes attempting to decipher the thread that still tied us together, and figure out how to get the knots out without severing it completely. I didn't know if such a thing was possible. I couldn't imagine life without my mother, but I could no longer imagine life going back to how it had always been.

Interlaced with my thoughts about Mother was the continued shock over Lucas standing with me, putting his arm around me, kissing me in front of the others. While it was something I'd recently started wishing for, it was definitely not something I'd seen coming. Oh, I understood that on the relationship scale a forehead kiss wasn't anything to hang your heart on, but I also understood that there had been genuine emotion behind the gesture. I couldn't make sense of it, and it only added to my whirling mind.

I was bone weary, yet knew sleep wouldn't come easily that night. I was flopped on my bed, staring sightlessly at the ceiling, still wearing my business clothing when the knock came.

My gaze focused and I noticed for the first time since entering my room that I hadn't turned on a light. I didn't bother to now and used moonlight to navigate to the door.

"Hey." Lucas filled up the doorway, his face in a shadow with the light from the hallway creeping past his shoulders.

"Hey," I replied, both happy and mystified to see him there.

"You up for a walk on the beach?" he asked.

I wasn't expecting that request, but it immediately sounded like exactly what I needed. "Let me change."

"I'll meet you at the top of the stairs." He gracefully moved out of the doorway and down the hall.

I shut the door and flicked on the lights. I didn't give much thought to what I'd wear or how I'd look. Tank top, shorts, flip flops. Ana would be proud of how casual I looked tonight and how little I'd thought about it.

Lucas leaned against the banister at the top of the stairs, dressed in similar attire, when I emerged from my room. I loved that he had so many different versions of himself, while still remaining true to who he was. He could be a beach bum, a biker, or a businessman, and it didn't take away from him in any way. I hoped to find a way to embrace my own variances.

He said nothing when I reached him, just held out a hand for me to take. I enjoyed the way our hands fit together, our fingers weaving and holding tight as we descended the stairs. I didn't have a lot of experience, but I didn't think friends held hands as much as Lucas and I did lately. I wasn't about to voice the thought. I wanted my hand in his.

We went out the side door and turned to the back of the house, making our way through the manicured gardens, to the seawall, down the stairs, through the marshy grass, and to the groomed sand. We didn't speak a word, and it occurred to me that I felt at ease with him. It was a bright spot in an otherwise upsetting day.

We kicked off our shoes as we stepped onto the sand. The sand felt cool under my feet, and I wiggled my toes, letting the coarseness rub between them. Lucas took hold of my hand again, and we started walking in the direction I'd walked the night I'd cut my foot. The memory of that night, trying to avoid Lucas and stepping on glass, made me grin to myself. We'd come a long way.

"Interesting day." His voice interrupted my musings.

I made a sound of amusement. "You could say that."

"How did things go with your mother? I didn't get any requests to launch bodies down the front stairs."

"It was . . ." I sighed. "To borrow your word, interesting."

"I'd like to hear about it."

I took a deep breath and worried my lip. It would be good to share but also painful, and I'd never shared with another person the details of my life this way. "Okay." I nodded at last.

I began speaking, and somehow it felt as though I was reliving the experience by watching it play out on a movie screen. The sounds of the beach faded, and I was back in my third-story room.

Our walk up the stairs from the ballroom had been frosty and heavy with expectation. The best way I could describe it would be like a roller coaster. Our life together as mother and daughter had been the long, slow, steep climb to the top, and the drop was looming ahead of us.

Mother had seated herself immediately on my bed and looked at me, inviting me to open the discussion. I'd faltered for a few moments, opening my mouth only to close it again, before finally saying the thing I'd always needed to stay and had never been able to.

"I feel like I'm living a life that was created for me, and it doesn't fit." I'd sat down hard on the window seat and dared to look to Mother to see how she was taking this.

"Success, security, a devoted parent, a good job, a nice home . . . yes, I can see how those things would be so uncomfortable," she'd replied sarcastically.

I'd taken a breath and looked out the window. I couldn't allow the swelling importance of this discussion to flip into emotional warfare.

I had to practice what I'd learned as a child and keep my emotions at bay. I'd gazed back at her after a few calming breaths, and my heart had pinched. She was aging. Her dark hair was becoming grayer. The lines around her lips had deepened. Mother had always been thin, with the sharpness of her personality mirrored in the sharpness of her body, and as she aged she seemed to grow even more so.

"I do appreciate all you've done for me." It was the first time, perhaps, that I'd said those practiced words and realized that I meant them. I did have a good life. While I'd been pressured into many of my choices, I'd avoided potholes in life and had landed in a stable place. "However," I said as she opened her mouth, "there comes a time when a child becomes an adult and flies the nest. I've never had that chance."

Mother had scoffed. "You talk as though I've smothered and mistreated you."

"Smothered, yes. Mistreated, well, that's harder to explain."

Her eyes had grown round before turning into slits. "How dare you accuse me of mistreating you. Was it mistreatment when I cared for you, paid for all your needs, saw to it that you had an education?" Mother had played deep, and I had expected nothing less.

"There are different ways to mistreat a person." My voice had begun wobbling, and I'd cleared my throat and swallowed hard. "Physically I have always been treated well. Mentally and emotionally, well, that's a different story, Mother." I'd cleared my throat again, feeling exposed and terrified to be verbally expressing things I'd only recently begun to openly think. "It isn't natural to control every aspect of your child's life, or to make her feel as though she'll never have your approval if she makes her own decisions." Then, I'd dropped what I saw as the biggest bomb of them all, the most well protected center of my existence. "I've always felt that your love for me is conditional on my behavior. That you'll only love me if I do what you say."

Her eyes had rolled and she'd pinched her lips. "Do you think you're the first daughter to have her life dictated by the adults around her? Do you think my parents allowed me to live wild and free, chasing after every whim? Of course not. I've been a good mother to you, leading you with my experience and loving you much more than I was ever loved. My parents would see my indulgences of you as a failure."

Instead of immediately responding, I'd watched a fleeting vulnerability flit across her face as she'd looked toward the wall. It was the first I'd heard of her upbringing. I'd never known my maternal grandparents. She'd never spoken of them. Now, instead of seeing the control and manipulation as a trait of hers, I was seeing it as a cycle handed down in our family. I didn't know how long it had been happening, but I did know it needed to end. Apparently, that part would be in my hands.

"I need to direct my own life from this point forward," I'd stated when she finally looked back to me.

"You will fail." Her words had left me feeling flayed alive.

"I've been given good instruction, as you yourself said. I'm asking you to trust me to take it from here."

"So far you've given me no reason to trust you. The first decision you've made for yourself was to run away to this island and dessert your mother."

I had stood my ground. "I'm asking for some boundaries."

Her eyebrow had risen. "Boundaries?"

My heartbeat had been strong enough to feel in my fingertips. "Yes. I'm asking you to respect my freedom to choose for myself. When I want your counsel or opinion on something I'll ask. Otherwise . . ."

She'd thrown up a hand, her face once again livid. "Otherwise, I can jump in the lake. You're trying to sugar coat it, but the message is the same: Butt out or get out. Well, here's something you need to understand. You can make your own choices, but you can't choose the consequences."

She'd stood in preparation to storm out of the room, but I'd thrown in one last word before the door had slammed behind her. "I do love you, Mother, and hope you can still love me, even if you disagree with what I'm doing."

The silence she'd left behind her had been loud and clear.

Gradually the sounds of the ocean waves brought me back to the present, and I turned to see Lucas looking directly at me. "I think I might need therapy," I said quietly, the words barely heard above the scraping of the sand beneath our feet as we strolled along.

I thought he might laugh, thinking I was joking. He didn't. "That's not a bad idea."

His reaction gave me courage to say more. "I don't know where to begin dealing with the fact that I've been held hostage my entire life. Taking those blinders off hasn't been pretty."

"It's not going to be easy to make the kind of changes you're hoping to make," he sympathized with me. "But, from what I've seen, you're up to the task."

I appreciated his vote of confidence. "When I think about the fact that it's been twenty-five years of non-stop manipulation, well, it's overwhelming. I'm doing now what most people do in high school. Pushing back against parents and finding their own beliefs and way of doing things. I'm such a late bloomer."

We were quiet again for a few moments before he changed the topic slightly. "I wanted to see how your talk with Lillian went, but that wasn't the only reason I sought you out tonight."

"Oh?"

"I owe you an apology."

My head whipped around to look at him. It wasn't easy to see his expression with just the moon for lighting, but he looked dead serious. "For what?"

"I shouldn't have jumped into the fray with your mother. I should have allowed you to handle the situation yourself and stayed quiet."

I took a moment to think through it. While I had really appreciated him being there for me, I hadn't analyzed how I felt about him asking Mother to leave, or attempting to go head-to-head with her. How *had* it made me feel? Protected or incapable?

My silence must have made him nervous because he started speaking again. "I don't want you to feel like you've traded one bossy person for another. If I made you feel that way this afternoon, I'm sorry."

I used our twined hands to tug him to a stop and turned to face him. He was so handsome looking down at me with those eyes that were more vulnerable that I'd ever known they could be. He cared. He cared how I felt. He understood how his actions could have affected me.

And I knew then. I knew where the line stood between protector and jailer. A protector was in it for the person they cared for. A jailer was in it for themselves. Yes, Lucas had been temperamental and a bit harsh with Mother, but it hadn't been because he doubted me or my abilities. It had been because he couldn't stand by and watch someone he cared for be hurt.

"You care about me." I didn't mean to say it aloud, but I whispered the words before I could swallow them back.

His eyes transformed into something I could be swallowed up in. "Yes."

I could barely breathe. Our gazes locked and everything else faded into the background. I had no words for what was happening to me—and only prayed that he was feeling it too—because I wanted this man to want me back. His face was close, his breath warm, his light eyes so incredibly beautiful I was lucky I didn't liquefy on the spot.

He stole any further thought out of my head by closing the distance between us, putting his free hand under my chin to tip it upward, and leaning down to press his lips to mine. It was an immediate explosion of sensation. My stomach swooped and I reached my free hand up to the front of his shirt, balling it in my fist. It couldn't be possible to live through this kind of pleasure. My bare toes dug into the sand, attempting to anchor me while my heart flew off into the darkness.

He released the hand he was holding and placed his palm on the small of my back as he pulled me in closer. My second hand joined my first, pressed against his chest for a moment before I slid them over his shoulders and around his neck. He was so warm and solid and real. I pulled myself against him, and I felt a small smile form on his lips before he deepened the kiss. His thumb caressed my jaw line for a moment, but much sooner than I'd have preferred he released me slowly and stepped back. When I opened my eyes my hands flew to my lips, almost as if to see if it had actually happened.

Lucas said nothing, just reached for my hand again, and tugged to get us walking. We walked without talking, the breeze floating between us, as we returned to the mansion. There didn't seem to be a need for words, and I was so grateful for the time to process and let my mind wander as I relived the kiss over and over. Sleep would not be coming easily that night.

CHAPTER 18

THE NEXT DAY I WAS A BLEARY-EYED SEE-SAW VICTIM, TOGGLING between heartache over the situation with my mother and the constant euphoria over Lucas kissing me. Both things were new and scary in their own way, and I couldn't settle on one tangible emotion or thought about it all.

I spent the morning with Eliza, catching up on all that had happened over the weeks while she'd been away. We spoke only briefly about Mother, and I said nothing about my exchange with Lucas the night before. I was keeping all of that close to my heart where I could wonder and dissect it on my own time frame.

When I entered the kitchen for lunch, I was relieved to find Chef Lou, Ana, and Marshall chatting it up in a relaxed way. It had been a week of stiff and uncomfortable silences, and as I watched them now, guilt, cold and hard, settled in my stomach. I knew without them saying anything that my friends had endured some sadness. I once again wondered how many of my budding friendships had been lost to Mother.

"Grace!" Ana noticed me before the others and jumped up from her seat. "Welcome back to the land of the free," she cheered. She ran to me and gave me a huge hug before tugging on my arm to drag me to the table. "We deserve a celebration, right, Marshall?"

"Sure do. What do you say to a night of dancing at the Warehouse tonight?" He smiled at me and reached across the table to pat my hand.

"Are you sure you want anything to do with me after what I put you all through this past week?" I looked at each of them, hoping my eyes conveyed my remorse.

"We're fine." Chef Lou surprised me by jumping in. "We had one week. You had many, many years."

"He's right," Marshall said.

"I don't . . ." I began.

"Now don't you start. As far as we're concerned it's over," Ana interrupted. "We're heading to the Warehouse at eight, and I expect you to be ready to go, fully styled."

"Fully styled?" I felt the icy guilt begin to melt.

"Fully." Ana nodded.

"I'm not sure what that means, but I'm suddenly worried that it might involve glitter," I joked.

"Glitter?" Marshall raised his eyebrows.

"A little extra sparkle never hurts." Ana's smile grew.

"It's a date," I said. Ana cheered and Marshall nodded happily. "I'll see you all tonight."

The rest of our lunch break was taken up with small talk and the usual teasing. I enjoyed re-submerging myself into the banter, but my mind was churning over Lucas. He'd kissed me yesterday, and I didn't know what to expect from here. We both had jobs to do, and heaven knew his kept him busy. Most likely too busy to text or call, but didn't people make time for all that? Was there some rule of etiquette that I was too inexperienced to know about? Even worse, did Lucas kiss a lot of women and I was taking it too seriously? I had, after all, kissed Jonathan on a total whim. Sigh.

After lunch I went back to my room and did my best to go over the plans for an upcoming bridal shower, but I couldn't focus. I was at a loss of what to do. Nothing sounded quite right. Eventually I decided to visit the mansion library and see what might catch my fancy. I'd passed the room many times but had never stopped to peruse the shelves.

While crossing the great hall toward the library I finally saw Lucas. He was passing from the conservatory through the ballroom, heading my way. He didn't see me at first, which gave me a moment to study him. He was on the phone, eyes down, watching where he was walking, brows furrowed, and tone tense. He looked every inch the powerful businessman I knew him to be. I wasn't sure if I should wait and hope for a minute of his time or continue on to the library. In the end I decided to keep going and not interrupt whatever he was dealing with. I wondered, of course, how he was and what he was thinking, but I also had enough pride to not grovel and beg at his feet for a few scraps of his time. Well, at least on day one. If another few days passed I'd probably be singing a different tune.

The library of Halstead House screamed wealth and splendor. The room was done in cherry wood bookshelves, with red and gold carpeting and gold and cream swirling wallpaper. Its position was off the great hall, just next door to the formal parlor. While there were many older, priceless books on the shelves, there was a shelf near the back corner with more contemporary books that I knew the household shared with staff.

I ran my fingers lightly over the bindings as I read the titles and authors' names. The smell of furniture polish and leather tickled my nose. I tried hard to focus, but I could still hear the deep tones of Lucas's voice just outside the doorway, and it had me on high alert. I loved the sound of his voice. Something about it was comforting and solid. He sounded in control and capable, a guy you wanted on your side during the hard times, a guy who got stuff done. Hopefully a guy who didn't dilly-dally with women's hearts . . .

After another moment or so I pulled my attention back to the shelves and picked a book that looked interesting. I wasn't a huge reader, which made it likely that I could pick any book and it would be new to me.

"Hey there," Lucas called to me from behind as he entered the room.

His greeting caught me off guard—I hadn't known he'd seen me—and I turned almost too fast, anxious to see him and speak to him. He came closer, still holding his phone in one hand, a tired look on his face.

"Hi to you," I said. "I hate to state the obvious, but you look tired."

"It's not called 'work' for nothing," he remarked.

"I suppose not."

He closed his eyes and took a deep breath before looking to me again. It seemed like he'd mentally shifted gears, leaving the phone call behind him and truly seeing me. His eyes landed lightly on my face, and the first semblance of a smile I'd seen from him appeared.

"How are you?" he asked.

"I'm good," I replied. "How are you?"

"I'm good too." He tucked his phone into his pocket and stepped closer. "Can we dispense with the small talk for a minute?" I nodded. "Good."

He reached out a hand and took the book I'd been holding. Not even bothering to look at it, he tossed it lightly to a chair nearby before tugging on my arm and pulling me close. His strong arms wrapped me in a hug, and his cheek came to rest on the top of my head. I was tucked in, safe and sound, and any tension I'd been feeling drained away in the comfort and confirmation of his embrace. I wasn't playing a one-sided game. Probably.

"You really doing okay?" he asked.

I snaked my arms around his waist and hugged him back. "I'm really doing okay."

"I'm glad."

We were silent for a few minutes, both lost in our own thoughts. I couldn't speak for him, but I was thinking that I would love nothing more than to crawl up in his lap and live there forever.

I broke the silence by saying, "Ana, Marshall, and I are going to the Warehouse tonight to go dancing. Do you want to come?"

His arms tightened around me for a moment, and I felt him sigh before answering. "You have no idea how much I want to say yes to that invitation."

"Don't feel bad. I'm sure you have other commitments, and it's very last minute," I hurried to reply, unwilling to cause him any guilt.

"I'm sorry, Grace. I wish my job was a regular nine-to-five."

I shook my head and pulled away to look him in the eye. His arms fell from around me, and I regretted the distance. "Truly, it's okay. I understand that your job and your life are intertwined. I shouldn't have asked. I don't want to put any pressure on you."

"No, please don't feel bad for asking. It's so much better to be asked than forgotten about."

"Don't feel bad for having to say no."

"Are we about to get caught in a guilt cycle?" His tone lightened and his eyes looked amused.

My face relaxed as I returned his look of amusement. "It looks that way."

"Well, the guilt stops here. We are not going to be people who guilt ourselves to death."

"Sounds good to me."

He grinned, and I kind of wondered if maybe there was a dimple under that well-groomed beard. "If you want to go dancing while I slave away at a business dinner tonight, you should definitely go dancing. Don't worry for a minute about me feeling left out."

"I won't. I'll probably forget you even exist until I bump into you the next time you're around." I shrugged playfully.

"I wonder if there's such a thing as taking this no guilt policy too far." He tilted his head.

I pulled a face. "I always thought guilt was all or nothing. You either feel it or you don't. But if it will help, I could possibly manage to feel five percent guilty over having such a great time tonight without you."

He nodded. "Five percent is pretty generous."

"I'm a generous person."

"I'm glad to hear you say that. I'm in the market for someone in my life who has a generous spirit."

"Are you now?"

"I am."

"How generous? I might know someone who'd be interested in the job." I could feel my smile growing as the natural banter between us happened. It felt beyond amazing. I actually had it in me, the ability to flirt and converse.

His eyes crinkled up at the corners as he stepped closer once again. I could feel the warmth of his body as his hands came to rest on my waist. "Generous enough to feel a little miserable without me around," he said before pressing his lips against mine in a spectacularly blazing kiss.

I wrapped my hands around his upper arms and pulled in closer, returning his kiss with more passion than I had before. It was happening again! His hands tightened, but he didn't wrap them around me like I wanted. I could have kissed him for a long, long time, but after a short minute he smiled against my lips and pulled away to look down into my eyes.

"Dancing tonight, huh?"

I nodded. "Dancing."

His phone interrupted anything else he may have said. He gave my waist a final squeeze and with a look of apology said, "I really hope you have a great time. You deserve a night of fun after everything."

"Thanks. Good luck to you too," I replied, gesturing toward his phone as he pulled it out of his pocket.

He answered briskly, his business voice back in place, as he walked out of the library. He turned at the doorway and gave me a final wave, which I returned, before he disappeared from view.

The book I'd been looking at was sitting in a plush leather chair next to me. I picked it up and sat down, opening to the first page. The words didn't penetrate as I thought over my conversation with Lucas. Was I a little disappointed that he couldn't come dancing? Yes. But not terribly so, because I was also unsurprised. He'd already taken time out of his schedule over the past week while Mother had been in town, and it had meant the world to me. It would be selfish of me to hope he'd continue to do so, especially when it wasn't like we were in an official relationship. For all I knew, this was how Lucas was with the women he was close to.

Nope. Scratch that thought. I knew Lucas better than that. He wasn't a Casanova. I knew that our affectionate moments meant something to him as well. I just didn't know what they meant, exactly. What I did know was that nothing had been said and no promises had been made. He had his life to continue to live. I had a new life to figure out. Hopefully the dance floor would take my mind off all of it.

* * *

The Warehouse was in full swing when Ana, Marshall, and I showed up that night. The festive feeling of a well-deserved weekend was in the air. We were lucky to find a small table and promptly sat down to order drinks and snacks.

After our orders had been delivered, Ana and Marshall scanned the tables and dance floor to see if they knew anyone there. I was already with the only people I knew, so I casually sipped my drink and enjoyed the opportunity to people-watch for a few minutes.

"Isn't that Olivia?" Ana suddenly said to Marshall, pointing her finger to a table on the other side of the room from us.

Marshall's head swung around. "Sure is." A slow grin spread across his face. "Not to be rude, but I'll be seeing you two ladies later." He unfolded his large body from the small chair he'd been sitting in, picked up his drink and his plate of onion rings, and ditched us cold.

Ana laughed. "He's been chasing that girl for months."

"Isn't she the one he took on the harbor cruise with us?" I asked, leaning to see past Marshall as he made his way across the room.

"Yep. They've been friends for a long time, but one day out of the blue—bam—Marshall suddenly woke up from a deep sleep and actually looked at her."

"And Olivia?"

"I think he's trying to wake her up from that same deep sleep." Ana wiggled her eyebrows.

"Is she good enough for him?" I asked. Marshall was a gem, and I couldn't stand the idea of him having his heart broken.

"Yeah. She's cool." Ana nodded.

"Who do you have your eye on tonight?" I asked her.

She pulled a face. "No one here who's worth my time."

"You and I could dance, though."

"Are you asking me to waltz, Grace? Because I like you, but I'm not slow dancing with you."

I chuckled. "No. But just so you know, I'd have let you lead."

Ana rolled her eyes. "Yeah, sure."

"I meant when a line dance starts, or a fast song, or whatever."

"I am so darn proud of you lately. You don't even know what the dances are, but you're ready to get out there and do them." She pretended to wipe a tear from under her eye, and I swatted at her arm.

"You're an idiot."

"True. Still, it's validating to see that I'm such a skilled therapist. Maybe Marshall will let me work with him next. He's got a few quirks to hammer out."

"Something tells me that if he can get Olivia to see him as a love interest, she'll take care of it."

We both looked over to where Marshall was sitting, chatting animatedly with the pretty woman I remembered from the boat. She was watching him and laughing, adding to the conversation and definitely engaged, but I couldn't tell for sure if she was still seeing him as just a friend.

"How do you know when someone is interested in you?" I asked quietly.

"He likes you," Ana stated.

My head whipped back toward her. "What?"

"Mr. Lucas Halstead. He likes you."

"I . . . I wasn't . . . I meant that as a general question," I stammered as my face warmed under her steady look.

"No, you didn't. You're wondering if Lucas is interested in you or not. He is." She popped a fried mushroom in her mouth and chewed calmly, as though she hadn't just made everything terribly uncomfortable for me.

"Ana, I . . ."

"He's kissed you, hasn't he?"

My face felt so hot that I covered it with my nerve-chilled hands and bent forward. "I don't know what you're talking about."

"No lies to your best friend, Grace. I know things. Look, I'm sure you're wondering about him. Time will prove me right. You need to try to relax about it and let things come together in a natural way."

"Relax? That's your advice to me?" I dropped my hands and looked back to her.

She nodded and popped in another mushroom. Without waiting to swallow, she spoke around it. "Yep. I know that patience isn't your best trait, but you're going to need to chill. It'll happen when it's supposed to happen."

"I go home soon," I reminded her breathlessly.

"Mmm. Maybe." She swallowed and took a sip of her drink.

"What do you mean 'maybe'?"

"Just what I said. Maybe." Another big gulp of her drink and she stood up. "A line dance is starting. You in?"

My mouth opened and closed a few times, my mind unable to track anything that had just happened. She grabbed my hand and tugged. I stood and followed her on shaking legs out to the floor, my mind still whirling.

"Grace." She said my name in a firm tone that snapped me back to attention. I looked over to where she was standing next to me. "Tonight is about blowing off some steam and having some fun. Leave it all at the door." I nodded. "Good. Let's shake it."

The music started, and I turned all my attention to learning the steps to a line dance I hadn't done the last time we'd been here. After a full rotation I had it down and was able to relax into the dance. My smile was broad as my body moved in unison with those around me. The rhythm beat in my chest, causing me to laugh. The combination of loud music and physical movement did its job of pulling my attention away from my worries and stresses.

The next two songs were also fast songs, although they weren't organized line dances. Ana and I stayed on the dance floor. While Ana could actually dance, I knew I was a complete klutz and most likely looked ridiculous. I didn't care. I waved my arms and shook my hips, and bopped my head around to the beat. My body was getting sweaty, my face warm and my bangs sticking to my forehead. It felt like freedom to stop thinking and simply move in whatever direction I chose. Ana teased me mercilessly, telling me she'd seen better moves from a monkey, but her eyes were smiling and we laughed together. When a slow song started we both breathed a sigh of relief.

"I did not have a fourth fast song in me," I said breathlessly as we headed back to our table.

Ana flopped down in her seat next to mine and took a big swig of her drink. "Amen."

We were quiet for a few moments, watching the couples sway together and getting our breathing back under control. I wished I had a fan to cool myself down with but made do with flapping a menu in front of my face.

"Marshall's out there with Olivia," Ana said, nodding toward the floor.

I looked and was happy to see them moving around the dance floor, him holding her close and her head resting on his chest. "I think her eyes might be opening," I said.

"Looks like it. He'll be no fun to live with if he's infatuated."

"Why not? I think it's cute."

"That's because you've never lived with a twitterpated Marshall."

"Twitterpated?" I grinned.

"What? You've never seen Bambi?" Ana replied.

"Nope. But I have heard the word before."

"You've really never seen Bambi?" Ana looked at me like I'd just announced I was from another planet.

"I haven't seen most of the Disney movies."

"Why not?"

"Think about it. None of them have moms. My mother could not abide a world in which there was no mother to run things."

"Are you serious?"

"Totally."

"No offense, but that's crazy."

"Totally," I said again as I burst into laughter that was both amusement and heartbreak combined. Ana laughed along, but the merriment didn't reach her eyes. After a bit, her hand reached out to cover mine where it was balled on the table. "I'm sorry," I finally breathed out.

"For what?"

"For being mental." I looked to her and she squeezed my hand.

"You're no more mental than the rest of us." The way she stated it was so matter-of-fact that I believed her.

"Thanks."

She shrugged and released my hand. "Would it help if I let you waltz with me?"

This time when I laughed it was a true, happy sound. "I think that might make things worse."

"Your call."

I chuckled again and leaned back in my chair. Silence descended between us, and I once again became aware of the music, the couples slow dancing, the cheery atmosphere. Marshall and Olivia were still swaying sweetly, which made me ridiculously happy for him.

"Grace?" A male voice behind me caught my attention, and I turned to see Jonathan standing near.

"Hi." I smiled up at him, but it was dimmer than the smile I'd been wearing earlier.

"I wondered if you were still on the island. How much longer will you be here?" he asked.

"Oh, I have a few more weeks," I replied.

"You want to dance?" He held out a hand, a hopeful expression on his handsome face.

"Careful, this one likes to lead," Ana joked, hooking a thumb in my direction.

"Ignore her," I said in response to the confused look on his face. I blew out a breath. I didn't really want to dance with him, and my hesitation showed.

"Come on." He snagged my chair and pulled it out, then reached out and took my hand, pulling on it to get me to stand. "It'll be fun. We're friends, right?"

"There you are." I heard Lucas's deep voice moments before I felt his arm wrap around my waist, his hand coming to rest on my hip.

Jonathan released my hand as Lucas turned me and leaned down for a kiss. It was no more than a peck, really. The type of kiss that long-time couples give to say hello or goodbye. Still, even though it was meant to be casual, it conveyed a primal message that Jonathan was sure to understand and that left me reeling, zings racing up my spine.

"Hi, Jonathan," Lucas said as he looked back up. He tucked me against his side and smiled at the other man, with cool eyes.

"Hi," Jonathan responded. His eyebrows shot up as he looked back to me.

I wanted to shrug or shake my head. I was as confused and surprised as he was, but I merely smiled in a friendly way. "It's always nice to see you," I said for lack of anything else to say.

He nodded slowly. "Yeah. Have a good night."

I turned to face Lucas, startled and thrilled to have him there, just as another fast song started. People flooded the floor. Lucas let go of my waist, and we turned to the table to sit down. Ana was nowhere to be seen. How was that possible? She had been sitting right here.

"Where's Ana?" I asked.

"Dancing." He tilted his head toward the dance floor, and I caught sight of her dancing with a man I'd never seen.

I turned back to Lucas and found myself caught by his gaze. "I thought you had a business dinner." A smile of pure delight bloomed on my face as it fully hit me that he was truly there.

His gaze warmed as he smiled back. "I played hooky."

"Was it the guilt?"

"That or the fear that some other guy would snatch you up." He pulled a face as he leaned an elbow on the table and reached to brush my bangs off to the side. "Which it turns out may not have been unfounded."

The words were serious, but his eyes were teasing and I warmed at the thought that he would care about that.

"I'm really happy you're here, but I'm sorry if you missed something important tonight."

He leaned closer to me. "I'm going to tell you a little secret. Are you ready?" I nodded, spellbound by his light eyes and all that intensity focused my way. "I have lots of money."

He stopped there and waited for, well, I'm not sure what from me. So I titled my head and said, "Yes, that's true."

"I'm not telling you this to brag or make myself sound like a jerk or something. I'm trying to make a point. Do you know what the one thing I don't have is?"

"I have no idea," I whispered. And I didn't. I wasn't sure where he was going with this. It was so unlike Lucas to lay it all out there in a way that could have been considered vulgar or arrogant.

"Time. Time is my most precious commodity. It's the thing I have the least of. Days pass and I can't get them back. So, instead of using that time for more business, I canceled everything and cleared my schedule. Tonight, if you still want it, my time is yours."

My heart crawled into my throat as what he'd said penetrated. He'd blown off everything else to give the gift of himself. He could have sent me flowers, arranged for me to go to a spa, or had Chef Lou prepare me a special dinner. Any of those things would have been kind. But they also would have been easy. Giving of his time wasn't easy. It was a sacrifice that required effort . . . and he'd done it for me.

"I want it," I managed to say.

He laughed, his entire face lighting up with happiness. "Well, that's a relief."

Ana returned to our table, breaking the spell as she flopped down into her chair. "I'm glad you could make it," she said to Lucas. "I think you'll enjoy seeing what a skilled dancer Grace is."

I rolled my eyes and blushed when Lucas looked back at me with curious eyes. "Really?"

I huffed. "No, not really. She told me I look like a monkey trying to catch a falling banana."

When Lucas's gaze swung again to Ana she snorted. "I really did, and I meant it too."

"I have skills in other areas," I protested.

"Which is a good thing," Ana replied. "Still, she's game for a dance if you are." This she directed at Lucas.

A line dance was starting, and he surprised me by rising from his chair and holding out a hand. "Shall we?"

I stood, took his hand, and reached out my free hand to snag Ana. She trotted along behind us and fell into line. This was, thankfully, one of the dances I knew. I wasn't sure what to expect from Lucas, but I should have known he'd be able to join right in. I doubted very much that he would have come out to the floor if he didn't know the moves.

Halfway through the dance Ana took a minute to lean close and whisper, "What'd I tell you? He likes you just fine."

"Stop it," I hissed.

"I have never, and I do mean never, seen Lucas Halstead at the Warehouse on a Friday night, or any other night, for that matter. I'll admit he knows how to line dance, but I doubt he learned it in a dive like this." She was forced to stop talking as our rotation put

Lucas within ear shot, but as we came around again, she picked up right where she'd left off. "He is a workaholic who doesn't take time for social stuff, yet, here he is. He made his move by coming here tonight. Now it's your turn. Make your move, Grace. No more sitting around watching life happen to you, remember?"

I bit my lip as I thought about what she was saying. She was right. Lucas had come for me. He had given his time to me. I squared my shoulders and nodded at Ana.

"You're right," I said.

"Usually am." She quirked a grin.

When the dance ended I grabbed Lucas's hand and walked toward the back doors to where I knew the veranda was. I could hear his low chuckle as he followed along obediently. The sound of it was like a pure shot of relief. He was okay with me stealing him away.

The veranda was crowded enough that I kept walking and took him down the steps. The shady area underneath, where Jonathan had taken me all those weeks ago, also had a few couples seeking privacy. I stopped and looked around for a minute before deciding an alley would do just fine.

Still Lucas said nothing as I dragged him around a corner and into a shady doorway. I stopped and turned to face him. His smile filled his entire face and shot straight to my heart. I'd had a few ideas of what I was going to say to him, but instead I put my hands on either side of his face, stood on tiptoe, and kissed him with everything that I had. I poured all my newfound determination into it.

The force of it caused him to take a quick step back, but he recovered immediately and pulled me fully into his embrace. At last he was kissing me how I wanted to be kissed by him. I sank into it, letting all my feelings pour out of me. One of my hands reached into his hair, the other ran over his close-cropped beard. I wanted to feel all of him under my fingertips.

Barely a minute later he unexpectedly tensed and pulled away. "I'm sorry, Grace," he said.

"For what?"

"I didn't mean to kiss you like that."

"You didn't kiss me like anything. I kissed you," I argued, confused and grumpy at him stopping things.

"Still . . ." He ran a hand through the hair that I'd just had my fingers in, and the sight of it incited anger. It was supposed to be my fingers doing that.

"Still what?" My chest felt tight as a horrid thought took root. "Do you not want me to kiss you? Is that what you're trying to say?" Had I been mistaken somehow?

"No, no." He took my hands in his. "You should definitely kiss me."

"So why did you stop?"

"We shouldn't be kissing like *that*."

"Like what?" I replied, puzzled, still a little miffed, and sinking down into mortification. I had very little experience. Maybe I was doing it all wrong.

"It's just . . . Grace . . . I'm trying to take it slow. You're in a vulnerable place right now. This is a lot all at once."

"So if a less *vulnerable* woman had dragged you out here, you'd kiss her without reservation?" I asked.

I'd meant it as a genuine question, but his face hardened. "That doesn't deserve an answer."

Shame made my face burn. He didn't deserve rudeness in response to his efforts to be a gentleman. Still . . . "What if I don't want to take it slow?" I said.

"I think it's best . . ."

I held up a hand and took a step back. "I hope you're not about to tell me what you think is best for me, because we agreed not to do that."

He folded his arms across his chest. "What about me taking it slow makes me such a bad guy? Because I don't want to risk our friendship, or your relationship with Eliza, or your efforts toward finding yourself and healing, I'm the bad guy?"

"You're twisting my words." I made a noise and looked away for a moment. Then a thought struck and I turned back. "You gave me your time tonight, right?"

His eyes narrowed, but he gave a succinct nod. "Yes." There was hesitation in his voice, but I didn't care.

"Well, I want to spend some of that time kissing in a dark alley where we'll probably get murdered, but at least we'll go out happy."

His face softened, and one side of his mouth tugged up as he reached out a hand and lightly brushed my hair out of my eyes. "I could think of worse things to be doing during a fatal mugging."

"Lucas, what do you want?" I asked quietly. "I mean really, actually want?"

His eyes traveled over my face, seeming to soak in every little detail. The cold, worried place in my chest began to warm and fill as I saw things in his gaze that I'd only hoped to see.

"I want to spend some of my time kissing you in this sketchy alley," he said at last.

I almost laughed with relief. "Stop trying so hard to protect me, then."

He shook his head and some intensity returned as he whispered, "Never."

Within that same breath he took my face in his hands and pressed a sweet, lingering kiss to my forehead that said more about his true feelings for me than he could have imagined. He moved to my cheeks, the side of my lips, and finally my mouth.

My hands trembled as I reached up to encircle his neck with my arms. I pulled myself closer against him so that our bodies were pressed together. He released my face and bent closer, his arms reaching around me to enclose me entirely.

As requested, he didn't hold back, and it was the stuff of dreams. I could never have imagined wanting another person the way I wanted all of Lucas. I wanted to know his thoughts, dreams, hopes, fears, and everything in between. It was dangerous, and heady, and terrifying . . . and I poured it all into him, letting him take it and taste it.

I couldn't say how long we kissed in that alley, because it didn't matter. Time was on our side for once. No one interrupted us—or mugged us, thankfully—and neither of us pulled away or asked the other to take it easy. I found something in Lucas's kiss that healed the sore spots inside of me, and I hoped that he found the same in me.

CHAPTER 19

"Something's wrong with me," I said to Ana as I flopped down next to her on the beach where she sat facing the water. The sun was just setting behind us and the waves were soothing. I didn't notice the beauty. "I can't focus." I dropped my head into my hands and continued before she had a chance to say anything. "I'm doing a terrible job of assisting Eliza. I haven't stopped to look at the stained-glass window even once or been to the beach in a week. I'm a wreck."

"Yep."

"Gee, thanks for your words of comfort," I grumped.

She chuckled. "You're not telling me anything I didn't already know. We've all noticed you moping around the mansion, obsessively checking your phone for messages."

"That's not what I'm doing." I pursed my lips in annoyance.

"It's exactly what you're doing."

"Don't you have some of your island therapist magic to make me better?" I raised my head to look at her.

Her smile was kindly amused. "I can't therapy away the fact that you're twitterpated."

"Not that again. I'm not a Bambi character. I have a little more dignity than that."

"Twitterpation is the kryptonite of dignity," she replied deadpan.

I decided to change tracks. "It's not like him being out of town is anything new, so it can't be that. He's gone all the time."

"True. But you weren't in love before."

I shot her a wide-eyed look. In two breaths she'd jumped from twitterpated to in love. It was too much even if something inside of me purred at the words. "I'm not in love with Lucas."

"Lies," she said out loud at the same time the word echoed in my mind.

"How can you be in love with someone after a few weeks, and a few kisses, and exactly zero dates?"

Her eyebrows shot up. "So you do admit you've kissed?"

I immediately blushed, as in tomato red. My mouth opened, but no words formed. Ana patted my leg, letting me off the hook. "I don't profess to understand all the ways love can happen, Grace. It just does."

"I refuse to lose control of myself over this 'who knows' situation and become a total fool." Too bad it already felt out-of-control, which was not something I had much experience with. Here I was, my first real love blooming inside of me, and it was wrecking my life. "I don't actually know if we're in a relationship or not."

"You don't have to have a label on something for it to be real."

I let that sink in. Lucas had texted me throughout the week, entertaining me with witty and sometimes sarcastic descriptions of his meetings. It had charmed me to feel him opening up. We'd spoken on the phone twice. Those conversations had been precious to me, and the happiness of answering the phone to hear his voice had tied my tongue to the point where I'd felt embarrassed about my stilted conversation. But Lucas had pushed on, comfortable and easy in himself, until I'd relaxed too.

"If this is what love feels like, I'm glad to have missed out on so much over the years," I finally said softly.

"Yeah, imagine how bad I was going through this at age fifteen, while also going through acne, hormones, and the misery of high school."

I laughed. "Maybe you're right."

"When does he get back?"

"Tomorrow afternoon."

"That's not too far off."

"I know. But he has a non-profit fundraiser dinner to attend that evening, so I'll maybe get a quick hello before he's off again."

"You're in danger of becoming greedy," she teased.

I bumped my shoulder against hers and she laughed. "I know. I know that Lucas isn't a person whose time I can demand. I know he's going a million directions at once. Trust me when I say that my mind is constantly spinning over this." Then I whispered the scary thought I'd tried to hide from. "How can I possibly compete with his life?"

"What do you mean?"

"He's so busy and his work is so important to him and the family. Can I actually carve out a space for myself in all of that? Does he want me to? It feels selfish to ask for more when I know the value of what he's doing, but . . . " I hesitated, and Ana jumped in.

"After everything you've been through, and all the changes you've made since coming here, if you don't think fighting for some-one you love is worth it, then you've learned nothing of real value." I was taken aback by the serious look on Ana's face as our eyes met. "I'm not kidding, Grace. If you give up because you think loving him will be inconvenient, then you don't deserve him."

I swallowed hard and looked away from the intensity in her eyes. "I think you misunderstand. I know he's worth it, Ana, and I'm willing to put in the effort and time. But aren't I worth it too? Aren't I equally deserving of someone who will fight for *my* time and walk over the speed bumps in *my* life? I don't want to be swallowed up into the shadows of his work, even if I do understand its demands. I don't want to be someone he only sees when he has a free minute." I shook my head as a lump rose in my throat. A deep breath helped calm me again. "Look, he hasn't even said how he feels about me, so we're talking about a whole lot of nothing at this point."

Ana's hand reached out and took mine. "Grace, you're worthy of love. You're easy to love. I shouldn't have jumped in with my opinions."

"Maybe you need listening lessons," I joked, and she grinned.

"Try to let it chart its own course, and I'm sure the two of you will figure it out."

"I hope so, because this past week has shown me that if we do take the next step, it's going to require sacrifice from both of us."

She squeezed my hand once before releasing it. We sat quietly side by side until full darkness had fallen. It had helped to talk to Ana, but it had also made things worse. Because now I had to decide what I was willing to risk for Lucas, and what I was strong enough to ask for.

* * *

The next afternoon I entered my room after lunch to find a dozen pink roses sitting on my desk with a note attached. The roses were beautiful, open and lovely, their perfume making the air around them smell amazing. I crossed the room and tore open the envelope, my heart pounding out a rhythm to the words "he's back, he's back, he's back."

I read the note with shaking fingers.

Grace,
I'd love it if you'd join me at the
fundraiser tonight. If you agree, the
dress is formal and we leave at 7:00 p.m.
Yes, this is a date. Please come.
Lucas

I didn't hesitate one moment. Lucas had asked me out on a date, and while I'd loved to have had him ask in person, I was thrilled that he'd taken the time to send flowers and leave me a handwritten note. Plus, I'd get to spend the entire evening with him. A few flutters of fear tried to creep in, but I squashed them back down. I was comfortable in a fundraising setting, having been involved in quite a few over the years. What I wasn't comfortable with was being someone's date. It was totally new territory. Oh, and I didn't have a dress.

Eliza and Ana made incredibly short work of hunting down an appropriate formal evening gown for me. The gown was beautiful. Ice blue in color with a wrap bodice and flowing skirt, it brought out the color of my eyes and set off my pale coloring in a flattering way I wasn't used to. Ana called her hairdresser friend Gwen, and she rushed over to join in the preparations. I knew she hadn't done it totally out of the kindness of her heart, and hoped that whatever Eliza had paid her wasn't too much.

When the ladies were done, my short hair had been swept back into a relaxed, loosely curled style held with sparkling fake diamond pins, a look that even I had to admit was becoming. I hardly recognized myself as I spun in front of the full-length mirror in Eliza's suite.

"You ladies have worked some serious magic here." I smiled my megawatt smile at them.

"We had a lovely canvas to work with," Eliza returned, coming to press a kiss to my cheek. "I hope you and my Lucas have a wonderful time tonight." Her eyes were sparkling with happiness, and I rushed to take her hand in mine.

"I hope you know I didn't come here to chase Lucas, or push myself into your household," I told her.

"Of course you didn't, but I do think our Mary gave a little push to you both from the other side."

I laughed at the idea of angel Mary's meddling. "She did always want me to meet her John Lucas."

"Now you know why." Eliza gestured toward her bedroom door. "Let's go. It's almost seven, and Lucas will be waiting for you in the great hall."

I felt like a princess as I took the long staircase down from the third floor to the first. Pausing at the stained glass window, I took a moment to be grateful for everything before making the last descent to where I knew he'd be waiting. His back was to me as I started down, but he turned upon hearing the click-clack of my heels on the wood.

I almost wished he hadn't turned. He was so handsome it made my heart flutter, and my breath become short. I watched his face closely as a smile grew. He held out a hand and started for me, his eyes seeming to devour me as we met at the bottom of the staircase.

He softly took my face in his hands and pressed a kiss to my lips, saying what words wouldn't have fully expressed. I felt the familiar tingle of being near him as it raced to the tips of my toes. It had been that way since the first time I'd seen him in the carriage house, and it was only in that moment that I understood it all. My heart had known where it belonged long before I'd even dared speak to this man.

"Beautiful Grace," he whispered against my lips as he pulled away. "I've missed you."

He took my hand, and we walked through the great hall, through the ballroom, through the conservatory, and out the side door. There was a car parked in the porte-cochere at the bottom of the stairs for the first time in my residence. I recognized the sleek opulence of Lucas's car and gave him a teasing look.

"First your motorcycle, and now this?"

"I promised Eliza I'd not lay even one strip of rubber." He threw me a mischievous look.

"It must have taken you a while to idle speed your way over here."

He opened the passenger door for me. "You have no idea."

I smiled up at him as the door closed. I was instantly enveloped in the comforting smells of leather and Lucas's cologne.

He entered his side of the car, started the engine, and pulled out—slowly—onto the street before saying, "I want to know everything about your week. What did you do, who did you see, where did you go?"

I laughed, surprised, and dove right in. I tried my best to make it sound like I hadn't been mopey and distracted. A girl has her pride, after all, and it wouldn't do me any favors to admit that I'd been hopelessly lost without him. It was too soon to feel that way. At least I thought it was too soon.

When I was finished, he returned the favor, and time flew. The drive to the fundraiser took us off the island and into Corpus Christi. I smiled to myself as we passed the movie theater where Ana and I had attended the first action show of my life. It was hard to believe that had been only two months earlier. Time on Lavender seemed to run differently than time anywhere else did.

Eventually Lucas pulled into a long drive edged by bushes and trees that led to a parking area in front of a sprawling Spanish-style mansion. Its arched, whitewashed walls and red tile roof seemed to go forever. The grounds surrounding it were immaculate and impressive in scope.

"Wow," I said as he came around to let me out.

"I'm afraid this might burst your bubble on Halstead House."

"Do you think they're looking for an assistant event coordinator?" I playfully stroked my chin as I looked over his shoulder at the house itself.

He reached for my hand. "I had no idea you were so mercenary."

I happily laced my fingers through his, overjoyed once again to simply be with him. I didn't care where we were or what we were doing. The feeling of his hand in mine was all I needed.

"I'll be the first to admit that we're probably too old for this, but I propose we play a little game tonight," Lucas said.

Pulled out of my thoughts, I glanced his way. "What kind of game."

"A getting-to-know-you game."

"With who?"

"You."

"Me?"

"Of course. Who else?"

"I thought you meant the people seated at our table."

He pulled a face. "Why would I want to play a getting-to-know-you game with them?"

"I don't know. Why would you want to play one with me?"

"Because . . . I'm trying to get . . . to . . . know . . . you." He enunciated each word slowly, and I was so caught off guard by his dry sarcasm that a laugh burst out of me. "I'll go first. Would you rather wear yellow or orange?"

"Um, orange."

"Why?"

"Yellow makes me look sickly," I replied.

He glanced over me in an intimate way that caused my face to heat. "I'm not sure you have a bad color."

"Liar," I said, pleased in spite of myself. "My turn. Dog or Cat?"

"Dog, for sure."

"Why?"

"They're just so happy. I'd worry a cat was trying to run a coup." His eyes crinkled at my laugh as we rounded a corner into an expansive courtyard.

If it hadn't been for his hand pulling me along, I would have shuddered to a stop. It was the most lavish scene I'd ever participated in. The arched and columned walls of the mansion surrounded three sides. Plants were everywhere, and lights strung from balcony to balcony. The red roof tiles, white-washed walls, and greenery blended into a beautiful backdrop for the black and white design of the tables and centerpieces.

"Wow," I breathed as Lucas guided us into the fray. "This is major."

"I know. It's a big one. The Alzheimer's Disease Research people do not mess around."

"I don't know where Eliza found my dress, but I'm terribly grateful she did," I said quietly. Nothing I owned would have worked at all.

"I'm grateful too, but probably not for the same reasons you are."

I was startled out of a response by the look in his eye. I recognized it as a look of masculine admiration, only I'd never had it directed my way. The tingles were back as he led us around the edges of the tables to an area off to the side where drinks were being served. I couldn't quite find my voice to compliment him back, even though I wanted to.

"Coke or Pepsi?" he asked, interrupting my thoughts.

"Coke. One hundred percent of the time. If Pepsi is all there is then I'd rather not drink anything at all," I stated firmly.

Lucas's lips curved up and he turned to the waiter. "You heard the lady. It's Coke or nothing."

"Oh, sorry. I thought we were playing . . ."

"We are." He handed me my glass. "We're also having a drink. Convenient, yes?" He reached for his own drink, and I realized I hadn't heard what he'd ordered.

"Is it Coke or Pepsi for you?"

"Pepsi, actually." He chuckled as I bit my lips. "But unlike you, I can be flexible when needed."

We stepped away from the table, drinks in hand, and I nearly spilled mine when his large, warm palm pressed against the small of my back to lead me away from the table toward a quiet spot to the side.

"People watching or center of attention?" he asked.

"People watching," I replied.

"Then tonight should be very entertaining for you."

"I believe so." I took a sip of my drink. "Toast or biscuits?"

"Biscuits. Hot with lots of butter."

"I'd add a little grape jelly to mine, but otherwise I'd choose biscuits too."

"You mean we might have something in common?" He grinned.

"Yep. Aunt Mary would be so happy." I chuckled. "So would Eliza, Ana, Marshall, and Chef Lou."

"We could make a lot of people happy if we manage to get along." He nodded. "Oh, pause. Incoming." His face immediately changed from an open and warm expression to his polite business one.

"John Lucas Halstead, I was hoping to see you tonight." An older man, neatly dressed, groomed, and about two inches shorter than me, bustled up to our side. "I heard you just got back from a hoteliers conference in Phoenix. I'd love to pick your brain on that."

"Hi, J.W. I'd like you to meet my date, Grace Burke." Lucas gestured to me, and the older man turned with a smile. "Grace, this is J.W. Porter."

"This one's much prettier than the last gal I saw you with," J.W. said with a wink in my direction.

I blinked a few times and looked to Lucas. His expression was calm, but I felt his body tense next to mine. I wasn't offended, just surprised at the tackiness of this J.W. person in saying anything about it. I'd done my internet research and knew that Lucas was popular with the ladies. Obviously, a man in his position took dates to events. Still, experience had taught me it was best to meet tactlessness with kindness.

"I'm going to take that as a compliment," I jumped in before Lucas had a chance to reply.

"As it was meant," J.W. responded with a small bow.

Lucas offered a small, polite smile to Mr. Porter and said, "I'm sorry to blow you off tonight, J.W., but Grace and I haven't seen each other all week, so I hope you'll forgive me for sneaking away with her and catching up. I'll call you later in the week."

Without waiting for any true response, Lucas took my hand and led us back past the drink table, where we deposited our two empty glasses. I stumbled along, having a hard time keeping up with his longer stride, feeling confused and a little worried.

"Lucas, you didn't have to do that. I know you need to discuss business with people tonight," I whispered, somewhat self-conscious about what had just happened. Was he angry?

"Ice cream cone or snow cone?" he asked.

"What?"

"Ice cream cone or snow cone?"

"Ice cream."

"Me too."

"What flavor?" I asked.

"All the flavors," he replied as we rounded a corner of the house and were immediately cast into shadows. The sun was beginning to set, and the twilight surrounded us.

"What . . ." I opened my mouth to ask, but stopped when he bent slightly and wrapped both of his arms around my waist, pulling me close.

"Kisses or hugs?" he asked in a quiet voice.

My heart thundered in my chest as his head neared mine. "Did you sneak me off to kiss me?" I asked. Delighted goosebumps rose along my arms.

"It's up to you. Kisses or hugs?"

I bit my lower lip as though thinking it over. "Kisses."

"Good answer."

His head bent over mine, and thanks to my heels I didn't have to push up very far to meet him halfway. I didn't care that my lipstick would be ruined, or that my chin might be red from the friction of his beard. All I cared about was that his arms were holding me tightly against him. Breathing became difficult, and I clung to him like a lifeline.

"I'd give anything to be anywhere else with you tonight," he whispered against my ear before placing a kiss on the side of my neck.

"I don't know, this place is kind of working out for me," I responded on a shaky breath.

He chuckled against my throat, his warm breath giving me those world-famous tingles. "Do you have any idea how many of these I've attended? You're the first person I've ever snuck away with."

I reached up and stroked his jaw, loving the way his beard scratched against my palm. "Maybe we could just hide out here for a while," I said.

In response he pressed another series of kisses to my willing lips. I wrapped my arms around his neck and clung tightly to him. I loved how solid he felt. He was strength, and warmth, and kindness, and it felt impossible that it could be real.

After a few more minutes he sighed and straightened up. His eyes roamed over my face and hair, his hand following to adjust anything that had been knocked out of place. "You ready to go back in there?"

"Only if we can sit by Mr. J.W. and get some more lovely compliments." I used my thumb to wipe a trace of lipstick from his lower lip before taking his hand in mine and tugging him back toward the gathering.

"He wasn't tactful, but he wasn't wrong." He pulled our connected hands up and kissed the back of mine. "You're much prettier than the others."

I was terribly pleased, whether I believed him or not, and my smile grew large. "Flattery or truth?" I asked.

"Flattery. Every single time."

"I'll remember that," I said.

"See that you do."

CHAPTER 20

"I never pictured you as the type to sit with her feet dangling in a fountain," I said to Eliza over a week later.

"If Mother and Father could see this, I'd be in more trouble than you can imagine." Eliza's voice was subdued as she tilted her head back and stretched her shoulders.

"Were your parents strict?" I asked. My toes lazily swished around in the cool water.

"No more so than any other parents of their generation," she replied. "Less so than I imagine Lillian was."

"My mother would never in a million years allow this moment."

This afternoon we'd hosted a luncheon for the local historical society. As Eliza was a member, the majority of the duties had fallen to me. However, as I'd watched Eliza and the other women circle around topics, and heard sharp words fly when emotions became heated, I'd come to appreciate that she'd worked just as hard as I had.

After cleanup Eliza had suggested we sit near the fountain in the garden, a favorite place of mine, and relax for a moment. The heat was at its peak, but Eliza had taken a chair from one of the lunch tables and told me to do the same. We'd placed them right next to the fountain rather than using the bench that was set back a bit. My mouth had dropped open as I'd watched her take off her shoes and stockings, hike her skirt to her knees, and put her feet directly in the cool water.

Eliza leaned her head back and closed her eyes, her face slightly tilted up toward the sun that filtered through the tree branches overhead. After a few moments of blissful silence she asked, "How is your mother?"

"I haven't spoken with her since she returned to Providence."

"Hmm. How long has that been?"

"Two and a half weeks now," I replied as the familiar ache bloomed in my chest.

"Is that the longest you've ever gone without speaking to her?"

"Before I came here, we talked every day."

Eliza opened her eyes and rotated her head to the side to meet my eyes. "Do you miss her?"

"I don't know how I feel about her."

I knew that I didn't feel right about the silence between us, but I also knew that I couldn't go back to how things had always been. My mind tossed it around constantly, jumbled thoughts criss-crossing during the quiet hours. Children love their parents, even though no parent is perfect, and while mine had been more difficult than most, I was no exception to the rule.

"Are you hoping to talk to her before your sabbatical is over, or wait until you return home?" Eliza asked.

"What do you think I should do?"

"My dear, there is no way I can tell you what to do. I didn't grow up in your household. I didn't have your same experiences. We don't have the same personalities. It really has to come from you."

I sighed and flopped my head back against the headrest of the chair. "That's not very helpful."

"What does Lucas say?"

I couldn't stop the smile that rose at the thought of Lucas. It had been the best week of my life since the fundraiser. He hadn't had to travel, and he'd kept his evenings free. We'd walked on the beach and had a few meals together in the kitchen or outside at a picnic table. He'd even taken me on a motorcycle ride along the seawall road that had left me breathless with an addictive mix of terror and excitement. We'd talked about so many random things, even sharing some of our more personal thoughts. What we had studiously avoided were the topics of my return to Providence and my relationship with my mother. He didn't want to pressure me, and I didn't know what to say.

"We haven't talked about it," I replied.

"Oh."

"What do you mean, 'oh'?"

"Nothing, dear. I just assumed you'd spoken about it."

I puffed out some air and looked away from her. "We're avoiding it." Eliza chuckled and I made a grumbling noise. "I should probably call my mother."

"No one is pressuring you to have a conversation or any type of relationship you aren't comfortable with."

"I'm her only daughter. She's my only family." It was a hard truth. If I wanted family, my mother was my only option. And I wanted family. I just wished it didn't have to be a choice between being controlled and being free.

"We're family too, in a way." Eliza reached over and patted my hand.

"Thank you."

Her head fell back again, her eyes closing. "Hard to believe that today was your last event."

I sat up straight, my feet flopping out of the fountain with a splash, my head swiveling quickly in her direction. "What?"

Her eyes slit open to look at me, and her lips curved up at my expression. "I know time flies, Grace, but you can't have totally lost track of it. You only have a little over a week left before you'll need to fly back if you want a few days to settle in and prepare to return to your job."

I looked away from her as my expression fell. How could it be possible that I had so few days left on Lavender? Eliza assumed I was going back, and that's because I hadn't said anything to the contrary. Heck, *I* assumed I was going back. No conversation had happened between me and anyone else to suggest otherwise.

A sharp pain shot straight through my heart and left my hands shaking as I thought about driving away and getting on a plane. I tried to hide it by putting my feet back in the fountain and clasping my fingers together in my lap.

"That went fast," I mumbled.

"Of course, you're welcome to stay if you can extend your sabbatical."

I nodded and bit my now dry lips. "I, uh . . ." I cleared the lump from my throat. "I don't think my superiors will allow that."

"I see."

She closed her eyes again, and I was grateful. I couldn't look her in the eye and not burst into tears. What was I going to do? Lucas and I were progressing and I was falling out of twitterpation and into love with him, but neither of us had broached the subject of my imminent departure. More than anything I wanted him to ask me to stay, but I wouldn't bring the subject up myself. He had so many people clamoring for him to do their bidding; I wouldn't be on the list. At the same time, I berated myself for not being honest with him about the fact that I'd stay in a heartbeat if he asked.

I suddenly stood, unable to sit for another minute as the anxiety rushed through my body. "I think I'll get changed out of this suit. Do you need anything else?" I managed to meet Eliza's eyes.

Her expression was one of kind understanding, and it nearly made me cry the tears I was attempting to blink away. "I'm fine. Go get comfortable and have a nice night off."

"I will. You too." I grabbed my chair and hurried away as fast as I could.

I hustled into the house with still wet feet, my arms wrapped around the chair, my business shoes forgotten by the fountain. The warm grass did a lot to dry my soles before I reached the steps leading up to the conservatory door, but there were still footprints on the cement as I climbed.

I loved Lucas, this I knew. I also knew—or at least thought I knew—that if he loved me back, truly, we could overcome the geographical distance between us. But, and this is where the devastation came in, for all I knew that love was one-sided. Sure, he kissed me, and held my hand, and told me I was beautiful. I knew he enjoyed my company, and I loved that he took off his society mask when we were together. Yet, there had been no declarations made by either of us. As far as I knew, this was a fun summer romance for him and life would go back to normal when I headed home. Did thirty-two-year-old men have summer flings? Another thing I didn't know.

It felt like a physical relief when I set down the chair in the ballroom and made my way to the elevator, where the doors closed me in to the cozy little box. I took a loud, deep breath and pushed it out equally loudly. I rotated my shoulders and head, wiggled my limbs, and willed my thoughts to calm. I was being ridiculous. I would handle this in a much more professional, analytical, logical way. I had been raised to avoid so much emotion. I could go back to that place and take a look at things from that head space.

My room was a welcome respite from the day. I changed out of my business suit and into a loose top and shorts. My bare feet were silent as I walked across the carpet to the dormer window that overlooked the entire island. I took a few moments to pull myself back together.

Yes, I was trying to come out of my cocoon, but that didn't mean I needed to abandon all aspects of my former self. There was value in being professional, hard-working, dedicated, selfless, and logical. There was a place in my new life for parts of the old me that had served me well. I drew on those parts of me now, and felt comforted as a cool reserve slid into place. I could think now.

A knock on my bedroom door pulled me from my thoughts. I knew that knock and wasted no time in answering it. I swung the door open and was greeted by the face and smile of the person I most loved in the world. A wave of tenderness washed over me, the tingles racing up my back as I took it all in. I hurried to put my arms around him and buried my face against him. My mouth pressed up against his neck, my nose against his jaw, and I inhaled his scent, tasting his warmth with my lips. I said his name on a light breath.

His arms came around me with no reservation, his palms flat on my back, pressing me against him. I felt his head rotate so that he could press a kiss on my temple.

"This is a nice way to be greeted." I could feel the vibrations of his low voice against my cheek, and it caused goosebumps to rise.

Still, I couldn't bring myself to say anything. Instead I moved my hands from his neck and into his hair, turning his head to meet mine. The kiss was electric in a way that the others had only hinted at. I heard him make a sound as one of his arms raced out to steady us against the door frame.

"Grace?" He pulled away from me, confused.

"Please, Lucas," was all I said as I pulled him back to where I wanted him.

His argument ended, and he lifted me off my feet to carry me further into the room so that he could close the door behind him, never breaking the kiss. I appreciated the effort toward privacy, as I was basically mauling him in the hallway.

All the emotion I'd been painstakingly burying for the past hour zinged to life at the feel of him, real and warm, against me. All the things I couldn't say coursed through me and passed on to him. I knew he could feel it, because I felt the loosening of control on his end too. He kissed me in a way he hadn't before, and I understood that even though I'd asked him to kiss me fully that night at the Warehouse, he'd still been holding back.

Annoyance, along with a sense of challenge, banked the flames higher, and I moved from his lips to scatter kisses over his jaw, his neck, his cheeks, until he finally pulled me in and tucked my head under his. I struggled for a moment, but it was fruitless. His strength far surpassed mine.

"Grace," he whispered, and I relaxed as he skimmed large hands up and down my spine, soothing us both. "I wish I could see what's happening in your head right now."

"I leave in ten days," I replied. He must have heard the bruised quality in my voice because he stopped caressing me and pulled me impossibly closer.

"That soon?" He sounded as dazed as I'd felt, and I was glad.

"Eliza told me that today's luncheon was my last event." I felt tears spring to my eyes as I said the words out loud. I cleared my throat and swallowed.

"Really?"

"Really."

"How do you feel about going back?" he asked. Finally, maybe we would get somewhere. I silently begged him to ask me to stay.

"I feel a lot of things."

This time his head bobbed up and down. "I'll bet."

That was it? No, 'please stay, Grace'? I sighed for perhaps the millionth time. I had no right to be angry with him when I couldn't say the words myself.

"What do you think about dinner out tonight?" I asked. I felt some tension drain from him and knew that I'd done the right thing in changing the subject. He wasn't ready for a big talk.

"I came here to ask you the same thing."

I pulled back so that I could see his face. "You mean you didn't come here to get attacked by your employee?" I grinned.

His eyes turned suddenly serious, and his hands left my back to cup my face. "You stopped being my employee a long time ago," he whispered, and then we were kissing again.

This time the desperation wasn't there. Instead it was so soft and tender and loving that I felt those tears well again. He said things so well this way. I wished he could say the same things out loud. I wished I could.

I clung to him for an extra second when he tried to release me. "Don't stop," I said.

He smiled and kissed me once more. This time I let go when he did. He brushed a thumb under my eye. I hadn't even realized some of those tears had escaped.

"You okay?" he asked.

I nodded once. "Hamburgers or pizza?" I asked.

"For the game, or for dinner?"

I shrugged. "Both."

"Hamburgers."

"Me too." I stepped out of his embrace entirely and tucked a strand of hair behind my ear. "My treat tonight. Let me grab some shoes and my purse and we'll go."

Dinner was relaxed and entertaining, and when we returned to the mansion neither of us wanted to call it a night.

"How about a game of cards?" I asked him as we crossed the grounds, arms around each other.

"What did you have in mind?"

"What cards do you have around here?"

His eyebrows pulled down as he thought about it. "It's been a long time since I played any card games. I have no idea. We can check out the cupboards in the family sitting room and see what we find."

We made our way through the kitchen and into the cozy and casual room reserved for family. I'd only been in the room once or twice, as it wasn't used regularly. The tans, creams, and reds that made up the color scheme created a welcoming feeling. I followed Lucas as he crossed to some cabinets near the television and opened them. There were some board games, a few stacks of cards, and some movies inside.

"Okay, Ms. Burke. Pick your pleasure. We have Uno, Phase 10, Skip Bo, or regular old face cards."

"Phase 10 it is."

He nodded and set the other boxes aside while he pulled out the deck and began to expertly shuffle. His long fingers were mesmerizing as I remembered the feel of them on my face and back.

"Cake or pie?" he asked, interrupting my mental wanderings, which was just as well, seeing as my heart rate was starting to pick up.

"Oh, um, that's an impossible choice."

"Come on, that's a cop out. Which will it be?" He grinned and dealt the hand.

"Well, I really love cake. Pie is more of an occasional treat. So, I suppose cake. You?"

"Apple pie all the way. Not the Dutch apple, though, with that brown sugar crumble on top. I like it lattice. Crust on top and bottom."

"What kind of monster doesn't like the brown sugar crumble?"

"Nowhere in the rules of the game does it say we're allowed to question each other's choices."

"Consider me chastised." I laughed. "Football or basketball?"

"I should say football, being a Texan and all, but in the spirit of honesty I'm going to say basketball."

"I'd say neither. I'm not sporty."

He jokingly looked me up and down and shrugged. "Agreed."

I swatted at his arm with the hand of cards I was about to play. "You're going down for that comment."

"Nice car or nice house?"

"Both."

"Against the rules."

I shook my head. "No, it's not. This is getting to know me. I want it all. I'm sorry if you can't handle that."

"I can handle it. Don't worry about me." He laid down a few cards and looked back up. "Beach or mountains?"

"I've always lived near water," I said while I drew a few cards, "so there's something about water that will always call to me. But I'll says mountains simply because it would be so different."

"Different is good. Providence is definitely different than Lavender," he replied.

"I can't believe how quickly it went."

Lucas glanced at his cards and played before looking back to me. "It really has gone fast."

"Too bad we wasted all that time circling each other when I first got here." I pulled a humorous face and he smirked back.

"We didn't waste time. We just needed to get to know each other."

"A little island therapy helped things along." The thought of Ana and her efforts caused a happy feeling to flutter, and I smiled to myself.

"Are you nervous about what's waiting for you back there?" He tried to sound casual, but I could hear the weight in the words.

"I suppose," I replied cautiously.

"I can't ask you to stay." His voice was low and quiet, his eyes fixed on his cards, and ice shot down to my toes. Here it was, my worst fears realized. He'd said out loud that he didn't want me to stay.

"Can't or won't?" I mumbled.

Lucas looked up and our gazes caught. "Both, I guess."

I tried to keep my face calm and my tone reasonable. "I see."

He set his cards down and leaned back in his chair. "You have a job that you love in Providence. Your mother is there, which I'll admit isn't a big draw right now, but she's your only family," he continued. "My work and my family are here."

"I understand that." I set my cards on the table too and sat up straighter, trying like mad to not choke on the giant wad of hurt forming in my throat.

"Your work is in Providence."

"Yes, you mentioned that already."

"So . . ." He spread his hands out and looked at me across the table.

I tried to smile, but my lips only wobbled. "The good news is that now we know where things stand, and we can move forward with no expectations or misunderstandings." I stood abruptly, my chair clattering to the floor behind me. "I think I'll head to bed."

"Grace, there's no need to be upset." Lucas stood too, his expression hardening.

My temper flared at the accusation. "What emotion would better fit this situation? You just said you wouldn't ask me to stay and reminded me that your work is here. How am I supposed to feel?" I folded my arms across my chest, the edge of panic making it nearly impossible to hold still, hoping with all I had that I could hold it together until I got back to my room.

"It's not like we didn't know this was coming," he said. "I've known since you arrived that it was a temporary thing."

I covered my mouth with both my hands as the reality crashed over me. "Oh my gosh. I'm nothing more than your summer fling." I barely choked out the lasts words before I had to start blinking rapidly.

"That's completely untrue," he said. The anger flooded out of him, leaving a look of misery on his handsome features as he came around the table and reached for me.

I darted back out of his reach. "This has to be the most humiliating experience of my life." The words were carried on a tormented breath as I continued to back out of the room.

"Grace, sweetheart, you're wrong." He tried to close the distance between us, but I scooted back again.

I reached the doorway and fled before he could say any more. I couldn't believe he'd called me sweetheart. It had been cruel and uncalled for. I heard his footsteps coming after me, but I ran as fast as I could through the kitchen, out of the great hall, and down to the basement. I took the twists and turns of the corridors as quickly as possible, all the while trying to tune out his voice calling my name.

I burst out of the side door and took off toward the beach. I hoped he thought I'd gone upstairs to my room. I needed him not to find me. My heart was fragmented. I wanted to be alone. My feet hit the sand, and I turned blindly in the opposite direction from what I usually took. The sand felt cold as it worked its way into my sandals. I left them on. Sand was the least of my worries. Right now, I was doing my best to keep the shattered pieces of my heart from littering the beach behind me.

After jogging along the sand for five minutes or so I stopped abruptly and crashed down onto my hands and knees. I was breathing hard, and tears flooded my face. I'd known it was a possibility to have my heart broken, but I hadn't been prepared for the reality of it.

I changed positions so that I was sitting down and hugged my knees to my chest, watching the water and trying to get my breathing calmed, but before I'd fully succeeded I saw a small figure coming my way. It was Ana. Tears fell again at the sight of my friend.

"Of all the . . ." she puffed as she came to where I was sitting and flopped down next to me. "If I'd wanted to chase a fool having a tempter tantrum down the beach I'd have gone to visit my nieces and nephews."

Her lack of sympathy rocked me. "Ana!"

"What?" She looked at me and pursed her lips. "I'm supposed to just pretend that it's normal for adults to run away and cry on the beach instead of talking it out?" She looked back out to the water and made another noise of annoyance. "Seriously, child. When we started your therapy program it was to help you loosen up a bit and help you stand up for yourself, not to turn you into this droopy mess."

I was too stunned to respond, but she'd certainly caused my tears to stop falling, so that was good I supposed. "Droopy mess? Ana, he broke my heart."

"No, he didn't."

My jaw dropped. "You weren't there. You have no idea what was said."

"Let me guess. He said he wasn't going to ask you to stay. It made you feel bad, so you attached it to your worth somehow rather than asking him why he wasn't going to ask you to stay and then talking it out."

"I . . ." Oh, how I hated that she'd pinned it so concisely. "It wasn't exactly that way," I hedged.

"Mm-hmm. That's why the poor guy was running around the house calling your name. Because he doesn't care about you."

"He said my work was in Providence and his work is here." I hiccuped a little as my breathing fully returned to normal.

"So, he told you something you already know."

"You're oversimplifying this."

She turned to look at me. "Okay, so tell me what I'm misunderstanding."

I couldn't meet her eyes. "He said that we knew this was coming and that he couldn't and wouldn't ask me to stay. I'm his summer fling."

She made a sound of annoyance. "Well, I suppose thirty-two is a good age to have your first ever fling." I didn't reply, just looked at her with raised eyebrows. "I'm saying, Grace, that I've worked here for ten years now, and I've never seen that man have a fling of any kind. He doesn't ever bring anyone to the house, much less spend every evening with them. He's been a total loner. A man doesn't suddenly go from loner to fling master. Especially in middle age."

"Maybe I'm his mid-life crisis," I harrumphed.

At this she laughed. "Fine. You're his mid-life crisis."

I replayed our conversation as we settled into quiet. Had I misunderstood something? Was Ana right and I wasn't seeing this how Lucas had meant it? I thought I'd taken him at face value, but then the look on his face when I'd stood and started out of the room flashed before my eyes. He'd looked stricken, and told me I'd misunderstood him. Had I?

"You know what you have to do here, right?" Ana asked.

"You're going to say I have to talk to him."

"Right." She stood first and pulled me up with her outstretched hands. "Come on, you watering pot, let's get you back so you can be a grown-up about this."

We started walking, and while I didn't feel peaceful, I did feel resolved to try to have this conversation again, without the theatrics. Because like it or not, she was right. I needed to decide for once if I was a wolf in sheep's clothing, or just a double stuffed sheep with illusions of grandeur.

I sniffled. "What happens if you're wrong, Ana, and he really does want this thing between us to end when I go back?"

"Then you can water the entire beach with your tears, and I'll have Chef Lou make you the biggest chocolate chip cookie in the world, and I'll eat dirt."

A small smile tugged at my lips. I reached out and grabbed her hand for a light squeeze. "Will there be earthworms in the dirt?"

"Yes. The slimiest ones we can find."

"That'll do."

We walked the rest of the way back to the house in silence. I was so incredibly grateful to Ana for seeking me out and whipping me into shape in the way only she could. We rode up the elevator together, and at the landing I turned to give her a hug.

"Thank you, friend. I needed that."

"The Great Island Therapist accepts your gratitude." She patted my back lightly.

"I'm going to go to my room and wash up a bit before I go talk to him," I said as I released her. She gave me a look and I chuckled. "I promise I will not go to bed tonight without talking to him."

"Good."

She disappeared down the stairs, and I turned to my room. I was sure my makeup was a disaster, and my clothing had sand on it. I wanted to freshen up and take a few minutes to try to tamp down on the nerves racing around all my limbs. I could do this. I wanted to do this.

Okay, what I wanted to do was run away. It would be easiest. I could check into that little Sand Dollar Motel and hole up until I could arrange a flight. I could call the others and say my goodbyes and head on home ahead of schedule. Then, I could spend ten days licking my wounds before diving back into my old life.

However, the thought of always wondering what could have happened if I'd been brave, well, I wasn't sure I could live with myself. No, I needed to take the bull by the horns and try to make peace with the man I loved. Even if he couldn't love me back, I couldn't leave things like this between us.

I entered the bathroom across from my room and washed my face clear of all the makeup before returning to my room and quickly changing into something clean.

I had just finished dressing when an insistent knock sounded on my door. Lucas was here. My heart crawled up and my stomach dropped.

"Grace?" he called.

I walked to the door as my heart picked up a bit, and opened it. His normally perfectly groomed look was gone. His hair was mussed, and he did not look like himself. I related to the feeling.

"Can I come in?"

I bit my lip and looked up at him. "I was on my way to see you, actually, but now I'm scared."

"Why?" he whispered.

"You know why."

"In or out?" He used our getting to know you game, knowing it would prick my heart.

I opened the door wider and gestured for him to enter. "In."

"Thank you."

He entered and turned to face me as I closed the door behind me and then leaned against it. We said nothing for several long moments, simply taking each other in. Just having him in the room with me made the soles of my feet tingle. I could feel the air heat with something inviting, and I knew it was the way I felt for him, oozing out of my pores. How on earth was I supposed to live without this man?

"Do you have any idea how worried I've been?" He reached out a large hand to touch my cheek with his fingertips. "I was scared that you'd decide to pack up overnight and go back to Providence early."

"I was lucky enough to have another therapy session with Ana. She talked some sense into me."

He choked out a laugh that sounded more miserable than amused. "I'll be sure to thank her." He pushed away from the door and took a step closer. I could feel the worry and the heat off him. I could also, somehow, feel the apprehension and stress. I could see it in the lines around his eyes, in the way the corners of his mouth were turned down.

He opened his mouth once and clamped it shut before starting again. "I had so many things planned to say. It was going to be a really impressive speech," he said. A corner of my mouth lifted, and I could feel my expression soften. "But the only thing I keep thinking, standing here looking at you, is 'don't go'. It's on a constant loop."

He took a step toward me until he was close enough that I had to tilt back my head to look at him. He reached for me, hesitantly, watching carefully to see if I was open to the contact. He had nothing to worry about. I was as open as humanly possible.

He pulled me close, and I could feel the tenderness, concern, and heartache all pour out of him in the way he touched me, running a hand over my hair and up my back. He tucked my head against his chest and laid his own on top of it. The familiar smell and feel of him nearly undid me. Almost without conscious thought, my own arms wound around his waist and held on. I prayed this wasn't going to end up being a goodbye.

"I don't know what happened. None of it was supposed to go this way," he stuttered out. He stopped and I could feel him shaking his head as if trying to clear it. "The first thing you need to know is the answer to your 'can't or won't' question. I said the answer was both, and it is. You see, I *can't* ask you to stay because I *won't* assume you want to give up your life for me. Do you understand?"

I snuggled my face in closer and nodded my head as I felt the first tiny flickers of hope begin to light. Still, I clamped down on it, unwilling to be hurt so deeply again.

"That conversation was a disaster, Grace. Can we try again?"

"Yes, please," I whispered against his shirt.

"Here's the truth. I've never felt this way about anyone else, and it's embarrassing to admit, but I wasn't sure how to put myself out there and open up the conversation. I didn't want to put pressure on you by asking you to stay when I know how much you've been through these past months. I'm so sorry that my hesitation and terrible wording earlier made you believe I didn't want you. I've waited a long, long time for you to come into my life, and I'd really like to keep you in it."

Before I could say anything else he dipped his head and kissed me like a man starving. His arms nearly lifted me off my feet, and I laughed with the joy of it all, which worked out all right because he moved his attentions to the side of my neck, below my ear, across my forehead, and back to my lips.

When I could feel the now familiar heat shifting to something more, I gently disengaged from his arms and took a step back, holding him away from me with a palm pressed to his chest.

"That's probably the best apology I've ever gotten." I smiled my megawatt smile at him, and he returned it with one of his own. I reached up to brush a piece of hair away from his eyes. "In case you were wondering, I made a mess of that conversation too. I assumed where you were going, but that was based on fear, and fear makes it hard to keep an open mind. I'm going to be brave now and tell you that I love you, Lucas. I'm not letting you go either."

Oh, yeah, I was a wolf. A wolf with a shiny coat who not only stepped out of the lambskin, but tore it up with her teeth. Roar.

His expression softened into one of utter affection and devotion as he leaned forward to place a very respectable kiss on my lips. "Thank goodness. I love you too. I think I knew something was happening to me that night you walked into the carriage house when you'd first arrived."

"Really?" My smile grew to fill my face as joy filled my heart. "I felt the first tingles then too."

He laughed and his face grew serious once more. "Are we okay? Truly?"

"Yes."

He took my hand in his and said, "Here are the things I know without a doubt. One, my life is so much better with you in it. Two, I can't let you go. Three, I'm willing to beg."

I squeezed his hand and smiled. "Here are the things I know. One, you're definitely worth giving up Providence for. Two, I'll probably try to make you feel guilty about it. Three, I can't let you go either."

He looked at me with more love than I could have hoped for. "I know you just said you'd give up Providence, but if you need to go back there to be happy, we'll find a way to make that work. If you need to be close to your mother, we'll find a way."

"What about the things you need?" I asked. "You said you needed to be on the island."

"Well, we've both agreed I royally butchered that conversation earlier. What I should have said is this. All I need is for you to be in my life, and the rest will take care of itself."

I couldn't resist leaning up to kiss him softly. "I'm kind of bummed that it took me twenty-five years to find you," I said when we broke apart.

"Imagine how I feel. I've got seven years on you."

"You think Mary is happy?"

"I think Mary is beyond happy."

He pulled me into a hug and I melted against him. "From now on if either of us have any doubts, or questions, or worries, we stop assuming and we talk about it. Deal?"

"Deal."

We sealed it with a kiss.

EPILOGUE

ONE WEEK LATER I WAS STROLLING ALONG THE BEACH AS THE SUN set. Lucas had gone out of town, and I'd had nothing to do but think, plan, and work out what I wanted my future to look like. It had been an unexpected gift—these hours alone. In my past life those hours would have felt lonely. Now they'd felt full of possibility.

Of course, most of those hours involved thinking about Lucas. He had become central to my happiness. After many discussions with Lucas when his meetings had ended each day, and even more time working out what *I* truly wanted, I'd called my employer in Providence and given my resignation. My boss had requested that I return and work until they could find a suitable replacement. I hadn't wanted that kind of open-ended commitment. We'd found middle ground, and I'd agreed to work for six weeks.

I'd called a realtor I knew and asked her to start up the preliminary paperwork to sell my condo. I'd use the month and a half back in Providence to pack and prep, and hopefully sell the condo quickly. The paperwork was ready to go, just awaiting my signature.

Eliza had been overjoyed to keep me on as an assistant event planner, and Lucas had been excited as I'd told him about the way things were coming together. It had made me feel like part of a team in a way I hadn't before. I was hoping he could join me for part of the time I'd be in Providence, because the thought of being apart for six weeks was depressing.

While I didn't know what would happen when I came back to the island to stay, I knew that it was a chance I was more than willing to take. My future started here, regardless of how it ended up looking.

I had less heartache over leaving Providence than I thought I would. Yes, I had loved my job, but I also loved event planning and occasional tours here on Lavender. The gulf area had a lot of history, and I knew I could find places to work, or volunteer, and be involved in the community outside of my work with the Halsteads. I was making a sacrifice but somehow knew it would come with immeasurable rewards.

The only sticking point that remained was Mother. I hadn't spoken to her yet. She was expecting me to leave Lavender to return to Providence any day now. That part, at least, was true. I would be heading back soon. However, she had no inkling that I wouldn't be staying.

I picked up small pebbles and tossed them into the ocean as I walked. I was barely strolling, enjoying the soft breeze, amazed at how it kept the air cooler than I would have expected. The oranges and pinks of sunset were soothing, and my thoughts shifted to Mother once again. I knew I had to call. It was my turn to reach out to her.

I sighed and chucked the last pebble out to sea. Time to stop procrastinating. My plans were in motion, and she deserved to know. I took my phone from my back pocket and dialed her number.

She answered after the third ring, and I felt a strange sort of tugging nostalgia at the sound of her voice. "Hello, Grace."

"Hi, Mother," I replied. "How have you been?"

"I'm fine. And you?" She sounded hesitant, like she was holding a shield in front of her. I didn't blame her. She'd felt attacked by my bids for freedom.

"Actually, I've been thinking a lot about all that happened while you were visiting the island. It got ugly. I hope we can clear the air and find some middle ground."

I thought I heard her exhale before she spoke. "I'd like to clear the air too."

"Good."

"What does clearing the air mean to you?" The words sounded forced, like they'd left a bad taste in her mouth.

I appreciated the effort and answered with direct honesty. "I want to make sure you understand that I meant what I said about there being some changes. We'll need to figure out a new relationship where I'm in charge of my own life."

"Then your opinions haven't changed since we last spoke?" Her voice was taking on an annoyed tone.

"I'd like you to be part of my life in a more balanced way if that's something you'd be interested in."

"I see."

"I also wanted you to know that I've handed in my notice and will be selling my condo. I'll come to Providence for about six weeks while I work it all out, but then I'll be returning to Lavender Island to live full time."

Her silence felt heavy and cold across the phone. I steeled myself, expecting the worst. Instead she only said, "Will you be able to make time for your lonely mother while you're here?"

I ignored the prod and answered simply. "I'd like that." I meant it. I truly did want to have her in my life if it was possible.

"Call when you're free. Goodbye, Grace." She ended the conversation unexpectedly.

I found that I wasn't too upset about not speaking further. I'd called to extend the olive branch, stood my ground, and she hadn't thrown a fit. That was all that could be expected at this point.

I put my phone back in my pocket and was thrilled to feel his presence before I heard him call out to me. "Grace."

My heart beat hard in my chest as I turned. He was jogging toward me, barefoot, dressed in casual clothing. He looked amazing.

"I thought you weren't back until tomorrow morning," I cried as he picked me up and spun me around.

"I was extremely motived to get back home," he replied.

He set me down and leaned in for a light kiss. I rested my hands on his chest and kissed him back as giddiness flooded me. He was the beginning of my new life.

He took my hand, and we started walking back in the direction he'd come from. "Who were you on the phone with?"

"Mother."

"Ah."

When it came to her, one word was often all that was needed. I filled him in on the details, and he told me about his travel day. The breeze kicked up his hair and blew mine into my eyes. The salted air and sounds of the gulls created a world outside of everything else. Twilight was on, and it was one of my favorite times of day in the gulf.

"I kind of sympathize with you mother, you know." He grinned. I bumped my shoulder into his side and made a face. "I know how she feels. You came into my life and threw my perfect world on its backside."

I laughed. "There's a lot of pressure in being the best thing that ever happened to you. I hope I can live up to it," I said dryly.

He laughed too and, like always, the sound of it pierced my heart. He didn't laugh enough. It was something I'd try hard to change.

Just ahead of us we could see two people hunched over a fire. It took me a moment to recognize them as Ana and Marshall. The smell of smoke and cooking fish reached me, and I tugged harder on Lucas's hand to get him moving.

Marshall waved first and I waved back. Ana's smile was open and welcoming when we came near the circle of chairs.

"Hey, Ana," I said, "I'm so glad you're here. I have something I need to tell you."

"Oh yeah?" She tilted her head to the side.

"Yeah. You're fired as my therapist."

Her shoulders slumped, and she pulled a face while Marshall chuckled. "I can't say I didn't see this coming. You're pretty perfect these days." She pretended to mope.

Now it was my turn to pull a face. "Well, I wouldn't go that far. Still, I don't think there's much else you can do to help me. The island is in my blood now."

Marshall stood and offered me the chair he'd been sitting on. "Here, Grace, have a seat. The fish is almost ready."

"Do you have enough for us?" Lucas asked.

Marshall nodded. "There's always room for a few more around my fire."

"I hope you mean it, because I'm planning to stick around for a while," I replied.

"Well, now, of course you are," Marshall replied, and Ana nodded. "The island always calls all its lost souls home."

"Welcome home, Grace." Ana reached over and patted my knee.

Lucas leaned down and kissed the top of my head. "Yes, love, welcome home," he whispered so softly that I almost didn't hear him over the cry of the pelicans and the swishing of the waves against the shore.

I dug my toes into the sand and watched the faces of those I'd grown to love as they chatted comfortably together. *I'm home, Mary,* I said to the sky. *I'm home.*

ACKNOWLEDGMENTS

My husband Steve, who has been working from home this past year while our family also lives through a major home remodel and a pandemic. Good news: We're still together! You're my sounding board, my continuing example of 'doing the right thing', and the guy who always steps up when I need someone to take the burden. You laugh when I dye my hair purple, help me look for houses in the Caribbean when I want to run away, and never make me do things I don't want to do. Thanks for twenty-two years of being my ride or die. It couldn't have been easy.

My four kids. You've lived behind sheets stapled to the ceiling, shared one small bathroom, made a basement bedroom into an apartment, and had so many of your norms taken from you. But you've shown me that you're strong, resilient, and filled with goodness as you get up every day and do your thing. Laughter still fills our home. You're going to take these experiences as building blocks, and I can't wait to see where you go from here. I love you all in every way.

My in-laws, siblings and spouses, and my nieces and nephews—boy do you make life fun. All the memes, Marco Polos, texts, and videos have brightened this year. All your prayers have lifted it. Thank you.

My "Queens." Together we're making it, and I'm so grateful for you in my daily life. I don't deserve you.

The lovely people at Cedar Fort Publishing, for endlessly and kindly answering my questions and continuing to teach me so much! Thanks for acting excited when I turn in a new manuscript! It makes me feel pretty good.

To my readers—it's because of you that my publisher gets excited. THANK YOU for pulling my books from the pile of millions. Thank you for your kind reviews, and for your messages, and for loving my characters as much as I do.

To my beta readers—as always, your input is incredibly invaluable! When I get too close to see the issues, you point them out and make the story better than I could have alone.

Last, a special acknowledgment to fellow author Sarah Adams. When I felt most insecure about this manuscript you gently took it from my hands, read it, and kindly settled my worries. Because of you I have the courage to put this out into the world, even though it's different from anything else I've written. True friends encourage and uplift. You're a keeper.

ABOUT THE AUTHOR

Aspen Hadley loves nothing more than a great story. She writes what she wants to read: clean, sassy, romantic comedy novels that give you a break from real life and leave you feeling happy.

Outside of writing, Aspen's number-one hobby is reading. Number two is sneaking chocolate into and out of her private stash without being caught. Other favorites: playing the piano, listening to classic rock, eating ice cream, traveling, a good case of the giggles, and riding on ATVs over the mountains and deserts of Utah.

Aspen shares her life with a patient husband, four hilarious children, and one grumpy dog in a quiet suburb in the foothills of her beloved mountains.

Scan to visit

www.aspenmariehadley.com